Happily Ever Witch

A Kinda Fairytale

Cassandra Gannon

Text copyright © 2024 Cassandra Gannon
Cover Image copyright © 2024 Cassandra Gannon
All Rights Reserved

Published by Star Turtle Publishing

Visit Cassandra Gannon and Star Turtle Publishing at
www.starturtlepublishing.com

For news on upcoming books and promotions you can also check us out on Facebook!

Or email Star Turtle Publishing directly:
starturtlepublishing@gmail.com

We'd love to hear from you!

Also by Cassandra Gannon

The Elemental Phases Series
Warrior from the Shadowland
Guardian of the Earth House
Exile in the Water Kingdom
Treasure of the Fire Kingdom
Queen of the Magnetland
Magic of the Wood House
Coming Soon: *Destiny of the Time House*

A Kinda Fairytale Series
Wicked Ugly Bad
Beast in Shining Armor
The Kingpin of Camelot
Best Knight Ever
Seducing the Sheriff of Nottingham
Happily Ever Witch

Frightful Loves
Love vs the Ooze Monster!

Other Books
Love in the Time of Zombies
Not Another Vampire Book
Vampire Charming
Cowboy from the Future
Once Upon a Caveman
Ghost Walk
Sexual Tyrannosaurus Anthology: Taming the Tyrant
Lizard by Cassandra Gannon

If you enjoy Cassandra's books, you may also enjoy books by her sister, Elizabeth Gannon.

The Consortium of Chaos series
Yesterday's Heroes
The Son of Sun and Sand
The Guy Your Friends Warned You About
Electrical Hazard
The Only Fish in the Sea
Not Currently Evil

The Mad Scientist's Guide to Dating
Broke and Famous
Formerly the Next Big Thing

Frightful Loves
Love vs The Beast!

Other books
The Snow Queen
Travels with a Fairytale Monster
Nobody Likes Fairytale Pirates
Captive of a Fairytale Barbarian
Sexual Tyrannosaurus Anthology: Lust and Fury by Elizabeth Gannon

*For my fellow nail polish addicts,
Who see the many, many differences between bubblegum pink
with micro-glitter and bubblegum pink without micro-glitter.*

Who understand the agony and ecstasy of using yellow creams.

*Who unashamedly pick the color of their new car based on how
close it is to their favorite shade of Chanel red.*

*And who know that it's right and just to blow this week's
grocery money on a bottle of Clarins 230, because owning the
fabled "unicorn pee" pigment is way more important than food.*

*We might be broke, crazy, and have no room in our Helmers, my
friends, but our manicures look amazing.*

"The time has come," the Walrus said,
"To talk of many things:
Of shoes—and ships—and sealing-wax—
Of cabbages—and kings—
And why the sea is boiling hot—
And whether pigs have wings."

Lewis Carroll- "The Walrus and the Carpenter"

PROLOGUE

Pick your perfect nail polish from our unlimited selection!
Burnt It All Orange: Hot, hot, hot! This illuminated polish is ideal for keeping warm on a cold night, because it's actually on fire. Containing all the burning colors and shifting shadows of a blazing inferno, it glows in an unholy conflagration for up to a week before your nails melt off.
(This product is not recommended if you work with small children or plan to ever grow fingernails, again.)

Happily Ever Witch Cosmetics Website

The Four Kingdoms
Wicked, Ugly, and Bad Prison
Seven Years Ago

"I'm not helping you set off a bomb." Marrok Wolf told him for the millionth time.

Trevelyan, Last of the Green Dragons, slanted him an aggravated glare. The Big Bad Wolf was one of a handful of people Trevelyan counted as a friend, but sometimes he wondered why he bothered. Marrok might just be the most moralizing villain ever born.

Unlike the wolf, Trevelyan wasn't willing to passively wait out his sentence. He couldn't. He had to get out *now.* Maid Marion had come back in time with news from the future. She'd told Trevelyan what would happen if he stayed in prison, beyond today.

Snow White, the lunatic doctor who ran the asylum, wanted one of Trevelyan's spells and he had no intention of giving it to her. If things continued on this course, she would kill him. That was completely unacceptable.

Trevelyan paced around the confines of his cell, morbidly aware of every second that ticked by. It was a literal countdown to his demise. The entire situation had spiraled out of control. He hated being out of control. And he certainly didn't want to die. He was too powerful to die. Too *important* to die. He was a dragon!

"I mean it, Trev." Marrok insisted, when Trevelyan didn't respond to his latest refusal to help. Even in his human-form, the wolf was some lupine-y mix of lazy and watchful. Topaz eyes stayed fixed on Trevelyan, revealing none of his undoubtedly infuriating thoughts. "I'm not going to blow anything up."

The two of them shared a cell in The Wicked, Ugly, and Bad Mental Health Treatment Center and Maximum Security Prison and had formed an alliance against the other inmates. From the beginning, it had made strategic sense. The enemy of your enemy is your slightly-less-hated enemy.

Marrok and Trevelyan were the strongest. Against each other, there would only be mutually assured destruction. But *together* they had total dominion. Young as they were, they were still more dangerous than all the other villains in the jail. The two of them ruled the Red Level. Since Red Level housed the worst-of-the worst offenders, that meant they ruled the entire WUB Club.

Well, *Trevelyan* ruled it.

To his way of thinking, Marrok lacked a killer instinct. Oh, he could hold his own in a fight, but he'd never have Trevelyan's ruthless need to win. Marrok got by on cunning coated in charm. He was surprisingly smart, for a sports star. Words and schemes and a glinting smile were his weapons of choice. Trevelyan relied on fear. People were so afraid of him, they rarely posed a problem. They just fell into line. He was willing to use his knack for intimidation to shield Marrok from the more aggressive monsters roaming the halls. The wolf therefore owed him some loyalty. It was obvious.

"We *are* bombing the prison." Trevelyan intoned.

The magic inhibitor on his ankle precluded him from casting any spells. He hated that. Deeply. How could the greatest villain in the world *be* the greatest villain in the world with no magic? It was impossible to reach his full potential without his powers. With his dark energy stifled, Trevelyan had reluctantly decided a bomb was his best option. It was vulgar, but he didn't need magic to make it work. He just needed bleach and hydrogen peroxide. Maybe some ammonia or vinegar to toss in the mix. Marrok was assigned to the laundry. Some of that shit *had* to be available down there. Why was the wolf complicating something so simple?

"The chemicals will catch fire, Trev. Or make poisoned gas. Or just fucking *explode*. It will kill hundreds of people."

"One hundred and eight people, I would guess."

At least that's how many he killed on his last attempted escape, in some other timeline, according to Maid Marion. This was a new plan, obviously. In Marion's original timeline, Trevelyan had died, too. That had to change, as he probably wouldn't get another do-over. He needed to *survive*, no matter what. And if he didn't have that bomb, his only option was doing something even more god-awful.

Trevelyan hated needing anything, but he needed the wolf. He needed help.

"I'm not killing a hundred and eight people." Marrok shook his tawny head, like the number was just *so* huge that it was crazy to even consider it. "No way. Not even for you."

Trevelyan was insulted. "Why the frozen-hells not?"

As a species, dragons were isolated and mistrustful. They didn't make allies easily. Or really *at all*. The fact that he'd accepted Marrok into his confidence was a huge honor for the wolf. He should be grateful. Their pact had started out as strategy, but now they had a genuine friendship. And friendship meant loyalty and loyalty meant setting off a bomb, so Trevelyan could escape.

It was crystal clear as a wishing well.

He didn't appreciate Marrok's squeamishness. It was madness to worry about the means they employed in order to reach the necessary ends. All that mattered was results.

All that mattered was *Trevelyan.*

"Well, for one thing, this plan could get me locked up for the rest of my life, if we're caught." Marrok was stretched out on his bed, one foot swinging over the edge of the mattress. "I can't be locked up in here forever. I have to find my True Love."

"Oh for God's sake..." Trevelyan rolled his eyes so hard it was a wonder he didn't catch a glimpse of his own brain. "I'm sick of you talking about this imaginary girl and your fantasy romance." Just about everybody had a True Love. Allegedly. The one person they were destined to be with. Also allegedly, most Bad folk knew their True Love the moment they met them. No one was quite sure why Good folk took a longer time to figure it out, while Bad folk could just look at their other half and *know* at first sight. They just blindly accepted the story.

Trevelyan thought it was all troll shit. He'd never experienced it and Trevelyan didn't believe anything he hadn't experienced for himself.

Marrok, on the other hand, believed in True Love without question. In his pitifully naive mind, some glamorous she-wolf was going to show up and propose at any moment. Marrok rhapsodized about the woman on a loop. Wolves were always fanatically dedicated to their True Loves, but Marrok rivaled Maid Marion's large, gargoyle husband when it came to obsession. Nothing mattered to him more than his True Love. Nothing.

"My True Love is not imaginary." Marrok insisted, right on cue. "I've felt her, for a long time. I know she's real and that she'll save me from my life. She'll *give* me a life. A family. A future. I won't do *anything* to risk her."

Trevelyan didn't understand why the man was so hung up on this ridiculous idea. Even if True Love had some basis in reality (and it probably didn't.)... so what? With so few of their species left, most dragons' relationships were rooted in practical, concrete, unsentimental concerns. They wanted a mate. A partner. You didn't need to *like* the person you mated with. You just needed to breed more dragons, and fight your enemies, and expand your family's power.

True Love matches were far more arbitrary. Assigned by fate and beyond a person's control. Trevelyan didn't accept *anything* was beyond his control.

Why should he settle for some random woman? He wouldn't. It was that simple. Dragons chose their own mates, based on logic and instinct. Love rarely entered into the equation. Even if they felt it, they would then *decide* whether or not to claim the person causing those feelings. They didn't just blindly submit to them. It was all about survival and empire building, which was a far superior system. Anyone rational could see that.

(Honestly, why was Trevelyan *always* the only rational person in the room? It never failed. Everyone else was a moron.)

"How are you going to find this wonderful, perfect, destined love, if you're stuck in here?" He tried, arching a brow at Marrok. Wolves were primitive. You couldn't always use reason with them, because they were primarily motivated by emotions. "For all you know, she's out there right now, fucking some other man. My plan gets you beyond these walls and looking for her."

Yellowish eyes stayed fastened on Trevelyan, not falling for it. "I'm out in ten months, anyway. I can look for her, then. If she's with someone else, I'm fairly certain I can coax her away." He gave a smug smile.

Trevelyan frowned, conceding that point. Marrok was the best-looking man in the Four Kingdoms. Everyone knew that. Even Trevelyan knew it and he hated to give anybody else credit for anything.

There was a downside to being so handsome. Marrok was constantly harassed by the WUB Club's chief administrator. Dr. White was a licentious bitch, who went after any male prisoner who caught her eye, whether they were willing or not. And Marrok had *definitely* caught her eye. It was a small miracle the wolf had kept himself out of her clutches, but could he sustain his luck? She was always pawing at him, seeking him out, and making suggestive remarks. Marrok detested her. Everyone in the WUB Club detested her.

Especially Trevelyan.

He hated that Snow White had any power over him. Not only was she plotting to steal his spell and then kill him, but the overly-sweet smell of her turned his stomach. So far, Trevelyan had ignored her innuendos and eluded her touch. The thought of *not* eluding her made his whole body contract in horror. *No.* He couldn't do that. He just... couldn't.

Not even imminent threats from Snow White's depraved appetite would convince Marrok to escape. It would be no better for him out there. Wolfball players were sold by their coaches for sexual shit, all the time. It was no wonder Marrok hated the sport that he was forced to play. Bad folk had no place to feel safe. To belong.

Trevelyan thought for a beat, looking for some kind of deal he could strike with the wolf. Nothing came to mind. Having his unknown True Love was all Marrok cared about. Trevelyan could perhaps perform some spell to find her, as a bribe. But that was far lighter magic than he typically used. Good magic rarely worked for him. He was too Bad to access the power of it. And he couldn't cast *any* spells inside the prison, so the entire idea was moot from the outset.

Shit.

Marrok raised his eyebrows in sardonic unconcern, seeing Trevelyan's increasing frustration. The wolf was always nonchalantly sure of himself. He was also even better at pissing people off than Trevelyan and that was a high bar to clear. It was what made him so dangerous. Like all wolves, Marrok knew how to exploit a weakness. Trevelyan had seen him convince opponents to destroy themselves, using nothing more than a taunting smile and some lie that the sap desperately wanted to believe.

The wolf might be a closeted do-Gooder, but he was also insidious.

Trevelyan's eyes narrowed, his thoughts going darker. He saw the man's intentions, now. Marrok knew that he had Trevelyan over a barrel. The plan wouldn't work without the cleansers from the laundry and only Marrok had access to them. The wolf thought he could stop him from escaping. Prevent him from killing anyone dumb enough to stand in his way. Stall him with all these pointless arguments.

It was a ludicrous notion. Nothing would deter Trevelyan from a goal. Once he decided something, it was *done*.

"You think you can outsmart me, wolf?" He asked quietly, danger in his tone. Deep inside of him, the dragon stirred.

"I think you need to rethink this plan." Marrok temporized. "Take some time."

There *was* no time.

"There's nothing to rethink. It's me or them." Trevelyan waved a hand at the wall and all the nameless, faceless, insignificant creatures beyond. "Which means it'll be *me*."

Why was Marrok so eager to save these worthless beings and this worthless cesspit? Everything and everyone in the Wicked, Ugly, and Bad Prison was nauseating. Dragons were scent-based creatures, so the stench of the place was sickening to Trevelyan. Awake or asleep it assaulted his senses and clouded his mind. Even without his impending death, he would be determined to escape. Wolves had a keen sense of smell, too. You'd think Marrok would understand his desire to get away from the odious odors.

Instead, Marrok slowly shook his head. "Don't do this, Trev. You can be *better* than this."

Frozen-hells, the man was exhausting. Trevelyan couldn't imagine the energy it took to give a troll's ass about "being better." "We're Bad, you colossal imbecile. This is how Bad people act. You might want to stay on the fringes of evil, pining for your precious True Love, but I'm an *actual* villain."

"What are you going to say to your True Love, when she finds out you did this?"

"I don't have a True Love!"

"Everyone has one."

"I don't. I don't even *want* one. I just want to go home." Wherever that was. The ancestral Green Dragon estate had been destroyed years before and everywhere else was unimportant. "I will rip through you, my fictitious True Love, and every single organism in the Four Kingdoms, if that's what it takes to escape."

Marrok watched him in stubborn silence.

Since they were supposed to be friends, Trevelyan decided to allow him one last chance to show some loyalty. He hadn't given Marrok all the details of why he needed to escape tonight, but why should he have to? The man should just do what he was told, goddammit.

"I *need* to get out." Trevelyan couldn't put it any plainer than that. They'd been arguing about this for two days and now it was the end of the line. "The best way I can think to do that is to blow a hole in the side of this prison and walk away amid the confusion." There wasn't time for a better plan and no one else in the WUB Club seemed capable of lending a hand.

(Why was Trevelyan *forever* surrounded by morons? Where did the smart beings hide? Had he killed them all, already?)

"People will *die* if you do this."

"I don't fucking care!" Trevelyan roared, pushed to his brink. Inside of him, the dragon was pacing too, in agitation and impotent rage. The lack of support from their friend bothered the monster, as much as it bothered Trevelyan. The dragon was the truest part of him and it was locked away, unable to surface with the magic inhibitor on his leg. That smoldering frustration drove his ire to even greater heights. "You need to have my back, the way I've had yours. ...Or else."

Marrok slowly blinked. "Or else *what?*"

"If you screw me over, I will make sure you regret it." Trevelyan stabbed a finger at him. "I've played fair with you, so far. That can change."

The wolf's head tipped to one side, like he sensed the atmosphere in the room shifting.

Trevelyan watched him with glowing green eyes. "If you're not with me, then you're against me. Countless others have learned that I am a real Bad enemy to have."

"I guess I'll learn it, too." Marrok's foot still swung with casual, animalistic grace, but his gaze had gone cold. "Because, I'm not doing jack-shit for you."

Trevelyan saw red. The wolf was trying to kill him. It was the only rational explanation. "You miserable little *fuck*. You think you can betray me and I'll just let it pass?"

"I think you're out of your mind!" Marrok snapped back. "I'm not betraying you! This plan is terrible and you're acting crazy. I'm not going to blow up this prison *with us still inside of it*."

"I will make sure we get out! I *told* you that!"

"You *can't* be sure and we both know it."

"I will be dead or free. I'm sure of *that*."

"What about everybody else? I won't let you kill a hundred people, just because you want to go home early!"

Trevelyan's restless anger and agitation reached a breaking point. He stalked across the small interior of the cell and hauled Marrok right off the bed. "How about if I just kill you, then?" He tossed the wolf up against the wall, prepared to slaughter him with his bare hands.

Marrok shoved him back. "You wanna fucking do this? Fine! We can fight it out." He lifted his arms in a mocking shrug, his expression aglow with self-satisfaction and fury. "But, no matter which of us wins, *you'll* lose." He leaned in closer, an infuriating smirk on his face. "Because there isn't a damn thing you can do to make me help you. ...And you know it, asshole."

Trevelyan hit him. What choice did he have?

It was hard to say which of them would've eventually won the fight, since physically they were evenly matched. But alarms went off after a few minutes and dwarf guards rushed in to pull them apart. Marrok's face was bruised and bleeding, as they wrenched Trevelyan off of him. Trevelyan imagined he looked much the same, but he was too enraged to feel any damage.

"I will take away everything you ever loved!" Trevelyan shouted, as they dragged him from the room. Betrayal burned at him, blocking out everything else. Marrok had been his friend. It went against his nature to trust, but Trevelyan had trusted him. The man's treachery burned like acid. "I will leave you with *nothing*, you bastard!"

"I could threaten the same thing, except you don't love anything!" Marrok bellowed back. "No one even likes you! You're an evil monster!"

"Who you just betrayed!" Trevelyan grabbed onto the doorway to pin him with a venomous look. "What do you think is going to happen, when I get out of here, wolf? What do you think I'm going to do to you, if I survive?"

Marrok had enough sense to look wary at that threat.

The dwarf guards finally pried Trevelyan away from the door

and hustled him down the hallway. One of them kept his hand on Trevelyan's arm, like he thought it might restrain him. Trevelyan sent the little fucker sailing headfirst into the wall. The other dwarves jumped away from him, like they'd been scorched. If Trevelyan had his powers they *would've* been. He had no tolerance for Snow White's lackeys or most of the rest of creation.

But he also couldn't afford to get send down to the dungeon. That would make his escape even harder. He closed his eyes, trying to quiet the dragon inside of him.

"Time for a one-on-one with Dr. Ramona." One of the guards muttered, still standing back in respectful fear. The dwarves knew to keep their distance from Trevelyan. *Everyone* knew to keep their distance from Trevelyan. "You know she always talks to inmates who can't get along with their cellmates. She'll want to make sure you two don't kill each other during the night."

Trevelyan wouldn't be there during the night. Dead or free. There were no other options.

He blew out a calming breath, his mind racing. The bomb wouldn't work. Marrok had ruined that plan. But today was Trevelyan's birthday. Dragons were strongest on their birthdays. He might not have his magic in the WUB Club, but there was another way to win if he had the strength to endure it.

The idea was repellent. Dirty and disgusting and beneath him, but it was the only way. It made his skin crawl to even consider it, which is why he'd been *refusing* to consider it. Until now, when it was literally life or death. Now, there was no choice. Trevelyan decided.

He ground his teeth together and blamed the wolf for what was about to happen. Marrok had caused all of this. One day, he'd pay. But for now, Trevelyan needed to survive until morning. That was all that mattered. *Him*.

Trevelyan was all that ever mattered to Trevelyan.

"Afterwards, I want to see Snow White." Hate swelled within him, even as his resolve strengthened. He could do this. He was a dragon! He could do anything. And then he'd get revenge. "Tell her I'm in the mood for company."

Chapter One

Pick your perfect nail polish from our unlimited selection!
Magic Apple Red: Gleaming in the most mouthwatering way, this color is an ode to those old-fashioned treats that grandma used to hex. Because family values, timeless elegance, and knocking off annoying princesses *never* goes out of style.

Happily Ever Witch Cosmetics Website

**Wonderland
The Heart Castle
Present Day**

"Is she a Good witch or a Bad witch?"
"She's *Bad*, of course. No such thing as a Good witch. You saw what she did to Queen Alice, right? Turned her into a log. That sure says Badness to me."
"You mean a frog?"
"No, a *log*. With twigs and branches."
"Why would a witch turn someone into a log?"
"Because she's frigging Bad, you idiot!"
Esmeralda the wicked witch drummed her perfectly manicured fingernails on the table. Under the glow of the intense spotlight, the holographic polish reflected a dozen colors at once. "Any chance we could hurry this up, fellas? Some of us have lives to live."
The two playing card guards flashed her identical frowns. They were big, square, flattened creatures with faces built into their bodies and arms like professional wrestlers. They were also seriously pissed that she'd blasted through a bunch of their

colleagues with her magic, so they weren't in the mood to be helpful.

God, Wonderland sucked.

If Esmeralda could just go back and undo the whole "Enspelling Alice" thing, she *totally* would. Sadly, magic didn't work that way. What's done was done and the best way forward was to talk to someone in charge. Someone who might listen to her. "I need to speak with --like-- your boss or something. This is all a *big* misunderstanding. We can work it out, if you find me somebody in authority."

Dismissing her request, they went back to discussing her like she wasn't in the room. ...The cramped, gray room, which looked exactly like all the other interrogation rooms she'd been dragged into over the course of her villainous career. And there had been a hell of a lot of them. Esmeralda got arrested with depressing regularity.

There were Good folk and Bad folk in the world. The Good folk held the power and the Bad folk took the blame. That's the way it had always been. Witches and trolls and all the other Baddies had been persecuted for as long as anyone could remember.

Ez was accused of crimes all the time, just because she was a witch. If she was actually guilty of half the atrocities she was suspected of committing, she would have been thrilled. Sadly, her Badness was mostly just on paper. It wasn't for lack of trying. She really, really wanted to be wicked. Magic just always seemed to go wrong for her.

She sighed in irritation.

If it would've helped any, Esmeralda could've explained to the guards that Queen Alice's log-ification was an accident. She had indeed been aiming to turn the vappy blonde into a *frog*, but her magic had misfired. It had been doing that a lot recently. Even more than usual.

Transforming Alice into an amphibian instead of a wooden lump wouldn't have gotten her off the hook in a court of law, but at least it would've made sense. A *log* was just plain silly. Hopefully, no one else heard about it or she'd be the laughingstock of the Cauldron Society.

Which she kind of was anyway.

Esmeralda had been born with level six magical powers. That was the highest level possible. People born with level six powers were always respected and feared. Except for Ez. She was basically unknown, aside from the occasional catastrophic screw up. No matter how hard she tried, her magic was undefined. Unpredictable. Uncontrollable.

She always had to work twice as hard as the other wicked witches to accomplish even the most basic villainy. And lately her magic seemed to be failing her altogether. The worst issues had started right around the time she'd escaped prison and they seemed to be even worse here in Dumpsterland. She'd been trying to come up with a transporting spell for hours and all she got was a headache.

Still, Esmeralda didn't like dwelling on her failures. Better to focus on something constructive. Like all the ways she would fix her crappy life.

1: Go home, hug her friends, and never travel more than two miles from the Enchanted Forest, again. 2: Figure out the glitch in her ginger-mutant spell, because their frosted fangs were still too runny. 3: Think of a perfect name for the new "X-ray-ing your fingertips while you wear it" nail polish she'd created for her online cosmetics shop. 4: Get the damn light turned off.

Only one of those items was doable at the moment.

"Do we have to have this lamp in my face?" Esmeralda held up a palm to shield her eyes from the high-intensity, detective-film spotlight they had trained on her. "What's the point of it? You took my fingerprints, my blood, and my mug shot... and I always look lousy in mug shots. I've been a great sport, but enough is enough. This whole thing is getting seriously old."

The light stayed on.

"Are you listening to me?" She looked towards the mirrored window on the wall to the left. Somebody on the other side was watching her. She could tell. "I know you're there. You're the one in charge, right?" She'd tried a hundred different ways to convince him to talk to her and now she was scraping the bottom of the barrel for ideas. "Come in here and face me, you fucking coward, because I'm done talking to underlings."

"Underlings?" One of the playing cards yelped in indignation. "You'll pay for your insolence, witch." The other guy snapped at the same time.

Esmeralda ignored their inanity, her eyes on the window. She wished she could see whoever was behind the mirror, but all she saw was her own reflection. Hell, that was okay, too. Esmeralda had a *tiny* bit of justified vanity. Green skin, crimson eyes, killer body... A girl could do a lot worse.

"Well?" She prompted, absently smoothing back her mass of black curls in the mirror. She looked mostly great, but her hair was all poufy and tangled. Dunderland was just too damn muggy and witches didn't do well with moisture. Direct contact with water melted them and --almost as terrible-- high humidity created frizz.

Luckily, the fancy tiara she'd liberated from Alice helped to mitigate the messy style. Sparklies made everything better. She touched the crown and arched a brow at the dickhead behind the mirror.

Nothing.

That pissed her off. This whole damn situation pissed her off, but being ignored was infuriating. She didn't do well with being ignored. Esmeralda had always been the annoying kid who threw paper airplanes until the teacher paid attention.

Her eyes narrowed at the faceless man. "You still don't want to talk to me? Then I guess I've got nothing to lose, do I? I'll just lean back in this uncomfortable chair and deal with my hurt feelings by singing. Loudly." She kicked her favorite boots up to rest on the table, settling in for the duration. "And FYI, I have a *terrible* voice and I only like country songs. You know the kind Pecos Bill sings, with long-lost True Loves and cheating exes. I hope you're a fan."

Evidently, he thought she was bluffing, because he still didn't answer.

Have it your way, asshole.

Two off-key verses, filled with wrong lyrics and lovelorn cowboys showed him that witches didn't bluff. No one could be more annoying than Esmeralda, when she really put her mind to it. Being a bitch was always more fun than being reasonable.

She was just getting into her bellowed karaoke set, when the door to the interrogation room slammed open. The damn light in her eyes meant she couldn't see the newcomer's face, but she sure as hell saw that he was massive.

And a walrus.

A fucking walrus? *Really?* God, why did she always meet up with the weirdoes?

Still, this was the closest she'd gotten to actually communicating with someone in power. "About time you showed up." She snapped. "I want to talk to you, in case you missed the subtle clues."

"I'm Commander of the Heart Kingdom Guard." He announced and she could already tell he was a jerk. The clothes were a dead giveaway. He was dressed in a fancy uniform, with a decorative sword at his side. Even with the light in her eyes, she could see every button and stay was straining under his colossal bulk. "You are a prisoner of Wonderland, witch."

"Who gives a shit?" Esmeralda retorted. "Look, all I want is a phone call." She held her thumb and pinkie up to her ear, mimicking the shape of a receiver. "You know? Tel-a-phone?" She carefully spaced out the syllables, in case these jokers were even more backwards than she thought. "Your men took mine and I want it back."

"Don't play dumb, you evil harlot." The Walrus spat out. Jesus, he actually used the word "harlot." "You enspelled our queen!" He was one of those guys who yelled every word and his huge tusks meant that all his Ss were slurred.

"Oh, Alice will be fine as a log. She's more durable now than she was before. Wood can last hundreds of years." Unless termites got it first. "Don't be so dramatic. Let's focus on the now. I want to go home."

There was a reason no one visited Wonderland, if they could possibly help it. Stuff just *happened* here, without sense or reason. The crazier you were, the crazier it all got. Some sort of insane magic bled out of the soil, feeding on anarchy and oddness.

"So can I call a lawyer?" She persisted when the Walrus just glowered at her. "I *am* entitled to a lawyer, aren't I?" It would probably be a giant, talking ostrich, but she'd take what she could get.

"Technology isn't working here, right now." The Walrus snapped, disregarding her request for legal representation. "We've made sure of that."

"What does that mean? You've got cameras going." She pointed to the blinking red light of the video equipment overhead.

"None of your business what it means! And you're 'entitled' to *nothing.* I should warn you that before Queen Alice hired me, I ran Wonderland's criminal underground. I *know* how to get the truth out of people, so I suggest you start talking, witch."

He was *that* Walrus? Crap. Better get her version out there, before she got herself shucked and eaten. Rumor had it that's what happened to his former henchman, the Oyster Brigade.

"I've been trying to tell you the truth for an hour." If he was willing to listen, maybe she'd finally get out of here. "First off, I'm not a spy or a terrorist or whatever else those nimrods upstairs were yelling."

"And yet you enspelled Queen Alice into driftwood." The Walrus paced around in agitation. "Did you think that would stop us? Is this all part of your secret plan?"

"None of this was a 'plan.'" Esmeralda sat up straighter and tried to see the Walrus's face through the glare of the interrogation lamp. "Mostly, I'm a fly-by-the-seat-of-my-awesome-leather-pants kinda girl."

"You're an about-to-be-killed-by-the-Queen-of-Clubs kinda girl!"

Who the hell was the Queen of Clubs?

"Let me just explain this from the beginning, okay?" Esmeralda tried. "I was in the Northlands, helping my friend Avenant woo himself a bride, and I fell through a rabbit hole. It transported me *here*." She jerked a thumb in the probable direction of the pastel lawn. "I fell through nothingness for a super-long time and then crash-landed at a garden party."

"Seventeen months."

"What?"

"You fell for seventeen months, using standardized clocks. Rabbit holes can compress time, so to you, it was only a few hours, but..."

"Seventeen months!" She interrupted at a shout. "*Shit!*" Her friends were going to be pissed. "So, I've missed like a year and a half?" She threw up her hands in exasperation. "If anything, *I* should be the one having the freak out here."

The Walrus wasn't convinced.

She let out an aggravated breath, trying to focus. "Fine. You know what? I will deal with it. At least, I'll have a lot of new documentaries to binge." Esmeralda liked watching documentaries while she worked. They were soothing. She reluctantly switched back to her story. "So, anyway, after I accidently fell into your yard, I tried to leave. But, your guards attacked and I *had* to attack them back. Anybody would've done the same." She paused. "Not for nothing, but did it ever occur to you that hiring a bunch of playing cards as soldiers isn't the brightest recruiting strategy?" Even her misfiring magic had flattened those jokers like they were --well-- paper.

The guards glowered at her.

So did the Walrus. "What about Queen Alice?"

"What *about* her? As I tried to walk out of this candy-colored nightmare, some snotty, blue-eyed bitch got in my face, threatening to arrest me. So I zapped her and she turned into a log. Super tragic. Not a dry eye in the house. At that point, your goons dragged me down here to answer for my nefarious crimes..."

He cut her off, looking suspicious. "Why didn't you 'zap' them, too?"

Because my magic crapped out.

"Because, I'm a peaceable girl. Once I realized my life wasn't in danger from you guys, I peaceably surrendered in a law-abiding way. Then those two locked me in this room," she gestured to the other guards, "and I've been bored ever since." She spread her hands. "The end."

"Not quite. You skipped the part where you took the Queen of Hearts' crown off of Alice's head." He gestured to the tiara she wore.

Esmeralda had forgotten about her new fortune in diamonds. It sat on her head, but she couldn't really feel it. She imagined it was enchanted to be weightless or something. The crown was blinged out like a disco ball, with a massive ruby heart right in the center. The look really worked for her.

She reached up to pat her wild hair and grinned. "Spoils of war. It looks great on me, right?" Esmeralda had a soft spot for sparklies and a moral compass that assured her that stealing them was A-Okay.

The Walrus turned to the playing cards. "Did you try to *take* it from her?" He demanded coldly. "Or do you want to aid this rebellion?"

The two guards exchanged a look. "Yes, sir, we did try to confiscate it, as you ordered." One of them finally mumbled. "But, it wouldn't come off."

That was true, but explainable. "The crown just got caught in my hair or something. It's totally the humidity."

They weren't even listening to her. For whatever reason, this seemed like it was going to be a whole big thing. The guards were cowering from the Walrus and he was trying hard not to rip them into pieces. Even with the lamp in her face, she could see this situation was deteriorating fast.

Esmeralda tried a different tactic. "Hey, if a little jewel theft is all that's standing between me and freedom, I'll just cut off some tanglier curls and pry the crown loose." As much as she liked the tiara, she was more than ready to leave this neon sewer of whimsy.

The Walrus acted like he didn't even hear her, looming over his men. "If the crown won't leave her head, we'll take off her whole damn skull. That's how that smirking cat stole it from the queen before Alice."

Esmeralda blinked. "Wait *what?*" Holy shit, she was about to be executed over a bad hair day! She surged to her feet. "You can't just chop off my head!"

"Oh, but I *can*." The Walrus turned to face her and she heard the certainty in his voice. "As soon as you give us what we need, we'll have no further use for you and I can do whatever I want. Who the hell is even going to miss you?"

"Lots of people!" Well, at least five. Esmeralda could hear her heart pounding in her ears. She struggled to find some scrap of magic inside of her. "I have a family."

She'd met Marrok, Scarlett, Avenant, Benji and Drusilla in the WUB Club. They'd been stuck together for group therapy sessions. Somewhere between yelling at each other nonstop, breaking out of jail, and overthrowing Cinderella, the six of them had become a family.

"The Tuesday share circle sticks together." She warned the Walrus, because it was a fact. "Believe me, you do *not* want to piss them off."

The Walrus didn't look impressed with the threat. "You belong to *no one*. No one cares enough to rescue a witch."

A spark of anger flashed to life inside of Esmeralda, eating through the fear. "Well luckily, we're damn good at rescuing ourselves."

That would have been an amazingly Badass thing to say, right before she blasted them all with her powers. Stuff of legends. Esmeralda could actually imagine herself repeating the words to Scarlett, once she was back home and they were laughing about this mess over cosmos and cheesecake.

Witches cast their best magic using their hands. She lifted her palms, giving the frog spell another go and *really* concentrating on getting it right this time. Putting all her effort into it. ...And absolutely nothing happened.

The jackasses just stood there, staring at her like she was crazy. Esmeralda lowered her hands and blew the bangs from her eyes in agitation. "Crap. In my head, that was going to be *super* impressive."

The playing cards grabbed her and hustled her from the room. Their flat fingers dug into her delicate skin. "Shall we take her to the dungeon, sir?" One of them asked the Walrus, as they half-carried her down the twisting hallway. All the walls were painted in alternating red and pink hearts. What sort of psychos decorated with alternating red and pink hearts?

"No, not the dungeon." The Walrus shook his head. "To the White Rabbit's lab. Let's get this over with."

"Lab?" That sounded even worse than the dungeon option.

"Um…. Let's talk about this idea, because it's a *terrible* idea. Whatever it is you want, I'm sure we can work it out without labs and decapitations."

"Dark Science is always conducted in a lab." The Walrus told her, like it was obvious.

"What's Dark Science?"

"What the White Rabbit used to bring you to Wonderland." He made a face. "Believe me, if there was another way, we would have gone with it. I knew you were going to be a pain in the ass."

Esmeralda's boots skidded on the ground, trying to find traction as the playing card guards propelled her through an unmarked door. They dumped her on the spotless floor, quickly stepping back like they were afraid of whatever lurked in the bright white space.

"What is going on?" A chirpy, hoppity male voice exclaimed. "It isn't time for her yet, Walrus. It's only Tuesday."

Esmeralda raised her head to look at the man talking… and yeah. He was a white rabbit. A bunny in a bowtie was beaming at her with buck-teeth and soulless pink eyes.

For real, Wonder-bland *sucked*.

"We're supposed to wait for the Queen of Clubs to arrive, before we wake him up. She gave orders." The Rabbit continued fretfully, gesturing to a calendar featuring topless mermaids pinned to the wall. "She won't be here until Monday."

Esmeralda automatically glanced at the calendar, but she couldn't read the damn thing. The days were all weirdly clumped together in twos and threes. And there were *eight* little date-squares, for the first week of the month. That didn't make any sense. Did they just add an extra weekday, somewhere in the middle?

The name over the eighth square read "Tove." Somebody had drawn a crown on the date with a bunch of stars around it. For some reason, it seemed like a threat.

"We need to get rid of the witch, *now*." The Walrus snapped. "Unless you'd prefer for the Queen to arrive and find one of Wonderland's tiaras in the hands of her enemies."

Esmeralda sat up, pushing the curls back from her face and sending them a glare. She had no idea who they were talking about, but what did it matter? There were only so many enemies a girl could handle at a time. "I'll get you both for this. Count on it."

They didn't seem intimidated.

"Oh dear, oh dear, oh dear..." The White Rabbit studied the diamond tiara and nervously bobbed his head. "Queen Alice was supposed to be holding onto it for safekeeping."

"The witch ruined that plan. Alice is now kindling. We need to move up the schedule."

"You want to wake him *now?*" The White Rabbit's voice dropped in fear. "It's not safe! *He's* not safe!"

"And the Queen of Clubs *is?*" The Walrus retorted. "At least his magic will be weakened. She'll be at full power, when she arrives with her army!"

"Even weakened, he'll be formidable." The White Rabbit wrung his paws. "If only I had more time, I could rig a magic inhibitor."
His? He? Him?

"We *don't* have any time!" The Walrus argued. "The damn witch arrived in the wrong spot, through that defective rabbit hole you created. She was supposed to land in the dungeon. Instead, she invaded Alice's tea party!"

"It wasn't my fault that it didn't work as expected. My calculations were right. The witch is the faulty variable. Either her or Wonderland. The magic here is very unstable. It must've..."

The Walrus cut him off. "Let's just get on with it. Hopefully, you haven't screwed this part up, too. He'll have no reason to fight us and the Queen needs him awake, sooner or later. We're doing everyone a favor, right?"

"You're not doing *me* a favor!" Esmeralda's eyes cut around the room, looking for an escape route. "What creepy shit are you up to in here?" All she saw was high-tech, ominous-looking, science-y stuff.

And a glass coffin with a guy in it.

"I didn't screw up." The White Rabbit insisted, still looking offended. "The Queen of Clubs hired me, because my science is *always* impeccable. And the Wicked, Ugly, and Bad Mental Health Treatment Center and Maximum Security Prison kept excellent records. I looked at all the blood tests, and conducted a mystio-physiological screening, and there is only one answer. It's not my fault that you don't like her."

"The witch has been nothing but trouble. Once she wakes him up, we'll kill her fast. It'll take me half an hour to get the execution ready and then we'll be home free."

The White Rabbit hippity-hopped over to hit some buttons on a blinking panel of switches. The sides of the glass casket slowly lowered. It wasn't a coffin, after all. It was some type of stasis box, keeping the sleeping guy inside suspended in time, so he'd wake up with his body functioning as normal.

Esmeralda stared at the unconscious stranger, her lips parting in reverence.

The Walrus rubbed his flippers together. "We'll get that damn crown off the witch's head and figure out a way to restore Alice ourselves, before the Queen of Clubs even finds out." He frowned. "You can use Dark Science to save Alice, right?"

"It would depend on how powerful the witch's magic is. Anything below a four, I can counter."

"Her file doesn't say her level, but I can tell that she's nothing much. No *way* is she as high as a four. However she enspelled Alice, she doesn't seem capable of repeating it. Just adrenaline and luck, probably." The Walrus snorted. "And *he* won't care what we do with her afterwards. Trust me. I've spent some time with this little bitch. Anybody would be glad to get rid of her"

The White Rabbit nodded, but didn't seem totally mollified. "The woman's score on my new Magic Matrix is very unusual. I've never seen anyone's magical powers rank so close to the center."

"Average." The Walrus intoned distastefully. "Told ya."

"That's not exactly what the score means..."

Esmeralda barely heard their jabbering. Her eyes stayed on the sleeping man, unable to believe what she was seeing. Unable to comprehend that she'd actually done it. After so many years of looking and hoping and *feeling* him out there... After longing for him for so long... After being so lonely and needing him so much... After all of it, she'd *finally* reached the only place she'd ever belonged.

It was him.

It was her True Love.

CHAPTER TWO

Pick your perfect nail polish from our unlimited selection!
Not What You Ordered Opal: Sorry! This polish is not the one you ordered. Instead, we're sending you a brand new concoction, filled with magical opalescent flakies and genuine piranha fangs. This mysterious gift is one of the most beautiful and dangerous products in our inventory.
Only you know if its amazing colors are worth the risk of having your fingers bitten off.

Happily Ever Witch Cosmetics Website

The Heart Castle

Esmeralda let out an amazed sound. She'd found her True Love.
She'd really found him!
She'd always known she could do it. The very first spell she'd ever cast had been to locate this man and, though it hadn't given her his GPS position, she'd felt his existence. Her whole life, she'd *known* he was out there. To be staring at him now was nothing short of magical.
Holy shit.
Everybody said Bad folk could just look at their True Love and recognize them. It was apparently true, because she looked at the dozing stranger and she *knew* he belonged to her.
Hopefully, he'd know it too, once he opened his eyes.
Why wasn't he opening his eyes?
"What's wrong with him?" She demanded, scrambling to her feet, afraid to even take her gaze off of his still form. "What did you do to him? Why is he asleep?"

"He was hit with sleeping gas." The White Rabbit told her, as if they were discussing the weather. "Only a kiss from his True Love can wake him. It's why you're here."

Bad folk did Bad things. They lived to perpetrate cruel and heartless acts. But, there was one overriding moral imperative that any Bad folk worth their salt followed: They all protected their True Loves.

Esmeralda didn't even hesitate. Didn't ask any more questions, because the answers just didn't matter. No one else even registered with her, now. There was no way she'd let her True Love suffer for even one more second. She headed across the room, her eyes on his slumbering face.

Jesus, she'd hit the jackpot with this guy.

He was *seriously* stunning, with his exotic features and long ebony hair studded with silver beads. It was hard to tell his height, since he was lying down, but he seemed tall and his body was awesomely beautiful. Muscular and broad and… naked.

Wow was he naked and the view was awe-inspiring.

She stopped by the bed, gaping down at him. Esmeralda would have been thrilled with the man, regardless of what he looked like. He was her True Love, after all. But having a *gorgeous* True Love was just adding a cherry on top of her good fortune. He even had a tattoo, covering most of the left side of his massive chest. Esmeralda liked guys with tattoos. She liked *everything* about this particular guy.

This was *her* guy.

She was stranded in Wonderlame, and her hair was a disaster, and she was about to be beheaded, but this was still the best day ever!

"I've been waiting for you my whole life." She whispered.

Leaning down, she pressed her lips against his.

For a second, nothing happen.

Then, he drew in a sharp breath and she felt him stir. His eyes blinked open, her kiss waking him from his slumber.

Esmeralda eased back, smiling down at him. "Hi." She said, overwhelmed with happiness and triumph… and lust.

The kiss had only lasted a second, but it still made her insides flutter. His lips had been soft and he tasted like magic. Passion was usually instant and overwhelming between True Loves, but this reaction seemed particularly strong. The man just looked at her and she was already ready to climb on top of him. Seriously, this guy was perfect!

His gaze locked on hers and recognition lit the vivid green depths. He must have been Bad, which was good! He clearly knew who she was without her having to explain the situation. Astonishment filled his expression. She had the odd feeling that this man didn't get astonished easily, but for a heartbeat of time he gaped like he couldn't believe she was really there.

"Hi." Esmeralda repeated breathlessly. She should think of something better to say. Something clever or memorable or seductive. And she totally would, just as soon as she stopped grinning like an idiot.

"It's... you." His deep voice seeped out like smoke.

A voice like that should've been whispering endearments and promises in the dark. It should've been ordering fancy desserts off a fancy menu in some fancy restaurant. It should've been reading audiobooks full of epic poetry and dirty sex. And now that voice was *allllllll* hers. For once in her life, her luck didn't suck!

"It's me." Esmeralda agreed, bouncing on the toes of her boots with excitement.

Something sparked in his green eyes, but it was gone too quickly for her to read. "My God." He slowly sat up, his gaze on her face. "I always thought it was bullshit. I never believed the stories about seeing your True Love and just knowing, but..."

The movement must have made him dizzy, because he abruptly stopped and pressed a hand to his forehead, like he had a hangover. "Shit."

Esmeralda winced, hating to see him distressed. "You should try and stay still." She wasn't sure how long it took sleeping gas to leave your system, but he seemed groggy. "I think you've been unconscious for a long time. You need to recover."

"Unconscious...?" Memories seemed to come rushing back. "From that fucking *gas*." He drew in a deep breath, his voice going harder. "Hold on. *No*. This isn't right."

"Not right?" What was he talking about? Everything was going great! She was ready to start planning their honeymoon crime-spree. "This is exactly what's supposed to happen when you find your True Love. I've read so many fashion magazine articles on it. Once you get some rest, we can..."

"No, things like this don't just happen. What *happened* to make this happen?"

She blinked at his accusatory tone. "I don't know exactly. I fell down a rabbit hole and they brought me to you. They said you were gassed and only True Love's kiss could wake you up. And so," she shrugged, "I kissed you."

"You kissed me?"

She bobbed her head.

"Because you're my True Love." It wasn't really a question, but he still seemed doubtful about the whole thing.

"Yes, I'm your True Love." She let out an amazed breath that she could really say the words to someone. That she *belonged* to someone. "I'm Esmeralda."

That would have been a perfect time for him to sweep her up in a romantic embrace. Instead, his expression darkened at her name. "Esmeralda." He repeated in a harsher tone. "The witch?" He looked her up and down, cataloging all the separate pieces of her. Something new and dangerous burned through his confusion. "*Marrok's* witch?"

"You know Marrok?" The Big Bad Wolf was part of the Tuesday share circle. He was Scarlett's husband and Esmeralda loved him like a brother. There was no denying that the guy made a few waves, but she was shocked by the fury she heard in her True Love's voice when he said Marrok's name.

"Trevelyan." The Walrus called from behind her, solicitation in his tone. "Can we get you anything? Coffee? Food? Clothes?" Esmeralda glanced over at the bastard and then back to her True Love. "Trevelyan?" She repeated warily.

He disregarded that cautious query. His attention switched to the other people in the room, as if he hadn't noticed them before. ...No, more like they weren't *important* enough to notice and it annoyed him they were talking now.

The beads in his waist-length hair jangled slightly, sounding exotic and seductive and somehow foreign. Like the music from a distant land. The last of the momentary softness faded from his eyes, replaced by cold suspicion as he watched the men.

The Walrus and the White Rabbit both edged closer to the door.

Esmeralda didn't blame them. The power dynamics had shifted. Even naked and barely awake, her True Love controlled the room. It suddenly felt like they were all prey who'd been unwittingly trapped with a very dangerous, very unpredictable predator.

"Who are you?" Trevelyan inquired and no one was fooled by his calm tone.

The White Rabbit made a small sound of dismay and cringed down into his bow-tied collar.

"Why we're your newest friends." The Walrus assured him with false joviality.

"I don't have any friends."

The Walrus held up his flippers in a gesture of peace. "You're wasting your time with the witch. She knows nothing important. *We're* the ones who saved you." His voice had a submissive "can't we please sit at your lunch table?" whine to it. "We can help each other."

Trevelyan kept staring at him.

The Walrus pressed onward, petrified but not giving up. "You have no idea all the trouble we've been through to steal your sleeping body from Neverland, and bring it here, and find your True Love, and wake you up..." He shook his head, like just listing all the steps was exhausting. "But *finally* you're conscious and now we can get down to business."

"Business?" Trevelyan echoed skeptically, not looking at all grateful about the rescue. Some of the tension left his shoulders, though. "You want to strike a deal?"

"Yes!" The Walrus seemed close to tears, thrilled the conversation had reached safer ground. "You hold the Blackest Magic in the world, Trevelyan. Our employer wants a spell."

Trevelyan.

The Walrus had said it twice.

Esmeralda felt herself start to hyperventilate. That couldn't be right. It just *couldn't.* Not even her luck was that terrible. She found herself shaking her head, refusing to believe that her life was *that* fucked up.

Maybe "Trevelyan" was a more common name than she thought. Maybe this guy was some other, better, *saner* Trevelyan, who maybe worked in a record store. Esmeralda liked guys who worked in record stores. They tended to be just the right amount of Bad. They'd help you transport your annoying roommate into space or something, but they didn't try to decimate kingdoms or slaughter all your friends. Record store guys were interesting, without being some crazy-ass lunatic bent on destruction.

Not like certain criminally insane, megalomaniacal, mortal-enemies-of-the-Tuesday-share-circle.

"You're not the Trevelyan who tried to kill Marrok and Scarlett, and help that depraved nutcase Cinderella conquer the Four Kingdoms, are you?" She asked, even though she already knew the answer. "That wasn't really *you*, was it?"

The Walrus was still blathering, but Trevelyan didn't seem to care and Esmeralda's heart was pounding in her ears, so she didn't hear his words. Their attention was locked on each other.

"I'm Trevelyan, Last of the Green Dragons." The deep angles of his face were hard, now. "Marrok betrayed me and betraying a dragon carries a death sentence."

She wasn't sure if that melodramatic statement was an explanation, a boast, or a threat. Regardless, it snuffed out the last of the excitement she'd felt over finding her True Love. All her dreams were crushed and he didn't care. The dragon was watching her like *she* was the one who'd done something wrong.

It was... devastating.

"I'd always hoped my True Love worked in a record store." Esmeralda heard herself say in a faraway voice. "And liked black cats, and going to sci-fi conventions, and working on spells together."

He was wrecking all her dreams! Did he not get that?

Trevelyan got to his feet, brooding, and dark and scarily big. He was still naked, which should've made him seem vulnerable, but it didn't. It made him seem dangerous. The tattoos that covered the left side of his chest were all of fire-breathing monsters and skulls. The illustrated flames somehow moved against his skin, like they were flickering and hot.

"I always hoped my True Love would be smart." He intoned. "So, it seems like we're both about to be disappointed, if you align yourself with the wolf. Only an idiot would get between me and my adversary." He loomed over Esmeralda, making her feel small and unsafe.

She'd been right before. He was definitely tall. ...And way, *way* too powerful for a witch with twitchy magic to stop if he went psycho. In his dragon-form, the guy would be fifteen feet tall and could breathe fire. In his human-form, he was ruthless and prideful and cold. Dragons were the most unpredictable, untrustworthy species in any kingdom. No one sane wanted them as a True Love. A girl would be lucky to survive the wedding night.

She automatically took a step backwards. Away from him. Trevelyan's jaw ticked at her quick retreat.

Esmeralda barely noticed. "Marrok didn't help you break out of prison, right? That's how he betrayed you?" Esmeralda had heard this story from Marrok. "You were going to burn down half of the WUB Club and he stopped you."

Having done time in the Wicked, Ugly, and Bad Prison herself, Esmeralda felt some sympathy for Trevelyan's desire to escape. In fact, she'd been part of a breakout, too. But when the Tuesday share circle fled, they hadn't bombed anybody.

"Marrok ruined my plans. Instead of a simple, clean-cut explosion, I had to sleep with Snow White to get out. I had to put my hands on her stinking body, wait until she fell asleep and then escape out a fucking window. Do you have any idea how degrading that was?"

The WUB Club's chief administrator had helped herself to half the prisoners in the place, so Esmeralda wasn't surprised by the angry words. Dismayed and furious, but not surprised.

She took a deep breath, trying to stay calm. "What happened

to you was wrong. *So* wrong and I'm *so* sorry. Dr. White was a psychotic, abusive skank."

"No shit!"

"None of this is important." The Walrus interjected. "The witch isn't a..."

Trevelyan interrupted him. "Stop talking." He ordered, not even glancing his way.

The Walrus stopped talking.

Esmeralda kept her attention on Trevelyan. "We erased Snow White's memory in the Lake of Forgetting. She's probably in some care facility, now. If you're still pissed at her, I get it. I do. I will *happily* help you find her and wipe her out of existence, altogether. I swear. But it was *not* okay to target Scarlett for any of that and you need to apologize to her. I mean it."

Trevelyan had the nerve to look insulted. "I was targeting the wolf. Scarlett was just a way to get to him. I didn't harm the girl."

"It's not fair to blame Marrok for what Snow White did."

"I blame him for what *he* did. Marrok was supposed to be my friend and he didn't have my back when I needed it."

"So you hold a grudge about it for years, plotting to get even? To come after Letty, when Marrok finally found her? To try and destroy the Four Kingdoms and everyone in it?"

"*Yes.*"

"But you can't do that!"

He gave a scoff of utter contempt at her protest. "Of course I can. I have darker magic than anyone in the world. Didn't you hear what that asshole just said?" He waved a hand at the Walrus, still not bothering to look his way.

"Hey!" The Walrus protested.

Trevelyan ignored him. "I'm a *dragon*. I can do whatever I want."

"Well, *I* don't want it! Are you out of your mind? That's my home and family you're talking about hurting."

That was not what Trevelyan wanted to hear. *"Nobody* will stop me from having my revenge against Marrok and everyone he claims as his own." He snarled, as if she'd suggested otherwise. "Certainly not a True Love, who I didn't choose or even ask for."

Esmeralda stifled a wince, refusing to show that he'd hurt her with his words. "You're not my first choice, either. My record-store guy wasn't a dick. He wrote me songs on his guitar. He was in a band. So it seems like we're both going to have to make some compromises."

"Dragons never, ever compromise. We *negotiate*, but we don't compromise."

"So start negotiating, then."

"I'm not negotiating! Not about Marrok. There is no middle ground in this war."

Her lips thinned. "Well, where does that leave us?"

He arched a snide brow, looking an awful lot like the judges always did, right before they passed sentence on her. "The wolf is my enemy. You need to decide whose side you're on: His or mine."

Esmeralda had no intention of doing anything that stupid. "Look, whether or not we chose each other, we're still True Loves. Let's calm down and talk about this in a reasonable..."

He cut her off. "Loyalty is what counts. Not True Love. *Loyalty*." He crossed his arms over his chest. "Are you standing with me or are you standing with your so-called 'family.' Decide."

Esmeralda gave up trying to reason with Trevelyan. It was no use. He wasn't going to listen. Not now, when they were both so upset. She stared up at her True Love --At this man who she'd waited for all her life-- and told him the truth. "Family sticks together."

CHAPTER THREE

Pick your perfect nail polish from our unlimited selection! Trustworthy Male Clear:-Like its namesake, this nail polish doesn't exist. Buyers will receive an empty bottle and a deep feeling of disappointment.

Happily Ever Witch Cosmetics Website

The Heart Castle

Trevelyan was evil. Not just Bad. *Evil*.

He took real pride in that distinction. You were *born* Bad. You had to *decide* to be evil. It took time and energy to build up the requisite skills. Fortunately, Trevelyan was a hard worker. Everyone who had ever heard his name feared him like a fucking plague, because he'd *proven* he was the worst son of a bitch in the world. When you dedicated yourself to a goal, it was always pleasant to see your efforts pay off.

He read over the file the Wonderland idiots had compiled on him, satisfied with what he saw. However the "Magic Matrix" worked, his powers apparently topped out the dark end. According to the White Rabbit's charts, Trevelyan's magic was ninety-eight percent wicked.

(Granted, that other two percent was confusing, but the number was low enough that he could pretend it wasn't there. Surely there was a margin of error. The technology was new.) No one tested had ever scored higher than him, according to the handwritten note in the margin. Despite everything, it was truly gratifying to see that his reputation remained intact even while he was in that damn mystical coma. Not a single magical creature anywhere was as horrible as Trevelyan.

That was the most important thing.

Of secondary importance was the fact that he'd been locked in a lab by miscellaneous creatures who had files on him. That was never a good sign. They seemed eager to accede to his demands, but he wasn't stupid enough to think they were really his "friends." Marrok had taught him the fallibility of allies. By his count, he had exactly one friend left and even that was stretching the definition of the word. Maid Marion was usually just a pain in his ass. She'd shielded him, when he'd escaped from prison, though, and saved his life with her warning about the WUB Club. So, Trevelyan didn't doubt her loyalty. Marion Greystone was the one being on the planet he gave a shit about.

Still, even if they weren't his friends, the Walrus and the White Rabbit had brought him all his medical charts, when he demanded to see them. And they'd left the room when he ordered them to, so they clearly wanted him appeased. For now. Who in the frozen-hells knew how long that would last, but he wasn't overly worried. They needed something from him. That was obvious.

And he *might* give it to them.

Possibly.

Being in a mystical coma for almost two years was extremely irritating. Trevelyan was predisposed to look favorably on those who woke him up, regardless of their motivations. So, he'd hear them out. If they begged, and paid a lot, and didn't piss him off maybe he'd make a deal. Maybe. Otherwise, he'd just kill them and get on with his life.

Then, of *far* less importance than all of the above, was the witch.

Marrok's witch.

Trevelyan had told the others to leave her alone with him and they had. Truthfully, they seemed grateful to be rid of her for a few moments. Maybe they thought he'd kill her and finally stop her talking. Now, it was just him and the woman, alone in the lab. So far she didn't seem any happier with him than he was with her.

"What are you reading?" She demanded, a suspicious frown on

her pretty face.

Trevelyan ignored her.

The situation would be simpler if the witch's attachment to Marrok was physical. Trevelyan knew it wasn't, though. Marrok had found his precious True Love and that smug bastard was the most moral Baddie ever born. He'd *never* cheat on Scarlett. Not even with a woman as beautiful as Esmeralda. No, the witch really did consider Marrok her brother.

Her fucking "family."

She wanted to stand with the wolf and his moronic group of morons, because she thought they were all super-terrific. That was much worse than if she was just having sex with the man. Trevelyan could counteract sex. He was very good at sex. Surely, better at it than *Marrok.*

(Not that Trevelyan had any firsthand knowledge on Marrok's skills, as they both preferred women. But you could tell just by looking at him that the wolf had no imagination, at all. In a sex contest, Trevelyan would completely win. He was sure of that.) Also, sex didn't mean very much. Sex was just sex. It came and went. Lately, it had been in the "went" column, if he was being honest. Even before the mystical coma, he'd been avoiding it for... reasons. But, what did it even matter? Only loyalty counted, in the long run. And Esmeralda's allegiances were tied to Marrok and her friends in the Enchanted Forrest.

So be it.

Trevelyan had given her a choice. He'd warned her that there were two sides to the war: dragon or wolf. Anyone who stood with Marrok would be mowed down along with him, when Trevelyan struck.

Even Trevelyan's True Love.

She wasn't his mate, after all. He hadn't decided that only she would do for him.

Mates were important to dragons, because they were the partners they *chose.* You and your mate stood together against threats, and went after the same goals, and fought the same enemies, because you were loyal to each other. Perhaps, you raised some children to perpetuate your line and increase your family's power. Your *actual* family. Couldn't be simpler. True

Love was an alien concept, but *loyclty* he understood.
Too bad the witch didn't.

"What are you reading?" She demanded again. "You might as well answer me. I'm hard to ignore. Ask any of my parole officers."

Trevelyan shot her a glare, still scanning back and forth between the files. One was his and one was Esmeralda's, both from the Wicked, Ugly, and Bad Mental Health Treatment Center and Maximum Security Prison. He understood enough of the WUB Club doctors' bullshit to know he was screwed. That reeking hellhole of a prison had taken his blood. It took *everyone's* blood.

And the markers in his exactly matched the witch's.

Trevelyan sighed in frustration. It had been pointless to even double-check the results. He didn't need the damn mystio-physiological screening to feel their bond. Bad folk instinctively knew their True Love. At least that's what he'd been told. Trevelyan had never believed it, until now. (He never believed anything he couldn't see, hear, taste, scent, or feel for himself.) But, he'd opened his eyes, saw Esmeralda and... recognized her. Somehow, though, he'd been hoping that the files would disprove what he already knew was real.

Why was his luck always so fucking lousy?

The woman was devoted to Trevelyan's mortal enemy, she seemed horrified to have him as a True Love, and she wasn't a dragon. Dragons *always* mated with dragons. What in the frozen-hells was he supposed to do with a mate who wasn't even a dragon?

She wasn't his mate. Obviously.

The witch might be his True Love, but there was no way he'd ever choose her as a *mate*. If he kept her, she'd surely just be an ancillary part of his life. Perhaps that would work. Trevelyan wasn't known for close relationships. Maybe he could just put her somewhere and forget about this mess.

"Whatever you're reading, you should probably stop." She persisted. "You look pissed and you *already* looked pissed, so maybe you should read something else, before you set something on fire."

That wasn't likely to happen for a while. His powers were too drained from the long sleep to take on his dragon-form. He could feel the monster stirring, but it wasn't able to emerge, yet. That did nothing to improve his mood.

"That White Rabbit is measuring Dark and Light magic on a continuum." He reported, since she wasn't going to stop nagging about the files. "These charts are full of information on his testing process. Did he tell you that?"

"He said something about a Magic Matrix, but…"

Trevelyan cut her off. "I scored very well on his new matrix. You… *didn't*."

That was more lousy news heaped onto the pile. Trevelyan lived and breathed magic. It was all he cared about and his non-dragon, disloyal, incredibly irritating True Love barely had enough mystical powers to make balloon animals. Thank God his parents weren't alive to see what had become of the family name. It would kill them.

"Like I give a shit about Professor Bunny and his fake tests." She was standing by the wall, watching him like he was a horrible nightmare made real. Which improved his mood, a bit. "We don't even know how they work."

"The Rabbit is weighing how much Good and Bad is in each of us." At least, that's what the files said. "Apparently, he's been listening to Marrok's Goody-Good True Love and decided that nobody is all one thing or the other. We're all a little bit Good and a little bit Bad." (Except Trevelyan. With the two percent margin of error, he was safely evil, through and through.) "The Rabbit wants to know exact proportions."

Esmeralda scoffed. "That's ridiculous. You can't break apart people into neat and tidy percentages. He's a quack! You might have noticed by his secret, underground lab, filled with incompetent henchman and bubbling test tubes."

Trevelyan sent her a look through his lashes. "Guess how wicked *your* magic is, witch."

"Magic and math have *nothing* to do with one another. You may as well ask me what imagination tastes like or how big the color blue is."

"Fifty-one percent wicked." He held up the graph so she could see for herself. "Your magic is barely half evil. Another point or two in the wrong direction and you'd be a fairy godmother." He arched a brow. "With the margin of error, you don't even *qualify* as Bad."

(And there was surely a margin of error.)

"Of course I'm Bad!" The witch objected, rightfully insulted by the alternative. "Do you have any idea how many times I've been arrested?"

"Being arrested a lot just proves you're *bad* at being Bad."

"Yeah, well, you were locked up in the same prison as me, dumbass. So look who's talking." She was genuinely affronted now. "Why are you even reading that crap? Some kidnapper in a bowtie gives you a stack of files and you just believe what he says?"

"The fact that I'm no longer in a mystical coma lends some credence to the man's scientific abilities."

"You're not in a coma, because *I* woke you up. Me! Esmeralda, the *wicked witch*." Her lovely crimson eyes narrowed. "And fifty-one percent is a *clear* majority."

"Fifty-one percent is fucking tragic." He flipped the file closed, totally discouraged. His head was pounding, but he wasn't about to show weakness by rubbing at his temples. "What *level* magical powers do you have?" Rankings gave everything context. Maybe she was somehow very powerful, which would offset the taint of Good. "The files don't say. Tell me it's above a three."

"None of your business." She gave her wild hair a toss and Trevelyan's attention instantly shifted.

He had no idea why she wore a tiara, but he liked the look of it in her thick tresses. Black curls bounced around the twinkling diamonds in unholy ways. The one promising part of this situation was the woman's undeniable beauty. Not even magic could've created a body as perfect as hers, a fact that she apparently wanted to show off in glorious detail. Her clothing was ridiculously small, revealing acres of lush, pristine skin. Witches had the most incredible skin of all the species. It was green and luminous and so soft that men fought to touch it. It was also extremely delicate. Bruising easily and melting in water. Like all rare and special things, it required care. Trevelyan had no idea how to care for anyone.

He also wasn't sure whether to be annoyed or pleased that Esmeralda was comfortable exposing so much of her translucent flesh to the world at large. Vast portions of her hourglass figure were on display, for anyone who cared to look. ...And *everyone* was going to look.

On the one hand, Trevelyan certainly liked the view. The woman was a work of art. (If you considered pinup calendars "art," anyway.) Again and again, his gaze went to the tall boots she wore, admiring the shape of her thighs disappearing beneath her too-short skirt. He'd always appreciated a woman's legs and hers seemed to have been sculpted from fishnet stockings and male fantasies.

But, contradictorily, it also bothered him that *other* men could behold her ample curves and radiant skin. Some cosmic force or another had given Esmeralda to Trevelyan. Her magic was ordinary, and she was his adversary by association, and he found her high level of Goodness to be dismal. But none of that made a bit of difference. Now that the witch was in his clutches, every other male needed to stay away.

Dragons didn't share.

"Tell me about that imaginary record store boy, again." He ordered, leaning forward on the bed. "The one you were hoping would be your True Love. Did he mind your powers were so very… average?"

"Fuck yourself, Trev." Crimson eyes gleamed. "Sideways."

He felt his body hardening under her challenging glare. Inside of him, the dragon roused. Liking her rebelliousness. Dragons were drawn to women who didn't just meekly obey. They desired strength.

They liked the hunt and the fight and the conquest.

For the first time since the WUB Club, the dragon focused on something beyond rage. It stared at the witch, from deep within Trevelyan. The smoke and hate in his mind cleared slightly. For a blessed moment, there was calm.

Perhaps things were looking up.

Trevelyan's tongue ran over the edge of his teeth, considering

Esmeralda with deeper interest. "You should be careful of what you say to me." He told her softly, just to see her reaction. "I've filled cemeteries with *actual* wicked witches."

She made a face at him, wholly unimpressed with that dark truth. "Oh, please. You're not going to kill me."

No, he wasn't. Everyone else was a possibility (even a probability), but never her. The True Love bond would never allow that and they both knew it. More importantly, he simply didn't want to kill someone so alive.

"We're connected." She continued, looking right at him. Meeting his eyes like she wasn't afraid. He far preferred that to her earlier alarm and small retreat from him. That had pissed him off, although he usually enjoyed inspiring terror.

It had seemed... wrong.

"You'd better start dealing with being my True Love, because we're in deep shit, right now." She paused, her tone going hard. "And if you *ever* threaten to hurt me again, I will drop-kick your ass right back into a coma. That's a goddamn *promise*."

Every drop of dragon blood in his body was pounding with desire, now. So few people ever defied him. Especially not small beings he could crush without even trying. It was fascinating.

"I am dealing with our True Love match quite well, I think." He said, all his attention riveted on her. "You're the one who's upset that you're not marrying a guitar player."

"I'm not upset!" She raged.

"Obviously." His eyes lingered on her shapely hips, as she paced.

He'd allow her to continue dressing as she pleased. Granted, other males were going to be an issue, but Trevelyan could just slaughter them all. Simple enough. Why should his enjoyment of her stunning body be impeded because weaker men didn't know their place? Trevelyan had never altered his own desires because of others and he didn't plan to start now.

He was the only one who mattered.

Esmeralda's wrath seemed to fade into something like sadness. "It's just I had so many dreams about my True Love. So many

ideas about the perfect guy..." She broke off with a sigh and put a hand over her face. "I have no idea what I'm going to do."
"Well, *you* might be stymied, but thankfully *I* can do anything I want." Trevelyan reminded her, insulted that she still longed for her fictional record store boy. Was she blind? "I have level five magic." That was pretty much as high as it went. "And my powers are ninety-eight percent wicked, according to the rabbit's matrix." He hesitated. "Not counting the margin of error, which I'm *sure* is two points. So, I'm not concerned about my future."
Esmeralda blinked over at him. "Level five?" She repeated, like she wasn't sure she'd heard him right.
"Yes."
"Not a six?"
"Few people have ever scored a six. Merlyn, of course. A sorceress, here and there. That dickhead from El Dorado. Perhaps a few others." And they were all Good, as far as he knew. Such a waste of magic.
"Oh." She crossed her arms over her chest, which just drew his attention to her bountiful breasts and skimpy top. The damn thing had less fabric than her underwear. Literally. He could see the edges of her lacy purple bra peeking out at all the seams. Her clothing choices were going to necessitate the deaths of thousands. It was inevitable. "Well, I guess level five is... nice." For no reason at all, she suddenly looked amused.
"Really."
Trevelyan's eyes narrowed, trying to understand her expression. "How low did you score?" He pressed again.
"A one." She held up her middle finger at him, pointedly flicking him off.
God*damn* but he wanted her.
It came over him in a crash. Nothing had ever felt like this and he reveled in it. Thankfully the two idiots who'd been there earlier had brought him a robe along with the medical files, because there'd be no hiding his growing desire, if he was still naked. Not that he cared about the "being naked" part. Dragons were the least inhibited species in any given kingdom. But he didn't want to scare the girl away.

...Unless he got to chase her.

Trevelyan slid off the edge of the bed he'd been sitting on, ignoring the way the edges of his vision dimmed. The long unnatural sleep was still wreaking havoc with his system. He took a deep breath and prowled towards her, forcing away the dizziness that spun around his head.

The dragon was watching her intently, now. Focused on the witch and intrigued by what it saw. Interesting. All parts of Trevelyan were being drawn towards this perplexing little creature. Well, that settled it then. He was definitely going to fuck her.

This time, Esmeralda didn't back up as he approached. Instead, she squared her shoulders to face him head on. It nearly made him purr in satisfaction. The woman was a fighter, beneath her showgirl veneer.

"This is crazy." She informed him. "We need to discuss what we're going to do about being True Loves, not compare our magical tests scores."

"Why don't we discuss what *you're* going to do about our being True Loves?" He retorted, moving closer to her. "*My* position is very clear: You stand with me or my enemies. You've apparently chosen Marrok," he spat out the name, "so *now* what are you planning to do?"

She glowered up at him. "I'm not great at making plans, but I guess..." She floundered for a beat. "I guess I'm going to stop you from destroying my home and family." She gave a firm nod, pleased with that announcement.

It made him chuckle, but it was a humorless sound. "*Nothing* will stop me from destroying the wolf." His fingers absently toyed with one of her unruly curls. "Certainly not you. More powerful people than witches have tried to keep me from my goals, yet here I stand."

She batted his hand away from her hair, which was both annoying and enticing. "Thanks to *me*." She insisted again. "You're standing here *thanks to me*. Because *I'm* you're True Love. Doesn't that mean anything to you?"

He shrugged. "It means you should be loyal."

"Loyal?" She repeated incredulously. "To you? Why would I be loyal to you, when you've been the worst True Love in the world, so far?"

Trevelyan's jaw ticked. He had been the soul of fucking consideration, as far as he could see. "Have I disappointed you, darling?" He asked softly and anyone else would've heeded the warning in his tone.

The witch didn't budge.

His hunger increased.

"You are *incredibly* disappointing." She assured him. "Too bad for you, I'm the toughest person you've ever met. I *deserve* a happily ever after. I *fought* for it and I'm not settling for less. So, I'm not about to let you screw this up for me." One sparkly fingernail poked at his chest. "Not yet. Not until I'm sure there's *no* hope, at all."

Trevelyan stepped even closer to her, crowding her smaller form. "Well then, you'd better start convincing me to keep you."

She finally noticed his arousal. It was hard to miss. Very hard. Those perfect lips parted in astonishment, jolted from her tirade. Her eyes jumped from his straining erection, then back up to his face. Generally, Trevelyan found innocence tedious and calculating, but for some reason her shock amused him. "What are you doing?" She blurted out, like she genuinely didn't know.

Trevelyan arched a brow. "Lord, tell me you're not *that* Good." "No, I mean..." Esmeralda shook her head. "You don't want to do this. Really." She swallowed. "It's just happening because of the True Love match. That's all. We need to *not* focus on sex. It will just make everything worse."

She was right, of course. About the True Love part, anyway. Supposedly Bad folk *always* felt overwhelming, automatic, mindless desire when they met their True Love. Trevelyan hadn't believed that rumor before, but now he was experiencing it himself, so it must be true. The wild pull he felt towards the witch could only be an involuntary mix of chemistry and magic. Obviously. That was the only explanation that made sense. It had nothing to do with Esmeralda as a person and everything to do with his body recognizing hers on a cellular level.

But who cared?

The desire was there and he needed to satisfy it. Carnivores wanted to *eat*, not discuss the menu. And dragons were definitely carnivorous. Trevelyan had always been a sexual being. He didn't give a shit about logic or reasons or thoughtful conversation, just being inside of her. Still...

His head tilted, taking in her beautiful, flushed face. "Does it matter *why* we have sex?" He asked, curious as to the source of her outrage. "Aside from the fact that we feel the urge, thanks to fate and biology?"

Her breathing had quickened, her full breasts rising and falling over the top of her tiny shirt. It would've taken a better man then Trevelyan to overlook her beaded nipples.

"Yes, it matters!" She snapped. "It matters to me, anyway."

"Why?"

Her eyes traced over his face, as if she thought he might be joking. He wasn't. In fact, he felt like he was missing something important and he hated that feeling.

"Because, it's empty to have sex with someone you don't like." She finally said in a quieter voice.

His eyebrows soared, unsure whether to laugh or curse at her naïveté. "That's it? Jesus, if I only had sex with people I *liked*, I'd never have sex, at all."

And no one in the entire universe had ever liked *him*, so that would certainly put a damper on things.

Esmeralda was silent for a beat. "My God..." She whispered. "You have no idea what I'm even talking about. None, at all."

He shook his head, ignoring that statement. "This pointless morality you're clinging to is the forty-nine percent Goodness dragging you down. You need to rise above that nonsense."

Most of her hostility faded and she looked almost sad for him. "Do you understand *nothing* about what having a True Love means, Trevelyan?"

He didn't appreciate the implication that *he* was the deficient one in their relationship. "I understand enough."

In fact, something new was just occurring to him. The witch was Bad. (*Barely* Bad, but Bad nonetheless.) So, if *he* felt this suffocating, instinctive passion... then so did *she*. The need in her must be rising to match his own.

Testing, he shifted so their bodies touched, his hard shaft nudging her. Demanding attention. Esmeralda gasped at the feel of him, causing more blood to rush to his throbbing flesh. Up close her skin was even more amazing. Like flower pedals. He wanted to touch it everywhere, just to feel the texture, but he was afraid he'd hurt her. Generally, he didn't give a shit about hurting anyone, but her skin was soft and delicate and so rare...

Against his will, a growl rumbled in his chest. The dragon wanting to possess her.

"Crap." Esmeralda muttered and arched forward like the sound enflamed her. "That is *not* helping. I'm trying to make you understand..."

"I understand that you want me, even though you don't *want* to want me." He interrupted, enjoying this more then he'd enjoyed anything in a *looong* time. "...And darling that just makes it even better."

"You really are the worst person in the world." She whispered, sounding dazed.

"I try."

"For real. I should forget about finding a way to make this mess work. I should just run away as fast as I can."

His eyes nearly crossed with lust at that spectacular image. "I truly wish you would." He whispered in her ear and she whimpered. It was like music. "Maybe you are a fairy godmother, because that's *just* what I want."

"I'm not talking about some twisted, dominance foreplay, Trev."

He barely heard her, more and more intent on his goal. Dragons were scent based creatures and Esmeralda's fragrance was the most intoxicating one he'd ever encountered. For a below-average witch, she smelled like concentrated magic. Trevelyan drew in a deep breath, amazed. *A lot* of concentrated magic. And her scent was different than the usual musk of dark spells that drifted around Bad folk or the light, fresh perfume of the Good. This was an impossible mix of *both.*

He'd never cared much for the banal reality of Goodness. Bad was so much deeper and more complex. It had a bitter aftertaste, though, that inevitably disappointed and made him long for something sweeter. Sadly, Good's aroma of sugar-and-spice was all an illusion. Trevelyan had always been perversely drawn to that beguiling whiff of sweetness, but the mouthwatering fragrance turned out to be frustratingly bland when you finally got a lick. Neither could completely satiate his appetite, which often left him confused and irritated and inexplicably... lonely.

Esmeralda suddenly seemed like the perfect solution to his quandary. The witch was nearly half Good. Dark and light came together inside of her to create something very special. Something new. Mixed with her glorious Badness, maybe Good really *would* taste as rich as it always promised. His head dipped lower, wanting more. Wanting to kiss her and...

Esmeralda did step back this time, emphatically shaking her head. "No."

Trevelyan's eyes snapped to hers. "What?"

Why would anyone say "no" to a dragon? He truly didn't understand.

Aside from those Good girls with the sparks in their eyes, he didn't recall anyone ever saying "no" to him. The last one of those vexing women had been Marrok's True Love, but he was pretty sure Scarlett Riding *would've* been agreeable, if he hadn't been playing up the menace for her idiot True Love's viewing pleasure. Trevelyan had gotten a bit carried away with the theatrics and frightened the girl. But he hadn't intended to *do* anything to her. Not really. And that certainly didn't explain why Esmeralda wanted to stop the game.

"No." The witch sounded resolved. "Absolutely, one thousand percent, unequivocally *no*." She stressed the word, the color high on her cheeks. "As in: this is not happening today. As in: it might not happen *ever*. As in: you've got this all backwards. You need to convince *me* to keep *you*."

Oh, Trevelyan liked the idea of convincing her. A lot. True Love matches were an unknown, but he knew *volumes* about sex. He was an expert, in fact. There was always a bit of teasing, when everyone was playing the game correctly. It added to the hunt. Supposedly sex between True Loves was the height of the sport. He didn't believe that yet, but he was willing to be convinced.

"Wonderful idea, darling."

Chapter Four

Pick your perfect nail polish from our unlimited selection!
All for You and Plum for Them: (Limited Quantity Available) Only one
bottle of this spectacular smoky-purple color will ever be made. No
surprise that you probably won't feel like sharing it.

Happily Ever Witch Cosmetics Website

The Heart Castle

Trevelyan closed the small distance that Esmeralda had created, backing her right into the wall.
That maneuver caught her off guard. "I don't mean you should convince me like *that*." She didn't seem scared to be caged in by a dragon, just flustered. That was interesting. "Jesus, you take everything in the *worst* way. I meant: I'm not kissing you, until you stop being a jackass."
"You've already kissed me."
"That was before I knew you were a jackass! I thought you were a *normal* True Love and I wanted to save you."
"And I'm very grateful." He assured her gravely.
"No, you're not. You're a deranged maniac."
"Well... that, too."
Muttering curses about his entire lineage, she attempted to squiggle free of him. "I'm *not* kissing you. When I kiss my True Love, it's going to be real. It's going to mean something. It's not going to be because some egomaniacal dragon is..."
Trevelyan ignored the baffling complaints, his hand shooting out when she tried to duck away. His palm went flat on the wall, his arm extended to create a bar and obstruct her path. She immediately tried to go backwards, but his other arm

moved to block that avenue, as well. It was lamentably simple to surround her, really. She could have put a bit more effort into her escape.

Esmeralda jolted as he kept her trapped and he felt her breathing get rougher. She was turned on by the game. (Not that it was much of a game. But even a small one was better than no game, at all.) She enjoyed being caught. He hummed contentedly at that promising sign. Such a Bad girl. He *liked* that.

And, now that he'd captured her, he could finally have her. Trevelyan leaned his head down to nuzzle her temple. Christ, she fit against him just like he knew she would. Every soft curve lined up just where he wanted it. He still hadn't touched her skin, but he knew it was going to be life-changing.

"Stop, Trev." She warned, breathlessly. "I'm serious."

"Oh, I'm serious, too, darling." He was *seriously* considering leaving her boots on when he took her. The image of it appealed to him. He *seriously* wanted those long legs wrapped around him. Now.

Inside of him the dragon growled, predatory and impatient. The monster was so much more involved in this game than it usually was with women. Typically, it barely noticed Trevelyan's bed partners. But the witch felt different. The dragon wanted to be inside Esmeralda, as quickly as possible. It wanted his scent all over her body, as a warning to others. It wanted that defiance melted into blissful submission.

Trevelyan couldn't agree more.

The lovely fragrance of her desire was rising, but he could see that she still wasn't ready to surrender. Hopefully, she'd carry out her threat to run. It was the fantasy of every dragon to chase down their willing, teasing, very Bad mate and then take her right where she'd been captured.

Not that Esmeralda was truly his mate, but...

"You really wanna play it this way?" She challenged, interrupting his thoughts.

"Absolutely, one thousand percent, unequivocally, *yes*." Trevelyan's mouth headed towards hers, again. "I'm enjoying this game." Her lips were so perfect. If she wasn't going to run, he'd fuck her right there against the wall and anyone who wandered in could see who she belonged to.

Her boot slammed down on his barefoot with a savage twist. "Shit!" Trevelyan stumbled back in shock, fairly sure the sharp heel had pierced his flesh straight through to the other side. Was she crazy? That really hurt! Was he bleeding? He tried to check the damage, but his equilibrium was still off from the sleeping gas in his system. Dots flashed before his eyes and he ended up toppling over onto the floor.

Shit.

He lay there for a moment, trying to rearrange the scattered thoughts in his pounding head.

"Game over." Esmeralda taunted.

Shit.

He let out a long breath of decompression. "That was playing a bit rough, witch. Even by my standards." Any reasonably intelligent person would've noted the edge to his tone.

Esmeralda just gave a snort, not at all apologetic over crippling her True Love. He'd been right before. She wasn't nearly as smart as she should be. "When I say 'no,' you take your hands *off*. That's not negotiable."

"My hands never touched you."

She hesitated, as if suddenly realizing he was right. "You did all that and you didn't even *touch* me?" She actually sounded insulted. "Why the hell didn't you touch me?"

"Witches have delicate skin." He muttered, wondering if he'd ever walk right, again. What had he ever done to deserve this kind of misery?

...Besides everything he'd ever done.

"Oh." Esmeralda digested his grudging explanation. "It's *not* that delicate. You can touch my skin, if you're careful. Well, *you* can't because you're horrible and I won't let you, but generally speaking..." She cleared her throat. "Point is, when I want *any* part of you to touch me, I'll let you know. And you need to *stop* when I tell you to stop. Understand?"

That seemed promising. Sort of. He held out a hand, beckoning her forward with a finger. "Come down here and kiss me, then. Teach me how you liked to be touched. I'm always open to learning new things."

She ignored his palm and her voice got harder. "I am *not* kissing you. That is not negotiable either, so don't even try it. *I will not kiss you.* Not yet and probably not ever."

Trevelyan didn't even like kissing. It was just a boring precursor to getting a woman naked. Still, that statement aggravated him. He let his hand drop. "Because I don't play the goddamn guitar?"

"Because I won't kiss someone I don't believe in."

"You want to *believe* in me? What the fuck does that mean?"

"Trust you. Respect you. Have faith that you won't deliberately hurt me. Have a vision for a future together. Know that you'll catch me if I fall. Or at least try. *Believe* in you, as a man and as a partner." She shrugged. "And right now, I don't."

Trevelyan's jaw locked at that ridiculous list. "This is Marrok's fault." He wasn't sure how, but he knew it was true. "The wolf and his bleeding-heart bride are filling your head with lies, and stupidity, and wholesome fucking values and it's..."

"Trevelyan!" The Walrus' alarmed shout came from the doorway. "Dear Lord, the witch is attacking him! Guards, come quickly! She's going to ruin everything!"

Oh for Christ's sake.

Trevelyan rolled his eyes in disgust, as a cadre of idiots stormed into the room. (He was *endlessly* surrounded my morons. It was like a curse.) He gave up on hiding his weakened condition and rubbed his aching temples, wishing the throbbing in his brain would lessen so he could make sense of the woman's pointless...

"Stop!" Esmeralda cried. "*Ow!* Let go!"

Trevelyan's head snapped up, the pain forgotten.

A mountain of a man in a heart-patterned executioner's mask had grabbed hold of Esmeralda and was half-carrying her towards the door. The witch fought to get free, but she was outweighed two-to-one. The man chuckled maliciously, enjoying her struggles as he overpowered her. His meaty fingers bit into her arm, digging into her delicate flesh and leaving angry marks.

What the fuck...?

For a beat, Trevelyan was so flat-out astounded that all he could do was gape.

Another man was hurting his True Love? Right in front of him? Another man was marring her perfect skin, and making her cry out in pain, and dragging her away? Right in front of him? Another man was trying to steal from a dragon? *Right in fucking front of him?*

Had everyone lost their goddamn minds while he was asleep?

"Get that crown back." The Walrus was telling the executioner. "It's on there with some sort of magic, so chop her head off. That should do it."

"You toothy son of a bitch!" Esmeralda raged at the Walrus. "When my family gets here, they're going to *destroy* you! Marrok is going to rip your heart out and nail it to the wall! Then, Avenant will bury you in ice forever and Letty will make sure everything you've ever owned is confiscated by... *Hey!*"

The scumbag executioner released her so suddenly that Esmeralda tripped over her own boots. Her crimson eyes swung around to stare at the giant hulk, who was now levitating two feet off the ground.

"Help!" The man vainly tried to get free of the unseen force suspending him. "Help me!"

Then, shit got *really* Bad for the jackass. His huge body went rigid. He screamed in agony, but no sound came out. It was more peaceful when victims suffered quietly, so removing tongues was always an advisable first step of villainy.

From Esmeralda's blank expression, it was clear she had no idea what was happening. Not even a glance in Trevelyan's direction.

Okay. Now, he was getting annoyed.

"Does no one here understand who I *am?*" Trevelyan asked very softly in the silence that descended over the room.

As if their heads were all connected by a string, everybody looked over at him. Which was excellent. Dragons did their best work with an audience. Deep down they were all attention whores.

"Does no one here understand *what* I am?" He continued coldly. "Do I need to show you? Would that help?"

He was still sitting on the floor, one fist extended in front of him. Very slowly, he twisted his hand in the air and the executioner's flailing body... deflated. It collapsed into liquefied mush, falling to the ground. It hit like a half-filled water balloon, sloshing against the linoleum in horrible jiggly ripples. Esmeralda scrambled backwards from the gelatinous mess, which was unnecessary. Nothing sordid was going to damage her precious boots. All the man's insides were still trapped by his flaccid skin. The witch didn't even bother to thank Trevelyan for his thoughtfulness.

"Holy *shit!*" She blurted out, her eyes wide. "What did you just do?"

"I removed all his bones, of course."

Trevelyan opened his hand and all two-hundred-and-six of them fell from the air above the executioner. They bounced off the man's dead body, clattering to the ground in a heap. His basketball-sized skull rolled around on its top, making a delightfully morbid sound that any dragon would've appreciated.

"Ninety-eighth percentile of evil." He informed his audience, just in case they hadn't heard the news. "Not counting the margin of error."

Esmeralda focused on Trevelyan and only Trevelyan. The Walrus' blubbery skin went pale. Two of the playing card guards took off running.

See? *That* was more like it.

Trevelyan gracefully rose to his feet, hoping he wouldn't faint from fatigue and ruin the moment. Using even that small bit of power had left him completely drained.

"Why did you do that?" Esmeralda whispered in something like wonder.

"I don't like other people touching my belongings."

For once, the witch didn't seem to have a ready answer.

"Now, explain why these men want to behead you." He continued pleasantly. "I can think of *many* compelling reasons, but I'm a bit curious as to which one they've settled on."

That jolted her out of her daze. "Because they're kidnapping assholes, that's why!"

"Why *else*? Something about that tiara, I believe."

The Walrus swallowed so loudly Trevelyan could hear his throat clicking from across the room. "The crown belongs to the rightful Queen of Hearts." He got out, edging towards the door. "Alice has been wearing it ever since some Cheshire Cat killed the last queen, but she was just a placeholder. It was never really *hers*."

"And why isn't Alice-the-placeholder wearing it, now?"

"Because the witch turned her into a log."

Trevelyan's eyebrows soared. "A log?" His gaze flicked to Esmeralda. "Dear *God*, darling…" It was a heartfelt lament for the sad state of her imagination.

Crimson eyes narrowed. "Well, I didn't know any good bone-removing spells." She snapped. "So I had to make do with way less theatrics."

He'd fought legions of knights with fewer balls than this woman.

The Walrus nervously gauged Trevelyan's expression. "We have to get Alice back into her body and the crown back from the witch. *Quickly*."

"Technically, Alice's energy is still *in* her body." Esmeralda interjected in a mulish tone. "It's just her body is a log."

A log.

Trevelyan sighed in exasperation. "Esmeralda, give the damn Walrus back the tiara, so we can get on with this mess." He would buy her another crown, if she wanted one so badly. Or steal one. Or create one with magic. Whichever was easier. Frozen-hells, his head (and foot) hurt too much for this nonsense.

"I can't give it back, genius. Trust me, I've tried. It's stuck."

"Stuck?" Trevelyan stalked over to try and remove it himself, because he never trusted anyone else's opinion or word. You could only believe what you experienced for yourself. Sure enough, though, the diamond tiara was firmly affixed to her curly head.

"Told ya so." She batted his hand away from her hair. "Quit it."

Trevelyan stepped back, frowning slightly. He wasn't sure what sort of magic was at work in the crown, but it was strong. He met Esmeralda's eyes for a beat, wondering what an ordinary witch could've done to trigger such a powerful enchantment. She stared back, sweet and defiant.

"You see?" The Walrus interjected in a more hopeful tone. "We need to decapitate her. It's the only way." He nodded at Trevelyan, sure that he'd just convinced him. "You see, right?"

"Beheading my True Love might remove the crown." Trevelyan allowed. "But it would also leave her without a head. Granted, she doesn't seem to use her brain for much, but her face is one of her best features."

"Aw gee, do you really think I'm pretty, Trev?"

Damn if Trevelyan didn't enjoy her sneering. What dragon could possibly resist so much fire? "You might do." He decided and barely dodged another heel through his foot.

The Walrus ignored the byplay. "Yeah, but... you don't *need* a True Love, anymore. You're awake, so she's served her purpose. We can get rid of her, now."

Trevelyan slowly blinked. The man still wasn't getting it. Was one dead body on the floor not enough? Was Trevelyan being too subtle?

The Walrus continued talking, heedless of danger. "Dragons aren't all sentimental about their True Loves, like wolves, and witches, and friggin' Midas. You won't care if we kill this mouthy bitch. That's what makes you the best at being Bad."

"No." Trevelyan corrected, his roiling temper achieving conflagration. "What makes me the best at being Bad is *I'm the fucking best at being Bad!*"

The last part came out as a reverberating roar. He might not be sure what he was going to do with the witch, but he knew for goddamn *certain* that no one was going to steal her from him. His powers were too weak to take on his true form, but the dragon was still within him. Always. And it was fully awake now, pissed that someone would threaten what was theirs. Green smoke began to rise from his skin and swirl around his body, a precursor to the transformation. That was enough to terrify anyone with a brain in their head.

The Walrus shrank back.

The remaining playing card guards froze in terror.

Esmeralda didn't even flinch.

Trevelyan ignored what that revealed about her IQ and advanced on the Walrus. "Now let me be very, *very* clear, because you seem very, *very* stupid." His voice echoed with flames and death. "What's mine *stays* mine, for as long as I want to keep it. No one takes it. No one threatens it. No one *touches* it."

The Walrus was too terrified to even move. Trevelyan got that reaction a lot.

"I could kill every person in this kingdom without even noticing they were alive, in the first place." Trevelyan went on ruthlessly. "And I will start with *you* if you ever --*Ever!*-- take... or threaten... or *touch*... my witch." If he'd been in dragon-form, fire would be coating that carefully enunciated threat. "She is just mine." The words sizzled the air.

Esmeralda seemed transfixed. Like she was seeing him for the first time. In a way, she *was*. The dragon was his truest self, so she'd better get used to it.

Trevelyan pointed at her for the Walrus' benefit, so there could be no mistake. So everyone could be crystal clear on the one and only rule that mattered. The line between life and death for every other man in the universe. "No one. touches. what's. *mine.*"

"Oh dear, oh dear, oh dear..." The White Rabbit came scampering back into the room. "This isn't going well, at all."

"You said the mystical coma would drain him." The Walrus frantically hissed. "Well, he doesn't look drained."

"He's stronger than I gave him credit for, but I'm sure his powers are completely depleted, by now." The White Rabbit's whole body shook with fear, belying his assurances. "He can't transform or he already would have."

"I'm not taking the chance. Gas him or something!"

"I can't use the sleeping gas, again. Spells only work once on a person." The White Rabbit fished a hypodermic needle from his waistcoat. "Here! I prepared this, just in case. You'll need to jab him with it."

"You're the scientist. *You* do it. Quick, before he escapes."

"The castle is enchanted so neither of them can leave. He's not going anywhere."

"We won't either, if he kills us!"

He was trapped in here? Trevelyan spared a glance towards the ceiling.

Fuck.

"This tranquilizer will knock him out." The White Rabbit insisted, like he was trying to convince himself of the plan. "We'll administer it to him and we can wake him up again, with heavy restraints in place."

Trevelyan's eyes narrowed, realizing the little bastard was about to send him back into a coma. He instinctively reached for his powers, but they weren't there. He was still weak and he'd already used too much energy.

Damn it, how was Trevelyan supposed to be a proper villain without magic? Brute force was so much messier, but it was the only option. Could he grab the needle from the Rabbit's hand before the son of a bitch used it? Hopefully, because he was about to try.

Dead or free.

Trevelyan started forward.

"Do it, now!" The Walrus yelled at the White Rabbit. "I *knew* this would happen! Everyone who's ever heard of this bastard knew it would happen! You were crazy to wake him up!"

The White Rabbit was outraged. "I *told* you we shouldn't wake him up without the Queen..."

Magic slammed out, like lightning flashes and the wings of birds.

Beautiful and electric and everywhere.

One second, Trevelyan was plotting a way to tackle the Rabbit and rip the syringe from his grasp. The next, the Rabbit was gone. So were the Walrus and the few playing card guards who had braved a return to the room. In their place was an impromptu barnyard of panicking pigs. The creatures raced around the lab, frantically squealing amid piles of clothing.

There was only one way that could possibly happen: The witch had just saved him.

Trevelyan slowly turned to look at her.

"Shit." Esmeralda muttered. "That damn spell *never* works

right."

Trevelyan had no idea what that complaint meant. Her magic seemed to have worked beautifully. It had been a massive blast of energy from someone with such limited talent, as a matter of fact. The witch might only be fifty-one percent Bad, but she'd made the most of it. He was fairly sure that she'd just transformed everyone in a forty mile radius into a walking ham. And her magic had been green.

To the Last of the Green Dragons, that was nearly as important as Esmeralda stopping their assailants. Magic came in many colors, but none of the other shades were *right*. (At least in Trevelyan's opinion and who else's opinion even mattered?) The witch's powers matched his own. Bright, sinister green that burned like unholy fire.

The dragon purred.

"Assholes." Esmeralda continued, glowering at the swarm of pigs. "I told you I'd get you sooner or later, didn't I?" She glanced over at Trevelyan. "You okay?

As far back as he could remember, no one had ever tried to physically protect him. Why would they? He was the greatest, darkest, most powerful villain around. He wasn't sure how to react to a level one witch stepping in to shield him from harm. His brain couldn't quite process it, so he instinctively fell back on what he knew: Pride and anger and lies.

"I didn't need your help." Trevelyan snapped. "I *never* need help. I had it under control."

"You're welcome, jerkoff."

Chapter Five

Pick your perfect nail polish from our unlimited selection!
Calling-in-Sick Canary: Perfect for those days when watching
afternoon soap operas and painting your nails in bed is just WAY
more important than your dumb job.

Happily Ever Witch Cosmetics Website

The Spade Castle

Why did jobs require so much work?
Lily Pleasance became the Queen of Spades because being a sheriff of the Swan Kingdom had been a constant pain in the ass. Confessions to listen to, and crimes to investigate, and whiny victims expecting her to solve all their damn problems. Being employed took up her whole day! The powers-that-be had ignored her helpful suggestion-box suggestions to just pay her and let her stay home. Dick-wads. So, she'd left for greener pastures.
Well, Fall-colored pastures, anyway.
She'd been wasting her talents with the snooty swans. Anybody could see Lily was made for bigger things and Wonderland had seemed like a real growth opportunity. She'd taken a job in the Kingdom of Spades' police department, with her eyes to the future. From there, Lily had worked her way up to queen, with a few strategic murders and well-deserved promotions. Now, she had a diamond tiara on her head and a great big castle of her own.
...And there was *still* too much damn work.
All the energy it took to get this job and, in the end, it was just as annoying as the last one. It wasn't fair. Lily ran a hand

through her dark hair and wondered if queens got vacation days. She needed a break, in some faraway land.

"The tea party was ruined." The March Hare told her, watching the flamingo-croquet match being played on the leaf-covered yard. He was a jittery human-sized creature, with a crippling addiction to Earl Grey that everyone was polite enough to ignore. "It's why we fled here, where we could have a civilized meal."

Tea had been quickly prepared upon their arrival. It was served outside, on the flagstone patio behind the castle. The Spade Palace was the most practical of Wonderland's four royal residences, more of a charming chalet than an ornate castle. It was constructed of gray stone, half-timber walls and tapered chimneys, giving it the look of an over-grown cottage. The thatched roof added an old-timey touch. It also leaked like a son of a bitch and made everything smell musty. Lily preferred to spend her days out in the crisp mountain air.

"The witch landed right on the table and started blasting guests with her magic. Can you imagine?" The March Hare continued, shaking his head in despair. "I'm not sure *what* Alice did after that. I was running in the other direction. Did you see Alice's reaction, Caterpillar?"

The Caterpillar exhaled vapor from his hookah. "Gads, no. I ran, as well. *Nothing* could save the party after the witch appeared. It was a social disaster, through and through. The Heart Kingdom will never live it down." He seemed perversely pleased with that harsh judgment. Probably because it would give him something to talk about for weeks.

Like the March Hare, the Caterpillar spent most of his time traveling from kingdom to kingdom. They were part of Wonderland's exclusive Tea-Partier set. The elite group was welcomed by all the queens, for their rich gossip, sharp wit, and flawless taste.

Sadly, Lily didn't have time to enjoy their jaded vitriol today. She hadn't been expecting their visit and she still needed to finish some dull reports. She flipped through the piles of financial documents she was supposed to sign off on, barely listening to them. "What is a lobster-quadrille and why am I paying so much gold for it?"

That money could go towards her raise. She deserved one, for all the work she did.

The March Hare and the Caterpillar exchanged meaningful glances, as if silently judging her *so* déclassé. It was no secret that they'd been hoping Grimhilde the wicked witch would become queen. She was semi-retired and had an estate in the Spade Kingdom, where she was hard at work on her memoir, said to be entitled *106 Uses for a Still-Beating Heart: Life Lessons from the World's Wickedest Wicked Witch.*

Personally, Lily planned to hire a ghostwriter for her own autobiography. No way was she putting in all the effort to type a manuscript, even if she was obviously a historic figure in the making.

In any case, the Tea-Partiers disliked witches. But they disliked everyone. And Grimhilde was President of the Cauldron Society. Such a notable title and lofty position appeased their snobbery and anti-witch sentiments. She'd gotten their vote for Spade Queen. Unfortunately for them, no one voted for queens and Grimhilde was too busy chronicling every second of her long, malevolent life to be interested in court politics. They were stuck with Lily on the throne.

The fact that Lily had worked her way up the aristocratic ladder rankled the Tea-Partier set. They endured her, because they were dependent on all the Queens for their livelihoods as judgmental gadflies. William --whose name was *never* to be shortened to Bill or Will-- was the worst of the lot. Thankfully, the condescending lizard wasn't presently there for tea. If it was up to William, he would rule *everything.*

Still, Lily didn't let any of their attitudes bother her. She aspired to their parasitic examples. Being a professional hypocrite looked way easier than doing paperwork.

"I should have the lobster-quadrille, then?" She guessed.

"You *must* have a lobster-quadrille, regardless of the cost." The March Hare insisted in a firm tone. "Not having one simply isn't done. Why it would be a never-ending embarrassment for the Kingdom of Spades."

"Never *ending.*" The Caterpillar concurred. "And you have

enough problems around here. If you cancel the lobster-quadrille, you might as well invite a witch to tea, like poor Alice."

That comment sent both him and the March Hare into a fit of world-weary chuckling.

Lily sighed and initialed the exorbitant estimate for the damn thing.

"I suppose the Heart Kingdom now falls behind the Club Kingdom, when it comes to places I most dread visiting." The March Hare lamented. "The Club Kingdom is filled with the unpleasantest people in Wonderland, no argument."

"Ghastly people." The Caterpillar agreed. "Even worse than the zealots in the Diamond Kingdom, who hate magic for no reason at all."

The Tea-Partiers were the one non-human group in Wonderland that not even the Gyre could completely exclude. They were too influential.

"Better those beachy bigots than the Club Kingdom's cold-fish citizens and those bloodsucking roses." The March Hare gave a shudder. "The gardener should be fired. But at least that murderous pigeon is just the *help*. No one's inviting him to tea."

"Thank God for that. He'd surely feed the other guests to his evil flowers or wear dirty overalls to the party. It would be a scandal!"

Lily ignored their byplay. "What about a brillig?" She asked, still consulting her papers. "Do I really need two?"

"You really need three." The Caterpillar scoffed, puffing his hookah. "They're positively mimsy!"

Lily should have become a nurse, like her mother wanted. It would have been so much less work. She okayed the brillig, as well. "I think we'll have to close some schools to afford it all, then." Otherwise, she wouldn't get so much as an extra coin in her pay this quarter.

The March Hare shrugged. "It's for the betterment of everyone. I'm sure the children will pick up reading and such, as they go along. But, a brillig is essential for the Spade Kingdom's future. *Every* powerful ruler should have one."

"Three." The Caterpillar chimed in. "She can't be cheap about it." He paused. "Not sure where she's going to find them, though. William already got the best ones for the Queen of Clubs."

The March Hare rolled his pink eyes. "That lizard is always social-climbing. It's unbecoming of a Tea-Partier."

Lily rubbed her forehead in agitation and crossed out a few schools on her budget. Why couldn't someone else deal with this crap? Wasn't the whole point of being queen that you could do what you wanted? Why did she never get to do what she wanted?

Leaves from the Tumtum trees drifted down, some of them landing on the table where they were having tea. Since it was always autumn in the mountainous Spade Kingdom, the leaves were forever falling. New ones just instantly grew to take their place. No one paid any attention to the phenomena.

Likewise, no one paid any attention to the serving hag who came plodding over with a fresh plate of apple pastries. Lily couldn't keep track of the castle's staff. It was too much work to even try. Still, this woman seemed completely unfamiliar. Maybe she was new? Jesus, why did someone hire a new servant who was six million years old?

"Wishing scones." The hag set the heaping tray onto the table. She wore the red-and-black, spade-patterned uniform of the palace staff. "You eat one and dreams come true."

"I wish for a trip to a faraway land." Lily muttered and grabbed herself a wishing scone. Apples were popular in the Diamond Kingdom, because they were always in season. The kitchen stuck the frigging fruit in everything. The apples in these pastries were perfectly baked and delicious. *That* must be why the hag was hired. She was a wonderful cook.

Even the March Hare and Caterpillar seemed pleased with the taste of the scones. They were stealing extras off the tray and hiding them in their waistcoats for later. Lily made a face. For people so free with *her* money, they sure were stingy with their own.

The hag stepped back and watched them all eat, with a contented smile on her mole-y face. Great chef or not, she

wasn't going to work out as a waitress. An old crone was not at all the kind of public-facing figure the castle needed. If she stayed, she would be confined to back-of-house duties, where no one could see how hideous she was. The Tea-Partiers hadn't said anything about her appearance yet, but it was only a matter of time before they started making jabs about how ugly Lily's staff was and how she needed to hire models to...
Her thoughts drifted off, as a strange sensation began swelling inside of her.
Painful. Burning. Terrifying. Air ripped straight from her lungs. Blood congealing in her veins. She couldn't breathe. Couldn't move. The half-eaten apple scone fell from her hand and hit the table, as she reached up to claw at her throat. It did no good. Panic set in, even as some small part of her brain continued to process what was happening.
Poison.
Beside her, the March Hare and the Caterpillar had both turned purplish-red, their own necks swelling up like inner tubes. The March Hare hit the ground, struggling for oxygen. The Caterpillar succumbed almost instantly, his dozens of legs sticking straight up in the air.
They'd just been murdered. All three of them.
Lily was still enough of a sheriff to solve this case. Her gaze cut over to the crone. "Poisoned apples..." Her mouth moved, even though her windpipe was too swollen for any sound to come out.
"Poisoned apples." The old woman agreed, understanding Lily's words. Her face was already changing, becoming more beautiful than the first snowfall. "Old family recipe."
In that moment, Lily knew what this was about. She helplessly gripped the tiara on her head, trying to keep it in place. If it came off, she'd know she was really and truly dead. If you were the rightful queen, your tiara could only be removed when you died. The blackened sapphire in the center was shaped like a spade. She felt it under her palm. Just as she could feel the crown becoming looser on her skull, as her life ebbed away.
The old woman moved closer, only she wasn't old, at all. Or maybe she was *very* old. It was impossible to be sure. Magic

kept her ageless. Diamonds glinted in her own tiara and, at the center, an onyx club gleamed.

"I told you they were wishing scones." Maryanna, the Queen of Clubs, smiled. "And my family is about to have *all* our dreams come true. I'll make sure of it." She lifted one lovely shoulder in a graceful shrug. "It's what a mother does."

Lily's eyes became sightless, no longer seeing the woman. Her chest stilled, her body shutting down. The very last thing she experienced was the Queen of Clubs' elegant hands pulling the tiara free from her corpse.

But by then, her mind was already in a faraway land.

CHAPTER SIX

Pick your perfect nail polish from our unlimited selection!
You Can Do Better Bronze: Keep scrolling. Don't let the appearance
of this seductive polish fool you. You deserve *way* more than this
irritatingly masculine shade, filled with aggravation, random color-
shifts, and itching powder. We're not sure why we even sell it. ...Or
why it's so damn tempting.

Happily Ever Witch Cosmetics Website

The Heart Castle

Esmeralda could do better.

She was *positive* about that. Trevelyan was a deranged maniac, who her family hated and the rest of the world feared. He was never going to be the True Love she'd dreamed of or even a pleasant partner to spend her life with. He was sarcastic, and dangerous, and only cared about himself. He could turn people into puddles of skin with the power of his mind.

But when the White Rabbit had threatened him, her magic had blasted the little rodent without Esmeralda even having to consider it.

"This is the first time I've ever *accidentally* overthrown a kingdom." Trevelyan mused, helping to search Alice's royal office. "Usually it takes more than an afternoon to usurp an entire land. You should feel proud, darling."

"We don't know that *everyone* in the Heart Kingdom was affected by my magic." Esmeralda muttered, although it sure as hell seemed that way, judging from the view out the windows.

For miles around them, there seemed to be nothing but very

angry swine and no people. She *completely* hadn't intended to make the spell that strong. Her powers were frigging impossible to deal with and Wonderland seemed to be making them worse.

Trevelyan gave a skeptical sound. "It affected everyone. ...Unless some of them were pigs to begin with."

"Hogs."

"What?"

"They're hogs, not pigs. Technically." Still not frogs, like she'd intended when she cast the damn spell. But at least it wasn't logs. Baby steps.

He squinted at her. "Of all the enchantments you could've used, why did you choose hogs?"

"What are you? The spell police? Shut up and search." Esmeralda snapped and reached up to touch the crown that was still situated in her curly hair. The longer it stayed stuck to her, the more concerned she became about what kind of magic was keeping it in place.

Why the hell hadn't someone warned her not to steal it before she stole it?

She cast a fuming glance at the portrait of Alice hanging on the wall, blaming the former-blonde for not giving her a heads up about the damn thing. The artist had captured her un-log-ified state perfectly. Alice's smug face was majoring in fake lashes, with a minor in concealer, and she didn't look at all repentant about screwing up Esmeralda's life.

Damn it, they had to find a way out of Wonderland.

The Rabbit hadn't been lying. The Heart Castle was enchanted. Trevelyan and Esmeralda couldn't get farther than the edge of the wide patios, without some mystical barrier stopping them cold. The dragon insisted he could knock down the spell, as soon as his powers returned. Esmeralda wasn't so sure, but there wasn't much of a choice except to believe him.

If and when they got past the invisible force field holding them prisoner, they had bigger problems, though. They didn't know how to escape Wonderland. They needed a map. So far, their search for one had been fruitless, but neither of them was ready to stop ripping shit apart.

That was the way it went with Baddies: Chaos reigned until they got what they wanted.

"The power you used seems unusual for a level one witch." Trevelyan went on, because he always wanted to talk about shit she didn't want to talk about. "That's the lowest score a magical being could earn and still be considered magical. And your spell was... big. Are you sure the tests were right about you?"

"I'm sure that my magic is twitchy." She answered without answering. No way was she telling him she was a level six. She wasn't telling him anything she didn't have to. "I'm not sure how I blasted them all into hogs, if you want to know the truth."

He didn't seem entirely appeased by that response. "Define 'twitchy?'"

"I get laughed out of the Caldron Society on a regular basis." That about summed it up.

"Am I supposed to know what the Cauldron Society is?"

"It's the international federation of accredited witches. They have wild parties, and plot world domination, and they're all snobs who hate me."

Trevelyan scoffed, as if the two-thousand year old institution of evil witchcraft was beneath his notice. "Do you think you'll ever be able to restore our new subjects to their former states or will we be ruling over a farmyard forever?"

"No way am I staying in Slumberland forever." Esmeralda dumped a useless stack of papers onto the heart-shaped rug. The entire interior of the palace seemed to be decorated in heart-shaped furnishings. And most of it was pink or red. "I'll figure something out.

That was the official-unofficial slogan of her life.

Most people were probably awed by the soaring asymmetrical architecture of the palace. Maybe Esmeralda would be too, is she wasn't a prisoner in its whimsical walls. The castle was interesting, in a strange and off-kilter way. According to some important looking papers she'd already trashed, it had been built by the fabled Wonderland Carpenter, who was a strange and off-kilter man.

The palace he designed was a bizarre mix of turrets, and balconies, and stairways that curved off at impossible angles. Nothing within its twisty walls made any sense. Tiny doors led to nothing. Hallways shrunk as you walked down them. Daisy chains of chandeliers randomly populated the ceilings, every which way. The pink and red furniture was all covered in pattern upon eye-popping pattern, style upon disparate style. It was probably one of the most unique castles in any kingdom. A real monument to creativity and art. Some people even claimed it had a sort of sentience.

Esmeralda got all that. ...She just didn't give a shit.

"You know, being stranded here indefinitely *could* be fun." Trevelyan lifted a shoulder. "We're basically the only ones left in this section of Wonderland, since you've enchanted everyone else. Shipwreck survivors on a deserted shore. It will be up to us to repopulate the whole land."

"I'd sooner procreate with one of the pigs."

Her scumbag True Love looked amused by that. "Hogs, darling. They're hogs." It was impossible to insult the guy. He seemed delighted by her snarking.

Trevelyan had ditched the robe, somewhere along the line. Now he wore an obnoxious ankle-length trench coat with decorative flames embroidered along the bottom hem. She could only imagine that he'd magically created it for himself with his recuperating powers, since it fit his wide chest like a second skin. It was so frustrating that he looked amazing in it and even more frustrating that she'd noticed.

The True Love bond between them was a real pain in the ass. The biological imperative to be with the man was drowning out all logical thought. Telling her that she should drag Trevelyan off to ravish his body, and trust him with her secrets, and protect him against all his enemies, and curl up beside him to sleep at night. Assuring her that everything would be happily-ever-after now that she'd found him. Insisting that this man was the *only* man and she should ignore all the reasons why he was horrible.

And there were a lot of big, blinking reasons why this jackass was horrible.

Trevelyan was a black pit of self-involvement, evil schemes, and hatred. Esmeralda was a smart girl. She could figure out a way to free herself from the prison/castle, escape Dunderland, and go back to the Four Kingdoms, alone. Running was the best play.

But, she'd wanted her True Love for *so long*.

The dragon might be a disaster, but he was her only shot at having her dream. How could she just walk away, after a couple hours, when Trevelyan was... hers?

"If we ever did have kids, you'd probably eat them." She muttered.

"Only the disappointingly Good ones."

Esmeralda dumped out another filing cabinet drawer, rummaging around for some clue on how they could leave Wonder-damned, once and for all. None of the countless makeup receipts or flamingo croquet fantasy league spreadsheets looked particularly helpful in finding an exit.

Trevelyan glanced out the window, towards the plaid, pastel lawn where all the curly-tailed denizens of the castle were presently rooting around for grubs. The hogs had no problems passing through the enchanted barrier. Only Esmeralda and Trevelyan were caged.

"Speaking of cannibalism..." He mused. "Perhaps we should consider cutting our losses and selling our citizens for bacon. I think their upkeep will be a drain on our economy."

"For the last time, we're not going to slaughter all the Heart Kingdom's residents." She was also pretty certain the spell was permanent, so none of the hogs would be helpful in giving directions. "Just keep looking for a map."

"This whole misadventure would be easier if any technology functioned." Trevelyan was ripping books off the floor-to-ceiling shelves, looking for anything useful. He flipped through an ancient tome entitled *In Search of Monstrous Crows* and then tossed it over his shoulder, moving on to the next volume.

"Wonderland is deliberately screwing us over, every chance it gets." Esmeralda waved a hand to encompass the whole horrible place. "It *wants* us causing problems, so it can cause *more* problems, so *we'll* cause more problems, and so on and so on, so it can thrive. It feeds off the chaos of the inhabitants. That's how the magic here works."

"And you're an expert on Wonderland *how* again?"

"Travel documentaries."

He made a distasteful face. "You must lead a very sad life."

"It's sure gotten depressing since I met you."

"I've certainly never been bored enough to watch a television show about *Wonderland*."

"Maybe you *should* have, since you're the one questioning why the technology is screwed up here."

"I just think a few computer searches would be extremely helpful, right now."

Esmeralda couldn't argue with that. "Or a phone." She missed her phone like some people would miss an arm. "The damn playing cards took mine when I was arrested. If you find it, tell me. I need to call my family. Like as soon as possible."

Trevelyan's head snapped around. "Call Marrok?" He sneered. "I don't think so. Possible will *never* come that soon."

"Pick a direction and fuck off in it, Trev. You don't need a map for that." She turned to jab a manicured finger at him. "But me…? I'm going *home*, just as soon as I find the exit. Count on it."

Green eyes narrowed, but he didn't argue. Another armful of priceless leather-bound volumes angrily hit the floor in a disorganized heap.

She frowned. "Some of those books could be really old and delicate, you know."

"So?"

Fair point.

They worked in silence for a few moments.

"What is Dark Science?" She asked, holding up a bunch of incomprehensible reports. "The White Rabbit was talking about it earlier and Alice has a whole file full of graphs about it."

"Manufactured magic." Trevelyan sounded disgusted, which put them on the same page for once "Unnatural spells, bought and sold by unmagical idiots who have no idea what they're doing. Camelot was screwing around with it a few years back."

Esmeralda winced. That was a terrible, terrible idea. "Well, I think that's how the White Rabbit got us both to Wonderland." She tossed the folder aside, feeling tainted just from holding it. Abandoning the filing cabinet, she headed over to search Alice's red lacquer desk. "It's your fault I'm even here in the first place, you know. They ripped me out of the Northlands, so I could wake up your sleeping ass."

"I didn't ask them to bring me to this cesspit. I'm evil, not stupid." Trevelyan gave up on searching the bookcase in favor of fixing himself a drink from the full bar Alice had set up in the corner. "Given the choice, I may have preferred a mystical coma, rather than visiting this dismal land."

Esmeralda rolled her eyes.

Trevelyan poured liquor into a heart-shaped glass. "To be honest, though, I can't imagine that *you* have anywhere else to be. The Four Kingdoms isn't much better than here. Is reuniting with Marrok and his do-Gooders you're only reason for wanting to get back? Or have you exchanged heartfelt promises with some starry-eyed guitar player, who you're longing to see again?"

"Is that your way of asking if I have a boyfriend?"

"It's my way of telling you… you *don't* have a boyfriend. If you had one before, he's history now." Trevelyan waded through the mess of books on the floor and sprawled in a heart-shaped chair, arrogance personified. "I'd be happy to break the sad news to him myself, if you'd like."

"You're such a dick."

Esmeralda was Bad enough to like his unapologetic possessiveness, though. She'd always wanted to belong to someone. True Loves belonged to each other, so it made sense to her that he wouldn't want to share. Even in their current state of mutual frustration and hostility, the bond was stronger than anything she'd ever felt. God knew, any other woman who came near Trevelyan would find herself transmogrified into a cockroach and then promptly stepped on.

Well, given Esmeralda's magical limitations, the bitch would probably be transmogrified into a hairy, slimy drain *clog,* but that would work, too.

Trevelyan held up his glass in a mock toast, casually unconcerned with life, insults, and hexes. "Come have a drink. We've conquered our first kingdom together, after all. Be it ever so humble, that's an occasion of note." He paused. "Or is *water* more the speed of forty-nine percent Good girls?"

"I'm fully Bad and I certainly don't drink water." She raised her eyebrows at him "duh" style. "I'm a witch. Unless it's mixed with something else, water will melt me from the inside out. Raindrops, bottled water, ponds, streams... anything that's *pure* water? That kills me. I even shower with magic, instead of that damn water from the faucets. It's basically acid to me."

He frowned slightly. It seemed like the full extent of her melting-when-wet issue hadn't occurred to him before. "Witches are *that* vulnerable? You're supposed to be one of the most powerful races. Surely, there must be a spell..."

Esmeralda cut him off. "Witches have incredible powers." Most witches, anyway. "But when you're given massive abilities, you're usually saddled with some massive limitations, too. That's how nature works. It's balance. At least that was what they taught us at school."

Esmeralda had never been a great student. She hadn't really understood most of the magic lessons, but "balance" was always a safe bubble to guess on a multiple choice test. Witches loved to prattle on about it and it seemed to be the answer to everything that didn't make sense.

Whenever she tried balance, though, Good magic tried to seep through and what kind of wicked witch wanted *that?*

"They're clearly teaching you horseshit in those witchy classrooms." Trevelyan decided. "No one can match my magical powers and I'm only limited when I run out of victims. That's the joy of *having* magical powers. I understand the principle of balance, but even someone with level-one abilities should be able to come up with a waterproofing spell."

"Or I could just not go swimming."

"If you're not up to the magic, I'm sure I can find a spell that protects you." He paused, his eyes skimming over her body in a way that should've been way more irritating than it was. "For a price."

She snorted at that lascivious suggestion. "When pigs fly."
He glanced towards the window and damn if one of the little porkers didn't sprout wings. Trevelyan's expression was one of taunting delight, as the hog took off and soared through the air. It made a "wee-wee-wee" sound of freedom, at home in the sky.

Esmeralda's lips thinned, refusing to smile. She hated to be bored and life with her diabolical True Love would certainly never be dull. "Aren't you supposed to be resting your magic, so it gets better?"

"Oh, but how could I resist an opportunity like that?" He defended, watching his porcine prank flap its feathery wings. "You would've done the same thing in my place."

Probably. Not that she'd ever admit it to him.

"And look how pleased that fat little piggy is. We should make them *all* fly. Easier to get them to market, jiggety-jig." He paused for a beat. "Or is it jiggety-jog?"

"You are incredibly unlikable."

"So everyone tells me." He didn't sound worried about it. "But I'm also incredibly talented at spells." He looked back at her. "I really can waterproof you."

"I'll pass."

He hesitated for a beat, not satisfied with her easy refusal. "Think about it for more than three seconds and you'll see I'm right. In the meantime, I can whip up something to temporarily shield you. My magic is recovered enough to do that much. We'll call it a favor."

"Nah."

Dark eyebrows compressed in frustration, his amusement fading. "I'm offering to save your life."

"What a hero."

His jaw tightened, probably because she wasn't falling for his crap. "You're being pointlessly stubborn. I'm the only reason you still have a head. You might show a little more appreciation."

"And I'm the only reason you're awake, remember?"

"I also saved you from the executioner."

"And I saved you from the demented Rabbit! We're totally

even."
Trevelyan didn't see it that way. "So you'll endanger yourself, just to avoid owing me a favor?" He demanded. "Just to prove a point?"
"It has nothing to do with proving a point. I won't make a deal with you, because I don't trust you. My imagination isn't vast enough to think of all the vile things you could slip into the spell."
"This is about *trust*, again?" He still seemed baffled by the concept of having faith in another person. "Why are you so hung up on this idea of 'believing' in others? I've never believed in anything that I can't experience for myself and I get along fine."
She snorted. "Yeah, you're living your best life, for sure."
"If Marrok could do magic spells, would you make the deal with him?"
"Yes." The answer was instant.
"Just that fucking simple, huh?" His voice was snide.
"Marrok would never hurt me."
"You think I would hurt my True Love?" Trevelyan made a considering face. "I'm not sure that's biologically possible. At least, on *my* end. You seemed fully capable of piercing holes through my foot, though. Those heels of yours are dangerous weapons. If anyone should be worried about their safety in this relationship, it's me."
"I don't think you're planning to kill me. I just think you're indifferent to my survival." All Esmeralda's pretty, romantic notions of True Love had died about two hours before. Now she was approaching their relationship the same way she'd enter a death-match with a centaur.
Green eyes met hers, his expression unreadable.
Esmeralda kept talking. "Once your energy fully recovers, you'll be capable of much bigger magic than water protections and hog spells. We both know it. You don't need me to help you. And I can protect myself. I've been doing it my whole life."
Trevelyan's fingers drummed on the side of his glass. "I don't need anyone." He assured her, his voice cold and unreadable. "*I'm* all that matters to me."

"Right. So, if we're going to deal with the True Love bond, we need to set boundaries and keep our expectations low. I take care of me and you take care of you." Unless he really needed saving, like with the Walrus. Then, she'd have to step in and do her best to help him, no matter what. ...Still, he didn't need to know that. "Fair?"

"Fair." He agreed, seeming relieved about the arrangement. She figured he would be. Dipshit. "We're stuck with each other. But, if this is going to work --and I'm not sure that it *will*-- we'll need to lead separate lives."

"Separate lives?"

"Yes. Your life is yours. Mine is *mine*." His eyes were hooded. "Although, there is some room for... overlap."

"Let me guess: We're naked and I'm agreeing with all the stupid crap you say."

"Great dynasties have been built on less, darling."

"I wouldn't build a tent with you, let alone a..." Her hand hit upon a rolled up tube of paper in the bottom drawer of the desk. "Map."

"What?"

"Map! I found a map!" She yanked it free and held it triumphantly aloft.

"Finally." Trevelyan stalked over to join her. He walked like a panther prowling, all feline grace and danger. "I was beginning to think we'd have to enthrall some idiot cartographer and force him to chart this damn kingdom for us."

"I'm not enthralling anyone, ever again." Esmeralda shoved everything else off the desktop so she could spread the map out on the heart-shaped surface. Alice's belongings hit the floor in a broken jumble. Between the two of them, Esmeralda and Trevelyan had decimated every square inch of the Valentine-y space.

Too Bad, so sad.

"People are always trying to enslave dragons, wanting to steal our magic. Case in point: The Wonderlandians who stuck us here." He gestured around them. "Why shouldn't we return the favor and enthrall some servants?"

"Because, everyone's a hog, for starters."

"Well, I'm sure someone else will happen along eventually and we can..."

Esmeralda kept talking. "Besides, *my* magic is the only one working at the moment and it doesn't work. Whenever I try to enthrall someone, it ends up in a big mess. Like he thinks he's a chicken and I have to spend six weeks feeding him corn, until the spell wears off."

Trevelyan arched a brow at her, saying nothing.

"I just wanted him to fix the roof of my gingerbread house, for a *reasonable* price." She defended. "He was overcharging me for the fondant! I wasn't trying to hurt him, just negotiate. But try explaining that to his stupid wife." She shook her head at the memory. "God, you never heard such whining. And the roof *still* leaks."

Trevelyan's mouth twitched upward. "What is it with your magic and livestock?"

"Oh, shut up, Trev." Esmeralda smoothed a hand over the curled paper, holding down the edge. "Alright, so we're here." She gestured to the bottom left corner of the map. "Heart Kingdom." She read off the short description of the place, printed under the name. "Perpetual spring rains, in this verdant and welcoming garden." She wrinkled her nose. "They misspelled 'reigns.'"

"Also, the armed guards didn't make me feel welcomed in the slightest."

"I don't see a way out of Wonderland in this region. At least, none that are marked." She cleared her throat. "So... then north of us is the Diamond Kingdom."

Trevelyan leaned forward to read the description of that land. Rather than step around her, he stood directly behind her. His arms came down on either side of her body. "Summertime is a beachy ball in the sandy kingdom by the lakeshore."

"That sounds horrible." Esmeralda shuddered with great feeling, studiously ignoring the heat of his body at her back. "Let's not go there. Lakes and witches don't mix."

"Are these lands seasonally themed?" Trevelyan asked, almost to himself. His finger traced to the right. "The Kingdom of Spades: A mountainous region, with colorful falls foliage abounding." He squinted. "What the frozen-hells does that mean?"

"Leaves fall in the autumn?" Esmeralda guessed. "And you fall off mountains?"

Trevelyan heaved a "God help me" sigh. "Just when you think Wonderland can't be any more irritating, it begins making puns."

Esmeralda couldn't suppress her amused snort in time. Shit. That was actually a little bit funny. He shouldn't get to be funny. It wasn't fair.

Trevelyan glanced towards her in surprise, realizing that he'd just made her laugh. Green eyes gleamed, as if he was pleased. Esmeralda ignored him and refocused on the map. This would be a hell of a lot easier if the guy just stuck to being unlikable.

"Right." She pointed to the top right of the map. "Last but not least, the Kingdom of Clubs: Icy snow here." She paused, translating that from "idiot" to "normal person." "I *see* snow here."

"We should find whoever wrote this map and kill them." He intoned darkly.

"Agreed."

"Dragons hate cold, you know. I'm not going through the Club Kingdom, unless there's no other option."

Esmeralda frowned, thinking. "Hang on. The Walrus was whining about someone named the Queen of Clubs wanting you awake. He seemed pissing-himself-scared of her. So did the Rabbit."

"I approve of her already."

Esmeralda turned to look up at him over her shoulder. "I think they said she considers us her enemies."

"Well, never mind about approving of her, then." Trevelyan shrugged dismissively. "But, if she hates me, why wouldn't she leave me entombed in my own body, sleeping forever under that spell? Why bring you here to wake me up?"

"Maybe she's an ex-girlfriend, out for a more visceral revenge. If she is, I'm *sure* I'm on her side. Just saying."

Trevelyan's head tilted, like he was weighing everything in his maniacally wicked mind. "I've never had a 'girlfriend,' in my life." He said absently. "I just sleep with women until I get bored. And I always get bored quickly."

Esmeralda made a disgusted sound and shoved him back, so she could wiggle out from between his body and the desk. Trevelyan obediently stepped away to let her escape his clutches. Maybe he was learning. *Maybe*. "The Walrus said they needed my magic. To help the Queen of Clubs, I suppose. That's her scheme."

"Help her do what?"

"I have no idea. And I have no intention of lending a hand, since we're enemies."

"*She* thinks you're enemies. You don't even know her."

"I'm willing to take her word for it." Trevelyan didn't look worried about having yet another person who wanted him dead. "When is the woman coming here?"

"Monday."

"What's today?"

"Tuesday, according to the weird calendar downstairs. All the dates on it are clumped together in twos and threes, though. I'm not sure how accurate it is. Next week has an eighth day added, with a little crown drawn on it. It must be important, because it's all circled in stars."

"Everything here is so *dramatic*," lamented the dragon who liked to remove people's bones and walk around naked. "Alright. So, we have approximately a week, before..."

"Shit!" Esmeralda cut him off. "The Queen of Clubs is sending an army on Monday." She'd only just remembered that part. It had been a busy afternoon. "Literally. They said an *army*."

He perked up. "Excellent. We can ambush them."

"Ambush an army?" Esmeralda blinked. "Are you out of your mind? We need to find a way out of here."

"So the Queen of Clubs can ambush *us* later? No. If my powers are back by the time they get here, I can fight them. We can..."

"I don't want to fight an army!" Esmeralda interrupted at a shout. "I just want to go home."

"And how do you intend to do that, exactly? Do you see a lot of exits on that map?" He gestured back towards the desk. "Do you know a way through the castle's force field that you're just not sharing? Explain your plan to me."

"I don't have a plan. I never have a plan. I just know *your* plan is terrible."

"Magic is the only way out of Wonderland. ...And we don't have any magic. We're stuck here until the Queen of Clubs lets us go or we kill her."

"When you're recuperated, you'll have plenty of magic." No one could match Trevelyan's abilities. She believed that. "You can bring down the invisible barrier, find a path out of Wonderland, and get me home. I know you can."

"Even if I had my powers, I wouldn't send you back to the Enchanted Forest." He made it sound like she was the crazy one.

Esmeralda gaped at him. "You're not going to help me get home?"

"Of course not." He leaned closer to her and lowered his voice in commiseration. "Dragons don't help damsels in distress. It's exactly the opposite, I'm afraid."

"Just when I think *maybe* you can be salvaged..." She made clawing motions with her hands, imagining grabbing his head and squeezing until it popped. "You're the most irritating, insane, aggravating..." She broke off with a frustrated sound.

"Use words, darling."

"Normal people don't hold their True Loves hostage!" She moved away from him, furious and hurt. "Do you seriously not get how psychotic this is? You can't just *kidnap* me!"

"I didn't. The Walrus kidnapped you." He shrugged in total innocence. "I'm simply not going to *rescue* you."

Esmeralda covered her eyes and took a deep breath, unable to believe what was happening to all her dreams. "You think I'm going to accept this shit? My True Love was supposed to be better than this! I thought you'd be so much *better* than this."

"Better?" He didn't like that word. "Like wolves and record store boys, you mean? I'm gratified to be left out of that esteemed group of imbeciles. All I've asked for is loyalty, but apparently that's far too much for you to give. So, we're both doomed to be disappointed."

"Loyalty?! Are you kidding me? You're plotting to abduct me, you fuckwit! How is that loyal?"

"I told you there are only two sides to this war. You chose Marrok's, remember? Everything that happens now is on *your* head, not mine."

"You're *such* an asshole."

"Your precious 'family' isn't going to rescue you from this mess, you know. I'm your best bet to stay alive. We've agreed not to save each other... But I'm willing to deal." Dragons loved to make deals. They were transactional creatures. Trevelyan's palms opened in a graceful sweep of enticement. "I'm happy to take your vulnerable little body into my very capable hands, if you make it worth my while."

Her eyes narrowed. "You really want to play it this way?"

Trevelyan arched a brow. "Oh, I always want to play." That was true. He seemed interested in anything that even hinted at a game, no matter how twisted.

Witches liked to play to, but she wasn't getting any deeper with this man. No way.

"Well, you're losing this round, Trev. I told you: I don't need your help. And I don't need Marrok to save me, either. I can rescue *myself*." She'd been doing it all of her life. This whole thing was fixable. She just needed to take it one step at a time. "Now, I'm getting out of this castle, *right now*, and there's nothing you can do to stop me!"

Muttering in the forgotten language of witches, Esmeralda headed for the door. There had to be a way through the force field. Some spell she could use or key she could turn. She would start doing every crazy thing she could think of, including hitting it with fucking *pogs*, until something worked and then... Outside thunder clapped.

And that's when it started raining.

CHAPTER SEVEN

Pick your perfect nail polish from our unlimited selection!
Don't Trust the Reviews Ruby: Give it a shot! Sure everyone else left
this polish a one star rating, but maybe that's because it was made
especially for you.

Happily Ever Witch Cosmetics Website

The Heart Castle

Esmeralda stared out the window, fuming over the torrential downpour. "I swear to God, you somehow did this. I *know* you did."
"Not even I can control the weather, darling. ...Yet."
Esmeralda's mouth thinned, not appeased.
"You said yourself that Wonderland is deliberately causing us problems." Trevelyan reminded her. "It seems like you were right. You wanted to run off and it stopped you." He regarded her with total innocence. "Maybe you pissed it off, when you were so mean to me."
Jackass.
It had been raining for hours, with no sign of letting up. "Perpetual spring" was pouring down all over the place. Off in the distance, thunder rolled in great lumps. The sound was incredibly odd and even more incredibly loud, as if the noise was knocking over everything in its path. And then there was all the damn water, clear and pure and toxic to her skin.
No matter how she considered it, there was no escaping the Heart Palace, even if she somehow got through the barrier. Not until the storm subsided. Esmeralda was reckless, but she

wasn't crazy enough to risk melting to death.

So, she was sticking with the dragon, for now.

"If you're worried about me fondling you in the night, you can sleep on the floor." Trevelyan offered in a solicitous tone, sprawled in a red velvet chair. "I won't mind."

"Fuck yourself, Trev." Esmeralda headed across the red wooden floor to the red canopy bed and began yanking down the red comforter. "In the depths of hell."

He chuckled.

The two of them were alone in a hideously decorated bedroom. Like Alice's office, everything here was pink and red and heart-shaped. The drapes on the windows, the chandelier on the ceiling, the sink in the connected bathroom, the light switch by the door, the door itself... all of it pink and red and heart-shaped. Even the dots on the pink and red wallpaper were tiny pink and red hearts. Esmeralda would've almost preferred to stay in the creepy science lab, rather than spend the night surrounded by all the cuteness.

Still, this bedroom was the best one she could find. The Heart Palace was a continuing fanciful nightmare. The first room she'd tried had had a Cheshire Carpet. It remained unclear if an actual Cheshire Cat had been enspelled into a rug or if a regular rug had been enspelled to act like a Cheshire Cat. Either way, it was odd. The smiling mouths covering its pink-and-purple surface inexplicably changed position as it talked.

And it *loved* to frigging talk.

How was Esmeralda supposed to sleep when the goddamn furniture was chatting about illegal chess moves? She couldn't. Switching rooms had been a no-brainer. Sadly not all roommates were so easy to avoid.

"Do you *really* intend to sleep in here with me?" She asked Trevelyan in annoyance.

"It's safer if we share a room, darling. Even you have to see that." He arched a brow. "No matter how much you enjoy blaming me for every little thing, I'm the only person in Wonderland who's *not* a danger to you."

"Aren't you?" Esmeralda continued stacking heart-shaped pillows in a long row along the center of the heart-shaped bed.

The heart-shaped mattress was the size of an average continent, so they could share it without touching.

Trevelyan clearly wasn't going to leave and honestly Esmeralda wasn't pushing hard for him to go. She hated rain. Since childhood, it had terrified her. Having someone else in the room, while the lightning flashed and thunder roared, was comforting. Even if that "someone" was an evil, stalking lunatic.

"Of course, I'm not a danger." He lounged there like he owned the whole castle. Elegant and plotting. "As I said, I'm biologically incapable of harming my own True Love."

There were a lot of ways to hurt someone without doing physical harm. He didn't seem to get that, but Esmeralda did.

"And I'm content to wait until you're ready, before I have my wicked way with you." He continued with haughty assurance. "The chase is always the most interesting part of sex."

"Then you're doing sex wrong."

His mouth curved. "Teach me the right way. I'm eager to learn. We can start practicing anytime you like."

Esmeralda scoffed at the idea she could teach him anything. "Just stay on your side of the bed, okay?"

There was no sense in telling him to stay off of it completely. He wasn't going to listen, just like he hadn't listened when she'd requested that he die of a horrible, wasting skin disease. Esmeralda needed a good night's sleep. Nobody could plot to escape an inescapable kingdom, and fight a mysterious queen, and deal with a pain-in-the-ass True Love without a nap. Unlike dragons who "never, ever compromised," witches knew when to pick their battles. It was probably why witches outnumbered Trevelyan's idiot kind a hundred-to-one. So long as he kept his hands to himself, he could stay in her room. It was the best option.

"You still seem upset." Trevelyan mused. "Do you want to talk about it? My mother said that you should never go to bed angry." He paused with a thoughtful frown. "But I think she just meant that you should kill all your enemies *before* bed. Mother hated procrastination. ...And her enemies."

Esmeralda fixed Trevelyan with a look over the wide expanse of

the heart-embroidered sheets. "Do you consider us enemies?"
"No." His smirk faded. "You're the one who wants to make this a fight, Ez."
"You're the one who's determined to wage war against my family!"
"Marrok is not your family. Note how he's not the one sitting here, offering to save your very lovely ass."
She did have a lovely ass. It was gratifying that he noticed. "How are you offering to save me? I'm the one who saved *you*. And you repaid my generosity by threatening to kidnap me."
"I didn't kidnap you. Feel free to leave whenever you like."
"Seriously, has anyone ever liked you? *Ever?*"
"Not that I'm aware of." His eyes traced over her body, like he was memorizing every inch. "Since we're being 'serious'... I have something very important to ask you and it needs a straight answer, right away."
"I seriously *am* being serious. You're the one who sees this whole damn thing as a joke." She fixed him with an exasperated look. "Well? What's your vital question?"
"Is your skin *naturally* that color?"
"Oh for God's sake..." She threw a pillow at him. "Why do I even bother with you?"
He dodged the fluffy projectile. "Well, it's a legitimate concern, given the amount of glamours available to your kind. You should keep your skin *exactly* as it is, either way. But, natural is so much better to fantasize about."
"Keep fantasizing. That's as close as you're going to get to it." Glamours were one of the few spells that always worked for her, but her current appearance was one-hundred percent Esmeralda. Not that she was telling anyone in Wonderland that she could change her looks at will, especially not her pain in the ass True Love. There was no advantage to it and Ez was a girl who liked to have an advantage.
"Wait," Trevelyan theatrically stroked his chin like something new occurred to him. "Level one witches can do glamours, can't they? I'll admit that I don't always keep up on what *lower*-powered beings are capable of." He paused with studious concern. "Is 'lower-powered' the correct term? Or do

you prefer 'magically disadvantaged?'"

"I prefer 'Esmeralda, The Majestic and Terrible.' Thanks for asking." She slammed some more ugly pillows into place, because the barrier between them could never be high enough. The rain continued to pound on the window, adding to her agitation. "God, once I escape from this shithole, I am never leaving the Enchanted Forest again."

"You'll probably reconsider that plan, once I burn the trees to blackened stumps and salt the ground beneath them."

"You really are the worst person in the world."

"I try."

"And the worst *True Love* in the world." She continued, casting a quick spell to change into a long night shirt that read "Dragon Slayer."

Trevelyan glanced at the front, where a cartoon dragon had been staked through the heart and a dancing witch celebrated her victory. His amusement seemed to deepen. "Maybe so, but I'm the only True Love you've got. And you're the only one I've got."

"For now."

"For*ever*." He didn't look thrilled about the fact they were each other's one-and-only, but he didn't look pissed about it, either. He'd been brooding earlier, but now he seemed to just accept it as fact. "We might quarrel a bit and play some games, but we're connected. Whether we like it or not. You said so yourself."

She stared at him for a long moment, searching his green gaze. Trevelyan stared back.

"I know." She finally agreed.

Tension seemed to ease from Trevelyan's wide shoulders. "And since we're stuck together, it seems reasonable that we attempt to strike a truce." He persisted. "We don't need to work *together*, obviously. You were right before. Every dragon --and witch-- for themselves is the best way to go forward. But there's no sense in us working at cross purposes, either."

That sounded doable. "Temporarily." She stipulated. Even a temporary truce with the dragon meant ignoring every sentence he uttered. She absently created a hair brush with her magic. "I doubt you can go more than twenty minutes without causing problems."

"Girls in glass houses shouldn't throw stones." Trevelyan watched with hooded eyes as she combed her thick mane of black curls. "Speaking of which, when the Queen of Clubs arrives, I'll be taking the lead. I'd prefer some answers from her, before you turn her into a hog or a log." He paused with a slight frown, as if he'd just realized that the words rhymed.

"You're accusing me of being magically violent?" Esmeralda scoffed, before he could question her about her misfiring magic. "Like you've been such a frigging peacemaker, since you woke up."

He'd set some harmless grandfather clock on fire earlier. Legit burned it to ash. It had smoldered straight through the floor and taken out at least six hundred square feet of castle. The damn thing had finally stopped warbling out the wrong time every two minutes, though.

"I don't have level one magic." Green eyes gleamed. "Even in my current state, I can figure out a way to deal with our enemies. You, on the other hand, are far more vulnerable to angry villains."

"Wicked witches are never vulnerable." She informed him, doing her damnedest to hide her fear of the storm.

"Just be more careful about who you piss off, alright? Especially if I'm not around to ensure you survive the battle." Esmeralda snorted, working the brush around the tiara on her head. She still needed to find a way to get the damn thing off. "Except you have no intention of heroically rescuing me, remember?"

"I'm mercurial." He made a languid gesture with one palm. "It's one of my defining characteristics, along with innate wisdom and great hair. I might change my mind, at any moment, and keep you alive. I *am* curious to see you naked and that's sure to be more fun if you're breathing."

Esmeralda made a face. "When you're around, *you're* usually the huge, angry villain I'm pissing off." She gave her hair a toss. "And I'm pretty sure *I'll* be the one who survives any battle between us."

His mouth curved into a less-mocking-than-usual smile.
Damn it, it was completely unfair how attractive the man was.
"What are you smirking at, now?" She demanded, attempting not to notice his miasma of sexual energy.
"I'm just thinking I've never wanted to fuck a woman more."
She leveled another glare at him. *"Really?"*
"Be fair, darling. If I said I *had* wanted to fuck a woman more, you'd be offended by that, too. A man can't win with you."
Esmeralda rolled her eyes and tossed her hairbrush towards the heart-shaped dresser. It broke the heart-shaped mirror above it, spider-webbing the glass.
Who cared?
"Your side of the wall." She pointed to the area on the right section of the bed. "My side of the wall." She pointed to the left section. "Got it?"
"'Wall' seems a bit dramatic, don't you think?" Trevelyan drummed his fingers on the arm of his chair. Scorch marks were left wherever the tips of them touched the velvet, like he just couldn't help himself. The man was addicted to arson. "If I wanted to get over that pile of pillows, what could possibly stop me?"
"You could get over the wall." She agreed, climbing onto her carefully delineated territory. "But you're not going to. Not if you plan on keeping your dick attached to your body. And not if you want this truce to last more than five seconds. And certainly not if you want to build any sort of trust with me, as we figure out what the hell we're going to do with each other."
He heaved a sigh and got to his feet. The exotic beads in his long hair jangled enticingly. "No other dragon has ever had to endure this much trouble from his True Love. I guarantee it. Most would have eaten you, by now."
"No other witch has ever gotten matched with such a colossal moron, so we're both making adjustments." She flopped down, wishing she'd saved one of the pillows for her head. "I just know you're going to screw this up. It's a waste of time to even try with you."
"You're the one being difficult, not me."
Esmeralda snorted. "Another lie." She pulled the covers up

and instantly felt safer from the rain. She had a morbid and not-completely-rational fear of ceilings leaking, so she always slept cocooned in blankets. It was why she'd paid that damn chicken-man to fix her roof back home and why she was so pissed that he'd done such a lousy job.

Building her house out of gingerbread had been a huge mistake.

"It's not a lie." Trevelyan began removing his clothes, without a drop of self-consciousness. When you looked like him, it was probably hard to be modest. "You're the one who's resisting the True Love bond and piling up pillows between us. I'm already resigned to our fate."

Her lips pressed together at that incredibly unromantic sentiment. She made a point of not looking at him, as he casually removed his shirt and revealed his intricate, enticing, possibly enchanted tattoos. "Are you really going to sleep in this bed naked?" She demanded, because that seemed to be the way things were going.

"Afraid you can't keep your hands off me?"

"I already saw you nude and I managed to contain myself."

"You kissed me, when I wasn't able to consent." He reminded her piously. "In some kingdoms, that's assault."

Insufferable ass.

Esmeralda took a deep breath and rose above his provocations. "Look, until I can believe in you, everything between us is empty. You have no idea how to be the True Love I want."

"So teach me."

Her eyebrows compressed at that surprising reply. "Teach you?" He'd been serious about that before?

"Yes. Teach me what you want. I'm willing to learn. Then, we can move past this nonsense and have sex."

Esmeralda snorted at the idea he could learn anything. He was smart enough, sure. But he didn't want to change a single molecule of his awfulness. "As far as I know, you've yet to tell me one true thing. So I'm not going to sleep with you, no matter how pretty you are. The end."

"My birthday is in May."

The non sequitur had her blinking. "Huh?"

"That's something true about me. Something you can *believe in.* My birthday is May 4th, and my favorite color is green, and your skin drives me crazy. I want to touch every inch of it." He paused. "Do you believe me?"

She was intrigued enough to sit up slightly, careful to keep her eyes on his face. "Yes."

"Well, that's a start on the trust building, isn't it?" He tilted his head. "Your turn. Tell me something true, Ez."

She studied his eyes for a long moment, wondering if he was worth the effort.

Trevelyan arched a brow. "Pretend I play the guitar, if it helps." It didn't. But, Esmeralda had to give him a chance. She'd waited too long for him to just give up without a fight. "I have no idea when my birthday is." She said at length.

"No?" He busied himself with taking off his pants.

"No. I was raised in an orphanage." Esmeralda kept her eyes above his waist. "Auntie Hazel's Home for Young Witches. No one ever told me my birthday."

Trevelyan's gaze slashed up to meet hers.

"No one hurt me there, but no one ever loved me, either." The words were simple and bare, because Trevelyan needed simple, bare words to understand anything important. "I stayed there for seventeen years, six months and a day. The other girls all got adopted over the years, but no one ever chose me."

His jaw tightened.

"Parents would show up with ideas of their perfect child and I guess I didn't make the grade." Her magic had always been frightening. She shrugged. "It got to the point where I stopped even going downstairs to meet the prospective adopters, because I knew they wouldn't want me. They *never* wanted me. I started daydreaming about my True Love, instead. About what he'd be like, and what we'd do together, and how great our happily ever after would be. Because, I wanted someone I belonged to."

Trevelyan stared at her, not saying a word.

"Do you believe me?" She asked.

"Yes." He said softly.

"So then don't screw this up." She flopped her head back down. "Your turn. Tell me something true, Trev."

He remained silent for a beat. "I'm not sure when my full magic will come back." He finally told her. It seemed like this honest exchange had changed something for both of them, because he wasn't taunting, for once. "I assume it will be a matter of days. But, it could be weeks. Months. No dragon has ever been under a sleeping spell for two years. Maybe it will never fully return."

Esmeralda shook her head. "It'll come back soon." She could feel the latent magic of the man from across the room. All the power was still within him.

"Without magic, I can't be a true villain. I can't be *me*."

The man was a deranged maniac, whether or not he was casting horrible spells. No one who met him could think different. "You're still plenty evil." She assured him. "Just give it time and your magic will heal."

"We don't have time. When the Queen of Clubs comes for us, I can't be sure I'll be recovered enough to defeat her. I have no idea how strong she is, but I'm... weakened." The word must have tasted terrible on his tongue, because his whole face compressed in revulsion. "When she sends people here, we may have to fight them together."

"I'm not going to be much help."

"You'll have to *try*. If she went through this much trouble to get me here, she is dangerous to us both. You might not trust me, but you can trust my instinct for survival. We have to *fight*. Always." He hesitated. "Do you believe me?"

Esmeralda sighed. "Yes. I don't like it, but I'll go with your idea. You probably know more about ambushing powerful enemies that I do."

"Undoubtedly. So, tell me something true, Ez: How is your magic?"

Esmeralda stared up at the hideous red canopy. "Not great." She admitted, reluctantly. "I told you, it's twitchy. I can do small things. But, I have trouble controlling it. I always have."

Trevelyan turned off the lights and crossed over to the bed, naked and gorgeous. Not that she watched him. Much.

"Describe the problem." He ordered. "Because we need to find a way to fix your powers. Quickly."

104

It was embarrassing to discuss, but it couldn't hurt to try. In the dark, it felt safer to say things to him. "Well, first off, I sometimes cast a spell and I get the *opposite* result."

"That's easily remedied." He settled on his side of the mattress. "Just cast spells for the opposite of what you want to happen."

"It's not that simple. Swarms of majestic bats become disgusting butterflies. Evil curses somehow help my targets lose weight. I once hexed my ex-boyfriend and the next thing I know the dickhead wins the lottery."

"Did he work in a record store?" Trevelyan asked without inflection.

"Yep. Now, he owns a chain of them, thanks to me." She huffed out an aggravated breath. "The Cauldron Society *loved* that one."

"I'll kill them all later, if you like. For now, focus on survival."

"You'll kill the entire Cauldron Society for me?"

"Not *just* for you. I also like killing people." He sounded bored. "Go on with your tale of magical woes."

"What else can I say? My powers are misfiring, more and more, all the time."

"Probably because you're focusing on them, instead of just letting the spells happen naturally."

"You'd focus on it to, if you were the most horrible wicked witch in the world."

"You're not the *most* horrible." He assured her in a tone that suggested there were, perhaps, one or two bigger screw-ups in the universe. Somewhere. "You can turn people into hogs, after all. That's quite an advanced spell for a level one practitioner." He paused. "You were *trying* to turn them into hogs, weren't you?"

Esmeralda stayed quiet.

Trevelyan laughed.

"Oh shut up, Trev." Esmeralda muttered, without any real heat. He had a wonderful laugh, damn it. Dark and rusty sounding, like he didn't get to use it a lot. But it warmed all the parts of her that she was trying to ignore. She also did her best to ignore the weight of his body on the bed. Even with the wall of pillows, it seemed oddly intimate to have him beside her.

...But not terrible.

She rolled onto her side, so she was facing the fluffy barrier between them. "Do you believe me?" She asked, wishing she could see him. "About the magic?"

"Yes." He was quiet for so long, she thought he'd gone to sleep. "You're forty-nine percent Good and trying to cast dark spells. Perhaps that's the problem. Wires are getting crossed, so you get butterflies instead of bats. You need to try some lighter magic."

Esmeralda was insulted. "Absolute y not! I'm a *wicked* witch!"

"I understand your horror, but this is an emergency. And you're only half Bad."

"Fifty-one percent is more than half. And you don't even know that damn Rabbit is right."

"I know that you've got *a lot* of Good in you. I can smell it."

Esmeralda winced a bit at that news. "No one else ever complained about my smell." She muttered defensively.

"You must not hang around with many dragons."

"There *aren't* many dragons."

"There are enough." He didn't sound thrilled to have more of his kind in the world. Dragons hated other dragons even more than they hated everybody else. "Hopefully, we don't meet any. You smell like poisoned candy. Tempting and dangerous. You'll start a war."

"Is that... a compliment?" She guessed skeptically.

"Of course it's a compliment. What woman wouldn't want to start a dragon war, just to see the flames?"

"Me. I don't want to set the world on fire."

He made a *tsk* of a sound, like she lacked imagination. "The Good in you truly does hold you back."

Esmeralda flicked him off again, even though he couldn't see it. "I'm going to sleep, now."

He disregarded that conversation ender. "It's just as well you're so drearily wholesome, I suppose. I want to bathe in the scent of you, so other dragons will no doubt feel the same. And I don't have enough power to kill a dragon right now."

"I'm pretty sure *I* could manage. I've been brainstorming ways to murder one, all day."

Another deep chuckle. "You are the only person I've ever spent hours and hours with, who's yet to bore me. Do you think that's because you're my True Love?" He kept talking, answering his own question. "That must be it. Some kind of biological response."

"Probably." He'd never bored her either and she wasn't known for her long attention span.

Another beat of silence. When he spoke again, he sounded more grim. "Other shifter species will also be able to smell you, to various degrees. Wolves. Lions. Coyotes. Possibly the centaur."

Esmeralda wrinkled her nose. The centaurs were barbarians. She didn't want them smelling her.

"Most assorted monsters will be able to scent *me* on you too, though. And then they'll know to back the fuck up. I have a reputation for lunatic violence and not sharing well." The bed moved like Trevelyan was trying to see her through the pillow-wall. "That's why it's important that you allow me to touch you, soon. It's not just about sex. I want my scent all over you, so everyone else stays away."

"Wow, that *swooshing* sound you just heard was me being swept off my feet."

He made an irritated noise. "You're being a child about this. I'm going to touch you sooner or later. We both know it. It might as well be now."

"You might as well blow me."

"Oh, sooner or later, I'll be doing that, as well." It was a sensual promise.

An image of that flickered through Esmeralda's mind and she mentally cursed. The True Love bond was making it hard to think for wanting him and picturing his dark head between her legs was not helping her cool down.

The dragon knew it, too. She could sense him smirking into the darkness.

Lightning flashed, jarring her from the unwanted fantasy. She flinched. "Trevelyan?"

"Yes?"

"Are you still going to be here in the morning?" The question was out before she could censor it.

The man wasn't the most reliable person she'd ever met. If the barrier lifted somehow, she could imagine him abandoning her in the Heart Palace and going his own way. Being stuck someplace all alone --while rain poured down and thunder rolled-- was Esmeralda's worse nightmare. If he planned on vanishing, she'd rather know now, so she could mentally prepare.

"Maybe." There was a negligent shrug in his voice. "When I inevitably run out on you, I'll be sure to leave a note, though."

"I'll be sure to do the same." Esmeralda pulled the covers over her head.

"Are you cold?" He asked, sounding confused. "I feel like you're wrapping all the blankets around you. If you need some body heat, you should come over to my side of the 'wall.' I guarantee I could keep you *very* warm."

Lord, but the man was easy to detest. "Good night." The words were like bullets.

A thoughtful silence, like he was still trying to figure something out. "You're afraid of the rain, aren't you?" He asked in a less mocking tone.

Shit.

"You'd be afraid of the rain too, if it melted you." She shot back.

"Well, you don't have to be afraid tonight." His assurance was grudging. "I'm not about to let you dissolve on the mattress beside me. It would be a mess in the morning."

"I told you, I don't want you casting a waterproofing spell on me."

"I didn't. But, I have enough magic to ensure that the windows stay shut and the ceiling stays dry."

"Are you going to try and demand sexual favors in return?"

"I can't, sadly. The spell is as much for me, as it is for you." He sighed tragically. "I'm not thrilled with the idea of getting wet, either. Keeping the rain out is only practical and the roof may not be sound. Nothing else in this abysmal kingdom is. Magic seems like the best option."

More silence.

"Thank you." Esmeralda eventually whispered.

She felt him start in surprise and it occurred to her that Trevelyan probably didn't get thanked a lot, because he didn't help anyone except himself. Esmeralda closed her eyes and felt strangely secure, curled up beside the biggest villain in the world.

"If you really wanted to show your appreciation, I could think of some ways..."

"Good night, Trev."

Her long-suffering interruption seemed to amuse him. "I rarely do anything 'Good,' you know. Even nights."

"I can wish you a *Bad* night, if you'd rather. I don't mind."

"No, I'll take what I can get, from you." He was smiling. She could tell. "Sleep well, darling. You're safe."

Esmeralda's eyes snapped open.

With me, you are always safe, my darling. I love you more than magic itself.

The voice and the words had played in her head a thousand times. Reaching out to soothe her through storms, as she'd drifted off to sleep.

Trevelyan.

It was really him. He was so powerful that he'd felt her fear and he'd responded with comfort. Only he didn't seem to know it. Esmeralda stared at the mountain of pillows separating them and, for the first time, she fully accepted that the man on the other side was her True Love. He might not work in a record store, but he was the one she'd been waiting for. He'd finally arrived. And he'd just said "good night" to her, sounding so much like she'd imagined he'd sound.

Maybe that was a sign.

Maybe this True Love match might work out, if she helped it along.

Maybe she *could* teach him.

Chapter Eight

Pick your perfect nail polish from our unlimited selection! Why Settle? Yellow: Every single shade of yellow is distilled into this magical multichrome polish. Because you don't have to waste your life wearing marigold, buttercup, and daffodil, one at a time. You're special and unique and --goddamn it-- you deserve the whole bouquet!

Happily Ever Witch Cosmetics Website

The Heart Castle

Trevelyan was half-convinced this was all some trick of Marrok's design.

That bastard could have sent the witch to Trevelyan just to fuck with him. To confuse everything and make Trevelyan's life infinitely harder. He certainly wouldn't put it past the wolf. Marrok had always been cleverer than his golden-boy looks suggested and he had a True Love of his own, so he must know how annoying they could be. If Trevelyan was smart (And Trevelyan was *very* smart. Ask anyone. Especially Trevelyan.) he'd walk away from Esmeralda before things got even more mixed up in his head.

So why was he searching all over the damn castle for her, instead?

He'd stirred at some ungodly hour and sensed that Esmeralda was missing. He wasn't sure how he knew it, given the mountain of pillows she'd erected between them, but he'd opened his eyes and known she wasn't in the bed with him. Instantly, he'd been wide awake.

He'd sat bolt upright, his head swiveling around to scan the

empty place where she was supposed to be and *wasn't*.
Women didn't leave his bed. Not that he'd ever slept beside
one before. He always left after sex. Always. But if he *had*
slept beside another woman, she would have been there when
he woke up. So why wasn't Esmeralda?

More importantly *where* was Esmeralda?

Something hot and cold and slimy had slid through his stomach,
as he realized the witch was wandering around without him.
The infinite list of Trevelyan's enemies had scrolled through his
mind. All the monsters who hated him and who would be
cackling with glee to get their hands on his Good little wicked
witch. Inside of him, the dragon went on alert.

Trevelyan had never in his life feared for another person safety,
so he refused to believe *that* was the emotion that crawled
through his gut. It was probably just some extreme form of
irritation that he was stuck with a True Love who was an early
riser. Anyone sensible would be devastated to learn that
horrific news.

He'd gotten out of bed and gone looking for her, because he
was *irritated*. With her, and with the dawn, and with the rain
which continued to pour down. He'd never thought much
about storms, but now they pissed him off. Once he got his
powers back, Trevelyan was putting an impenetrable protection
spell on Esmeralda, whether she liked it or not. At least until he
figured out how to control the weather.

After fifteen minutes of searching up and down heart-patterned
corridors, the witch had still been missing. By that point,
Trevelyan had been getting *very* irritated. Where the fuck *was*
she? Dragons loved a good chase, but only when two people
were playing. It seemed like he was the sole participant and
that Esmeralda had vaporized into thin air.

The dragon had been going wild. It wanted the witch found.
Now.

So did the rest of Trevelyan.

He'd been all but running, when he reached the kitchen and
finally saw the mass of black curls. Trevelyan had skidded to a
stop, his heart hammering with... irritation. He braced a palm
on the doorframe, trying to calm down and speculating on if the

wolf had sent Esmeralda to drive him purposefully insane. At the moment, he was leaning towards "yes."

"Hey Trev." She said cheerily, her back to the door. She just seemed to know he was there, the same way he'd known she was missing when he'd woken up. "I made coffee."

The dragon eased at the sound of her voice.

The rest of Trevelyan didn't.

"There are some fancy smoothies in the fridge, too." She went on. "They all say "drink me" though, so I'm pretty sure they're poison. Why else would you want some random person to drink your stuff, unless you were testing a poison?"

He had to agree with that analysis. He spared a brief look at the refrigerator, where someone had pinned up some useless daily affirmation that read, "Believe six impossible things before breakfast!"

"Dear God... If you wrote something that adorable, I'm going to kill myself." He muttered.

"I *didn't* write it, as a matter of fact. But I don't think it's adorable. I think it's a dare."

"A dare?" He read the words again, suddenly seeing the challenge in them.

"Sure. You say you don't believe in anything you can't see and smell and hear, right? Well, this is daring you to believe in something *impossible*." She smirked. "It knows you can't do it."

"I could do it, if I wanted to." Dragons could do anything. Their DNA was magical. Literally.

"No, you could not. If you had a *week,* you couldn't do it."

"In a week, I'm certain I could..." He stopped and rubbed at his forehead.

What was he doing?

He should bellow at her for almost *irritating* him half-to-death, or demand to know what she'd been thinking wandering away the minute he closed his eyes, or stalk forward and seal his mouth over hers, kissing her until she was begging to climb back into bed with him.

(He Badly wanted to kiss her, probably because she was refusing to allow it. Kissing itself had always struck him as juvenile and unnecessary. He wanted Esmeralda's lips against his, though, and he was pretty sure he could convince her to accept his own.)

But all of that would have revealed more than he was comfortable revealing. Or feeling. Because he wasn't feeling *anything* except irritation. And now a lot of it was directed at himself.

What had just happened to him? Why had he reacted so strongly to the idea of her being gone?

The woman could take care of herself. She'd told him so. It had been an immense relief when Esmeralda suggested that they skip all the tedious bits where they protected each other. After all, it would surely be *him* protecting *her* and why should he bother? She wasn't loyal to him. She'd sided with her precious "family," not Trevelyan.

If she left him, he'd get on just fine without her. He'd always been fine without her before. So there was no need to be awake at this hellish hour, acting like he'd lost a limb until he saw her again. It was just misfiring biological instincts.

They were leading separate lives.

He could sleep late and she could go do whatever the frozen-hells she wanted, with her glorious body and "impossible beliefs."

Trevelyan straightened. "It's too early for coffee or poison. I'm going back to bed." One day in her company and it was already affecting him. This was a worrisome precedent and he needed to...

What was that smell?

He stopped short and looked around the messy kitchen. If Wonderland thrived on chaos, it must have been in its glory with Esmeralda taking up residence. The witch had ripped apart all the cabinets and piled things everywhere. Pots, pans, and teapots covered the floor. Half of them were now broken. Also, one of the walls had been blown out, so a jagged hole connected it to the next room. Apparently, Esmeralda hadn't been able to find the doorway to the dining room, so she'd just made her own. Logical, really.

It was the palace architect's fault that such drastic measures were needed to negotiate the Heart Castle. The Carpenter had built it all topsy-turvy, with invisible doorknobs and endless spiraling hallways. Then, he'd just expected visitors to deal with it.

Villains didn't "deal" with other people's bullshit. They made other people deal with *their* bullshit.

The smoldering drywall and pulverized masonry weren't the source of the strange smell, though. The scent was chemical. His eyes swept in the other direction and spotted an array of small bottles lined up on the pink countertop. They were the only neat and orderly things left in the room, and all of them were filled with black goo. *That* was the smell.

"Do I even want to know what you're cooking?"

"It's not to eat, dingus. It's nail polish."

"Nail polish." He repeated with absolutely no context of how such a thing fit into his life. "Why?"

"Because I make nail polish for a living. It helps me think and right now I need to think of a way out of here."

"Your job is *nail polish?*" He was momentarily stunned and it took a lot to stun Trevelyan, Last of the Green Dragons. "Your job can't be nail polish. You're a mostly-wicked witch, for Christ's sake."

"I'm a *very* wicked witch who runs an internet business."

"Nail polish." Trevelyan pinched the bridge of his nose, developing a migraine. "My God... For the life of me, I can't imagine a more useless profession."

"I create beautiful things that my customers like to buy and wear. Every day, I get to make people happy. Have you *ever* made anyone happy? Even once in your whole life?"

His jaw ticked. "It's not my job to make people happy."

"Then maybe your profession is even more useless than mine."

"My profession is villainy, so at least there's always a market for it." He stalked over to examine the colorful little jars of nonsense she'd brewed up.

Esmeralda dashed in front of him to protectively shield her creations, like she was afraid he'd begin smashing them against the walls.

Trevelyan glowered down at her. "If I was intent on

destruction, do you *really* think you could stop me?"

She scowled right back at him. "Don't screw up my work. I'm trying to perfect the formula for Bow-Before-Me Black. The polish is color-matched to the exact shade of remorseless evil."

He glanced at the bottles and made a considering face. "I wouldn't say it was *exact*, but the un-remorsefully evil --like *you*-- probably won't be able to see the difference, like I can. It's very slight." Very *very* slight. Very, very, very...

Shit. Maybe it was exact.

He glanced at her.

She arched a brow.

"It's close enough." He allowed and left it at that.

Esmeralda seemed to relax. Deciding that her ebony lacquer was safe around him, she shifted out of the way, so he could move closer to the bottles. "What do you really think?" She pressed, like his opinion actually mattered. "I already did a manicure to test it." She held out her hands for him to examine. "Is it perfect or not?"

Even her hands were sexy. How was that possible?

Trevelyan took his time in deciding about the quality of her work. Nail polish was a horribly harmless profession for a witch, but if she was going to do it, she might as well be the best. The inky shade she'd created was a fair representation of remorseless evil. And it certainly looked lovely on her delicate fingers. And cosmetics did have prices that bordered on villainy. That was always a plus.

"It's perfect." He decided grudgingly.

Esmeralda sent him a beaming smile, free of ulterior motives. It took him a moment to process what the strangely innocent expression even meant.

She was happy. He'd made her happy.

Trevelyan couldn't say why that appealed to him. Why should he care if he made anyone happy? He'd just told her how pointless it was. Esmeralda's smile did something strange to his insides, though. The lack of guile and the sweetness of it were unique. At least, in his experience.

Who would smile up at a dragon with such... virtue?

He was the best at being Bad. He should be repulsed to see

even a hint of virtue aimed his way. Instead, some organ flipped in the vicinity of his chest. Yes. This was *extremely* worrisome.

"Are you hungry?" Esmeralda asked. She was wearing those tall boots again and her skirt was even shorter today. "I was going to make treacle pancakes. I already mixed the batter. You can have some, if you want."

Trevelyan found himself nodding like an idiot.

"Great!" She shined another cheery grin his way. The woman was definitely a morning person. "I love baking. I have a ginger-mutant recipe I'm working on, too. We can eat those later, because I already know this batch isn't right. They're never going to become a sentient cookie army, eager to do my bidding."

"Cookie army?"

"Yeah. Wouldn't that be cool? But the spell is very complicated and I think I'm using too much cinnamon in the dough. For now, they're just a snack."

She headed for the stove, the diamond tiara twinkling.

That glittering headpiece distracted Trevelyan from his lustful fascination and gave him some foothold back in sanity. Maid Marion sometimes wore a plastic beauty queen tiara around, but that seemed to be some kind of empowerment statement and/or Marion being predictably eccentric. (Her brain didn't work like other people's, which was doubtless why Trevelyan was so fond of her.) Esmeralda's tiara, on the other hand, was studded with valuable gemstones, imbued with a colossal dose of magic, and assholes seemed willing to kill for it. Why?

"Maybe the Queen of Clubs is after that damn thing." He gestured at her head. "The Walrus was determined to get it off of you." Crowns held a lot of power, in the right hands. Or the wrong ones.

His eyes narrowed thoughtfully. Ambushing the Queen of Clubs was the best option he currently had, but it wasn't his *first* choice of countermoves. Trevelyan liked to play offense. If his enemy wanted something, then he wanted it, too. It was leverage. The question was: What was the Queen after? The tiara?

Esmeralda snorted. "Hell, the Queen of Clubs can have this crown, just so long as she sends me home. It keeps catching in my hair, anyhow."

Home. To the Enchanted Forest.

Trevelyan's mood darkened. "We also need to put some rules in place, if we're going to try this True Love thing." He decided out of the blue, mostly just to piss her off. Because he was pissed off and why should he be the only one?

"I hate rules. Pretty sure I mentioned that."

"This one will be simple. I want to outline some monogamy exclusions." Trevelyan sat down, ready for a fight. Fights made sense to him. "Obviously, having a True Love will dramatically narrow the variety of my sex life." He believed in loyalty, even if she didn't. "I expect mostly I'll be touching you."

Esmeralda scoffed at that assertion, not looking his way.

"But there is a small group of women, I'm still going to need to pursue. Not romantically. Just for sex. It's a long term science project of mine." Trevelyan dropped that gauntlet and sat back, waiting for the explosion.

"So, you want to put rules in place to date other people?" Esmeralda clarified, still focused on her pancakes. She didn't sound peppy, anymore. He perversely missed her galling early-morning brightness, now that he'd ruined it.

"No. I don't want to *date* anyone." The very idea was revolting. "But I sometimes see women with a strange spark in their eyes. And I want to try one of them, to see what it feels like up-close. It shouldn't take long. The women all seem to be Good, so I'm sure I'll get bored quickly."

He *always* got bored quickly. There were a few Good women -- just a handful-- that intrigued him, though. When he looked into their eyes, there was an intense light shining out. Unguarded magic, beckoning with the promise of something special.

Life and purity and ideas.

That spark was rare and bright and Trevelyan coveted it. He wasn't sure why, but it felt important. He'd never been able to touch anyone who actually possessed it. The women tended to have fanatically obsessed True Loves, which led him to believe he wasn't the only male who could sense the unique sparkle in those girls.

Esmeralda was quiet for a beat, flipping pancakes.

He frowned, still waiting for a fight that didn't seem to be coming.

"I'll take guitar players." She finally decided.

His brows slammed together at that completely unexpected response. "What?"

"For my monogamy exclusion." She sent him a casual glance over one shoulder. "I'll take guitar players."

What the hell?

"No." The word was out before Trevelyan even considered it.

She seemed annoyed. "What do you mean 'no'?"

"I mean *no*. You can't fuck a guitar player." Was she out of her mind? The thought of any other man touching her... Putting his scent on her body... Leaving his fingerprints on her petal-soft skin... The dragon moved inside of him, again. Furious, now. Claws raking. Wanting out, even though his powers were still too weak to transform. "No, Ez." The command was final and accompanied by an ominous swirl of smoke.

Esmeralda didn't notice. "You pick your non-monogamy dates and I'll pick mine, alright?"

"I told you, I'm not dating anyone! It would just be sex."

She plated her pancakes with a shake of her head. "Oh, I'm for sure going on dates with mine. I enjoy dates. Dinners and flowers and shit. I think it will be fun."

Was Trevelyan losing his mind? It seemed the most likely explanation. "That is not how this works."

"Why do *you* get to decide how this works?"

"Because it was my idea in the first place! You're not following the rules." Honestly, he hadn't considered the rules himself. He'd just been trying to annoy her with a spur of the moment idea, and she'd turned it all around, and now it was chaos. Why did she have to be so difficult?

Esmeralda sighed. Loudly. Like Trevelyan was the one being completely unreasonable. "I told you, I *hate* rules. What's wrong with my 'guitar players' choice?"

He tried to think, but it was hard through the dragon's roars and the frantic thudding of his heartbeat. She couldn't go to another man. He wouldn't allow it.

"Your choice of guitar players is much too broad a category, for one thing. There are minimal women with that spark in their eyes. There are *millions* of guitar players." And all of them would kill to get her into bed, beaming up at them with virtue and seduction. "So, that's hardly much of an exclusion."

She set the breakfast in front of him, like they were discussing nothing more pressing than maple syrup or powdered sugar.

"Okay, that's sort of fair." She allowed.

Finally, she saw reason!

"I'll choose cute, male, guitar players, with great smiles. That's my type."

Shit.

Trevelyan shook his head emphatically. "No."

Esmeralda disregarded that logical argument and sat down across from him, contemplating her perfect man. "I really only need one boyfriend, if he's the right one. But I don't think I should limit myself to numbers, at the beginning. I'll need options to choose from."

"You can't have *any* boyfriends. A boyfriend isn't casual. You're completely missing the point of *casual sex*."

"I don't like casual sex."

"Good! Because you're not having that, either."

"I should get a vote. And I want one cute guy with a great smile, who plays guitar. And maybe he lets me do his nails sometimes. That would be fun." She stared off at nothing, like she was imagining the musical motherfucker already. "And he owns a record shop. And he's kind to me."

No, no, *no*.

"'Kind?'" Trevelyan repeated scathingly. "You want someone *kind?*"

She got defensive. "Well, you want someone Good, so…"

"I don't want her for anything *kind*, though. I haven't wanted anyone *kind* since I was thirteen and had the passing desire to corrupt the prom queen. I quickly came to my senses and just fucked my algebra teacher, instead.'

Esmeralda's lips parted. "Your teacher slept with you? When

you were *thirteen?* That's against the law in every kingdom I know of."

"Also, the experience was horribly mediocre." He shrugged the matter aside, because he didn't like discussing Mrs. Clyburn. The dragon got restless just thinking about her.

The witch still seemed concerned.

Trevelyan wasn't sure why he'd even brought this up. He quickly refocused on what mattered. "Anyway, it's not like I want to *keep* any sparkly-eyed girls. That's the point. I have no desire for a long-term commitment to their reeking Goodness." The very idea was repellent.

He just wanted to find out what made those glowing girls glow. It was simple curiosity. Now that he stopped to consider it, he couldn't muster much enthusiasm for his science project anyway. Sleeping with them would be tedious. None of the women would smell as perfect as Esmeralda did. None of them would keep his interest for hours, waiting to see what she'd say next.

That's what he wanted. To have someone who never bored him and smelled like poisoned candy. He was a dragon! Why shouldn't he have exactly what he wanted? Why should he have to settle for less than everything?

Apparently, Esmeralda planned to use the monogamy exclusion to find an actual partner, though. Someone to spend her time and attention on. Someone she desired for his talents and goddamn niceness. Someone to give her loyalty to. Someone she *chose*.

She wanted to select another mate.

NO.

The dragon roared so loudly that Trevelyan's whole body jerked.

Esmeralda didn't notice. "I feel like you're micromanaging me, right now." She told him, around a mouthful of food. "You want to sleep with sparkly girls. I want my guitar player. That's a fair deal. You said yourself we needed to lead separate lives."

"I never said that."

"You did to and you know it."

He had said it. He didn't care.

A strange calm settled over Trevelyan. Every single part of him —all the deep and evil hollows-- sighted on the witch. And he decided. Just that fast.

Because, it wasn't a choice, so much as Trevelyan realizing it was the only possible option. Esmeralda wasn't getting another mate. She was *his* mate, whether either of them liked it or not. He wasn't sure why it had to be her. Perhaps it was the damn True Love bond. Perhaps it was the green color of her magic, pitifully weak as it was. Perhaps it was the way she'd happily smiled at him, when he complimented her nail polish creations. But whatever the reason, all of Trevelyan's instincts told him that she was the one.

Esmeralda would do for his mate.

He'd *decided*.

As soon as the choice was made, he felt the dragon relax. For the first time since the WUB Club, the monster's fury fully dissipated. The relentless prowling stopped and the smoke cleared. The dragon watched Esmeralda with arrogant pleasure, content with their prize. Soothed.

Trevelyan drew in a deep breath, astonished at how much better he suddenly felt.

Yes. This was the right path. The only path, really. Sooner or later, Trevelyan would've gotten himself a mate, anyway. It might as well be the witch. He could comb the world over and not find another woman so ludicrously bold, after all. At least their children would have some fire.

Esmeralda forked up another bite of pancake. "Hey, do you think we should tell each other, before we have sex with new people? It might slow things down, if there's any instant chemistry. Like, if my cute, smiling boyfriend had a concert and I was just incredibly drawn to his creativity and kindness. I don't want to have to go and find *you*, before I strip his pants off."

Trevelyan tilted his head at a predatory angle.

Anyone else in the universe would have stopped talking at that point.

Esmeralda kept talking. "But on the other hand, a quick chat between us might be smart, too. To make sure neither of us is feeling left out." She shot him a vaguely concerned look. "I don't want you to feel left out, Trev."

"Oh, I plan to meet any and all guitar players you want to bed. Introduce me to the boys."

"Yeah?"

"I insist, darling." His eyes glowed. "I'll kill them, right in front of you. Then, I'll fuck you myself, still covered in their blood and ashes." His smile wasn't particularly friendly. "I think we'd both like that."

She glanced at him, not looking worried about the charcoaled fate of her precious record store clerks.

"I'll even bring flowers, if you like. We can make a date of it. I know you enjoy those."

"Funny."

"Only I'm not joking." His tone was ominously soft. "I will brutally, instantly, *savagely* slaughter any man who touches you. I thought I made it clear yesterday, but I'm happy to prove it again. And again and again and *again*."

"So that's a rule, too, huh?"

"It's the *only* goddamn rule."

Esmeralda chewed her pancake. "I hate rules." She repeated. "Maybe we should table the discussion of monogamy exclusions, until you're not so crazy."

"This is as sane as I get. We're finishing it *now*." He wanted no ambiguity. "Dragons don't share."

"Neither do witches."

Trevelyan considered that, breathing hard.

"This whole thing was your idea, so I don't know why you're having a big, dramatic meltdown. It's just sex, right?" One black eyebrow arched. "Like you're going to have with those Good girls. If you can have yours… I can have mine."

He stared at her.

"Payback's a witch, baby." She wrinkled her nose. "I know you hate puns, but how could I resist that one?"

Trevelyan suddenly realized that she was trying to teach him something about being a True Love. Just like he'd told her to, the night before. Rewinding the conversation, he saw how she'd boxed him in and he understood the lesson. If he kept pursuing those girls with the spark, Esmeralda would find another man. She was smart. Sooner or later, she'd give herself to someone before Trevelyan could stop her. And it would destroy him.

Just like him sleeping with another woman would destroy her. True Love bound them too tightly to allow for casual sex or guitar players. The flames of that betrayal would consume them both. They could have separate lives, but not *entirely* separate. He couldn't just stash her somewhere and go about his business. No. He would have to see her. Spend time with her. Keep his scent on her. Ensure no other man came near her. It was just the two of them, forever-after.

Holy *shit*.

Esmeralda smirked, seeing that she had his full attention. "You push me, I'll push you back, Trev. Do you believe me?"

He met her eyes …and believed. "Yes."

On the plus side, he was already on his way to completing that daily affirmation's idiotic dare. It was before breakfast and he believed something impossible. He believed that he'd never sleep with another woman, ever again. He didn't even want to. He just wanted his too Good, mostly powerless, annoying little mate all to himself.

This was going to take a second to process.

Esmeralda took in his turbulent expression. "Sucks to suck." She told him with no empathy whatsoever.

Trevelyan's eyes narrowed, regrouping. He couldn't win this argument… but it also wasn't a total loss. He still received what he most desired. Dragons liked to make deals. If he agreed to this bargain, Esmeralda would have to forsake all other men, record store owners included. He would have her loyalty in this, at least. And that was the most important thing. Well worth giving up his science experiment with sparkly-eyed girls. A choice between Esmeralda and any other woman was no choice at all.

The witch was his mate. Just his. Something far darker and Badder than True Love told him so.

"No exclusions, for either of us." He offered flatly. "Total monogamy. Happy?"

"Why, I've never been happier in my *whole* life." She drawled out sarcastically.

Triumph filled him at the testy agreement. The dragon settled inside of him, purring in satisfaction.

Just his.

Trevelyan jabbed a finger at Esmeralda, wanting the last word. "If you expect me to be completely celibate, you're kidding yourself, though." She saw that was insanity, right? She saw that she needed to submit to the inevitable. "A chase is fun, but you're going to have to sleep with me soon."

"No, I don't."

Trevelyan was honestly flabbergasted. Who had ever heard of one mate refusing another? "Even if you don't 'believe in me,'" his tone was mocking because that whole idea was ludicrous, "your resistance makes no sense!"

She casually flipped him off.

Did she not understand that this had already been decided? He tried to break it down into her cultural framework. "We're True Loves. In some kingdoms, that means an instant marriage." He snapped his fingers to illustrate the speed of the bond. "Witches sleep with their husbands, I'm sure."

"Only if our husbands aren't dickweeds." She retorted. "Also, we're *not* married. You can tell, because we never signed a marriage scroll in front of a wizard and had a big reception with a cake."

No wizard or scroll or cake could tell Trevelyan if he was married or not. Only he decided that.

"And we're not getting married, either." Esmeralda continued. "And even if we were getting married, I *still* wouldn't sleep with you, after your little detour into sparkly-eyed Good girl obsession."

"I just told you I'd give up my experiment, didn't I?"

"Yeah, but I hold a grudge." She shrugged like there was nothing in the world she could do about it.

He made a frustrated sound. "I haven't had sex in two years!" Longer. Ever since the incident with Snow White, he'd been... off. He'd forced himself to sleep with that psychopath, so she'd let her guard down and he could escape. It had been the only way to survive, thanks to Marrok. But the distasteful incident hadn't faded from Trevelyan's mind as quickly as he'd expected. Esmeralda was the first woman in forever that he felt real desire for and she was completely wasting it!

"You were *asleep* for two years." Esmeralda rolled her eyes. "I think you can get through the sexual deprivation. Eat your pancakes, before you give yourself an aneurism."

Trevelyan had rarely been so frustrated. "Why I want to keep you is a total mystery to me, right now." He shoved away from the table, ignoring the breakfast she'd made.

Esmeralda blinked. "You want to keep me?" She repeated in a less flippant tone.

"I *am* keeping you." That part was decided, although he was sure that he'd regret it bitterly. "I'll be in Alice's office."

"Again? Why? We tore that place apart...?"

He cut her off. "Stay where I can hear you, if you yell." He ordered. He wasn't going to come rushing to her rescue, even if she *did* call out, of course. No way in the frozen-hells. Let Marrok do it, since she loved him so much. Maybe when she realized that the wolf wasn't able to help, Esmeralda would finally come around to the winning side of the war.

"Trev, what are you up to now?"

He kept walking, his mind switching back to something he could control. Something that made sense. He needed to look at every book on those damn shelves (and floor), until he figured out why that tiara was so important.

"Trevelyan." Her tone was insistent and a little desperate, not liking his brooding exit. "Tell me something true. Right now."

He stopped, but he didn't turn around.

Esmeralda waited and he could feel her tension, like she was worried he wouldn't play. He shouldn't. He was irritated. And it really was a strange game, since no one could win. Plus, he hated giving her unvarnished information, because it left him feeling... *irritated.* Technically, he could've stayed within the rules simply by telling her it was raining outside. That was true. But that wasn't how the game went and they both seemed to know it.

He stared at the pink-plastered wall in front of him. "I have to touch you soon." He rubbed a hand over his face and gave into her demand, for no logical reason. "It's not just because I want to. And I *do* want to." She had no idea how hot his desire was raging. If she did, she'd hide. "It's also a biological need. I *need* my scent on you. Dragons are scent-based creatures. I even think in smells, half the time. I can't relax until I can scent myself all over your body, so everyone realizes who you belong to."

"There's nobody else here. Who's even going to know what I smell like?"

"*I'll* know." And who else even mattered?

Esmeralda digested that for a beat.

"Do you believe me? About the need?"

"Yes." She cleared her throat. "So... it would just be touching?"

"For now."

"Alright. Give me a couple hours, so I can stop being so mad at you. Then, I'll consider it." It was a grudging acquiescence and they both knew it.

He closed his eyes in staggering relief. There was no other word for the emotion. "Tell me something true, Ez." He ordered, still not turning around.

Esmeralda thought for a beat, coming up with a baldly honest fact to share with him.

Taking his turn was the best part of this game. Also the worst part. Trevelyan was incapable of not striking out at people who pissed him off. Esmeralda had sounded distressed, when she discussed her childhood. So, now he was going to burn alive every single prospective parent who'd refused to adopt her. Who'd made her feel unwanted at that fucking orphanage. Surely there would be other people he needed to massacre as well, once she began sharing more with him. If they'd mistreated his mate, they would all die. Horribly. It was a matter of principle.

She cleared her throat. "When you told the Walrus I was yours, I felt..." She trailed off uncomfortably.

"Aroused?" He finished for her, reading it in her scent. He liked this confession, so far.

"Yes. And scared. I've never belonged to anyone. Not in my

whole life." She swallowed. "Do you believe me?"

"Of course. How could you possibly belong to anyone else? You're mine." Any other man who thought to claim her would be dead within minutes. Less, once his powers returned.

"I'll be yours, Trev. But only if you're mine." She shook her head. He heard the thick curls moving. "And I don't think you're mine. I think you only belong to *you*."

"No. I'm all that's left of the Green Dragon line, but *that's* what I belong to." Trevelyan had loved his parents, for all their homicidal tendencies. Perhaps *because* of their homicidal tendencies. He always wanted to make them proud. Their pitiless example was an inspiration of blood and flames and fear. "I'd consider allowing you to join my family, if you weren't aligned with Marrok and his horde." He shrugged, like her preference for the wolf wasn't a constant nagging irritant, grating along his very bones. "You're the one refusing to show any loyalty, not me."

"That's an interesting read on the situation. Not at all self-serving."

"Can I help it if the truth supports me and not you?" He was baffled as to how she could see this any other way. "I gave you a choice and you chose to side against me."

"You want to eviscerate the Four Kingdoms!"

"No. I'm *going* to eviscerate the Four Kingdoms. But, if you're standing in it at the time, I'll give you one last chance to move out of the way first." He finally looked at her over his shoulder. "See? There's really no need to be scared of belonging to me. I can be merciful."

Esmeralda's pretty fingernails, painted like remorseless evil, drummed on the tabletop. "I'm not scared of belonging to you, Trevelyan. I'm scared you're going to screw this up and break me into pieces."

His forehead creased. Nothing in his life had prepared him to respond to a statement like that. He was ninety-eight percent Bad. Not breaking things went against all his instincts and they both knew it.

Esmeralda stared back at him, beautiful crimson eyes solemn. "Teach me not to, then." He finally told her and went stalking out of the room.

Chapter Nine

Pick your perfect nail polish from our unlimited selection! Divorce Day White: Bright and fresh! This ivory polish celebrates the three most important clean sweeps you can have when reclaiming your singlehood: Clean nails. Cleaned out closets. And taking that bastard to the cleaners.

Happily Ever Witch Cosmetics Website

The Diamond Castle

The mermaid was the first to die.
She'd lived in the Pool of Tears, the huge lake at the center of the Diamond Kingdom. Nautical creatures didn't do well in the relentless heat of the open sand. Mermaids were supposed to frolic in waves and sing at starfish. Those cheerful airheads couldn't stay on dry land for long, which was why this kind of punishment was so damn effective against her. The iridescent colors of her enchanted tail withered in the unrelenting sun and her lush body crumbled into the dunes.
It was just what the Queen of Diamonds wanted.
The row of condemned prisoners was both an object lesson and a cheap source of entertainment for the Diamond Kingdom. The mermaid hadn't let them down on either front. She'd perished faster than even the bookies expected, keeping the deathwatch interesting. She also went out begging for water, ensuring that no one was eager to repeat her mistake.
The mermaid had played a prank on the royal yacht. As the rowers rowed, their oars became stuck in place, like the water was glue. It had stopped the boat's forward progress and caused a lot of panic on board. The mermaid had thought it

was hilarious. Clearly, she'd had the IQ of a beach ball. She was promptly arrested and sentenced to death for her temerity. She'd used magic, after all.

The Queen of Diamonds didn't like magic, because she didn't have any. The woman was human and part of some un-magical sect calling itself the Gyre. They hated anything that even hinted at enchantment. Bluebeard had never heard of the bigots before, but it seemed to him that Wonderland was a damn stupid place to live if you didn't like magic. All the talking animals would be a constant irritation, right? Maybe that was why the Queen of Diamonds kept killing everybody.

By the second day, a sheep with knitting needles stuck in her woolen hair and three shrieking elves had joined the mermaid. All of them had committed magical offenses, as well. Unable to withstand the scorching temperatures of the deadly beach, they lapsed into unconsciousness and slipped away. They were the lightweights. Or maybe the lucky ones.

Everyone else hung on through the night and into the next golden afternoon. Their bodies were staked to large poles, their arms suspended over their heads. They suffered from heat stroke and dehydration, with the Pool of Tears just a few hundred yards away. The cruelty just made it more fun.

Two mock-turtles perished the following evening. Not even their shells could give them adequate protection from the searing sun. Then, a sentient nesting doll went. Each of its little pieces perishing, one-by-one, biggest to smallest. Then, a wizard, who prayed to gods nobody had ever heard of. Then, a regular human magician. That dumbass had hosted an unbirthday party. He should've known better. On the sixth day of the execution, the ogre finally gave in, his huge body lax in the unbreakable chains.

That just left Bluebeard.

"You'll never get rid of me! Better Good folk have tried and I'm still here!" Bluebeard bellowed up at the Queen of Diamonds' massive sand castle. He'd lived on the sea for so long that going without fresh water was commonplace. He could endure thirst better than any of the dead pussies surrounding him.

"You invaded our land, with your dirty magic!" The Queen of

Diamonds shouted back from the safety of her shaded porch. The nasty bitch was lounging under a harlequin-patterned umbrella, drinking margaritas and willing him to die. She was bone-skinny, with yellow hair, and sunscreen smeared all over her nose. "You'll pay for what you've done!"

"I don't even want to be here! I fell through a rabbit hole, back in the Four Kingdoms. I *told* you that."

Not that it had helped his case. Rabbit holes were magical too, after all.

"The Four Kingdoms is filled with evil magic!" The Queen of Diamonds shrieked. The tiara on her head glinted. A gigantic diamond-shaped garnet was situated in the center, with hundreds of brilliant white stones surrounding it. "Everyone there is tainted."

"Hey, I'm right on board with hating that shithole! I'm pretty sure I have a death sentence back home, too. But, there's no reason to kill *me* for *them* being dicks! I don't even have any magic."

That was a lie. He had magic, but nothing worth dying over. Well, unless you were one of his six wives, anyway. He couldn't fight or fly or do anything that would help him out of this mess. No one else even understood his abilities. If he directed his mystical energy towards the Queen of Diamonds, all that would happen was...

Hold on!

His eyes widened, as it suddenly occurred to him that he *could* whammy his way free. He should've thought of it days ago! Bluebeard's colossal powers were limited in focus and big on results. He couldn't do a lot, but he was real, real lucky with the ladies.

Bluebeard's magic was all about marriage.

It dropped the panties of his many fiancées, got him plenty of free drinks from well-wishers each time he got engaged, and convinced scores of rich women to say "I do." Even if they didn't technically marry him, with all the troll-shit laws and whiny parents getting in the way, he could still *convince* them they were married. That was just as good, most times. He'd had six legal wives, but his temporary "wives" numbered in the thousands.

There was no reason his gift shouldn't work on the Queen of Diamonds.

"You are looking lovely today, your highness." He smiled widely, his magic pulsing out over the sand, aimed right at her. "We should go to dinner, tonight."

A familiar blank look came over her face. His spell had reached her, even over the distance separating them. "Dinner?" She repeated in a faraway tone. "With me?"

"I long to be with you. Forever and ever." Sincerity radiated in his voice. "I want to marry you. Today! This minute. We've waited long enough."

The other spectators of the execution stood in uffish thought and exchanged baffled looks. Bluebeard ignored them. Nothing would get in the way of his proposal to his newest bride.

He vaguely wondered if she was *already* married. Well, he could make her forget that interloper quick enough. No one could remove a wedding band, except the person it belonged to. But, Bluebeard's magic was unique. Specialized. He could make the ring invisible, so that not even the individual wearing it knew it was there. His magic hid the ring on a person's finger, as soon as he erased their spouse from their minds.

He really should get more respect from the other villains, because *no one* could do what he did.

"Marriage?" The Queen of Diamonds' voice rose in a hopeful, excited way, her hands clapping together.

Sure enough, the wedding band glinting on her finger vanished into nothing. Her current husband might protest such a hasty end to their royal union, but no matter. Breakups zipped right along when you had an axe to cut through red tape and the inconvenient ex's neck.

"Say you will!" Bluebeard begged. "Make me the happiest man in Wonderland."

"Callooh! Callay! Yes, I accept!"

"I hoped you would." Bluebeard told her honestly. "We'll have a wedding, as soon as I'm untied. I *love* you..." What the fuck was her name? "...my dear. I want to spend the rest of my life with you." Which wouldn't be much longer if he didn't get out of the sun pretty damn quick. His citrus-colored captain's uniform and turquoise beard were baking him alive. "Hurry! We haven't a moment to lose. Our whole future is waiting!"

His upcoming-wife was dazzled by the very idea. "Let my husband go!" The Queen of Diamonds sprang to her feet, her face alight with beamish joy at her impending nuptials. "And someone find me a red and white wedding dress. Oh, this will be positively mimsy!"

Whatever the hell that meant. "Positively." He agreed anyway. "You'll wear red and white too, of course." Not even married yet and already she was bossing him around. Typical. "And the cake will be red and white. And then we'll…" She stopped mid-word, like she was frozen.

Everything in the Diamond Kingdom appeared frozen, in fact. The spectators, the water of the Pool of Tears, the scorpions skittering around the sand. Even the air went still. As if time itself had just… stopped. The only two things still moving were Bluebeard and a stranger in a gigantic, purple hat.

Bluebeard was in the middle of his own execution and whatever was happening was still the worst thing that had happened all day. He could already tell. No question.

The newcomer frolicked up the steps to the sand castle's porch, nonchalantly twirling a katana-style sword in his hand. He stopped directly behind Bluebeard's betrothed. "Off with her head!" He shouted happily and swung the sword at the Queen of Diamonds' throat.

It sliced through skin and bone. No way could she survive that kind of blow. Bluebeard cringed. Shit. This was going to put a real damper on the wedding plans.

The Queen of Diamonds kept standing there, even though she was already dead.

The hatted-man's head tilted in confusion and then he laughed. "Oh! That's right. I forgot." He patted his torso, feeling for a large pocket watch hanging from a chain. He depressed the stopper on the top of it.

And time restarted.

Jerking back from her frozen state, the Queen of Diamonds'

head finally slipped from her neck. Blood spurted out everywhere, her body collapsing like a puppet with the strings cut.

The reanimated citizens of the Diamond Kingdom screamed at the sight. Most ran away in panic and confusion. His former-future-wife's decapitated skull hit the ground, rolling into the sand face-first, and Bluebeard knew the engagement was definitely off.

Damn. He sagged back in his restraints. So close.

The wedding-crasher-who'd-killed-the-bride grinned like a lunatic. He *was* a lunatic. He wasn't that big, but he pulled attention to him like he was lit with a spotlight. And that pocket watch thing was a neat trick. The stranger seemed middle-aged, with thick, white hair. He covered it with a ridiculously large top hat, but furry tufts still popped out all over the place. Bluebeard wore captain's regalia every day of his life and even he thought it was weird as hell.

But not as weird as the lunatic's eyes.

His pupils were spirals. Fucking *spirals*. Curving black lines, cutting through solid white. No irises, no pupils, just the gentle, constant movement of the curly-cues as he stared down at Bluebeard. Each tick of the pocket watch's second hand seemed to match pace with the swirl of his eyes.

Those bulging eyeballs, synched with that damn watch, scared Bluebeard more than anything he'd ever seen. And he'd had fifty-eight divorces.

"Hello, Bluebeard." The crazy guy said in a merry voice. "I'm the Mad Hatter."

Perfect name for the nut. Bluebeard had to admit it, even through his fear. Branding was everything in the modern world and this lunatic had nailed it.

A red-headed, bland-looking teenager dashed by. The Mad Hatter's horrible eyes sighted on her. Instantly, she was on the ground, screaming. Her whole body seemed to shrivel in on itself, as if it was being sucked dry by some unseen force. Within seconds, all that was left was a mummified husk, dressed in a modest apron.

"Delicious!" The Mad Hatter sucked on his fingers, like he'd just enjoyed a satisfying meal. "Good magic refreshes me, you know. Even these bigoted humans have a bit, whether they like it or not. And I do enjoy the taste of fear and innocence, dolloped on top."

"I taste terrible." Bluebeard assured him, quickly. "Hardly any innocence, at all."

"Oh, you've been a troublemaker, alright." The Mad Hatter wagged a damp finger at him, in a scolding manner. "When we rigged that rabbit hole to bring you to Wonderland, we didn't expect you to crash down in the Diamond Kingdom." He tut-tut-ed, like Bluebeard had deliberately screwed up his plan. "It took us days to find you."

"Sorry." Bluebeard got out, because what else was he supposed to say?

"No harm done. We needed to get this, anyway." The Mad Hatter picked up the sparkly crown from a puddle of blood, shaking off the gore. He casually tossed it in the air and caught it again. "Mimsy news, my friend. Maryanna the Queen of Clubs would like to speak to you."

"Is she married?" Bluebeard asked, always ready to give romance another go.

"She is!" The Mad Hatter grinned with festering insanity. "To me, as a matter of fact."

Well, scratch that idea, then.

"Congrats." Bluebeard wished he'd just died with the mermaid. It would've been way less painful than whatever befell him next. He already knew it was going to be a bloodbath. "Sure. Sounds... mimsy." There was nothing to do but nod and play along with the madness. "Let's go meet your Mrs."

Chapter Ten

Pick your perfect nail polish from our unlimited selection!
Rotten Choices Orchid: You know that feeling you get after you've just had sex with someone you *really* shouldn't have had sex with? Well, now it's a color!

Happily Ever Witch Cosmetics Website

The Heart Castle

Esmeralda was looking for her phone.
The stupid playing card guards had stolen it from her, when she was arrested. They'd lugged her down to the basement, locked her in an interrogation room, confiscated the phone, and put it... *where* exactly?
She had no idea.
Esmeralda blew out an aggravated breath. She'd been searching all around the lower level of the castle, where they'd held her after her initial arrest. So far, she'd found nothing of interest. Not even architecturally. Down in the bowels of the castle, there was less weirdness and gilding. The Carpenter must not have wanted to waste any of his creative energy on the Heart Kingdom's prisoners. They were no doubt grateful for his restraint.
Esmeralda didn't much care about the frabjous decorations or lack thereof. She just needed to make a damn call. And maybe blow off some steam. Doing significant structural damage to the castle's foundations was a great stress reliever. Her magic might be misfiring, but it could still blow things apart. She blasted the doors right off the hinges, as she moved from room to room.

Esmeralda had made it as far as the cell where the Walrus had interrogated her, but no phone was lying around. Also, no computers or landlines. Wonder-Why-I'm-Here-Land was truly the most dismal kingdom in the universe.

"What in the frozen-hells is that lettuce-y, corkscrew, sailboat-ish thing in the other room?" Trevelyan asked from the doorway.

That was a "rog." Her twitchy magic had accidently invented it, during another failed frog-spell debacle. Formerly, the rog had been a heart-shaped fire extinguisher. Now, it was a glob of disparate parts and uselessness. Her powers really were getting weirder and weirder. It was like Wonderland fed into their natural affinity for chaos.

"It's *cabbage-y*, not lettuce-y." The rog was an embarrassing freak of nature, but precision was important. Esmeralda glanced Trevelyan's way, not at all surprised to see him. She'd been timing it. "You're early."

"It's been two hours."

"It's been one hour and fifty-six minutes." At least, according to her gold, borogrove-shaped wristwatch, which was expensive and accurate. It had to be. She'd stolen it from Cinderella. Scarlett's stepsister's wholesome blondness and cupcake-y dresses hid a twisted soul. ...But, that depraved nutcase had had some incredible jewelry. Cindy didn't need such an awesome timepiece to count off all the centuries of her prison sentence, so Esmeralda had taken it for herself. Diamonds looked great with any manicure.

Trevelyan leaned a shoulder against the slightly-destroyed door jam. "Alright. We can chat for the next four minutes, then. I'll start." He lounged there, evil and gorgeous. "Is there a particular reason you're down here in the gloom?"

"This is where they brought me for interrogation. I'm looking for where they put..."

He cut her off. "Interrogation?"

"After they arrested me, yesterday. They had questions."

His eyes flicked around the edges of the small room and his jaw tightened. "The Walrus interrogated you? Here? Alone?"

"There were a few of them. He was in charge."

"What did they do?" His voice sounded eerily calm. It made the hairs on her arm stand up.

She looked over at him, wary.

"What did they do?" Trevelyan repeated in a more demanding tone. "Did they put their hands on you?"

"No. I mean, the playing card guards dragged me down here, but no one really hurt me. They just held me here and threatened me."

He didn't seem appeased. His eyes went to the lock on the door and his mouth thinned.

Esmeralda frowned at him, trying to read his mood. "I turned them all into hogs." She reminded him. "Why are you upset?"

"I'm not." He shrugged, but it was more like an agitated roll of his shoulders. "I just don't like the idea of anyone else touching you." He cleared his throat. "Sexual frustration is making me... irritated. It's your fault."

Now he sounded more like himself.

Trevelyan seemed keen to change the subject. "So, you've never had sex with someone you didn't like?" He asked randomly. "Not ever, in your whole life."

"Not ever in my whole life." She confirmed.

"And how many men have you liked?"

"None of your business! Do you hear me asking you how many people *you've* slept with?"

He rolled his eyes, like the question was ludicrous. He probably couldn't even count that high. "But you'll sleep with me, even though you don't like me, right? Since we're stuck with each other and *only each other* for the rest of ever-after?"

She wasn't sure whether he was nagging about the monogamy thing because it bugged him or because he wanted to remind her that she couldn't go date a guitar player. Somehow she thought it was the latter. "Today, I'm not going to sleep with anyone, *including* you. I agreed to consider letting you touch me, so you could get your scent on me. That's it."

He seemed okay with that, weirdly enough. "Have you considered it, then? You said you'd get over being mad, after a couple hours."

"And it's only been *one* hour and fifty-seven minutes."

"Will you be finished hating me, sometime over the next hundred and eighty seconds?"

"I'm considering it." Esmeralda arched a brow. "Have you considered ways you're not going to screw this up?"

"Yes."

"Really? What did you come up with?"

"I'm going to be kind."

"Kind?" She echoed and wondered if she was hallucinating. *"You?"*

"Yes. I can do that."

"No, you can't." She scoffed, because he absolutely couldn't.

"I'm a dragon. I can do anything. I can be extremely... kind." Just saying the word was killing him. He made it sound like a fatal disease.

"Trev..."

He cut her off. "Your skin is delicate. I understand that. And you yourself are very," he frowned a bit, like he was delivering a dire prognosis, "virtuous. You'll require special handling, so I don't break you."

Esmeralda pinched the bridge of her nose. "I swear to God..."

"It's not my fault that you're the way you are. I'm just reporting what I see."

"I'm a wicked damn witch, you moron. I'm not virtuous." If Grimhilde, President of the Cauldron Society, heard him, Esmeralda would never live it down. "Virtuous people are Good and I'm Bad."

"Barely." He waved a palm, forestalling her protest. "Whatever you call it, you're different than most of the women I fuc..." He stopped mid-syllable. "Most of the women I've been *involved* with."

She didn't miss the last minute word substitution. The dragon really was trying to be kind. It was a doomed effort, but she appreciated the attempt. Esmeralda was marginally encouraged.

"Obviously, it will take some time to adjust to your peculiarities, but I'm confident I can do it." He went on. "Dragons can do anything. And it's not as if either of us has much of a choice."

"We're stuck with each other." She agreed snarkily.

Trevelyan frowned, like he wanted to argue with that phrasing, but she was just repeating his exact words. He cleared his throat, instead. "So we can try touching, then?"

Esmeralda checked her watch. Close enough. "Alright."

He blinked at her casual agreement. "Really?"

"Sure."

There was *maybe* some progress with his attitude...? Maybe. And Esmeralda's body was constantly on fire for the man, so her own desires needed to be taken into account, too. In fact they were the *most* important consideration. She really wanted him. And all her instincts screamed he was the one she'd been waiting for all her life. He was her True Love and that bond was rock-solid, right from the jump. And Trevelyan was a very possessive guy. Having his scent on her would calm him down and possibly make him less of a handful. And she really, really wanted him. Did she think about that consideration, already? Because, she *really* did and nothing else seemed to matter. Anyway, this plan was worth a shot. "Want to go upstairs?"

"No." His brows compressed, suspicious of a trap. "You could change your mind on the way."

"I'm not going to change my mind, dumbass."

"We should do this here." He insisted and came striding into the room. "Replace whatever memories you have of this room with something more pleasant. If I had been awake, you would *not* have been trapped in here. I promise you that a thousand percent."

"You would have heroically saved me, even though we live separate lives?"

He frowned.

"Didn't think so." She snorted. "You know, I'm only *in* Wonderland, because they wanted me to wake you up. If you hadn't been in that coma, I wouldn't have been kidnapped, at all."

"Blame Marrok. He's the one who doused me with the sleeping gas." Trevelyan stopped in front of her. "Shall we establish rules, before we begin? I know you hate them, but I'd like to get through this without you piercing my other foot with your heel."

Whatever, just so she got some relief.

"No sex. Not even oral. And I'm not putting my hand down your pants. I'm willing to negotiate the rest."

His expression lit up.

"Except kissing." She said before he could even suggest it. "I already told you that I'm not kissing you until I believe in you. And I honestly don't see that happening. Ever."

He closed his mouth and sneered dismissively. "Kissing is overrated, anyway. I'll endure the loss."

"Super." She crossed her arms over her chest. "Well? What rules do you want?"

"I want to touch your skin." He decided without an ounce of hesitation. The man was never shy about what he desired. "I want to take your clothes off and I want to put my hands all over your body. I want my scent to cover you."

Her head tilted, thinking that over. Generally speaking, Esmeralda didn't like a lot of touching. No witch did. Their skin was sensitive and when other people handled it, there were usually unintended bruises and abrasions. You got used to it, but it wasn't fun. Honestly, sex was better if you tied the guy down before you began. They were usually all for it and things went a lot smoother. Still, the idea of Trevelyan's large, elegant hands on her body was intriguing.

"Define 'all over.'"

"Everywhere." The word was unequivocal.

She swallowed, thinking.

He watched her.

Esmeralda took a deep breath and made up her mind. "Okay." This would be a good learning opportunity for him, if nothing else. "But, my underwear stays on and your hands stay on top of it." She needed relief from the sexual tension, but not *that* much relief.

"Underwear is off."

"On."

His eyes narrowed. "On to begin with." He finally tried. "But I have the option of taking it off, unless you specifically tell me no."

Since Esmeralda was one-hundred percent going to tell him no, it seemed safe enough to agree. "Fine." She took a step closer to him. "You were right before, about my skin being delicate. You could hurt me and not even mean to."

His eyes met hers, listening.

"I'm not asking you to be kind. I think that's impossible. But you need to stop if I tell you to." She stressed. "Be careful with me."

"Yes." He agreed quietly.

"And I'll be careful with you." Esmeralda leaned down to unzip her boots.

Trevelyan's mouth curved at that promise, like he was amused by the idea of needing care. "Thanks."

"You're welcome."

His breathing got rougher as she stepped out of her shoes. Without the high heels, she didn't even reach his shoulder. He stepped closer to her, looming over her body. The predatory posture had her heart rate speeding up.

He chuckled, like he could sense her nerves. "Last chance, darling."

Asshole.

Esmeralda's blouse and skirt hit the ground next, because she never could resist a dare. She stood before him in her red lace underwear. "I'm all yours." She offered.

He swallowed hard, his face no longer mocking. He hesitantly reached out, so his fingers brushed against her arm in the lightest touch imaginable. "My God." It was a whisper of awe. "You're so *soft*. I didn't believe..." He trailed off, mesmerized by her.

Esmeralda's eyes drifted shut, overcome with sensation.

Witches' skin was always sensitive, but now it felt like every cell was awakened. Trevelyan's fingers left a trail of fire wherever he touched. Tingles were racing up and down her body.

Esmeralda couldn't breathe. She hadn't expected it to feel like this. It hadn't felt like this with anyone else.

A small sound escaped her, as she tried to orient herself in the maelstrom.

"Mine." He whispered and his touch got more certain. "Just mine."

His large hands ran over every inch of her body. Everywhere. Between her fingers, and the back of her neck, and the curve of her stomach. Places that shouldn't have been erotic, at all, except everything was erotic when Trevelyan did it. Flames burned her from the inside out as he learned every curve. And that's when she realized that he wasn't just touching her.
He was *claiming* her.
Surprised by that realization, Esmeralda looked up at him in sudden uncertainty.
He made a soothing sound, his hands never leaving her skin. "No, no, no..." It wasn't a threat. More like a croon. "Don't pull away. Don't tell me to stop." He shifted closer, like he was afraid she'd flee. "You're safe."
She hesitated, wanting to believe that reassurance. She *felt* safe, but...
"You're safe." He repeated, seeing that his simple declaration had calmed her. "You're always safe with me."
With me, you are always safe, my darling. I love you more than magic itself.
The words he'd said a thousand times in her head, when she was scared, flashed through her mind. Esmeralda stared up at him in wonder.
"There we go." Trevelyan smiled slightly, pleased that she'd responded to his promise, even if he didn't fully know why. "I might be a monster, but you belong right here in my claws."
Did she?
He turned her around, so he could explore her back. Esmeralda felt him slipping off her bra. She was supposed to tell him to stop, but she'd forgotten how to talk. Thick, slow, liquid pleasure was filling her. Drugging her. So all she could do was stand there and soak up the wonderful sensations on her skin. The man was magic.
"Beautiful." Trevelyan made a sound of pleasure, moving her so she faced him, again. "Christ. You are the most beautiful woman I've ever seen. Every inch of your skin is perfect. I could drown in it."
He grazed her nipples, causing them to tighten into almost painful points. Instinctively, she tried to pull away. Her skin

was too delicate. It usually ended up hurting when someone touched her like that and her body knew it. Trevelyan's fingers didn't relent, but they also didn't injure her. They felt amazing, in fact.

"It's alright." His touch was gentle. ...And territorial. Even in her daze, she recognized the greed and want in every stroke. "I can learn to take care of you. I already am. I see what you like. I can give it to you."

She slowly relaxed again, because he was telling the truth. He was giving her exactly what she liked. She hadn't even *known* she liked it, but he'd figured it out. No one else could do what he did. It was all Trevelyan. Her forehead came forward to rest against his shoulder, unconsciously trusting him and asking for more.

He pulled her right up against him. "Oh yes…" His voice was deeper than usual. Darker. "So soft and beautiful and sweet."

Only Trevelyan would think a wicked witch was sweet.

Esmeralda melted into his palms. She had never felt so relaxed or so aroused. Everyplace he touched was simultaneously soothed and enflamed. It was a revelation.

She sighed in languid surrender.

He purred in satisfaction. "That's my Good little mate."

Her body grew accustomed to the feel of his fingers and the strength of his hands. Her skin warmed to him the way it never had before. Began to associate his touch with nothing except pleasure and care. The desire to shy away, worried about rough handling, vanished. So did the desire to ever be touched by anyone else. Which was no doubt his intent. Making sure she responded to him so completely that no other man was ever going to be able to get close to her again without it feeling wrong.

He was such a tricky bastard.

She gave a slight whimper, almost over the edge and all he'd done was touch her skin.

Trevelyan shuddered out a breath. "I completely get the attraction to Goodness, now." He dipped his head to nuzzle her temple. "I get why men go insane to have it. You're so beautifully Bad, but with this little bit of sweetness that…" He trailed off and swallowed thickly. "The sweetness just kills me, Ez. It's all over you and it kills me."

She didn't jolt when he brushed the inside of her thigh. Was her underwear gone? When had he done that? She had no idea. She just shifted her legs and let him touch wherever he wanted. Lost in him.

"That's it." His voice was pure seduction. "Let me in." Fingers caressed and then eased into her warmth. "You know I belong here."

She gave a gasp at the feeling of him inside of her. And then he started moving them in *just* the right way and... Oh God... Her head went back, trying to breathe.

Oh *God*.

Esmeralda's hands instinctively came up to grasp his shirtfront, hanging on.

He gave a snarl that belied his calm, coaxing tone. "Give me everything. That's all I want. Just every single piece of you."

She knew what he wanted. He wanted her to come against his hand and it was probably going to happen. He was absolutely the *worst* man in the world, and her whole family hated him, and she couldn't trust him, and she was helpless to stop the tightening of her body. The hot/cold sensations of pleasure. She made a sound of need and surprise and dismay, caught off guard.

"That's it." He pressed even deeper, taking more. Demanding compliance. "You're so tight and wet. Come all over me, just like you're supposed to."

Oh Jesus... The orgasm was *definitely* going to happen, unless she figured out a way to tell him to stop. She should tell him to stop.

Right?

Esmeralda glanced away, trying to think...

"No." Trevelyan's free hand found her chin, keeping their eyes locked. "Look right at me." His intense gaze stayed on hers, his big fingers stroking deep, touching every part of her. "I want you to know who you belong to, my darling."

The "my" part of the endearment was all it took. The exact word he'd always used in her head, filled with possession and tenderness. The one she'd dreamed of all her life.

Esmeralda exploded. "*Trev!*"

Green eyes glowed hot, watching with villainous satisfaction as she came apart in his arms. "Just mine." He said again and, in that second, Esmeralda believed him.

As her body went into meltdown, Esmeralda's magic pulsed out. Lights dimmed all over the castle. Flickering off and then blazing back on, brighter than before. Pleasure wracked through her, her back arching towards him as tremors shook her. It was the greatest orgasm she'd ever had and she'd been researching pleasure spells since she was fifteen. Finally spent, she lagged forward, breathing hard. She would have collapsed, except he was holding her up.

Strong arms caught her and she felt lips graze her temple.

"Next time, I'll be all the way inside of you, Mate." He said into her ear. "I'll have *all* of your fire."

She shoved against him, barely keeping her balance.

What the *fuck* just happened?

"Did you use a spell to do that to me?" She demanded, panting for oxygen.

He didn't appreciate the accusation. "No." The word was absolute. "You *know* I didn't."

That was true. Logically, she did know it. It had just been *him* fogging her mind. She ran a hand through her hair. "Well, however it happened, that was a mistake."

Trevelyan ignored that assessment. "Speaking of magic..." He drawled out and she could hear the suspicion in his tone, so different than the gentle voice he'd used when he touched her. "You just blacked out half the kingdom, without even trying. Seems like quite a feat for a level one talent."

She grabbed her clothes. Her magical abilities were the *last* thing on her mind. She'd just let Trevelyan stroke her to orgasm, for God's sake. That was not what she'd intended. She was pretty-almost-sure of that. Maybe he hadn't used magic, but the man was messing with her mind.

Her eyes fell on the blinking red light of the security camera, situated on the wall. Oh shit... "Do you think they're still recording down here?" She blurted out.

"What?" He was visibly confused by her panic and distraction.
"Do you think there's a tape of us doing that?" She hissed, zipping up her skirt and gesturing to the camera.

"A film of me getting you off, you mean? Oh, that would be fun to watch." Dragons enjoyed showing off their conquests, so he clearly wasn't worried about videotaped evidence of her crying out in pleasure. ...Just so it was *his* name, she was calling.

"No, it would not be fun! I have to find the damn thing before someone sees it."

"Why? Are you afraid the hogs are voyeurs?"

"I just don't want anyone getting the wrong idea." She fumbled with her boots.

"Wrong idea?" Trevelyan sank onto the edge of the table, lounging there like it was a golden throne. "The citizens are all pigs, darling. They don't *have* ideas, thanks to you." He arched a brow. "And, if they *did*, I think their theories about what happened in here would probably be right. Really not much of a mystery as to what I just did to you."

"That's not the point!"

"It's the only point. Honestly, everyone *should* understand that you're mine. I'd take you right in front of them, if you'd allow it." He waved a dismissive hand. "Let them all know that I'm the only one who can..."

She cut him off. "I don't *want* everyone to know! Is that so hard to understand?"

Sudden comprehension lit his features. "Oh..." His head tilted, his eyes growing sharp. "You're worried about *Marrok*."

"Not just Marrok specifically. My family in general." No one was going to approve of her sleeping with the dragon. Not until she got him tamed, anyway. Esmeralda could already envision the screaming and death threats on both sides of the wedding aisle. "I just think it would be smart f they didn't see videotaped evidence of..."

"They are *not* your family." He interrupted, his voice ice cold.

"They *are* my family." She tugged on her shirt. "And they hate you. With really compelling reasons."

"You think I give a shit about their feelings?"

"*I* care about their feelings!"

Trevelyan was seething, now. "You give all your loyalty to *them*." He surged to his feet and swung an arm in the general direction of the Four Kingdoms. "To others. Never to me."

"Everyone who's mad at you is *right* to be mad at you, because you've hurt them!"

"The wolf is going to lose. Deep down, even you must suspect it. I have more magic, and more focus, and more fucking hate in me than he does. *I'm* going to win this war."

"You might." Esmeralda had boundless faith in the dragon's abilities. You couldn't be within half a mile of the man and not feel his colossal energy, even when it was still healing. It was entirely possible that he would destroy the Four Kingdoms, in the end. "But it doesn't matter."

"Of course it matters!" Trevelyan met her eyes, as if willing her to understand. "I'm going to burn the Enchanted Forest to the ground, Esmeralda. It *will* happen. You're on the wrong side of this fight."

"No, I'm not." Her voice was calm. "Even if you win... you'll still be wrong."

His expression darkened. "*Fine*. Stand with my enemies, if it makes you feel righteous. It makes no difference to my victory, just to your own virtuous little fate. I'm not rescuing you from your own stupidity."

"You'll never rescue me from anything, Trev. You said so yourself. Not unless it's super easy. Or you're super bored. Or you feel like killing someone. Or you want something from me in return. When it really matters, you are *not* going to save me. You'll let me fall."

His eyes snapped to hers, watching her silently.

"It's alright." She wasn't angry about his nature, just realistic. "I'm not asking you to catch me. I told you, I can rescue myself."

Growing up in an orphanage had taught Esmeralda not to expect too much from others. No matter what the True Love bond was trying to convince her, this man was not built for picture-perfect happily-ever-afters. That wasn't something she could teach him.

She sighed. "I just need you to see that the loyalty I feel for the

Tuesday share circle... It comes from trust. You think they're two different things, but they're not. Loyalty comes from believing in someone. I can rescue myself, but --if I couldn't-- my family would rescue me. I *believe* in them. Do you see?"

He didn't say a word.

Esmeralda tried delivering the lesson, again. "Marrok and Letty and Avenant and Benji and Dru are looking for me, right now." She believed that with her whole heart. "Sooner or later, they'll find me. That's why I will always support them. Because I trust them to support me back." She paused. "Also, you're completely wrong about --like-- *everything*, so there's that, too. But, the point is, when they arrive, I'd appreciate it if you didn't mention anything... *private* happening between us."

The fact that the dragon was her True Love was going to go over like a spider in whey. The news would be a lot better coming from Esmeralda than from Trevelyan. He wasn't great at holding conversations.

Trevelyan smiled, but it was all menacing teeth. "Well, I don't plan on talking to them, darling. I plan on killing them. So, I'm sure that it will be easy enough to keep our True Love match a dirty little secret, until after they're all dead in the ground. Whatever makes you happy."

She made a face. "This isn't about your ego. This is about me wanting to keep graphic details of our sex life private.

Especially from the guy I consider my brother. Just because you feel like bragging to Marrok about..."

He went stalking out of the room, before she could finish. "Are we done? I'm going back upstairs to research that damn tiara."

"The tiara, again? What are you...?" Esmeralda winced as the door slammed shut behind him.

So much for being kind.

CHAPTER ELEVEN

**Pick your perfect nail polish from our unlimited selection!
Longing-for-Something-Stupid Chartreuse: Face it, you're not going
to be able to wear this color anyplace. It matches nothing you own.
The formula is impossible to deal with and your friends think you're
crazy for even looking at it.
...So why are you falling so hard for this horribly inappropriate shade?**

Happily Ever Witch Cosmetics Website

The Heart Castle

It took Esmeralda the rest of the afternoon to find the security office with the video from the interrogation room. Then, it took her another hour to figure out how to watch the damn thing. Because, *of course* she was going to watch it. She wouldn't have intentionally made a recording of her and Trevelyan rounding third-base, but since one just happened to exist, she might as well take a look, right?

Right.

She was fast-forwarding to the sexy parts, when she suddenly heard her phone ring.

Letty was calling her! She recognized the Pecos Bill song she'd picked as a ringtone, just to annoy Marrok. Scarlett adored that musical cowboy, which made Marrok all pouty and randomly jealous. Esmeralda's gaze cut around the TV monitors and old-fashion recording equipment in the small space. Where was her phone hidden?

She began banging open the drawers of the metal desk, frantically rooting through them and haphazardly dumping their contents onto the floor. And there it was! Second drawer from the top. Her sparkly green baby.

Esmeralda gave a choked sound of deep emotion, grabbing up her phone and sliding a thumb across the screen to answer. "Letty?"

"Ez!" Scarlett shrieked. "Oh my God! Is it really you? Are you alright?"

Esmeralda's hand tightened on the phone, relief swamping her. "Letty." She closed her eyes. "I'm okay. I am just *so* glad to hear your voice."

"I'm glad to hear yours! Are you in Wonderland?"

"Yes! How'd you guess?"

"Midas. He got me the best tracker in the known-kingdoms to hunt you down. Trystan Airbourne's been searching for you *everywhere* and you show up in that hellhole?"

"I'm not here deliberately. I was frigging kidnapped! I was falling through a rabbit hole and crash-landed in this crappy place yesterday. Then a Walrus and a White Rabbit..."

Scarlett cut her off. "Do they have Marrok?"

"Marrok?" Esmeralda frowned. "No, why would they have Marrok?"

"He's gone." Letty's voice cracked. "He was abducted from the Enchanted Forest and taken to Wonderland. It *has* to be somehow related to what happened to you, because it's just too big a coincidence otherwise."

"Someone kidnapped the Big Bad Wolf?" Marrok had been a professional Wolf Ball player. He was huge and could turn into an even huger bipedal wolf, covered in scary looking mist. "How in the world did *that* happen?"

"I don't know exactly. I just know that he's *gone*. Whoever took you, took him, too."

"I'm in the Heart Castle. I've sort of turned everyone here into hogs, but I know Marrok wasn't one of them." Her magic would never hurt her family, even when it was misfiring.

"You made the Walrus a hog? Well, that's a good start. My grandmother will be thrilled. So will Midas."

"Yeah, but he's just a lackey of someone called the Queen of Clubs." Esmeralda thought for a beat. "I've been gone over a year." Not that it had aged her. To Esmeralda, only a few days had passed. "Why do you think Marrok was just taken yesterday?"

"Probably because you just *got* there, yesterday. This is all some bigger plot. Trystan Airbourne's positive Marrok was taken to Wonderland and you're there, too. It's all connected!"

"Trystan's the tracker guy? Do I know him?"

"I doubt it. You'd remember if you did. He's a gryphon. So the wings stand out in a crowd."

"Holy *shit!* You've got a gryphon looking for me?" That was kind of a big deal.

"I have *everyone* looking for you! Only Trystan can't find a way to reach you, now. Someone has locked up Wonderland, tighter than a drum and it's *always* hard to get into Wonderland." Scarlett was talking too fast. "The phones and internet aren't working. It's a miracle I got you on this one. I have an evil fairy helping me boost the signal, but I've been calling you for hours and this is the first time it connected. No one knows what's going on and I just *have* to find Marrok, Ez."

"Of course." Esmeralda nodded. She wanted him found, too. He was her brother.

"I know he's still alive. I would feel it if something happened to my True Love. I just need to..." She trailed off with a sob, trying to hold herself together.

"Wherever he is, I'll find him." Esmeralda vowed. "Tuesday share circle sticks together, right?"

Scarlett sniffed, like she was trying not to cry. "Right."

"So, I will get Marrok. Wonderland isn't that big. I will track him down, just as soon as I escape the force field surrounding this castle."

"Force field?"

Esmeralda made a face. "It's a thing. Don't worry about it. You just find a way to get us out of Wonderland."

"Trystan's husband is going to figure out that part. He's the best knight ever, apparently."

Esmeralda's eyebrows rose. There was only one "best knight ever" and everyone knew it. "The gryphon's married to Sir Galahad? Wow, I used to watch his TV show all the time, in prison. He's amazing! And he's got puppets."

Scarlett gave a watery laugh, knowing that Ez was trying to cheer her up. No matter how much time had passed on Letty's end, their relationship was deep enough to resume without even a pause. "I doubt Galahad's bringing puppets, but he *is* amazing. I'm confident he'll figure out a rescue plan. He's talking about using some portable, rabbit hole creation device thing to get the two of you..."

"Three." Esmeralda interrupted before she thought better of it.

"Three? Who else is there with you? Bluebeard?"

"No. Jesus, is that asshole kidnapped, too? Why would anyone want him?" As a villain he was strictly B-list. He just killed wives and pranced around in his dumb pirate-captain's uniform.

"Bluebeard vanished the same time you did. Odds are, he's in Wonderland."

"Wonderful." That was sure to be Bad and not in a fun way. "Who else is with you, then?"

Esmeralda was silent for a beat. "Trevelyan." She muttered, not seeing a way around the truth. It would be easier coming from her now, then from Trevelyan later.

"The dragon!" Scarlett shouted, her tears forgotten, as she took in this new twist. "How is he even awake? My God! *He* could be the one who took Marrok!"

"He's not. The Queen of Clubs nabbed Trev, too. I think that's why she brought me here, actually. To wake him up from the mystical coma." Better to just rip off the bandage. "Trevelyan is my True Love."

Silence.

Esmeralda winced and stared up at the stained ceiling, wishing it would fall and crush her. It would be way more pleasant than this part of the conversation.

"That man is *evil*, Ez." Scarlett finally said in a serious tone. "He scared the hell out of me in the Westlands."

Esmeralda knew the broad strokes of that encounter, but not the gory details. "What exactly did he do?" It was no doubt terrible, knowing Trevelyan. "Was it a spell?"

"A spell? No, mostly it was dire threats."

Okay, for the dragon, that wasn't *too* awful. It was a low bar.

Her True Love was an undeniable shithead, at times. "I'm sorry, Letty. Really. He's horrible. I'm working on that."

"You think he could've cast a spell on me, if he'd wanted?"

"Oh, I'm *positive* he could've." He must have been pulling his punches, because Scarlett wasn't his real target. Knowing him, it had been a big, tantrum-y show for Marrok's benefit. "I watched him evaporate a guy's bones earlier. Dark magic is his go-to problem-solver."

Scarlett was the cleverest person Esmeralda knew and now she was thinking hard. "Are you *sure* that he's your True Love? It's not some trick he's pulling?"

"He's not tricking me. Believe me. He's *desperate* for a way out of this arrangement." The man was pissed as hell over her "disloyalty." "Trevelyan doesn't think I'm Bad enough for him."

Scarlett snorted, because she'd been hearing the same criticism all her life. "If he's your True Love, then there *isn't* a way out. Not unless you both agree to stand before a wizard and formally dissolve the match. Does Trevelyan want to do that?"

Esmeralda wasn't kidding herself. "He'd probably go for it, if I offered."

"He hasn't suggested it, though?"

"No."

"It seems like a pretty obvious solution to the problem. If he hasn't mentioned it, maybe he doesn't think there *is* a problem."

Esmeralda hadn't considered that. "He did say," she cleared her throat, "that he planned to keep me."

"Do *you* want to keep *him?* That's what really matters."

"I'm not sure." Esmeralda rubbed at her forehead. "I mentioned he's horrible, right?"

"Yep."

"And selfish. Arrogant. Oblivious. Prone to childish dramatics. Thinks he's always right." She closed her eyes, because the list went on and on. "He told me to teach him how to be a better True Love, so I'm seeing if he can be salvaged, before I decide what to do next. Right now, I'm not very hopeful."

"Why do I hear a 'but' coming?"

"But, I've *always* wanted my True Love, Letty. You know that. I just can't give up without a fight. And I have heard him in my head before. Trevelyan's voice. I just didn't know it was him."

"Your magic is strong, Ez. But it's sometimes... twitchy."

"I know, but not about this. Not about *him*."

Scarlett mulled all that over. "He said you should teach him how to be better?"

"Yes. And how not to break me."

"Well," Scarlett's tone turned grudging, "it's not a terrible sign, if he wants to learn."

"And he never bores me." Esmeralda hated being bored. "And he flips the hell out whenever I even hint about dating another man. And he promised not to sleep with any other women."

"You're sure he's sincere?"

"Yes." Esmeralda didn't doubt his word on that front. "If Trev didn't want the deal we made, he'd say something. He's not afraid to advocate for himself, that's for damn sure. It was actually his idea. He hates sharing. Like... a lot."

Scarlett made a "huh" sound, gears turning in her head. She'd always been good at strategies. "I'm not thrilled with this, as you can imagine. Maybe he refrained from evaporating my bones, but I still don't like the man. If he's yours and he's attempting to be better, though, I will *try* to reserve judgment."

That was more than Esmeralda would have done in her place, but Scarlett was always too Good for her own good. The Trevelyan news seemed to be calming her down, as a matter of fact. She must have a new plan.

"Wonderland is a dangerous place." Scarlett went on, as if confirming Esmeralda's thoughts. "Trevelyan is at least some protection for you there, because he's an absolute, literal monster. You're his True Love, so he *has* to look out for you."

Esmeralda rolled her eyes. "No, he doesn't."

"You don't think he'll keep you safe?" Scarlett was startled by that idea. Possibly because her True Love was a protective, doting, sweetheart to her.

"We've established an 'every dragon and witch for themselves' kind of relationship." Esmeralda shifted uncomfortably. "I can look out for myself, though."

For some reason, she didn't mention Trevelyan's powers were

still healing. He wouldn't like Letty knowing about that and it wouldn't matter in the long run, so it seemed best to just keep it quiet.

Scarlett sighed. "I know you can take care of yourself. But, you and Marrok are both in danger and I want my family home. Can you trust Trevelyan to help make that happen, *at all?*"

"No." The answer was instant. "He might help me find Marrok, but only because he'll want to kill him at the end."

Scarlett was silent, thinking some more. "Marrok beat him once before. He can do it again, if he has to. I'd prefer him to face Trevelyan, rather than this Queen of Clubs bitch. Especially if you're there to mediate."

"Mediate?" Esmeralda scoffed. "With those two?" She had no idea how Marrok had survived the last battle. He'd either been incredibly lucky or Trevelyan hadn't been fully invested in killing him. "Trev will walk right over me to have his revenge."

"True Love doesn't work that way. Trevelyan might *think* it does, but it doesn't. The bond is straight through your soul. You own some part of him now, whether he likes it or not."

Esmeralda waved that aside, because none of the usual True Love stuff applied to the dragon. Trevelyan wanted to live "separate lives." That kind of precluded a soul-deep bond.

"What about Marrok's reaction, then? He despises Trev. Even if I perform some miracle and keep Trev calm, how am I going to stop Marrok from going wolf on my True Love?"

"I have no idea." Scarlett said honestly. "But I trust you. If you say Trevelyan can be salvaged, I'm going to go for this plan. It's the best option for Marrok and for you. They were friends once. Maybe the two of them can..." The phone was losing the connection, Scarlett's voice going in and out.

Esmeralda raised her own voice, like that might somehow compensate. "I will find Marrok, with or without Trevelyan. I *will*, Letty."

"Thank you." Scarlett told her sincerely. "...so happy to hear your... I love you, Ez."

"I love you. And I will see you soon. I promise."

"Just be safe and remember..." The call failed.

"Fuck." Esmeralda gave her phone an irritated shake and then

set it aside. "Alright. We'll try again, later." If it worked once, it would work again.
Probably.
In the meantime, she needed to find a way out of the castle. That was the next step. She'd tried breaking every window in the damn place and it hadn't helped. The rain had stopped, but she remained stuck. The farthest she could go was the wide veranda overlooking the hedge maze. The remnants of the tea party she'd crashed were still set up on the plaid, pastel lawn. She could see them, but she couldn't walk down the sweeping steps to reach the ground.
This palace was *not* going to be her red-and-pink tomb.
Sooner or later, she'd find a way out. It was just a matter of persistence and Esmeralda was the most persistent witch in the west.
In other news, the video monitor had finally started showing something interesting. Esmeralda slowed her fast-forwarding, her gaze on the screen. It showed Trevelyan touching her naked body for *ages*. She looked great. That was important to note. But the whole experience took way longer than it had seemed, when she'd been experiencing it.
And Trevelyan looked enthralled by every single moment.
She would've expected him to be smug or smirking or distracted by something shiny, every once in a while. The man didn't have the longest attention span. But, nope. He was positively *enraptured* by her. It wasn't even lust. That was there, sure. But Trevelyan's expression seemed like... more. She had never seen him so fascinated and content. Not even when he was ripping out the executioner's bones. In that moment, she really had owned the dragon.
And what a fabulous monster she'd caught for herself.
Esmeralda's gaze stayed on his face, watching Trevelyan run his palms over her skin. She saw her own head fall onto his shoulder in dazed rapture. And she saw his eyes flutter closed in response to her show of faith. His face buried in her hair and a tender smile played around the edges of his lips. For several heartbeats he didn't even move.
He just... held her.

Like she was precious to him.

Like a man with ninety-eight percent Badness, might possibly be tamed.

Like he'd protect and care for Esmeralda, happily ever after.

She decided not to erase the video. Instead, she stacked her chin in her palm and enjoyed Trevelyan revealing some of his secret thoughts to the hidden camera. When she'd climaxed, there wasn't an ounce of snide-ness in his expression. Just pleasure. He'd loved making her come. Loved that she'd trusted him with everything.

The tape flickered, as her orgasm messed with the electricity, but it didn't stop recording. So she saw him glance up at the lights. He knew she'd caused the disturbance, which meant he knew she'd lied to him about being a level one witch. But instead of being annoyed, he just held her tighter and smiled. Then, he'd licked the taste of her right off his fingers, a dragon relishing his greatest treasure.

Esmeralda's mouth curved. Maybe she *could* teach him something about love. Maybe he wanted to learn. Maybe he just needed a little push out of his "separate lives" comfort zone to see the bigger picture.

Her phone *bing*-ed with a text message from Scarlett and Esmeralda glanced down at it.

Can't get call through again. Maybe this will work. Just did five minutes of research on Trevelyan & already found a problem. Did you know there's another woman, who's offering a MASSIVE reward for his safe return?

CHAPTER TWELVE

Pick your perfect nail polish from our unlimited selection!
Forty Proof Lime: Yep, it's alcoholic! This frosty-umbrella-drink-colored polish gives you just the strength you'll need to suffer through another day of dealing with morons.
(Must be twenty-one to purchase or have a reasonably good fake ID.)

Happily Ever Witch Cosmetics Website

The Heart Castle

Alice's office had no books about Esmeralda's tiara. The castle's library was far more useful, though.

Once Trevelyan broke some locks, and ignored some direly written warnings, and dismantled a few magical safeguards, he was able to access all of the Heart Kingdom's most interesting tomes.

Like everything else in the very pink Heart Palace, the library was very pink. It soared three stories high, with wide open balconies and tall windows. The stained glass in the towering panes depicted red-armored knights slaying dragons.

Damn bloodthirsty knights.

Trevelyan shook his head in disgust, half-reading through the dry magical ruminations of some half-assed wizard and half-fantasizing about his seductive little mate. Well, it was more like 70/30 Esmeralda fantasies. Even that was giving the dead wizard more attention than he deserved.

Trevelyan munched on one of the ginger-mutants Esmeralda had made, pleased with life. He had been pissed when he left her downstairs, however it was difficult to stay that way. The day had been an overall success. His new mate was wonderfully fearless, with an intriguingly virtuous smile, and a mouthwatering scent.

Plus, she could bake.

The ginger-mutants may have been a lackluster army, but they were amazing cookies. In retrospect, it had been a huge mistake not to eat those pancakes the witch made that morning, because they were surely exceptional, as well. As annoyed as he was with Esmeralda for her inexplicable preference for mangy wolves, he gave her full points for her culinary efforts.

And her body... Dear God, her body was the stuff of all his evil daydreams.

That was the main source of his buoyant mood. Trevelyan had thought he'd become jaded about most every sexual activity, position, and fetish under the sun. He'd been wrong.

Esmeralda changed *everything* for him, just by standing there in her pretty underwear. The sinful softness of her skin, and the hesitant sounds she made as she slowly surrendered, and those wide eyes looking up at him in surprise and wary pleasure...

Trevelyan gave a hungry growl at the memories. He hadn't simply *touched* a woman since he was a young teenager, before he'd even fucked Mrs. Clyburn in the algebra room. (Not that he was going to think about her. Thinking about his teacher always annoyed him, for some reason.) Dragons were sexual beings. *That* was the point. They came of age early and they didn't wallow in the preliminaries. There was always an expectation that touching would lead to something more interesting. Why else would you do it? It would be a waste of time.

But, just having his hands on his Good little wicked witch had been better than sex. *So* much better. Time spent with Esmeralda wasn't wasted, no matter what they did.

After experiencing it for himself, Trevelyan was now a convert to the awesome power of True Love. He fully believed it was worth all the hype. (At least in bed.) Having your True Love in your arms did indeed reset the bar. It made sex... better. And he hadn't even *had* sex with Esmeralda, yet. It was going to be revelatory, when he was fully inside of her. He could already tell. The witch's beautiful, green magic flashing out as she came around his fingers had captivated him, forever-after. And she had *a lot* of magic.

No way was Esmeralda a level one witch. Not even a level two. Trevelyan wasn't sure what the hell she was up to, with that obvious lie about the strength of her powers. Did she think he wouldn't notice? Lying to your True Love was charmingly Bad, though. Considering her forty-nine percent Goodness, he'd take whatever hints of villainy he could get with the girl. It showed she was at least *attempting* to be devious and immoral. You couldn't ask for more than that, really.

And whatever her magic level, Esmeralda was his mate. Just his. It was already decided and it wouldn't change. Ever. So, the lie meant little. It didn't matter how powerful she secretly was, because he was keeping her anyway.

...Level four magic would be nice, though. Or at least level three.

Red frosting from the ginger-mutant's fangs dripped onto the pages of the ancient Wonderland spell book. Trevelyan ignored the damage. Who else would ever read it, anyway? It wasn't like the hogs could use the library.

Really, it was for the best that the tome was doomed to linger forever, stained and ignored, on a shelf. The wizard who'd written it was some magical hack using the preposterous pseudonym "Lyon N. Unicorn." (God save him... Trevelyan was *always* surrounded by morons. Even when they were long dead, they managed to find him.) He was annoyed by the wizard's many typos and all the useless shit the man included in his potion recipes.

Why the hell would you put porcupines into a fertility brew? You wouldn't. Not unless you wanted slow, prickly children. He rolled his eyes and turned another page. Stupid people should never perform magic. It led to all kinds of...

And that's when he saw the crown.

A thousand percent of Trevelyan's attention zeroed in on the illustration, his head tilting to one side. It was Esmeralda's tiara, linked with three *other* tiaras, so they formed a continuous circle of diamonds all around the head of whoever wore it. At the center of the tiaras, each of which made one side of the full crown, there was the emblem of a playing card suit. Hearts, the one Esmeralda now wore, was in the back. Diamonds and Spades on the left and right. And right up front was Clubs.

Well, look at that.

Trevelyan's gaze scanned the paragraph of text, under the picture.

The Unified Crown of Wonderland: Each tiara selects a worthy bearer. When donned by a chosen woman, the enchantment will trigger and it will become permanently affixed to her head. Those who wear the tiaras will be recognized as the queens of each Kingdom. However, when the proper spell is cast and Wonderland recognizes its true ruler, the four tiaras will join automatically and the Empress of All Wonderland will be anointed. She will reign over all four lands and bring peace and prosperity to the entire kingdom.

So, the Queen of Clubs was after the tiara. He'd been right. (No surprise.) In fact, she wanted *four* tiaras. She wanted Trevelyan to perform the "proper spell" and reunite them. She wanted to rule all of Wonderland, as an empress.

Trevelyan's eyes narrowed, as the full ramifications of the passage hit home. No wonder the Walrus and the White Rabbit had been panicking earlier. Esmeralda was wearing the Heart tiara and it wouldn't come off. It was enspelled right to her pretty little head. It had *chosen* her.

According to the book, that meant Esmeralda was now the rightful Queen of the Heart Kingdom. As her mate, that meant Trevelyan was the *king* of this accursed place.

He looked around the be-hearted hellscape and made a face. Ugh.

Luckily, Esmeralda was a quarter of the way to acquiring *all* of Wonderland for them. Always pleasant news, when your mate was a success in her career. True, it wasn't much of an empire, but surely there was something lying around they could export or exploit. And being called "Emperor" had a certain cachet. *Marrok* wasn't an emperor. It could only benefit the entire Green Dragon line (which was presently only Trevelyan) if they ruled over a gigantic kingdom of cowering peasants, who made them lots of gold.

It was decided.

They would take over Wonderland.

He flipped to the next page of the book, satisfied with his new plan. Kill the Queen of Clubs. Acquire the other three tiaras. Become Emperor. Build a new and better castle. Have sex with his mate on their piles of money. What could be a better happily ever after?

Chewing on his sixth ginger-mutant, he scanned more rambling about the "proper spell" that would unite the four tiaras into one big, shiny crown. Lyon N. Unicorn had apparently created this enchantment, so it shouldn't be too hard to master, once Trevelyan had his powers back. Whatever magic was needed, he was confident that he possessed it. The Queen of Clubs had been right about that much, at least. He was a dragon! He could do anything.

The words "sealing wax" suddenly jumped out at him, from the middle of the page. Trevelyan's stomach knotted, his assurance fading away.

Oh *fuck*.

A loud buzzer sounded, causing him to jolt in his pink-cushioned seat.

"You have accessed restricted materials from the royal library and damaged them." A mechanized voice said, from somewhere overhead. "If you have the proper authorization, please say your pin number now."

Trevelyan glanced up towards the roof, aggravated by the interruption. "Piss off." He muttered distractedly. "It's just frosting."

His mind was spinning, trying to decide if he was being paranoid or if the universe was legitimately out to get him. As far as he knew, there was only one spell that mentioned "sealing wax." This must've been where the enchantment originated, typo and all.

Was Snow White involved in this mess?

Another buzzer and then the automated voice returned. "That pin is not recognized. If you have forgotten your pin, please answer the following security question to retrieve it: Why is a raven like a writing desk?"

Well, that was an easy riddle to solve. "I don't give a shit about either one of them." See? Simple.

Another buzzer. "That answer is not recognized. Please stand by."

Trevelyan made an irritated noise and got to his feet, preparing to go find the alarm system's controls and rip out all its wires. As a villain, he respected general pandemonium, but he needed to focus on the damned spell. There wasn't time for jangling Wonderland nonsense.

His mind was on the WUB Club. A shudder of distaste went through him, as he recalled Snow White. When he'd slept with her to escape prison, she'd been talking about "sealing wax." But, not for herself. No, it was her...

The laser beam cut off Trevelyan's thoughts. It also cut apart the chair he'd been sitting on.

He barely managed to jump out of the way before the intense red light sliced from some hidden point in the room and did its very best to kill him. The library table, where he'd been reading, split in two and collapsed inward, the edges of the wood burning from the intensity of the laser's heat. The remainder of his delicious ginger-mutants slid to the floor.

"Son of a *bitch.*" He shouted at the disembodied voice. "You just ruined my cookies!"

"Please stay where you are. The security team is on its way."

Security team? That didn't sound very promising.

Behind him, metal grates slid open, like the doors of an antique elevator. Trevelyan turned to see two clockwork men chugging out of the opening. They were shiny brass automatons, with steampunk gauges all over their chests and snazzy red bowler hats on their pressed-metal hair. One hat read "Tweedledee" and one read "Tweedledum."

Great. What was *this* madness?

The robots' primitive faces jerked this way and that, light-bulb-eyes scanning the room. Both of them sighted on Trevelyan at the same time and they started forward in stiff unison. They were about the size of humans, only they reminded him of wind-up toys. The automatons' gyros and motors whirred, as they moved closer.

Those animated noises were quickly drowned out by the sound of all the bullets being fired. Frozen-hells, they were *armed* robots! Trevelyan went diving for cover, behind a bookshelf. The Tweedles' limbs might only have a few points of articulation, but there were old-fashion, gangster-style submachine guns soldered to their three-fingered hands. The drum magazines matched their rounded bodies. Trevelyan wasn't sure if that was an aesthetic choice or if Tweedledee and Tweedledum had simply been manufactured decades before. He hoped it was the former. If they were a newer invention, he still had the opportunity to track down their builder and kill the asshole.

He slowly inched along the rows of priceless tomes, while the Tweedles resumed scanning for him. Their guns silently swung around, waiting for the next opportunity to fire at his vital organs.

Magic would be very helpful, right now. Magic was *always* helpful, but never more so than when you were being attacked by clockwork assassins. Unfortunately, his energy was at low ebb, because he was using his rejuvenated powers to restore his injured powers faster. Every bit of healed magic went to heal more magic, in a continuous circle. Trevelyan had thought that was fairly clever. Possibly it had been a miscalculation. How could he fight evil androids without magic?

"Trev?" Esmeralda called from the doorway to the library. "Who is Marion Greystone and why is she looking for you?" Inside of him, the dragon finally deigned to stir. It was far more interested in the witch than in the metallic-killers hunting them. "Do not come in here!" He bellowed back at her, peering through the stacks of academic magic journals to keep an eye on the Tweedles.

Their heads had already ratcheted in the witch's direction, but they didn't fire at her. Apparently, he was the only one targeted for death. The intensity of his relief over that fact caught him slightly off guard.

Esmeralda took offense at his very sensible order. "I'll go

where I want!"

"Well, you don't want to come in *here*. Trust me." He headed up to the second floor, hoping the Tweedles didn't have the technology to climb stairs.

"Why not?"

"Robots are shooting at me." There was no sense in hiding it. Instead of retreating, Esmeralda came forward. He could hear the tapping of her very sexy boots on the pink marble floor.

"Robots? Lord, what have you done, now?"

"Why are you automatically blaming me?"

"Because you must have done something to piss them off. I *don't* have robots shooting at me, because I *haven't* done anything to piss them off. Logic, dummy."

"That's not logic, it's..." He stopped talking when another laser blasted from the ceiling and fried a shelf of wizard periodicals directly in front of him. Shit. He forgot about that thing. "Also, there's a laser." He tacked on and went the opposite way.

"Lasers and robots." Her eye roll was audible. "Whatever. I want to know who Maid Marion is to you. I remember Marrok once telling me she's his financial advisor."

"She's a friend of mine." Trevelyan stayed low to avoid more gunfire, trying to steer clear of the open balcony. The Tweedles were able to get up steps, damn it. They were already following him, shooting wildly as they came closer.

Esmeralda barely paused in her harangue. "You don't have any friends." Her voice echoed, shouting to be heard over all the weaponry. "You said so yourself."

"I lied. I do that a lot. I'm ninety-eight percent evil."

"Well, how close a friend is she? Because, it turns out she's been taking care of your body, since you were doused with that sleeping spell. The Walrus kidnapped you from her damn house." Esmeralda headed up the stairs. "And she's offering a fuck-ton of gold for your safe return to Neverland Beach. Like *so much* gold, that I think I might just drop you on her doorstep and cash in on the reward myself."

"Marion predates the lesson your precious wolf taught me, about friendship being a crock of shit." Trevelyan had never questioned Marion's loyalty and he appreciated knowing that he'd been right. (He usually was, of course.) While he was in the coma, she'd looked after him. It warmed him, a bit.

"This has nothing to do with Marrok." Esmeralda declared hotly. "This is about *you.*"

Fighting robots without magic meant a lot of defensive play. Trevelyan *hated* defensive play. He needed to go on offense. Glancing around, he tried to reason out a trap. "I like to think everything is about me." He agreed.

"I like to think you're a colossal idiot, because you *are.*"

"Are you mad about something in particular, darling?"

"No!"

"You must be mad or you wouldn't have come here." She was braving machine guns to storm into the library and scream at him. That hinted at deep feminine anger.

More footsteps, as Esmeralda continued tracking him down on the second level. She was like the relentless clockwork hitmen, only in six inch heels. "How long have you known her?"

"Marion? I've known her for…" Jesus, how did you calculate time when you were in stasis for two years and she had traveled through time? "…awhile."

"Have you slept with her?"

"Is *that* what this is about?" He laughed, finally figuring it out.

"Have you? Yes or no?"

"No." He darted to the left to avoid another sweep of the laser. "I have not slept with Marion." He'd half-heartedly tried years before, but she'd turned him down. Now, he never even considered it.

"I don't believe you have any platonic, female friendships, Trevelyan. I've met you."

"Can we talk about this after I'm done with the robots? I'd like to enjoy your jealousy, without so many distractions."

"We'll talk about it, right now! And I'm *not* jealous. We're supposed to have a monogamy deal, though. I gave up guitar players for you, so you need to give up this Maid Marion girl."

He settled on an offensive strategy and headed down a long aisle, knocking ancient scrolls and grimoires off the shelves as he moved. Scholarly vandalism should draw the Tweedles' attention. "We *do* have a monogamy deal. But, if you get

Marrok, then I get Marion. That's only fair."

"He's my brother!"

"And she's my sister!" It wasn't until the words left his mouth that he realized they were true. He saw Marion as a sister. He had a sister, not of his blood. Did that count as believing an impossible thing?

Yes.

He was winning the dare from that cheery affirmation on the refrigerator door. That was two out of six impossible things already and it wasn't even dinnertime.

"Your sister?"

"Marion and I were in prison together. You know better than anyone the bonds that can build."

Esmeralda was quiet.

"Marion got sent back in time ten years. Then, she saved my life, because I saved *her* life in the original timeline." He gave his head a shake. Even he was getting confused. "Anyway, now she's rolling in cash and treats me like I'm fourteen. And she's married to her True Love. You have nothing to worry about, alright? Can we drop this?"

Although, it was thoughtful of Esmeralda to be so possessive. A man liked to know he was wanted.

Esmeralda remained silent, as if she was trying to sort through that convoluted explanation. "You saved her?" She finally said and her voice sounded strange. "You deliberately went out of your way to protect this woman?"

The Tweedles were closing in on him, one on either side of a long aisle of priceless manuscripts. He was cornered. ...Or so they thought.

"Actually, it wasn't me that helped her. It was the *other* me. From her timeline." Trevelyan climbed up the shelves like a ladder.

"I have no idea what you're talking about and I don't want to." Esmeralda snapped. "One of you is *plenty*. Why are you always mixed up in so much weird shit?"

"I make a lot of enemies. God knows why."

"I can make you a list of reasons, if you'd like." Her voice changed, becoming less irritated. "Hey, speaking of enemies, did you know Bluebeard's in Wonderland, too?"

"I have no idea who that is."

"He's a jackass with turquoise facial hair and middling powers. I'm sure he hates you. Everyone always does. We'll probably have to kill him, if he shows up."

"Fine." Trevelyan couldn't care less.

"So, does Maid Marion have that spark in her eye, you were talking about earlier?" Esmeralda asked, back to her main focus. "The one Good girls sometimes have and you want to science experiment with?"

She did. Trevelyan wasn't stupid enough to admit it, though. "Stand back, Ez." He called out instead. "I'm about to make a mess." The Tweedles were directly under him, trying to get a clear shot, as he perched on the top of the bookshelf.

Trevelyan jumped to the next bookcase over, shoving the one he'd been standing on with his foot. It toppled down on top of the robots, flattening them beneath the massive weight. The shelves hit the next bookcase in line, as it fell. And that one hit the next, and that one hit the next, in a domino effect of cascading paper and wood and deafening sound. The final bookcase went right over the library balcony, bending the decorative metal and then exploding onto the floor below. Trevelyan smirked.

It wasn't an elegant win, but he'd take it.

Dropping back down to the ground, he stalked towards the trapped Tweedles. Esmeralda turned the corner, just as he'd exposed their gyrating heads. Their blinking eyes saw him, but their guns were trapped beneath the debris and there wasn't time for them to crawl free.

Trevelyan stomped down on their faces, crushing their mechanized brains with his heel. Their clockwork bodies slowly stilled, jittering madly and then going silent. Trevelyan smashed them a few more times, just to make sure. Enemies could never be dead enough.

Esmeralda frowned. "Well, that was a little much."

"Muchness was required. They don't have no-kill shelters for murderous robots. Best to just put them down."

She wrinkled her nose and forgot about the crazed security

force. "Anyway, you're saying Maid Marion is like your family? That's it?"

Trevelyan considered that question. Family meant everything to dragons. And for a man who was the last of his line, it meant even more. "Yes." He finally decided, dusting his palms together. "She's my *only* family."

The witch was welcome to join him too, but instead she'd cast her lot with the rejects in the Enchanted Forest. She couldn't be in both camps. You were either with Trevelyan or you were against him.

Esmeralda crossed her arms over her chest, hearing the exclusion he'd built into his reply. "Why do you want to turn everything into a fight?" She asked, as if she hadn't raged into the library looking for one herself.

"I'm not 'turning' anything into a fight. Fights come at me and I respond to them straight on."

"That is such troll shit…"

She didn't get to finish that insult. The laser targeted Trevelyan again, its red beam aimed right at his head. He always forgot about that damn thing. He automatically dodged, not sure he'd be able to get out of the way fast enough.

And then approximately ten million gallons of liquid dumped down on Trevelyan and everything else in a four yard radius. The laser cannon was blasted right out of the ceiling and propelled downward, as it was power-washed from its perch. The giant weapon shattered into the pile of destroyed bookshelves, broken and dark, adding to the mountains of rubble on the floor.

Trevelyan stood there, dripping wet.

Water.

For one terrible instant, that was the only thought in his head. Water, water, *water*. Motherfucking water was *everywhere* and Esmeralda would be melted.

Desperation seared through his brain, like a blowtorch. *"Get back!"* He roared and his eyes jumped to her, frantic to see if she'd been harmed. She seemed okay, but what if she was splashed? What if it pooled at her feet? What if more fell from the sky? "Run!"

She stared at him, not running. Her head tilted to one side, when she saw his expression. "I'm fine." She promised softly. "Calm down."

"Don't let it touch you!"

"Only pure water burns witches and this is..." She cringed a bit and cleared her throat. "It's kind of... rum."

The breath wheezed out of him. She was okay. It was all okay. Except...

"Rum?" He sniffed at the sleeve of his jacket, smelling the liquor now that his initial panic had started to ease. "Why am I covered in rum? And," he picked up new scents, his mind whirling, "black tea and fresh lemon and sugar cane? Wait, is this... *grog?*"

She shrugged, like she had no idea what he was talking about. Trevelyan's eyes narrowed, angry at himself and at her. Mostly her. "It had to be your magic that did this, because it sure as hell wasn't mine." He flicked some of the sticky alcoholic concoction off of his fingers.

Given every single option in the world to stop a laser beam, *grog* would've been the last weapon he picked. No. Scratch that. He never would have thought of it *at all*, because it was insane.

"Yes, fine! It was my magic." She allowed. "But, it wasn't really my fault you got a little damp."

"I'm soaked in *grog!*" He would simply never get over it. "What the fuck, Ez?"

"I told you my powers are twitchy! I don't know why they did that, okay? I just..." She made a frustrated sound. "I should've just let you get zapped." She went flouncing off, unwilling to continue listening to his very rational critique of her bizarre spell-casting choices.

Trevelyan's heart was still pounding from thinking she'd been hurt. Feelings he wasn't choosing to feel had swamped him and he didn't like it. He couldn't even classify them all. He didn't *want* to. He hated anything being outside of his control, so he just ignored whatever the True Love bond and the dragon were screaming in his head.

(And since when did the monster inside of him and the True

Love bond agree with each other? Why were all the different parts of him siding against him, now?)

"I'm going to smell like a distillery for days." He complained at Esmeralda.

She smelled like Trevelyan, though. Well, mostly she smelled like *her*, thank God. He loved her Good/Bad fragrance. But now, his scent was all over her, marking her as his. No other shifter-species could miss who she belonged to. That brought a sense of satisfaction and began to soothe the edges of his temper.

"You're welcome, dick face. Glad I could save you."

"I didn't ask for your help."

"Well, *Maid Marion* wasn't here to lend a hand, so I thought I'd better do it!"

Trevelyan reluctantly snorted at that delightfully bitchy retort.

"You're exactly like the Cauldron Society." Esmeralda ranted. "None of you ever think my magic is special enough. But once I get my ginger-mutant army to do my bidding..."

He cut her off, his voice going arctic. "Anyone who says you're not special, I will burn at the stake. I promise you a thousand percent. I've wiped out covens of witches in the past and I'll do it again."

She paused, looking back at him.

"Just give me a list of names and it's done, my darling." *Nobody* insulted his mate. Certainly not a group of pompous bitches in pointy hats.

"Now you're trying to make me like you." She accused with a sniff. "It's not going to work."

"Of course not. No one ever likes me." He shrugged that ridiculous idea aside. Nine times out of ten, he even annoyed his honorary-sister. "But I like *you* and that's all that really matters. So, your enemies are my enemies." He arched a brow. "...Unlike some people, I'm loyal."

She flipped him off with one Bow-Before-Me-Black-tipped finger and kept walking.

Christ, but he liked her.

He even liked that she'd instinctively helped him, although he would've been fine without a bath in high-proof spirits. With

Esmeralda, he would take whatever small bit of loyalty he could get. She was attached enough to be jealous of Maid Marion and flood half a library for him. That was progress.

"You're getting a waterproofing spell, whether you like it or not, Mate." He shouted after her, wanting the last word in their argument.

Inside of him, the dragon had yet to calm. The creature was infuriated, roaring, and pacing, and raking its claws. It was obsessed with the witch. It couldn't stand that their mate had been in danger.

The monster was right. This couldn't keep happening. He wasn't about to let goddamn water threaten Esmeralda ever again, because it was threatening *him* by proxy and nothing threatened Trevelyan, Last of the Green Dragons. That was the reason for his burst of panic, when he'd thought water was pouring down on them.

It wasn't about her. It was about *him*. Obviously.

Trevelyan was all that mattered.

Instead of agreeing with his supremely levelheaded command, Esmeralda scoffed at him. "Fuck yourself, Trev. With a chainsaw."

He liked the woman's fire, too. He really did.

He sucked some of the grog from his thumb. Perfect mixture. He preferred bourbon to rum and even he was impressed with the cocktail. Esmeralda could cook, mix drinks, looked like a centerfold, cursed like a sailor and was capable of crushing laser beams with her odd magic. No wonder he was keeping her, regardless of how irritating she got.

The dragon was in complete agreement. It huffed, but began to settle down, feeling Trevelyan's resolve to claim their witch. The sooner she was fully mated, the happier it would be. And it was wise to keep a dragon happy. Esmeralda should really know that, by now.

Trevelyan ran his tongue over the edge of his teeth. He'd always been mercurial and it was hard to stay angry at a woman with an ass as lovely as Esmeralda's. He was able to nurse a grudge for years, but not with her.

The last of his anger cooled, partly because the dragon was

quieting. (He'd forgotten how much easier it was to think, without the beast constantly raging.) And partly because it was silly to be upset over his mate trying to help him. No matter how ill-conceived her spell, it at least showed she cared. And *mostly* because he simply wasn't ready for the witch to leave his sight, yet.

He liked being with Esmeralda. Even when he knew they wouldn't be having sex in the immediate future, he still wanted her around. It was very strange.

Luckily, he knew how to get her attention back on him and only him, where it rightfully belonged. "Don't go, Ez. I've got a secret to share with you."

"I don't care!" She yelled back, heading down the stairs to the bottom floor, picking her way through the huge mess they'd made.

Yes, they definitely needed a new castle. This one was getting systematically ruined, one room at a time. What could you expect when you locked a dragon and a wicked witch inside of it, though?

Trevelyan stood by the balcony, watching her storm off. *Such* a lovely ass. "I think you might want to know what I know." He sing-songed tauntingly. "Since it's about you..." It was a dare and neither of them could resist a challenge.

She hesitated.

He slowly smiled.

That beautiful crimson gaze swung back his way, just like he wanted. "Alright, what's your big secret, wiseass?"

He leaned over the railing, loving this game. "Guess who's the new Queen of the Heart Kingdom, darling?" Green eyes gleamed. "I'll give you a hint: She's mated to the handsomest dragon in all of Wonderland."

Chapter Thirteen

Pick your perfect nail polish from our unlimited selection!
Not Mint to Be- This is the exact same color you keep buying, and
keep hating, and keep buying again. Only now it's got a cuter name!

Happily Ever Witch Cosmetics Website

The Club Castle

Dragons liked power and hated rivals. It was a fact of their species.
All the various color lines dedicated a great deal of time to conjuring up horrific new ways to destroy their enemies. And dragons had *a lot* of enemies, so a horrific number of their horrific ideas got tested out in a number of horrific real world trials. Because they were also arrogant, dragons were further convinced that only other dragons posed a *real* threat to their own power. Whenever possible, most of their most horrific ideas were tried out on their own kind.
Consequently, no one understood how to hunt dragons better than dragons.
If you were rich and cruel and needed a dragon captured, hiring another dragon to do your dirty work was the smartest plan. Especially if the dragon you needed captured was Trevelyan. Anyone who'd ever met Trevelyan had a motive to hurt him. He was the most hateable man in the world.
There was a fan fiction site on the internet entirely devoted to furious death-to-Trevelyan daydreams, where authors of every known species fantasized about ways to kill him. Florian of the Blue Dragons, son of Ferdinand and Brandgomar, often lurked there, taking thoughtful notes on the more creative tortures.

Unlike many dragons, Florian was an intellectual. An academic. He didn't care much for hands-on fighting, but he excelled at strategy. He was hired, at a steep hourly rate, to advise kingdoms with dragon problems.

And Wonderland had a dragon problem.

When word reached the wintery Club Kingdom that Trevelyan, Last of the Green Dragons had somehow defeated every single person in the Heart Kingdom, the Queen of Clubs was displeased. Florian was summoned to help her remedy the situation. Immediately.

Since she was paying double his usual rate, he'd dropped everything and come to Wonderland. Selling his magical services to help capture other dragons was the best way to stay free himself. Plus, he was bright enough not to boast about his strength or flash around his powers. That helped, too. People hired Florian, but no one had ever tried to enslave him. He was professional and discrete. As a bonus, his job paid very well.

Dark Science allowed Florian and his assistant to bypass the barriers. A quick word with the Queen of Clubs --who'd told him Trevelyan *must* be taken alive, no matter the cost-- and then Florian went straight to the soldiers' barracks.

The most important part of his new assignment was prepping the Club Queen's army for the battle to come. Because there *would* be a battle. If Trevelyan was breathing, he'd fight. And if he fought hundreds of men would die.

Maybe more.

Florian wouldn't be among them, of course. He'd allotted three hours for this job and then he was leaving Wonderland. Hopefully forever. He was a consultant, not a combatant. He would simply prep the knights for the slaughter they were about to face.

And what better way to prep people than an informative slideshow?

Wonderland was a technological wasteland, but Florian had brought his own meticulously prepared computer presentation, which hopefully this motley crew of knights would be able to follow. Most of them were humans. Not the brightest species. He'd have to use very small words and lots of pictures.

Impeccably dressed in a navy suit, Florian stood on the makeshift stage that had been erected for him and clicked the button to begin his presentation. The first slide was projected on the large screen behind him, the title direct and unsentimental:

How to Kill a Dragon without Dying Yourself

"As you know, your upcoming mission was to go to the Heart Kingdom and collect Trevelyan. The timeline still stands, but there has been a slight change of plans. The Green Dragon was supposed to be asleep, when you arrived." Florian adjusted his wire-rim glasses. "Now, he's awake."

The knights began whispering amongst themselves, panic on their faces. The barracks suddenly smelled of fear. There were legions of men stuffed into the huge room, so it was overpowering. Barracks weren't the cleanest places anyway, so adding even *more* odors over top of the unwashed socks and sweaty bodies was just disgusting.

Florian made a fastidious face, vaguely repulsed by the stench. Other people tended to baffle and annoy him, but never more so than when they lacked proper hygiene.

Beside him on the stage, Haigha snorted in grim amusement, enjoying the knights' overwhelming terror. Misery always brought a smile to his face.

Haigha was Florian's cousin. Also his nephew. And also maybe his cousin, again. The family tree of Blue Dragons didn't have a lot of branches. They distrusted outsiders and tended to mate within their own group, which led to complicated relationships. Everyone was related to everyone. Repeatedly.

The other Blue Dragons had pressured Florian into giving Haigha a job as his assistant, after the other man had nearly died from some stupid stunt or other. Their working relationship wasn't exactly meant to be. The two of them looked similar with golden hair and vivid aqua eyes, but their resemblance was only skin deep. Where Florian was stoic and scholarly, Haigha was a violent idiot who craved conflict.

The idea of crusading against Trevelyan invigorated Haigha. He wanted to make a name for himself. To be feared and admired. No matter what the Club Queen commanded, Haigha had no intention of bringing Trevelyan back alive. He planned to ride into the Heart Kingdom and kill the mightiest dragon in the world.

Regardless of the outcome, that wasn't going to be great for Florian's business.

"Trevelyan's magic will be low, because he was in a coma." There was nothing Florian could do to stop Haigha's idiocy. Instead, he'd do his best to prepare him and the Club Kingdom's soldiers for the coming battle. "And he'll be facing four thousand, two-hundred and seven of you. The situation isn't hopeless. But Trevelyan's literally been designated as 'A Scourge of All Lands,' by three international bodies, two of which he's since wiped out of existence. So, I want you to understand *exactly* who you're up against."

He clicked to the next slide, which showed an attractive dark-haired couple, dramatically posed in stylish clothing and expensive jewels.

"Trevelyan's parents. You've possibly heard of the Seven Cities of Gold? There were *Eighteen* Cities of Gold before the Green Dragons got it into their heads to begin claiming them." He flipped to a new picture, which showed an endless battlefield filled with towering flames and piles of corpses.

Haigha grunted in appreciation of the brutality.

"The knights of every neighboring kingdom were sent to stop their reign of destruction." Florian went on. "The Green Dragons eventually fell. Fifteen knights survived. Total. They stumbled towards their homes, spirits broken, but grateful to be alive. ...They would have been better off dying with the others."

The audience exchanged worried glances at that news.

Florian advanced to the next slide, because there was no use sugarcoating the truth. "*This* is what became of those unlucky bastards, after Trevelyan found out what happened to his family and tracked their killers down."

Soldiers gasped at the graphic images on the screen. Their hands came up to shield their eyes, even as the ungodly pictures burned into their brains forever. A few vomited.

Haigha lost his smirk, as he took in Trevelyan's wrath. "Is that a head sticking out of there?" He whispered, his lips barely moving. "Or part of the intestine?"

"I have no idea *what* that is." Florian told him honestly. Anatomy had never been his best subject. Neither had art. And the grisly mass of flesh was some disquieting mix of the two. It was almost beautiful in its grotesque creativity.

"Holy shit." Haigha crossed his arms over his chest to hide his shudder of revulsion. "Trevelyan's always been a psycho." Florian moved on with his presentation and everybody heaved a sigh of relief. "After the death of his parents, Trevelyan embarked on a life of rootless, conscienceless crime." He gestured towards the object on screen. "This is the ever-playing harp from the Enchanted Realm of Melody. Everyone who hears its perfect music is compelled to dance. It was destined to only be strummed by a pure-hearted champion, who would use its gentle music to bring peace to all the world." The assembled knights relaxed slightly, looking up at the picture of the lovely, silver instrument. The graceful curve of its body and the magical shimmer of its strings calmed the eye.

Next slide.

People cringed at the ghastly new image on the screen. "Then, Trevelyan killed the pure-hearted champion and used the sacred harp to murder a pack of fire imps." Florian announced. "As you can see, he made them all dance until they died of starvation. It took days. Their corpses are *still* dancing. The harp plays on and on and on. Instead of bringing peace, its perfect music accompanies the endless gyrations of the fire imps' exposed bones, as they clank together. Forever."

"Why?" A knight in the front row whispered brokenly. Florian adjusted his glasses. "Why did Trevelyan ruin the world's best chance at eternal peace?" He shrugged. "The imps claimed their fire was better than a dragon's. Trevelyan took it as an insult."

"Everybody's got something to say against dragons." Haigha muttered, not feeling sorry for the fire imps. "It's bigotry." None of the assembled knights seemed to see things that way. Their faces were haunted.

"Misuse of magic is where Trevelyan really excels." Florian

continued. "His powers will be weakened on Monday, but don't underestimate him. The malevolent spells he casts are unusually inventive. Notable highlights include," he changed slides, "that time he made everybody on Sarras two-dimensional."

Soldiers screamed at the soul-scarring picture.

Next slide. "When he did away with gravity in Bisnagar and suffocated forty people in the low atmosphere." Next slide. "Rabid tadpoles in the drinking water." Next slide. "Stealing the moon." Next slide. "Vanishing the entire town of Paititi." Next slide. "Somehow erasing a week from everyone's memory."

"I don't remember that." Haigha complained.

"Exactly."

Men were openly sobbing, now. Growing more and more terrified about the monster they were about to face, as the photographic evidence of Trevelyan's cruelty mounted. It was an understandable reaction, but also noisy.

Florian sighed in annoyance and looked out the window, while the knights got control of themselves. Outside, he could see the Queen of Clubs' famous white roses. He'd heard of them, of course. They were cultivated by the palace's gardener, a pigeon named Pat. The precious blooms couldn't survive on the frigid water from the palace wells, so Pat fed them with fresh, warm blood, instead. Carnivorous horticulture was his specialty.

Florian wasn't sure how Pat got the blood, but he very much doubted the people sacrificed to the plants volunteered for the job. They were probably dragged into the flower beds kicking and screaming. The Club Kingdom was known for having the most unpleasant people in all of Wonderland, though, so losing a few wasn't much of a tragedy.

And the roses *were* lovely.

"Shut up!" Haigha bellowed at the weeping knights. He shoved his way to center stage. "Forget this shit." He waved a disparaging hand at the presentation screen. "Nothing in the past matters, because *now* we're going to make Trevelyan pay!"

Frightened soldiers blinked up at him, willing to listen to any scrap of hope he offered. Wanting to hear how they might survive the week. They probably *wouldn't* survive it, of course, but fools often desired pretty lies over ugly truths.

"You don't need this damn slideshow." Haigha told them, his voice filled with conviction. "You're men! Knights! You know how to fight and win!"

Heads began bobbing in agreement.

"They *do* need to listen to my slideshow." Florian argued, because adequate preparation always had an observable impact on results. "It's important that we review Trevelyan's strengths and weaknesses, so the knights are able to..."

Haigha cut him off. "They out number him *four thousand to one!* You said so yourself. Not even Trevelyan can defeat four thousand knights. Especially not when *I'm* there to help bring him down."

Haigha's confidence had a rousing effect on the men. They began to exchange smiles and nods with each other.

"We need to be out in the field!" Haigha decided. "Not stuck in some fucking classroom, learning ancient history."

The soldiers cheered, thrilled to not have to look at more crime scene photos.

Florian knew it would be impossible to stop his cousin/nephew/cousin. Still, he had to try. Otherwise, he'd never hear the end of it at family dinners. "We've only just gotten started on my presentation. If you wait a couple hours before you begin pummeling each other, you might learn some techniques to help you fight Trevelyan more effectively."

"Cannons seem like they'll be plenty effective to me." Haigha scoffed. "We've got those, don't we?"

"Yes. Hundreds of them. But..."

"Let's go, men!" Haigha hopped off the stage. "We've got weapons to assemble."

The Club Kingdom's knights marched towards the exits, heads held high, and filled with renewed bravado.

Puffed up with self-importance, Haigha moved to follow them. He loved it when he was the one in charge. He had dreams of being the most famous dragon in the world. They would never come true, but he clung to his delusions like a Wolfball player who'd never been quite good enough to make the big leagues. The idea of defeating Trevelyan in epic battle was irresistible to his caveman brain.

"Haigha," Florian called, giving logic one last chance, "I'm leaving Wonderland, right now. If you don't come with me, you're fired. I have no intention of being here, when Trevelyan realizes what's happening. He might not have all his powers, but he's still the very best at being Bad."

"Not for long. Soon *I'll* be the best." Haigha kept walking. "Go back to your library, Florian. When I bring back the head of the Green Dragon, I don't want to have to share any credit with a pussy like you."

Florian watched him leave, with a resigned shake of his head. Now, he was going to need a new assistant. And the Club Queen would *not* be giving him a glowing recommendation. And Christmas at his grandparents was sure to be awkward as hell.

This is what he got for hiring a relative.

CHAPTER FOURTEEN

Pick your perfect nail polish from our unlimited selection!
Growing on You Green: At first, you're going to hate this weird jelly polish. But as its enchanted properties turn your fingers into tiny topiary gardens, you might just find it unexpectedly growing on you. Literally.
(Note: Manicure will require regular pruning and a heavy dose of bug spray.)

Happily Ever Witch Cosmetics Website

The Heart Castle

"Most women would be thrilled to become a genuine queen." Trevelyan drawled out, delighting in the witch's adorable sulking and superior baking skills. "There's really no need to mope over your royal fate. Although you look delectable doing it, so don't stop on my account."

Esmeralda flashed him a look that promised painful death. Trevelyan smiled. He was back in the palace kitchen, playing with his pretty little mate, and watching her make more ginger-mutants. She wore a black-cat patterned apron and those high heel boots and a very sexy frown. Off the top of his head, Trevelyan couldn't imagine a place in the world he'd rather be. There surely *was* one. Somewhere. But, damn if he could think of it.

"The Heart Kingdom is a nightmare wrapped in pink tchotchkes and Cheshire Carpets, Trev. You *really* want to stay here?"

"It's a starter home." He allowed, waving a dismissive hand. "This hideous castle is a steppingstone to bigger things. We control twenty-five percent of Wonderland already! Even you have to admit that's impressive, considering we weren't even trying."

"This dopey kingdom was begging to be overthrown by the first villains who came along." She set about adding almond-sliver claws to her dessert army. These insidious ginger-creatures were much like the last batch, only their fangs seemed a bit sharper and there was less cinnamon in the dough.

Trevelyan snatched one up for himself, because they were delicious and because he relished the fact they belonged to him. His mate had baked cookies. They were therefore *his* cookies. It was obvious.

"Stop eating all my minions." Esmeralda chided. "I'm trying to enspell them to do my horrible bidding."

"You're adding too much Badness for that." He chewed on his cookie, enjoying the taste of her exquisitely sugared magic.

She sent him a baffled frown. "It's a nefarious spell. Of *course* I'm adding Badness."

"And that would work fine, if you were ninety-eight percent evil... like me. I'm sure I could easily whip them into an obediently homicidal rage." He shook his head. "But you're powers aren't dark enough to enslave baked goods. Under your command, the ginger-mutants are sweet and defiant. Like you."

Esmeralda scowled at that news.

"I'm sure confronting your forty-nine percent Goodness is difficult." Trevelyan commiserated. "No one likes to admit their flaws. But, if you practice a bit with lighter magic, I think you'll see quite an improvement."

"What would you know about light magic? You hate it!"

A fair point. Trevelyan embraced blackest villainy as a lifestyle, but still... "If I had access to a whole different source of magic, I would use it." He told her honestly. "Even if it was Good. Extra power is extra power. For dragons, power means survival."

And really, Goodness wasn't *so* repellant, when the witch was the one who possessed it.

Esmeralda sent him a stern frown. "I'm only casting Bad spells. I'm a *wicked* witch."

Trevelyan sighed at her stubbornness. Yep. Sweet and defiant. "Well, if you won't even get ginger-mutants under control, how do you intend to properly subjugate Wonderland?"

"Oh, I'll leave all the subjugation to you. If you're determined to be emperor, fine. Go for it." She shrugged expansively. "But, I'm too busy for the day-to-day grind of tyranny. For real, I'm launching a new nail polish color next week."

"Which color's that?" He asked, interested in how her mind worked.

"I'm calling it, 'Gold. Really.'" She nodded in anticipation. "Because it's gold. Really."

"You're selling a nail polish made of liquid gold? How much will that cost?"

"Who cares? The look is incredible." Putting a price tag on her art was clearly beneath her. "Anyway, I can't be distracted from my vital work on the bottle design to rule stupid Wonderland."

"I'll take care of building our empire." He assured her helpfully. "I'm a natural leader."

Esmeralda didn't seem convinced. "What are we going to do with Wonderland, after you conquer it?"

"Burning it to the ground and starting fresh seems like a wise first step."

"You always want to burn everything."

He hoisted himself up onto the counter beside her trays of cookies. "Dragon." He reminded her simply.

"I'm not sure that's a winning leadership style. People will bitch at us, if we incinerate everybody."

"Not if we incinerate *enough* everybodies. They'll be no one left to complain." Trevelyan glanced towards the window. "Or you could enspelled the dissidents into pigs. That would work, too."

"*Hogs,* you deranged maniac. And I'm not making you anymore pets."

"They're not pets. Just uncooked banquets."

"I saw you give that flying one an apple." She crossed to the oven and checked her timer. "Don't deny it."

He made an "ummm" sound, because she'd caught him. "I'm

fattening him up for the slaughter."

Esmeralda's mouth curved, her lovely crimson eyes finding his, and lust hit Trevelyan like a hammer. He wanted to kiss her. He wanted his mouth slanting over hers. He wanted to swallow the soft sounds she made. He wanted their breath mingling. Kissing had never been important to him before. Dragons liked to fuck their bed partners into submission, so kissing seemed very tame. And pointless. ...And oddly intimate. Trevelyan had always avoided intimacy. Having someone too close made him uncomfortable.

Now, things seemed different. Now, he wanted everything that was rightfully his.

There were many logical reasons for his change of heart. Obviously. Kissing was a territorial marking, for one thing. It warned other males away. If he kissed her often enough, rivals were sure to get the message. *That* Trevelyan understood and it was more than enough reason to justify kissing his Good little wicked witch in every single way she'd allow.

Esmeralda said she *wouldn't* allow it until she "believed" in him, though.

Why? It was all incredibly irritating. In fact, the more he thought about it, the more irritated he became. Why shouldn't he be allowed to kiss his True Love? Sappy cowboys wrote country songs about kissing your True Love! It was part of the natural order.

"Come here, darling." He caught hold of her as she walked by him. "The time has come to talk of *many* things."

"It has?" She asked suspiciously, but she didn't resist as he maneuvered her closer. "What 'many things' do you want to talk about?"

He shifted his stance on the counter, so she was standing between his legs. A dragon's primary instinct was to capture its mate, so the monster inside of him rumbled in pleasure. God, it was like a whole different beast now that Esmeralda was there. The raging fury was replaced with satisfaction. Contentment.

"Let's begin with an obvious one: When are you going to believe in your successful, brilliant king?"

She leaned closer to him, like she was relaying a secret. "If you'll believe in *me*, I'll believe in *you*."

He frowned at that confounding answer. "I think you're just playing hard to get, with your stubborn resistance to the inevitable." His fingers slipped down to untie the apron at her waist, for the sheer fun of removing some of her clothes. "I mean, surely you believe in me enough by *now*. How long could it take to see how spectacular I am?"

"About the length of time it takes to get a lobotomy, I'd guess."

"Is this because you don't have sex with people you don't like? Does that rule apply to kissing, too?" His mind kept going back to her twisted predilection for kindness, because it was worrisome.

She didn't move away as he tugged her apron free and it hit the floor. "How come you've never suggested dissolving our True Love match?" She inquired out of the blue.

Trevelyan's attention snapped to her face.

She raised her eyebrows at him, questioningly.

He didn't trust this tangent. He didn't like the suggestion that he could lose his mate. He didn't want it to even be a *possibility* that Esmeralda could get rid of him. "Why would I mention something that will never happen?"

"It *could* happen if we both signed a scroll and a wizard abolished the bond."

"No wizard has the authority to take you from me." He said in a serious tone. "I don't care about lawful magic. I don't recognize *anyone's* authority to steal what's mine."

Esmeralda didn't seem upset by that news. If anything, she seemed to relax beneath his hands. Like his unyielding words had reassured her somehow.

Still, Trevelyan was uneasy that she'd considered the idea of ending their match, at all. "Why haven't *you* suggested dissolving the True Love bond?" He asked warily.

"I still have hopes you can learn to play guitar."

That almost made him smile. "I should warn you, I'm not musically inclined. ...But I am difficult to get rid of." She needed to understand there was no escaping him. It would save lives. "If it came down to the line, I would kill every single wizard, in every single kingdom to keep you."

She blinked.

"I will *never* give you up." He couldn't be clearer than that. "This is the truest thing I've ever told you. Do you believe me, Ez?"

"Yes." Esmeralda nodded. "I'm pretty sure I'm not going to give you up, either."

"'Pretty sure?'"

"I told you, I'm still deciding whether or not to keep you."

He didn't like her hesitation. At all. She was still standing in his arms, though, so he decided not to push it. There were other ways to convince her that Trevelyan was her one-and-only mate. "If you understood how amazing I am at kissing, this wouldn't even be a question."

"I would be out of my mind to kiss you. You're *for sure* the worst person in the world."

Trevelyan's hands caressed her perfectly perfect ass. "I try." He said modestly. "But I'm also very open to deals. Tell me what you want and I'll make it happen. I'm ready to progress to the part where your tongue is stroking against mine in helpless submission."

"I thought you didn't even care about kissing."

"I care that you're denying me something that's mine." Obviously, *the principle* of the situation was his main concern. It was a matter of fairness! And ensuring he didn't die celibate. And keeping other men away. And other very important things he couldn't exactly think of. *That* was why it bothered him so much that she wouldn't kiss him. His eyes drifted down to her lush mouth. Obviously...

From Esmeralda's expression it was clear that she'd now somehow cast *him* as the Bad guy in this discussion. Granted, he was the Baddest guy in *every* discussion. But, not this time. No. *This* time, Trevelyan was being the soul of reason, while she was deliberately toying with him.

"My kisses are *mine*, jackass." She informed him loftily. "*I* decide who gets them."

"Well, then hurry up and decide *I* should get them. I'm tired of waiting." He paused, considering her words. "Decide *only* I should get them, while you're at it, because we have a deal about monogamy."

"Kissing doesn't count as sex." She argued mutinously, staking out an absurd position simply for the sake of being difficult.

"We never agreed to that."

"We're agreeing to it *now*, unless you want guitar players dead in the streets."

She made a face at the warning.

"I'm very serious, Esmeralda. I'll start picking off those kind, friendly, musical assholes *before* they kiss you, if that's what it takes to keep you all to myself."

Still standing in the V of his legs, she arched a brow and didn't look concerned. "You're going to preemptively kill the kindhearted guys who might kiss me, *and* all the wizards in existence, *and* the Wonderlandian masses, *and* annihilate the entirety of the Four Kingdoms?"

"Oh, I'm sure I'll kill *everybody*, one of these days. …Except you." He leaned forward to brush his lips at the very corner of her mouth. As close as he could possibly get to a kiss without inciting her wrath. Esmeralda drew in a quick breath of desire and he nearly purred. "You smell too pretty to savagely murder, regardless of how frustrating you are."

That comment earned him a reluctant sound of amusement. "You really are ninety-eight percent evil, Trev."

He loved it when he made her laugh. It warmed something inside of Trevelyan to hear it. Dragons craved warmth, so that was obviously why her laughter would matter. That was the only reason it had become a goal.

Obviously.

His hand brushed the skin of her inner thigh, savoring her small jolt of surprise when she realized he'd worked his way under her sinfully short skirt. "Give me your word you won't kiss anybody else."

"Will *you* kiss anybody else?"

"No." His fingers slid higher. "When dragons make a promise to our mates, we keep our word. I promised you monogamy and that's what you'll get. A thousand percent."

Her eyelashes fluttered down, as his thumb stroked her inner thigh. "I won't kiss anybody else either then. One thousand percent."

Trevelyan gave a hum of pleasure at how simple it was to secure her agreement. The witch might not be willing to kiss him, but she clearly wasn't plotting to kiss some other man in his place. "Let's go upstairs, for a while." He suggested enticingly. "Wouldn't that feel... *Good*."

She gave an unconscious nod, leaning a bit closer to him. "That's it." He nuzzled her temple. "We don't have to kiss, if you don't want to. Just let me have the rest of you."

She swallowed. "I'm not going to sleep with you today. I'm still teaching you how to be a True Love."

"And I'm studying *so* hard. Don't I deserve a reward?"

"Pray you never get what you deserve, dickhead. It'll be painful and grisly."

His head dipped down to whisper into her ear. "Submit to the inevitable and I'll show you how very wicked I can be, my darling. You don't have to do anything but say yes. I'll hold you down, and make you come, and we can pretend you had no choice, at all."

His adorable little witch liked that threat. He could tell by the way her breathing changed. How very, *very* interesting.

"Of *course* you're into dominance games." She complained, just to be contrary.

He was into all games and he flat out *adored* this one. Adored having Esmeralda's undivided attention. Adored her bantering with him, like she enjoyed his company. Adored trying to lure her into Badness. Adored her helpless arousal, as he stroked her exquisite green skin. His thumb grazed the cleft of her body, through her dampening underwear. Esmeralda gazed up at him in virtuous pleasure.

He adored that part most of all.

Trevelyan's hands had done so many violent things to so many screaming people, but the witch trusted them against her delicate flesh. She wasn't scared of him, at all. She believed he wouldn't break her. ...And he believed it, too.

That *had* to count as a third impossible thing.

In his shrunken heart and twisted soul, Trevelyan knew he'd die himself before he harmed his mate. Despite his history of

endless selfish cruelty, he believed it without question. He might delight in the suffering of the rest of the universe, but *never* the witch. Esmeralda was the one person who was forever safe in a dragon's claws. He knew it as deeply as magic.
"I can *always* top myself in depravity." He told her anyway.
"It does seem to be a particular gift of yours."
He shrugged with arrogant assurance. "Let me show you my *real* gift." His fingers pressed higher, his touch gentle. "Say yes and we can play any game you want."
She bit down on her glorious bottom lip, like she was actually considering it.
Trevelyan almost had her. "Would it help at all, if I owned a record store?" He offered, wanting to push her over the edge and into his bed. "Because I'm sure I can steal one."
"No, but it would help if you weren't such a despicable..."
Someone else entered the castle.
Trevelyan stopped playing, as a new presence vibrated along all his senses. His head snapped around, knowing a strange male had just crossed into his domain. His hands instinctively tightened on Esmeralda. Inside of him, the dragon snarled in lethal warning, hating another man near their mate. Trevelyan couldn't agree more.
Esmeralda blinked, seeing his lethal shift in focus. "Trev?"
"Somebody's here." He pushed off the counter and faced the door, wondering if he had enough energy to kill the newcomer at a distance. Best not to risk it. There was only a lone man approaching. He'd just wait for the intruder to draw near and then strike. One-on-one, Trevelyan could kill anybody, weakened magic or not. "We're the only two trapped by the barrier. Someone else just walked right through it."
"Who would want to come *here?*" Esmeralda asked in confusion.
"Knowing Wonderland? Someone ridiculous and horrible."
"We have days before the Queen of Clubs arrives and everyone else is a hog. Maybe it's Bluebeard. I *told* you he was around here someplace."
Trevelyan waited, saying nothing.
"Yoo-hoo!" The visitor poked his head into the kitchen. He was

an anthropomorphized lizard in a morning coat. "Ah! *There* you are." His gaze was on Esmeralda. "You must be the Queen of Hearts. ...For now, at least." He chuckled like that was quite witty.

Trevelyan's head tilted. "Who are you?"

"I'm William. Not Bill. Not Will. *William*." He strolled into the room, absently twirling a walking stick, like he owned the castle. "Since you're new, I thought I'd pop by and give you the what's-what on how we run things here in Wonderland."

"How *you* run things?" Esmeralda crossed her arms over her chest, in a distinctly unwelcoming way.

Apparently, William wasn't used to dealing with any real villains, because he didn't make a hasty exit at her tone. Instead, he smirked in a condescending way, still thinking he could direct this conversation. "Well, the Tea-Partier set *is* Wonderland. Surely you've heard of us. Everyone who's *anyone* has heard of us."

"I haven't heard of you." Trevelyan intoned.

That earned him an imperious glare. "And you are...?"

"Esmeralda's mate." The witch might want to keep their True Love bond a secret from Marrok Wolf and the rest of the universe, but Trevelyan planned to make it very plain who she belonged to. "The *King* of Hearts."

Esmeralda rolled her eyes, still not thrilled with their new titles.

"Well, the Tea-Partiers are *the* cultural organization of Wonderland." William declared, focused on his own agenda. "Nothing happens without our input."

Esmeralda's eyes flicked Trevelyan's way, her meaning clear. He nodded, because she was right.

William had to go.

"All the queens are happy to host us." The gossipy gatecrasher was already making himself at home. "Even over in the Diamond Kingdom, where they're ever so fussy about magic. The Gyre is gaining a foothold there. Have you heard of them? Humorless group."

Trevelyan had heard of them. The Gyre were violent zealots. If even one of those bastards was in Wonderland, it was too many. Trevelyan made a mental note to go clean up the

Diamond Kingdom, once he was free of the force field. He wasn't about to have humans who hated magic encamped near Esmeralda.

"Tea-Partiers go to all the best palace functions and help to keep things civilized." William went on, testing a random shelf for dust with one long finger. "Tradition, you know. Not even the Gyre can stop that. The March Hare and Caterpillar tragically perished, so now I'm the unofficial head of the organization."

The lizard didn't sound too sad about their passing. This was clearly a power grab, as he exploited the deaths of his friends for personal glory. Trevelyan could respect the self-centered heartlessness of the plan.

But William still had to go.

Trevelyan and his witch controlled Wonderland. No one else. Not the other queens. Not the Tea-Partier set. Not the hogs on the lawn. Just him and Ez. Any ambitious courtiers contemplating a grasp for control, needed to be swatted down. Hard.

The annoying lizard sighed in dramatic regret. "The entire social season might be ruined now, of course, with only two queens left to organize any truly fashionable gatherings. I'll need to take charge of the planning or everything will be a nightmare." He paused, as if a terrible thought had just struck him, his eyes rounding with worry. "How many brilligs do you have?"

"Three." Trevelyan reported, because he was fond of brilligs and so few people ever asked about them. "Three together help to aim their teleporting."

"Well, at least you know *that* much."

"Teleporting?" Esmeralda interjected. "Wait, you have three of those teleporting, mushroom things and we're not using them to get the hell out of here?"

"Well, they're not *on* me." Trevelyan defended. "I keep my brilligs at my sister's house." Hopefully, Marion wouldn't go poking at them too much. He had a lock on the door to his room for a reason.

Esmeralda sighed in disappointment and returned her attention

to William. "So, what happened to the other queens?"
"The Queen of Clubs picked them off, according to rumor, and took their crowns." William gave a *tsk* of regret. "Such a shame about Lily, especially. She was a bit of a rustic, but she knew how to take direction. Her brilligs promised to be positively *mimsy* this year."

Trevelyan made a considering face. "How big are they?"

Esmeralda threw her hands up in exasperation. "That Club bitch is killing all the other queens and stealing the damn tiaras, Trev. Who cares about brilligs?" She looked up at him like that was somehow his fault. "Are you *sure* about this plan of yours?"

"More sure than ever. If she's got the rest of the crowns, it becomes one-stop shopping for us. They're all centralized in one place. Once we kill *her*, we'll control everything."

"Oh, she'll be hard to kill." William opined, needing to dominate the conversation. It was always a lousy idea to draw attention to yourself, when you were an idiot surrounded by predators. But, that was one of the downsides to being an idiot: You missed the fact that you were prey. "Maryanna's got level five magic."

That wasn't welcomed news. Trevelyan preferred enemies who were weak and mewling.

Esmeralda shot him a pointed look. "Level five." She mocked. "I heard him. Don't worry. I'm a *higher* level five, I'm sure."

"And Maryanna's husband is..." William twirled a triple-jointed finger next to his temple to indicate the man's instability. "Not our sort. The 'Mad Hatter' they call him, and rightly so! He wears a top hat, no matter the occasion. Usually crushed velvet and purple, which is just *beyond* gauche." He looked at Trevelyan's long coat, his judgmental eyes sighting on the embroidered flames at the hem. "Fashion sense is sadly lacking in *some* people."

Trevelyan's answering smile was all glinting teeth and psychotic threats. "Oh, this should be fun..."

Esmeralda put a restraining hand on his sleeve, anticipating his next move. "The snobby lizard guy is giving us information about the crazy people who want us dead." She murmured.

"Don't kill him, until he stops being useful."

"He has three minutes to finish imparting his vast knowledge." Trevelyan kept his eyes on William. "Then, I'm having fun, regardless."

"I have *no* idea what Maryanna sees in old Hatty." William continued, heedless of his life winding down. "My own late wife was the very apple of my eye. But if she embarrassed me socially, I would have divorced her on the spot! And she would have done the same, for me." He nodded righteously.

"Standards are *so* important in any marriage."

Trevelyan and Esmeralda stared at him.

William's nose wrinkled in distaste. "Maryanna positively *dotes* on her maladjusted husband, though. Bad folk always take the whole 'True Love' bit *far* too literally, don't you think?"

"No." Trevelyan and Esmeralda said together.

William didn't seem to hear them. "Maryanna could do so much better. Hatty uses some off-brand pocket watch to stop time, instead of investing in a noteworthy model. And he eats the most disgusting things you can imagine! Goodness, for example. Sucks it right out of people. And he slathers mustard on absolutely everything!"

This hatter ate Goodness? How? *Why?* It probably tasted revolting. Well, Esmeralda's would surely be delicious, but... Her muttered curse cut off his culinary contemplations.

"Wonderful." Another accusatory glance at poor Trevelyan, who'd really done nothing at all to deserve the blame. "Now, we've got some asshole in a purple hat, who eats Goodness and controls time."

"All hatters control time to some extent, darling. It's all they really have to fall back on, magic-wise."

"And it's plenty!"

"And don't even get me started on the daughter." William jeered, caught up in the Club Kingdom's soap opera. "They say she has amnesia, but I'm here to tell you she was *always* a bit off. The poisoned apple doesn't roll far from the tree."

Trevelyan frowned slightly. Amnesia?

"Speaking of food," the lizard picked up one of the cookies -- *Trevelyan's* cookies-- and took a large bite, in what had to be

deliberate provocation, "when's tea?"
Trevelyan's eyes narrowed, his heroic patience evaporating. Dragons... didn't... share.
Why the hell was that so hard for other people to understand? Trevelyan was a shit-ton of joy to be around, so long as you didn't cross him. Why did everyone always want to cross him? Invade his territory? Challenge his authority? Steal his motherfucking cookies?
Esmeralda groaned, knowing William's end was nigh. "Trev, *don't*. I can make more ginger-mutants..."
"And those will belong to me, too." He interrupted righteously. It was obvious!
Esmeralda didn't think so. She existed just to vex him. "How do you figure they're yours, when *I'm* the one who baked them?"
"Whenever my mate cooks something, it's *mine*." He spelled out. "I don't have to give away a single cookie to some interloper. Every male on the planet would agree with me on that rule, Ez. It's a universal law."
(Unless your honorary-sister just happened to bake red velvet cupcakes and you just happened to eat them all. Then, her whiny gargoyle husband was simply being petty for objecting.)
Esmeralda scoffed at Trevelyan's very logical and nuanced explanation. "I hate rules. Especially the borderline sexist ones. Since when do you care about them, so much?"
"Since they're *my goddamn cookies* being stolen!" He'd rarely been so pissed off.
"I say... the hospitality in this kingdom is sadly lacking, under you two." William tut-tut-ed. "Why, Alice would have offered me oolong and wabeberry tarts long ago." He paused. "I take lemon and one sugar in my tea. Hop to it."
Esmeralda squeezed her eyes shut, as their uninvited guest drove the final nail into his coffin. "It hasn't been three minutes." She tried a little hopelessly.
"Close enough." Trevelyan took a step forward.
It was time for William to go.
Rather than run for his reptilian life, William frowned like he was going to ask for the manager. "What did you say your

name was again?"

"Trevelyan, Last of the Green Dragons."

William's eyes widened. The echoes of Trevelyan's endless crimes must have carried into Wonderland. His skin paled in horror, as he suddenly realized who he was facing.

Trevelyan's mouth curved.

Piggybacking off the ginger-mutant spell was simple. Esmeralda had done most of the work already, so it took very little of his recuperating powers to seize control and twist it to his liking. Her magic was green, the same as Trevelyan's. Their powers were always going to be somewhat compatible, but this was... effortless.

It shocked him how the edges of his powers blended into hers. He barely even had to think about the witch's energy to manipulate it. It flowed as easily as his own. They almost seemed like one. He had no idea how that was even happening, but it felt glorious.

The fathomless darkness of his magic spurred the normally sweet and defiant cookie-creatures into fearful action. Rising from their baking trays, they flung themselves at William. Icing fangs biting, raisin eyes narrowed in maniacal fury, almond claws gouging flesh... It was a massacre.

The snotty lizard screamed in soul-rending terror and pain. The noise was slightly garbled, because the cookie he'd been eating had latched onto his long, lizard tongue and wouldn't let go.

The sight of all the mayhem improved Trevelyan's mood. "It really is a lovely spell you've concocted, darling." And nowhere *near* what a level one could brew up. It was beautifully intricate and pulsing with chaotic energy. He was certain now that she was at least a level three. He had no clue as to why she'd lie about it, though. Most people wanted to appear *more* magical, not less. "Amazing work for someone so powerless."

Esmeralda missed his sarcasm. She was occupied with being endearingly pouty. Giving up on William, she focused her villainous attention on more worthwhile matters. "I know! All the ingredients are *perfect*. But then why doesn't it ever work for me?"

"You just need to find the right balance for your magic. That's all." Trevelyan slipped a soothing arm around her. He'd never attempted to reassure another living creature, but it came easy for him with his mate.

She rested her head against his shoulder, accepting his comfort. Trevelyan breathed in her scent.

Just his.

Swarmed with rampaging ginger-mutants, William was in a panic. Trying to brush them off was futile. There were bakers' dozens of them. The would-be usurper ran mindlessly out of the kitchen, through the palace, and into the yard, leaving a trail of cookie crumbs and blood behind him. Hard to say how far he'd get. The little frosted monsters were doing their best to devour him whole.

"Is he going to live?"

"Oh, I hope so. At least for a bit. I enjoy leaving my victims to suffer, even more than killing them outright.

"Maybe we should have given him warning, before we sicced the cookies on him." Esmeralda mused.

"I told him my name. That *was* his warning."

"We could have gotten more information out of him, if you'd waited."

"He was boring me." Most everyone bored Trevelyan, except his devious little witch. Why was she hiding her magic level? It was very intriguing. "Surely you didn't expect me to share my oolong with that dull, thieving lizard."

"It wasn't really going to be an issue, because we don't *have* any oolong."

"We'll make some." Tea sounded like a marvelous idea to Trevelyan. "And we can have some of those wabeberry tarts he was talking about, too."

One dark eyebrow arched. "Do you know how to make wabeberry tarts, Trev?"

"No... but the ginger-mutants just ran, ran, as fast as they can. I doubt we'll catch them, now. And we're going to need *something* to go with oolong." He tried a beguiling smile. "Do *you* know how to make wabeberry tarts, Ez?"

Her mouth twitched. Forty-nine percent Goodness or not, she was still delightfully Bad. And sometimes it seemed like she enjoyed his company as much as he enjoyed hers. Was he imagining that?

"I'd have to figure out what a wabeberry is first, but yeah." She told him. "I've seen every baking documentary there is. I can probably make some tarts. Maybe we should try *not* to enspell them to life, this time, though."

"No promises, my darling."

Esmeralda laughed.

Trevelyan grinned, his heart beating faster in his chest. He wasn't imagining it. He definitely wasn't boring her, either.

Chapter Fifteen

**Pick your perfect nail polish from our unlimited selection!
Teal-ing Me Lies: Is it blue or is it green? This tricky bitch will keep
you guessing.**

Happily Ever Witch Cosmetics Website

The Heart Castle

There was a huge golden mirror in the royal bedroom.
The damn thing was hideous, heart-shaped and hypnotic.
Esmeralda found herself staring into it and somehow seeing
more than just a reflection. She couldn't really explain it. It was
showing an exactly reversed image of the royal bedroom, just
like it was supposed to. Only she had the weird feeling that it
wasn't the royal bedroom reflected in the glass surface. It was
something else.
Some*where* else.
Trevelyan came up behind her. He'd been off on his own, for
the last couple of hours, and he looked exhausted.
"You okay?" She asked in concern.
"I'm fine. My magic is just..." He shrugged in frustration that
his powers weren't back.
"Don't push your energy." She warned. "It has to heal."
He grunted, his eyes on the mirror. "That thing is unsettling."
"I like unsettling décor. That thing is just *creepy*." Esmeralda
corrected, allowing him to change the subject. He clearly didn't
enjoy talking about his weakened condition. "I don't trust
Wonderland. It likes to generate craziness. I don't want a big
mirror watching me while I sleep. I think it might be
enchanted."

"Big mirrors often are." He rested his head on her hair, his arms coming around her waist. "More importantly, they go *over* the bed, not beside them. Everyone knows that."

"There *is* a mirror over the bed."

"Yes... I noticed that, too." His voice was full of dirty ideas. He must not be *too* exhausted.

"Is that why you insisted we sleep in here?" She guessed. "The room we had last night was fine. Hideous, but fine. This one is hideous and creepy."

Trevelyan shrugged. "The other room has somehow turned into a holiday party. I'm unclear as to why, but I doubt you'd want to sleep there. The furniture is drunk and singing carols."

Egg*nog*.

The party was serving spiked eggnog. She'd forgotten about that little mishap. Damn misfiring magic. If it wanted to get stuck on alcohol today, it could've at least made some kind of frog-flavored moonshine. That would have been *some* progress with the spell.

"Besides, you're the queen, now." Trevelyan went on, oblivious to the annoying lack of frogs. "Why shouldn't we claim the royal suite?"

"Because it's creepy? Have I mentioned that?"

"But no pink-and-purple rugs are lecturing us about a hippopotamus. So, there are still worse places we could be in this abysmal house."

They were currently situated right next door to the chattering Cheshire Carpet. Esmeralda could hear it talking to itself about Tove, that extra day on Wonderland's calendar. The rug was either crazy or lonely. Maybe both.

"The walls are too thin, in here." She said pointedly. "Plus, you set one of them on fire and now everything reeks like smoke."

He made a *tsk* sound, dismissing the scorched paneling behind them. "The smell is a small price to pay to assume your rightful place, in the rightful bedchamber. Royalty means a life of sacrifice."

"If it did, you wouldn't be so pleased to be king."

He smiled at that retort. No cruelty or mockery in his expression, just amusement. Like he enjoyed bantering with her. "Touché, my queen."

As always, Esmeralda was struck by the absolute perfection of the man. The exotic angles of his face were all placed like he'd been sculpted to represent the idealized image of an invincible hero from legend.

Or the fabulous monster who killed the invincible hero and ate him.

"You're so beautiful, Trevelyan." The words were out before she could stop them and she wrinkled her nose. "People probably tell you that a lot."

"Just so *you* tell me, Mate." He nuzzled her temple.

The beads in his hair made gentle sounds that soothed her and he was so *warm*. She found herself relaxing into his hold, her body recognizing it was safe and protected in his hands. Her body was so stupid. Trevelyan wouldn't catch Esmeralda if she fell. He wanted separate lives. But he was bitching at *her* about loyalty, all the time? Hypocritical dick.

"I'm beautiful, but you're still thinking insults about me." He rumbled into her ear.

"How do you know what I'm thinking?"

"I'm watching your face in the mirror. Don't ever play poker. We'll lose our new kingdom within three hands."

"Would that be such a terrible thing?" The news that she was now the Queen of Hearts continued to not thrill her. Sure, it was always nice to be anointed sovereign ruler of all you surveyed, but when it came to enchanted castles, location was everything.

"Wonderland isn't prime real estate." He allowed, as if reading her mind.

"Exactly! There's still time to overthrow some other, less colorful, not-so-annoying realm." That was doable, with a dragon on her team. They loved empire building. "One with fewer hogs, un-charcoaled walls, and better internet access."

"Every great dynasty has to start somewhere, Ez."

His teeth grazed her throat, careful not to damage her skin. Esmeralda tilted her head and allowed him better access to her neck. The dragon liked that. His touch grew bolder.

"Once we control all of Wonderland, do you think this damn

tiara will finally come off my head?" She asked, slightly breathless. "Wearing the same accessory forever sounds awful."

"According to Lyon N. Unicorn's book, you'll be able to remove the unified crown at will. We just need to kill our enemies and conquer the other three lands, first. No need to worry about a fortune in diamonds limiting your fashion choices, for long."

Considering Trevelyan was Trevelyan, she took heart at that assurance. The man could kill anyone and conquer anything. "We have to get out of this damn palace." She reminded him. "That's the initial step to world domination."

"I'm working on it." His palms slid under the black silk nightgown she'd created just to torment him. The matching robe was trimmed in distinctive feathers. He glanced at her through his lashes. "Did you pluck these from my flying pig?"

"That little brat was chewing my favorite boots. I cast a costuming spell, as a warning."

He smiled again.

She sniffed, feeling the need to defend herself. "They're not actually his feathers. They just *look* like them. You're going to have to teach your pet some manners, if you want to keep him in the house."

"You're the one giving lessons." His hands traveled to her breasts, touching her through the silk. "I trust you'll keep us both in line."

Esmeralda watched him caress her body in the mirror and bit back a moan. The sight of his palms on her increased the eroticism. Her head fell back against his shoulder, surrendering to the dragon.

He made a contented sound, scenting her building desire. "That's my Good little witch." He murmured. "I'll take care of you."

He would never take care of her. Not the way she dreamed of. Not without a lot more training. "I'm a *wicked* witch."

"Compared to me, you're a literal angel." His fingers skimmed over her nipples. "That's alright, though. I like you, anyway."

His touch was absolutely magical.

Magic. Shit. Force field. Marrok.

Esmeralda tried to stay on topic. "I *really* need to get out of the Heart Castle, Trev." She'd been trying to come up with a plan all day and she was still stuck on the very first step: Escape. "My powers are healing. Not as fast as I'd like, but I can cast some spells, if I push hard enough."

"Don't push or you'll hurt yourself." She reiterated. She wanted out of their pink-and-red cage, but not at the expense of Trevelyan. "Is that why you look so tired? What spell are you casting that's so important?"

"Not one that will open the force field, I'm afraid. But, I'll be able to rip through it soon. I'm sure of it."

"The sooner the better." Once she was free of the Heart Castle, she could save Marrok and everyone would be happy. ...Except Trevelyan. He didn't know about her intention to go looking for the wolf, yet. He would be pissed about the whole idea.

That thought doused her dazed pleasure like a bucket of witch-melting water. Esmeralda had no issue with fibs, obfuscations, and outright deceits about most things, but any lies regarding Marrok seemed like a betrayal. Or at least that's how Trevelyan would see it. Betraying her True Love felt wrong and not in a fun way. Just... *wrong*.

The dragon sensed her guilty flinch and raised his head. Green eyes locked onto hers in the mirror, seeing her discomfort. His head canted to one side, suspicion dawning on his face. "Tell me something true, Ez."

She bit down on her lower lip. "You won't like it."

"Tell me anyway."

She debated for a beat and then gave in. "Scarlett called earlier. I found my phone and talked to her. That's how I learned about Maid Marion. Letty said Wonderland has been locked up by some very powerful magic and she can't get to us. No one can get in here."

He went totally still, his expression shuttering.

"Do you believe me?"

"Yes." His tone was flat, not looking very interested in the mysterious enchantment cursing the entire realm. "Did you tell Scarlett about our True Love bond?"

That was his first question? "Yes."

He blinked, like her instant answer startled him. "I thought you wanted to keep my existence a deep, dark secret."

"No, idiot. I just didn't want you doing a video presentation of our sex life. I explained that."

He gave a skeptical snort, but she felt some of his tension ease. "Did Scarlett promise to pray for you?"

"She took the news better than I thought." Probably because she'd been distracted by Marrok being MIA and she'd been thinking of ways Trevelyan could somehow help them. ...Which would never, ever happen.

"What about Marrok?" Trevelyan demanded, as if reading her mind. "What did *he* say?"

Esmeralda winced again, dreading this part. She decided to just get it over with, the quicker the better. "Uh... Apparently, Marrok has been abducted and brought here to Wonderland. I assume by the Queen of Clubs. Scarlett would like us to go rescue him."

There! She'd done it.

There was a beat of absolute astonishment.

Esmeralda squeezed her eyes shut. Waiting.

Trevelyan burst out laughing. News of Marrok's abduction was apparently the most hilarious joke he'd ever heard. He laughed so hard he had to lean against her to stay upright, his whole body shaking with mirth.

"It's not funny! He could be in real trouble."

More laughter. Absolute gales of it.

Next door, the muffled chatter of the Cheshire Carpet stopped, like it was trying to listen in. The rug was definitely lonely. Personally, Esmeralda would have been grateful for the solitude.

Esmeralda shoved away from Trevelyan and headed for the bed. "Jackass." She began stacking pillows down the middle, like she had the night before. He'd just lost his chance at sex for at least twelve hours.

"Oh frozen-hells... that is just... *glorious*." He sighed in something approaching true bliss. "Marrok's gone and got himself wolf-napped." More hilarity ensued.

Esmeralda tossed her feathered robe aside and climbed into

bed. "You know, *you* were kidnapped, too."

"I was unconscious, at the time. What's his excuse?" Trevelyan wiped at his eyes.

"Scarlett isn't sure how he was taken. I just know that I have to save him."

Trevelyan blinked. "What?" He must've missed that part of her confession, amid his chortling.

"I have to save Marrok." She repeated slowly. "I can't just leave him a prisoner here in Wonderland, can I?"

"Of course you can! I'm not lifting a finger to help that treacherous fuck." The refusal was instant and certain, all amusement gone. "Let him rot."

"Hence me saying: *I'm* going to have to save him. Scarlett suggested you could help, but I knew better. Notice how I didn't even invite you."

"I'm a goddamn villain." He snapped, disregarding her words.

"So are you, by a one point majority. Villains don't save people."

"Really? If Maid Marion was kidnapped, wouldn't you go looking for her?"

He scowled.

"I thought so." She nodded, feeling righteous. "And I will do the same for my honorary sibling."

"My honorary sibling isn't an asshole. I'm serious, Ez. Marrok is going to die when I kill him, anyway. It's pointless to rescue him from the Queen of Clubs."

She wasn't going to waste time arguing about it. They'd never agree. "Also, Scarlett made some deal with Kingpin Midas. He's sending Sir Galahad and Galahad's gryphon husband to find us all a path out of here." Maybe that would calm him down. "Trystan Airbourne is supposed to be the best tracker in the world."

Trevelyan was briefly distracted. "Sir Galahad married a gryphon? Didn't he kill them all? He's the Butcher of Legion."

"See, *I* think of him as the pretty blond man with the adorable puppet show."

"I hate that show. It was far worse than the massacre he led."

"You believe that because your soul is black and shriveled."

He grunted, but didn't deny it. Instead, he began stripping off his clothes. Esmeralda studiously avoided looking at him, because it would just tempt her to forget she was mad. "In any case, I don't care who opens a door for us... even if it *is* a knight." He decided with a derisive twist of his mouth. "This might be the realm I plan to own, but I don't enjoy being confined here. I like to be in control."

"No kidding."

"I told you I won't save Marrok and I mean it. Dragons never, ever compromise."

"So you've said."

"Because it's true! Now, are you joining me and leaving Wonderland, with the murdering knight and his husband? Or are you staying here to die with the wolf?"

"Neither and both. I'll go with you, *after* I rescue Marrok."

"I'm not waiting for Marrok." Trevelyan's voice was contemptuous. "I'm leaving this kingdom, until I'm sure no one can trap me in it again. Lesser species always try to imprison dragons. We don't like it."

That was a fair analysis, actually. It was why the Queen of Clubs had brought Trevelyan to Wonderland, in the first place. If you were a royal scumbag seeking magic, enslaving a dragon was a great idea. Dragons were hard to capture, sure. But even if you took devastating losses in the fight and large swaths of your lands were uninhabitable for generations, it was often worth the risk. If you succeeded you'd have a magical weapon like no other and chances were you'd be able to hold it forever. It wasn't like people were lining up to help captured dragons. They had no friends or allies.

"You *should* go." She told him and meant it. "The Queen of Clubs will target you again, as soon as she realizes you're free of the Walrus and the White Rabbit. She needs your magic for something. She doesn't care about me, at all."

Very few people cared about Esmeralda. That wasn't self-pity. That was reality. And she wasn't about to lose one of them to the Queen of Clubs. She *would* save Marrok.

Trevelyan's clothing hit the floor with more force than necessary. "There are a hundred other lands where I can fully recuperate my magic and plot my counterattack. I'm not about to stay on the Queen's turf and play *her* fucking games. She can play *mine*." He barely looked Esmeralda's way. "You can do whatever the frozen-hells you want."

He waved a hand at the creepy mirror and it went vanishing into the hallway. Even in the midst of his tantrum, he recalled she didn't want it watching her while she slept. That softened her.

"I said I would come with you." She reminded him. "But I need a little time."

"It's a very risky idea to wait."

"What choice do I have? Marrok's life is at stake. Literally. The Queen will keep him alive for a while, because why else take him, at all? She could've just killed him in the Enchanted Forest, if that's all she wanted. But Marrok can piss off *anybody*."

He grunted in sardonic agreement.

"Sooner or later, she'll murder him just to shut him up." Esmeralda estimated Marrok had about a week before he got himself dead. "You know that, Trev."

Naked, Trevelyan flopped down on his side of the mattress. "Well, I wish you luck, darling. Let me know if you need advice on how to survive the dungeon of our super-powered nemesis. I can give you some tips on trapping rats to add extra protein to your gruel."

She wasn't going to ask him to help her. Not for anything. There was no point. Esmeralda wasn't upset over it, just pragmatic about his nature. They'd settled on an "every witch and dragon for themselves" rule and she would stick to it. It was safer, anyway. Relying on Trevelyan would always be a dead end. She'd figure out how to rescue Marrok, the same way she figured out everything else: Alone.

There was some connection between her prideful self-reliance, Trevelyan's refusal to compromise, and the downfall of dragons as a species, but she wasn't in the mood to figure it out.

"Tell me something true, Trev." She said, ready to change the subject.

A long pause. So long, she wasn't sure he was going to play.

"I don't like this pillow wall between us." His tone was disgruntled, now. "I want to be able to smell you."
"You can smell me just fine from over there, I'm sure."
"I want to be able to hold you, then. You're my mate."
"I'm not having sex with you. You were a jerk. It killed the mood."
"That was Marrok's fault, not mine."
She ignored that lie.
Trevelyan sighed and tried again. "I told you I would wait for sex. But, the damn pillow wall means that you don't trust me not to push for more, even though I *told* you I wouldn't."
Realization dawned. When dragons gave their word to their mates, they meant it one thousand percent. That's what he'd been insisting earlier. He clearly expected her to trust his promises and it upset him when she didn't.
"Your feelings are hurt." She translated.
"Dragons don't get hurt feelings. Don't think so virtuously. No. I just… don't like the pillows."
His feelings were definitely hurt. Crap. She detested him, at the moment, but she still couldn't stand to see him unhappy. Damn True Love bond. Esmeralda reached behind her, grabbed some of the pillows and chucked them across the room.
"Better?"
Instantly, big arms were dragging her backwards, through the remainder of the wall. She wound up against his tattooed chest. "Much better." He breathed in the scent of her hair and she felt his whole body relax. "I need this. Do you believe me?"
"Yes."
It was impossible not to believe him. He was holding her so close that not even a magical spell could have pried her loose. She wasn't sure if all dragons were so physical, but hers needed constant touching to be content. If Trevelyan was awake, his hands were on her.
Grudgingly pleased with the situation, she let him wrap himself around her.
"Tell me something true, Ez."
She decided to go big. "Alright. You've held me like this before."

He hesitated, like he was trying to recall that moment.
"When I was younger. In the orphanage." She explained.
"Whenever it rained, I would get so scared. It wasn't a very sturdy building. Sometimes it leaked."
His grip got even tighter.
"In order to calm down, I would imagine my True Love holding me." Protecting her.
"The guitar player?"
"No, dummy. *You*. Sometimes, when I was really, *really* scared, I could feel you. It was the only way I could sleep. At first, I thought it was my imagination, but once there was a terrible thunderstorm. I was so terrified that I think my powers must have reached for you. I think they *found* you, wherever you were. In your own bed, in your own house. I swear, I felt your arms around me and I heard your drowsy voice reassuring me. ...And I was finally able to relax. After that, I heard you a lot. Always the same words."
Silence.
"Do you believe me, Trev?"
"Yes." He whispered. "What did I say?"
With me, you are always safe, my darling. I love you more than magic itself.
"Maybe it was your powers." She speculated, instead of answering. "Maybe you felt me, someplace in your head, and you reached for me, too."
"No. It was your energy conjuring an image of me. Sensing who your mate was and soothing you. A very rare phenomenon. ...Especially, for a level one talent."
She ignored that dry remark. His explanation didn't sound quite right. "It was both of us," she theorized, "on one long connection, with you on one end and me on the other."
He absently rubbed his chin against her head, like a panther marking his territory. "To do that --over such a long distance and without even knowing each other-- our powers would need to be fully melded."
"So?"
"So fully melding powers is impossible. Did you pay no attention at all in school?"

"Not really." She'd been a terrible student. None of the magic lessons ever seemed to make sense for *her* magic, so it was all just theoretical bullshit. "Honestly, I learn best from documentaries. But you co-opted my ginger-mutant spell easy enough. That worked."

"There is the potential for magic connecting, if the colors are close. Ours are almost identical, which is very... stimulating." His voice was dark and lustful. "But they still can't *fully* meld. No one's can."

The rules of magic never much interested Esmeralda. No rules did. As a little girl, she'd been scared and he'd felt it. Young as they'd both been, they'd connected. That was just fact. The hows and whys were immaterial to what she knew had happened.

"Besides," Trevelyan continued on, sure he was right, "if I'd have felt you, anywhere in the entire universe, I'd have come for you."

That surprised her. "You would've?"

"I chose you as a mate. I *decided*. No one else will ever take what's mine and hide her away in some leaky shack. Not without a fight."

She smiled a bit. "You'd fight Auntie Hazel, the half-blind proprietor of the orphanage for me?"

"Why not? I'd win."

"You'd win against *anyone*. I doubt an old lady with level two powers would be much of a challenge for you."

He made a pleased sound. "All the better."

That made her snicker.

"You are the only person who never bores me, Esmeralda. So, I intend to ensure you're alive and unmelted, for the foreseeable future. Even if old witches and rainstorms attack you."

She snorted. "Careful. You're inching towards agreeing to keep me safe."

"Well, I wouldn't go *that* far."

"Didn't think so."

"I just enjoy the novelty of having a mate." He lazily shrugged. "If I ever change my mind about keeping you, I'll leave you a note before I run off. I promise."

"I'll do the same." She snuggled closer to his naked body. He was aroused, but he wouldn't push for more than she was willing to give. She trusted him in that, at least. "Tell me something true, Trev."

"I know why the Queen of Clubs wanted me awake."

Esmeralda's eyebrows compressed. "You do?"

"There's a spell I was working on, many years ago. No one else had ever been able to get it right. I thought it would be a challenge." She felt the tension return to his muscles, as he thought about it. "It's why Snow White targeted me in the WUB Club. Her stepmother wanted me to cast it. I think she still wants it."

"Her stepmother is the Queen of Clubs?"

"That would be my guess. William mentioned a daughter with amnesia. And I imagine the woman is none too pleased that I escaped without giving Snow White the key to the spell." He made a sound of dragon-y superiority. "The idiot wizard who wrote it was a terrible speller. There's a typo. That's the whole mystery."

"You solved a spell that no one else could solve?" She smiled up at him. Nobody could match Trevelyan's magical talents. "That's amazing!"

"It almost got me killed." His tone went far away, like he was recalling something he'd prefer to forget. "I *hated* Snow White. I didn't want to touch her. I swear to you, I did *not* want to do that, Ez."

Her lips firmed and she rubbed his arm in commiseration. "I know."

She was going to kill that abusive bitch, whether Snow White lost her memory or not. *No one* hurt her True Love. Esmeralda was pissed at his damn algebra teacher for taking advantage of him when he was a kid and Snow White was just as horrible.

"Everything I did, I *had* to do." He insisted, like she'd been arguing otherwise. "Even that damn bomb that Marrok refused to help me set off... What other option did I have? Just sit there and die? Snow White would have *murdered* me. She did the last time through. Marion warned me to get out of prison anyway I could. It was freedom or death. Do you believe me?"

"Yes."

He hesitated at the simple reply. "Really?"

"*Really.* I'm sorry you went through it, but I'm glad you escaped. Anything you had to do to survive, I'm *glad* you did it."

"Marrok disagrees."

"He's always been nobler than us." She loved the wolf, but he liked to play by the rules, far more than she did. Esmeralda hated rules. "You should have killed Snow White, once you had the bitch alone. That's what I would have suggested, if I'd been there."

He gave a snort of amusement. "You would have, I think."

"Yep. I'm all-the-way Bad, Trev. I don't care what the Rabbit's Magic Matrix says. And you're even Badder than me. You want me to cry because we do Bad things?" Esmeralda made a face. "No. I don't give a shit, just so we win."

He pressed his lips to her hair and said nothing. He just held her.

She ran her thumb over the back of his hand, soothing him. After a while, Trevelyan spoke again. "The Queen of Clubs likely took Marrok, because the wolf pushed Snow White into the Lake of Forgetting. And before that, he refused all of the doctor's sexual advances. Repeatedly. The woman was fixated on him and he only ever cared about finding his True Love. He wouldn't so much as look at Dr. White. Not even to get out of prison."

"Marrok is insanely in love with Letty. Even without the True Love bond they'd be together. But, the True Love bond is *so strong* with wolves. I think he was married to her in his head, before they even met." Esmeralda envied that kind of commitment. Given a choice, her own True Love would be halfway to Oz, by now.

Trevelyan scoffed dismissively, hearing the wistfulness in her tone. "Dragon's might not know much about love, but we know *loyalty*. The wolf isn't capable of it. That's all that should matter to a mate."

That video tape from their interrogation room tryst had given Esmeralda hope, but she still wasn't sure she could teach

Trevelyan what she needed him to learn.

"In any case," he went on, "Marrok hurting her stepdaughter has no doubt pissed off the Queen of Clubs. He's probably not her favorite person. She and I remain enemies, but we do have that in common." He hummed in appreciation. "I hate both sides of their fight, so I win either way."

Esmeralda "accidently" elbowed his spleen, ignoring his amused chuckle in response. "Scarlett was the one who yanked Snow White into the water and gave her amnesia, you know. But all of us in the Tuesday share circle like to take some of the credit."

"I don't blame you. It must have been a lovely sight to see." He was quiet for a moment. "My share circle was on Tuesdays, when I was locked up, too."

She liked that. "Tuesday share circle sticks together."

"I killed at least two of the members of mine. The only 'sticking' they did was to the bottom of my shoes." He paused. "Wait… Bluebeard might have been part of my share circle, now that I think of it."

"You said you'd never met him."

"I can't *remember* him, per se. I just recall beating him to death one session." He made a "huh" sound. "Did he *live?* How disappointing."

"Black and shriveled soul." She reiterated with a sigh. It was a wonder he could feel anything at all, through the steady diet of vengeance and horror. The man was just a *huge* makeover project.

"Your turn, Ez. Tell me something true."

She pursed her lips. "I've been thinking about the 'separate lives' part of our True Love bargain."

"What about it?" He didn't seem pleased with the new topic.

"Our relationship is going fine. Except for the part where you refuse to kiss me, we're not having depraved sex, and you insist on saving that whiny wolf, we don't need to change anything."

They didn't? Was he completely oblivious as to how relationships worked?

"I just want some clarification. Like I said, I hate rules. So, I'm not great at figuring them out. I need to be sure we're both on the same page."

"Alright." He was still wary.

"Do you see us living together, after we get out of here?"

"*Yes.*" The word was emphatic. "You are in my bed and in my arms, from now on. Separate lives isn't physical distance. It's..." He floundered for a second, like even he didn't know what the rule meant. "We're just separate."

"So, we don't have to tell each other everything?"

"What aren't you telling me?" He demanded instantly.

"Trev, just..." She sighed in exasperation. "I felt guilty earlier about not telling you about Marrok's kidnapping, right away. Alright? Do you believe me?"

"Of course. You're weighed down with virtue. It's you're forty-nine percent Goodness at work."

Esmeralda rose above that provocation. "I don't like feeling guilty. I need to figure this out for the next time. So, as long as we don't sleep with anyone else and we live together, we're within the 'separate lives' rules? Is that it?"

He hesitated, as if defining the clause made him extremely uneasy. "I mean... you're my mate. There are certain things you *should* tell me."

"Like what?"

"I don't know. *Things.* You're supposed to be the one teaching the True Love lessons. Why am I having to explain this?"

She *was* teaching him a lesson. He just didn't understand it.

"You should tell me all the things you're thinking of stealing, and what horrendous goals you're scheming towards, and who you want dead." He went on in agitation. "What a dragon's mate *always* tells him."

"What if I don't want to tell you any of that? Would that be against the rules?"

"I don't see why you wouldn't want to tell me *everything*." He complained. "I'm wonderfully wise. Instinctively intuitive. Endlessly empathetic."

"You just laughed about my brother being taken hostage by an evil queen."

"It was funny!"

"Remember when you promised to be kind? What happened to that?"

"I *am* being kind. At least, when I remember to try. You're the one stirring up trouble."

"The 'separate lives' thing was your idea! I just want to know the stupid rules."

She could all but hear his brain working, trying to figure out a way to win this unwinnable discussion. Either he agreed to share with her or he agreed she didn't have to share with him. There was no middle ground.

"If either of us feels guilty about *not* telling something, we should have to tell the other about it." He said very carefully.

"How's that?"

"No! You never feel guilty about anything. It would be me doing all the confessing and you keeping all the secrets."

"That seems like a workable solution to me."

"Dream the hell on." She scoffed. "We're either doing fully separate lives or we're not. I'll let you choose which."

"Well, we need separate lives." He decided without even stopping to think about it.

"Fine." He'd chosen wrong, but that was his problem. "We're still monogamous and living together, but we don't have to feel guilty about not sharing things."

"*Fine*." He bit off, annoyed that she'd boxed him into a deal that he couldn't fully control. "Fuck. You have to complicate everything."

She stared into the darkness, already plotting. "Tell me something true, Trev."

He brooded for a beat. "I believed three impossible things today." He sounded irked at her, but proud of his accomplishment. The man loved to win dares. "Do you believe me?"

Esmeralda shook her head. "Nope."

"It's true! Three more and I'll have beaten that smug note on the refrigerator. I told you I could meet the challenge. Dragons can do anything."

"So can witches."

"If it doesn't involve snorkeling, diving, or a hot tub." He snarked, continuing to pout over his loss on the "separate lives" debate. "It's insanity for you to be so defiant about a waterproofing spell. Pointless, stubborn recklessness."

"Coincidently, that's what 'Trevelyan' translates to in the forgotten language of witches." She drawled sarcastically. "Pointless, stubborn, recklessness. Maybe it's a sign of your wonderful wisdom and instinctive intuitiveness that you somehow guessed it."

He sighed loud enough to part her hair. "You drive me crazy, Mate. I have no idea why I decided to keep you."

"It doesn't much matter, since you still haven't answered the more important question."

"And what question is that?"

"How are you going to convince *me* to keep *you?*"

CHAPTER SIXTEEN

**Pick your perfect nail polish from our unlimited selection!
Doomed Maroon: Don't even bother loving this one. It won't end
well...**

Happily Ever Witch Cosmetics Website

The Heart Castle

Bombs shook the castle, waking her up.

At first, Esmeralda thought it was Trevelyan. When you were living with a dragon, a little destruction was expected.

Honestly, the same could be said for witches. The Heart Palace had lost two stories, tons of pink walls, and a fancy little turret, since they'd moved in. Cannons firing were a bit unimaginative, but not a huge surprise from Trevelyan.

Except, she could still feel her True Love's large body wrapped around her.

One leg was tossed over her thighs, his arms encircling her, just in case she tried to escape the bed. He'd disliked the news that she still hadn't decided to keep him. Trevelyan was possessive and egotistical. Her hesitancy seemed to baffle him. Or maybe it worried him. Either way, he'd gripped her tightly all night and she didn't mind in the slightest.

Esmeralda opened her eyes. So then what was all the noise...?

Another explosion rocked the building.

Trevelyan pulled a pillow over his head, with a drowsy curse. He wasn't a morning person. "Ez, if you're going to blow stuff up, wait until after lunch. The sun is barely..."

She cut him off. "It's not me. I think someone's outside, attacking us."

He let out a groan of total aggravation. *"Why?"*

"Well, we've taken over the Heart Kingdom, and turned everyone into hogs, and wrecked the royal castle, and you have that super-secret spell..."

"No, I mean why are they attacking us at *six a.m.?*" He reluctantly rolled to his feet, running a hand through his long hair. Beads chimed together. "Someone's going to die for getting me up this early, I swear to Christ."

The tattoos on his chest stretched around to his back. Elaborate visions of monsters and skulls and fire. They were gorgeous. Exotic and dangerous and she was certain now that the flames of them moved. Magic and beauty were just a part of the man.

Naked and fuming, Trevelyan prowled over to the glass doors, leading to the balcony of the royal suite. Whoever was out on the lawn, they'd just pissed off an evil dragon. Never a great idea.

Esmeralda followed him, grabbing up her feathered robe as she went. No sense in being underdressed for whatever the hell was happening. "Hang on, don't you think you should...?" She trailed off with a gasp, getting her first glimpse of the sight below.

The army had arrived.

Hundreds and hundreds of soldiers were stretched out as far as the eye could see, covering the pastel hills of the Heart Kingdom. Some of the newcomers were knights on horses. Others were various animals and playing cards and dwarves. One of them was a Dormouse riding a hippopotamus.

And all of them were emblazoned with a huge club on their flags and uniforms.

Even Trevelyan hesitated for a beat.

"Oh no." Esmeralda scanned the huge force sent to kill and/or capture them. "I thought the Queen of Clubs wasn't attacking us until Monday?"

"I guess the calendar was right. Days really do happen two or three at a time in Wonderland."

Her lips thinned in frustration. "The magic here is deliberately screwing with us. I'm telling you, Wonderland thrives on anarchy. It *likes* us causing problems, because it wants us to push back and contribute to the chaos."

"I'm about to make it real happy, then." Trevelyan shook his head in disgust. "I hate knights." He waved a hand and low-slung black pants appeared on his glorious body. "Stay here." He stepped out onto the balcony, two stories above the invaders, and crossed his arms over his chest. Mostly-nude and unarmed, he still looked invincible to her. "Alright." He called to no one in particular. "Which of you bastards wants to die first?"

Well, that was one way to begin the parlay.

"Maryanna, the illustrious Queen of Clubs demands your surrender!" The Dormouse on the hippo shouted back, magic boosting the volume of his squeaky voice. He was a squirrelly-looking little thing, in full battle-armor. "Comply immediately or pay the price!"

"I'm Trevelyan, the illustrious King of Hearts. Soon-to-be Emperor of all Wonderland." Trevelyan's voice rang with authority and promise, as if he wasn't intimidated by the battalions of men surrounding him. As if he was in complete control. "I demand *your* surrender or I will kill… you… all." Each word was spaced for emphasis.

The unexpected retort caught the Dormouse off guard. Muttering began amongst the army as they tried to figure out what to do next. The fact they weren't already charging the castle hinted that the dragon's reputation for manic violence preceded him. Even knowing he was weakened, they were wary.

Trevelyan's favorite feathered pig was perched on one of the castle's chimneys, scared of the invading horde. The other hog-citizens were probably lying low, as well. Esmeralda wished she could join them.

Instead, she moved to stand beside Trevelyan on the wide balcony. "It's the two of us against *thousands*." The sheer scale of the invasion was staggering.

He frowned, as if surprised to see her next to him. "Two of us?"

"We're True Loves. It's always the two of us, when the army shows up to attack." At least as far as she was concerned.

Trevelyan blinked.

She arched a brow. "No one's ever fought at your side before?"

"Just my family."

Esmeralda raised a shoulder. "It's always smart to stick with your family." She'd told him that the first time they'd met and she believed it. "Unless they're jerks, of course. Then, you choose a new family and begin again." No one got that philosophy better than an orphan.

He cleared his throat, not fully understanding her, and refocused on the invaders. "Well, I'm a dragon and you're a witch. So, that evens the odds, a bit."

"A dragon with weakened powers and a witch with twitchy magic. I don't think your original 'ambush them all' plan is going to work. Maybe I should try bargaining." God knew, *he* couldn't do it. Trevelyan's negotiating skills would get the Heart Kingdom blown into a crater.

"Queens never make bargains. Not with assholes."

"Of course we do. I make bargains with *you* all the time."

He slanted her a sideways look.

"Let's at least *talk* about giving them the damn spell." She persisted. "It will buy us time, if nothing else."

His façade of physical invulnerability stayed in place, but his tone got more urgent. "I can't. It will unite the four tiaras and ensure the Queen of Clubs controls Wonderland."

"So?"

"So, *I* want to control it." He paused and then reluctantly revealed the real problem. "Also, in the wrong hands, the spell has the potential to end all of existence."

Her mouth dropped. "And you've been messing around with it, as a goddamn puzzle game?!"

"I never *cast* it, though. I was just passing time. One of the ingredients doesn't even exist!"

"Shit." Esmeralda tried to think. They couldn't retreat, because the force field locked them into the castle. They couldn't stay put, because the frigging army would bring the building down around them. They couldn't give in, because the spell the Queen of Clubs wanted might end the world.

They would have to fight.

Shit.
"How many of these men can you kill, with your powers depleted?" She asked him, getting more serious about the situation.
"I don't know." His eyes swept over the countless soldiers, his jaw tight. "Maybe enough to scare the others away."
He didn't sound sure. And Trevelyan *always* sounded sure. That probably meant they were doomed. It seemed like he was now willing to reveal some private doubts to her, though. That was the one promising sign, in the midst of disaster. With a dragon, you had to take all the positives you could get.
Esmeralda took hold of his palm, her fingers locking with his. He was still for a moment. Then, he slowly gripped her hand back.
The Dormouse started shouting again, reaching a strategic decision. "On behalf of Maryanna, the illustrious Queen of Clubs, I refuse your offer! If you don't yield to our mighty will, we will bomb you into…" His words stopped with a sudden resounding snore. His tiny head tipped back, his eyes closed and his breathing deep.
Esmeralda pursed her lips. "I think the Dormouse just fell asleep, midway through his dire threats."
"I told you it was too early for a battle."
With or without their narcoleptic general, the Queen of Clubs' army prepared for their next attack. Cannons were being reloaded and aimed straight at the Heart Palace. Fuses were lit. Knights stepped back, counting down to the bombardment. This was going to happen and it was going to be terrible.
"Trev." She whispered.
"I *hate* knights." He grumbled again. "They killed my parents. Did I ever tell you that? Those bastards kill everything."
His magic arced out, way more than she'd ever seen Trevelyan use before. The shadowy churning of bats' wings, mixed with showers of brilliant electric sparks and the snapping of massive teeth. All of it a vivid, malevolent green. Precise and sizzling with power, the charge of it made her skin tingle.
Esmeralda had been around witches her whole life, but she'd never felt energy like the dragon's. It was huge and deadly and

treacherously beautiful. Dark, but *alive*.

And he was in absolute control of it.

Despite her imminent death, Esmeralda's body went damp. This was him *weakened?*

Trevelyan jerked his free hand up, like he was conducting a symphony. Every cannon on the field suddenly pointed straight into the air. Shouts of panic sounded from the soldiers, but there wasn't enough time to fix the artillery. Instead, the cannons fired their heavy loads towards the sky.

Esmeralda's eyes followed the projectiles' trajectory, up, up, up... And then down, down, down. Countless cannonballs fell right onto the Queen of Clubs' forces, decimating the lines. Men ran in every direction, trying to escape the barrage. Hundreds of them died, all from a single wave of Trevelyan's palm.

"You're spectacular." Esmeralda murmured, awed by all the lovely destruction.

The army began to flee in terror, soldiers yelling as they retreated across the plaid landscape.

"That's all I had." Trevelyan swallowed, breathing hard. "I used too much last night."

"What spell did you...?"

He cut her off. "I usually have *fifty times* this much power. I just can't recoup my magic fast enough, yet." Tremors of strain ran through his large body.

"It was enough. Look!" She pointed to the terrified army, running for their lives. "They don't know that your powers are gone."

"His powers are gone!" A deep voice bellowed from the field. "Don't you remember that damn slideshow?"

"Slideshow...?" Esmeralda began in confusion.

Then, a big, blue dragon came into view and nothing else much mattered. The twelve-foot creature dominated the battlefield. Even his own side was intimidated by his arrival. Their frantic retreat slowed.

"Get back in formation!" The newcomer ordered again. "Stand fast or I'll kill you myself!" And, just to prove he meant business he shredded some random human with his claws.

"*Now.*"

The soldiers weren't sure which dragon they were more terrified of. The one on the ground with them seemed to win, because he was the more immediate threat. The knights reluctantly faced the castle again.

Beside her, Trevelyan stiffened. "Haigha of the Blue Dragons, Son of Haddock. *Fuck.*"

Somewhere in the transformative smoke that swirled around Haigha's huge body, there was a figure that was both man and monster. An imposing, unstoppable beast, with animalistic features, and clawed hands, and eyes that glowed like aqua flames.

When it came to super-weapons, nothing beat a dragon and the Queen of Clubs apparently had one.

"Crap." Esmeralda whispered.

"Where the frozen-hells did Haigha come from?" Trevelyan was still trying to catch his breath. "I thought that bastard was dead."

"You think a lot of people are dead, who turn out not to be dead."

"I'm eternally optimistic. It's my nature."

"Any chance Haigha might want to not attack us, if you talk to him?"

"That will just make him attack faster. He doesn't like me. Nobody ever likes me."

Something in his voice had her shifting closer to him. "I like you. ...Most of the time."

He glanced at her.

Esmeralda dug deep for some kind of serenity. "Things could be worse." She shrugged, looking on the bright side of their certain demise. "At least it's not raining."

Trevelyan's gaze ran all over her face.

"You and me, Trev." She reminded him and squeezed his hand.

He slowly nodded, like he'd just made some decision. "You and me, Ez. *We're* all that matters."

Esmeralda smiled at him. "Sounds about right."

"It does." He took a deep breath and looked back at Haigha.

"And we won't die in Wonderland, of all places." His voice was scathing. "I won't allow it."

"Well, that's a relief. Quick, go tell the angry dragon."

"We're not going to tell that inbred moron anything." He shook his head and she saw the whatever-it-takes, kamikaze determination that had gotten him out of the WUB Club lighting his face. "We're just going to kill him."

Haigha's inhuman voice boomed out, his attention on Trevelyan. "My pussy cousin's research must have been right. Your powers must be depleted. Otherwise you'd be in dragon-form, fighting like a deranged maniac."

"Damn Florian and his damn books." Trevelyan muttered.

"Poor, Green Dragon." Haigha mocked. "You're as weak as the humans. Let's see you steal the moon again, *now*."

"You stole the moon?" Esmeralda asked, not even surprised.

"I gave it back." Trevelyan defended grouchily.

Haigha kept talking, loving his moment in the spotlight. "Oh, I've waited years for this. For a chance to finally take out the mightiest dragon, once and for all. Without your magic you're *nothing*."

"That isn't true." Esmeralda promised, just in case Trevelyan took the insult to heart. "You're the best at being Bad. That's got nothing to do with your powers. You're just a horrible fucking person, through and through."

His mouth curved at the pep talk. "You think I can be a deranged maniac, even without my magic, huh?"

"You *are* a deranged maniac." She assured him. "Your mind is filled with villainy. You can come up with a plan to beat these guys, because you've got way more than just your evil magic going for you."

"Yes..." He agreed slowly, like a brilliant idea had just occurred to him. "I've got *your* evil magic going for me."

"Huh?"

"*You're* going to kill him, Ez."

"Me?" She scoffed, incredulous at the idea of slaying a dragon in her nightgown. "No, that's not the sort of plan I meant. I meant a plan that would *work*."

"Ready the next attack!" Midnight smoke swirled around Haigha, sustaining his transformation and obscuring the details of his monstrous body. It was just as well. Who wanted to see every inch of the dragon come to kill them? "Destroy Trevelyan and that useless..." He stopped suddenly, sniffing the air and his gaze whipped towards the balcony.

Towards Esmeralda.

"Goddammit." Trevelyan said quietly. His body shifted, so he was in front of her. He didn't even seem to notice that he did it.

Esmeralda's brows shot up in amazement.

Haigha chortled. "Oh Green Dragon... I wondered why you put your scent all over some worthless True Love. I can smell you on her from here. Only mates should be marked that lavishly." He inhaled deeply. "But now, I don't blame you for your weakness. You *had* to mark her, didn't you?"

Trevelyan's grip on her fingers tightened.

"You were given a True Love who smells like poisoned candy, just begging to be stolen. Sweet and wicked and tempting." Haigha made an approving sound. "I hope you enjoyed her while you could. ...I certainly will." He turned his attention back to the troops. "Don't harm the witch. I want her for myself." Flames enunciated that licentious threat.

"Esmeralda is not a weakness. She's about to slaughter you, right here in this garden, you chauvinist fuck."

Haigha shook his huge head. "No witch can stop a dragon."

"Mine can." Trevelyan was back to sounding very, very sure. If you didn't know better you'd believe his claim.

Esmeralda knew better. "No, I really *can't*." She whispered fiercely.

Trevelyan didn't listen to her, his gaze fixed on Haigha. "If you're so certain my mate and I are helpless, why did you bring an army to take this castle? Why isn't it just you?" It was a taunt. "What kind of dragon needs *knights* to fight his battles?"

"You smug son of a bitch! Once I kill you, *I'll* be the dragon everyone fears! *I'll* be the darkest power in the world."

"You'll be dead in two minutes." Trevelyan scoffed. "Then, I'll go have coffee with my mate and forget you even existed."

Esmeralda was close to hyperventilating.

Haigha looked increasingly rageful. "*End the Green Dragon*

Line." He screamed the words like a battle cry.

The Dormouse roused himself from his slumber. "Wait... the Queen of Clubs wants Trevelyan alive." He protested with a yawn. "Nobody cares about the witch. You've got it all backwards."

No one listened to him, either.

Haigha's orders seemed to propel the surviving soldiers into action. They came in waves towards the castle, an impossible force of trained killers and an evil dragon and a hippopotamus. Crap, crap, crap.

"Can't you do something like you did with the ginger-mutants?" She asked Trevelyan desperately.

"I was piggybacking on *your* magic. *Your* spell. It has to be you, Ez." He was trying to appear confident, but he was clearly worried. "You need to cast something *now*."

"I can turn some of them into hogs, maybe?" Esmeralda offered, because she was pretty sure she could do that. ...Or maybe she'd accidentally send them on a very long *slog.*

"Only Haigha matters." Trevelyan insisted. "He *cannot* put his hands on you. If he gets close, you fucking run."

"To *where?*"

"Just get out, anyway you can. The things he will do to you..." Trevelyan's jaw firmed and he shook his head. "No. *No.*" She could see his mind racing. "Maybe we can make a hole in the barrier big enough for you to fit through. You're small."

"What about you?"

He ignored that, his gaze flashing over to her, again. "What level is your magic? And don't give me that shit about it being a level one. Level ones can't blackout a kingdom from an orgasm and whip-up ginger-mutant spells."

Esmeralda didn't answer. Her attention stayed on the gigantic blue dragon, stalking closer and closer. The Queen of Clubs' men scampered out of its path, as it came galumphing forward. Haigha ate some of the escaping knights, anyway. Just grabbed them up in its massive jaws and crunched down, snicker-snack. And he wanted her brought to him, so he could...

"Ez!" Trevelyan's voice was insistent. "Is your magic a three?"

"What? No."

"A two?"

She impatiently shook her head and then realized she should've lied.

"Higher?" He guessed, not giving her a chance to change her mind.

"I can't control it, so it doesn't matter!"

Trevelyan's head tilted. "Four?" His tone was different, now. More focused. "*Five?*"

"It's high, okay? But just technically."

Trevelyan stared at her. "Six." It wasn't a question. It was a whisper.

She winced.

His breath came out in a whoosh. "You're a six? You're sure?"

"Only on paper! I have never been able to accomplish anything huge with my magic. I swear it. It never works the way it's supposed to."

He gaped at her, completely ignoring her frantic explanations and the rampaging horde. "The WUB Club didn't notice that you were a motherfucking *six?!* They put a *level six witch* in with the other prisoners and they didn't know you'd eventually escape?"

"Well, I didn't tell them what level I was! None of those idiot doctors knew much about magic. They couldn't be sure what I can do. I'm not even sure!"

"*I'm* sure." Trevelyan's laugh was triumphant. Exuberant. "I've never been so goddamn sure of anything."

She glanced up at him in surprise.

Trevelyan didn't notice. He scanned their enemies. "Oh, this will be fun." His slanted smile was like something from a conquering barbarian centaur, watching a city burn.

"I'm happy you're happy, but my misfiring magic won't stop a couple thousand knights."

"Yes, it *will*. You have more power than anyone else in this kingdom." He looked baffled by her hesitation to use it. "My mate is a *level six* witch. You are absolutely *not* going to lose to some half-assed humans in metal hats. I won't allow it."

"None of the spells I cast go right! I explained all this, but you're not listening..."

He cut her off, remembering their earlier conversations. "Cast a Good spell. Like we talked about. See what happens."

"I'm not casting a Good spell! I'm a *wicked witch!*" Esmeralda could barely think straight.

"Ez, you have to…"

Haigha blew out a plume of white-hot fire, drowning out his words. It incinerated half the hedge maze. The flames jumped fifty feet in the air, the heat intense enough that the Queen of Clubs' men began screaming in fear and pain. Scores of them were charred to ash.

Esmeralda's eyes went wide. There was no way she could stop this. There was no way *anyone* could stop this, except Trevelyan. "Are you sure you can't turn into a dragon, right now?" She asked desperately.

"I'm *positive*. If my dragon could get out, he'd already be fighting. He's in a rage." Frustration and fury were etched into the harsh angles of his face, despite his confidence that they'd somehow win this battle. "I would kill Haigha myself, if I could. Gladly, my darling."

She nodded, believing him.

"It has to be you." He persisted. "*You* need to do this. If you won't use a Good spell, then *yes*… turn him into a hog. Or a log. It doesn't matter, just vaporize him."

Esmeralda kept her eyes on the blue dragon. "Vaporize him?" She echoed blankly.

He held her hand in a death-grip. "You're a fighter. Just like me. *Fight* that son of a bitch for us."

She didn't know a spell to vaporize people. Why would she know how to vaporize people? She mostly did glamour spells. Those tended to work best for her. Magic to change her hair color, and create nail polish, and transmogrify stuff.

Could she do one of them… bigger?

Haigha prepared to burn the bottom levels of the castle. If those went up in flames, how would they escape? How could they get out even if he *didn't* burn them? They were trapped in the Heart Palace.

Trevelyan leaned closer to her ear. "Darling, if you vaporize Haigha for me, I will rip your clothes off and make you come harder than you've ever come in your life."

Haigha disintegrated.

Esmeralda didn't think about it. Didn't even move her hands. It just happened. Her lips parted in shock, as the massive dragon vaporized into the air. The rest of the Queen of Clubs' army gaped at the smoky blue remnants of their unstoppable monster, trying to figure out what happened.

Trevelyan purred in villainous pleasure. "My wicked little mate." He pressed a kiss to her temple, like he just couldn't help himself.

"That was an accident!"

"Nonsense. I inspired you. Like a mentor for sex and evil." His eyebrows compressed. "My God... Evil sex mentor might just be my calling. I'll fuck you in every way imaginable, while you call me 'sir' and show me all your incredible, green magic."

She gave a slightly hysterical laugh, because what else *could* she do with the man? "You really are a deranged maniac."

"A deranged maniac... *sir*." He corrected gravely.

"Charge!" The Dormouse spurned his hippo forward. "Kill our manxome foes!"

No longer worried, Trevelyan released Esmeralda's hand and leaned forward, with his elbows resting on the railing. Casually slouched there, he enjoyed the view, as thousands of armed men roared forward. "If I promise to make you come *twice*, will you vaporize every single one of these armored assholes?"

"That's a lot of guys, Trev."

"You can do it." He looked positively jovial. "I want to watch your magic destroy legions of knights, so I can masturbate to it for the next fifty years. Go as big as you can." His eyes narrowed slightly. "I hate knights."

And he'd loved his parents. His devotion to them was a hopeful sign for his continued emotional growth. This would make Trevelyan happy. And save their lives. And honestly it *would* be fun.

Like Auntie Hazel always said: If you weren't having fun being a wicked witch, you were doing it wrong.

Concentrating hard, Esmeralda focused on repeating the transmogrifying spell, only *bigger*. Much, much bigger.

Ruthlessly pressing down all the Good inside of her, Esmeralda let loose with a full torrent of Bad. Everything she had blasted out. Green magic scorched the air, like forked-lightning, and birds in flight, and death itself. A swirling tornado of evil electro-charged the entire Heart Kingdom.

And the whole army turned to mist.

Every single knight, Dormouse, hippo, and cannon was just... gone. All at once.

Trevelyan made a sound that resembled sexual release and his head tipped back in ecstasy. "Oh *God*, yes."

Dissipating into the air, the invading force became a thick rolling cloud of yellowish-gray vapor. The haze smelled of industry and ozone. Diffusing the sunlight, it obliterated the view for miles. Hanging over the gardens, it slowly drifted through the smoldering hedge maze, a thick, polluted blight on the pastel scenery.

Esmeralda wrinkled her nose, realizing what her *big* transmogrifying spell had actually done.

Trevelyan scented the fumes. "Smog?" His brow furrowed, piecing it together. "Log. Hog. Grog. ...*Smog*."

"But still not a single frog." She muttered.

His mouth curved, as he finally recognized what was happening with the rhymes. Something glinted deep in his eyes. Some kind of spark. "Regardless, the army was soundly defeated... as if you'd wielded a *flog*." He offered in false commiseration.

"Oh, shut up."

"Why, it was a spell worthy of any *blog*. Everyone watching was *agog*!"

"Shut *up*, Trev."

He chuckled, but the sound was much more tender than usual. He moved to stand beside her, again.

"I told you, my magic is unpredictable." Esmeralda defended. "But at least they're gone. You're welcome, dickhead."

He touched her back, rubbing gently. "You did very well, my darling."

That mollified her. "Yeah?"

"I didn't know it was possible to feel proud of someone else's actions. But I am *very* proud of you."

She blinked up at him. Literally no one had ever said that to her before. No one in her whole life.

That dragon-green gaze met hers and she saw he was serious. "Because I'm a level six?" She guessed.

"Because you *fought*. Your magic is different. Good and Bad mixed together and competing for supremacy. I felt it. But you managed to make it work. I'm not sure another being alive could have done what you just did. Not even me." His hand slipped lower, caressing and demanding. "I am more turned on than I have ever been and you're still clothed."

"You promised to rip my clothes off of me." Esmeralda reminded him with a pious expression. "I'm expecting you to keep your word."

"I always keep my word to my mate. A thousand percent." Trevelyan's breathing was growing rougher. His fingers slipped under her nightgown, finding the edge of her underwear and her damp flesh beneath. Without warning, one finger pressed inside of her. Taking the territory he wanted.

Esmeralda jolted, her head falling onto his shoulder.

"My mate." His voice sounded deeper and echoing. More like a dragon's. "Just *mine*."

For people with powers, magic was always kind of an aphrodisiac. For Trevelyan, it seemed like even more than that. *Her* powers excited him. The strength and feel and color of them. Esmeralda realized that he now considered her magic his. Just like her cookies were his. Just like *she* was his. Possession was a part of the man.

Tendrils of smoke curled off of him. They felt exotic and erotic against her skin. She couldn't wait until Trevelyan had enough of his powers back to coat her whole body in that magical, dragon-y essence. And he *would*. She'd make sure of it. His green magic was so much like hers, but different, too. Savagely elegant. Precise and lethal as a blade, it moved like a natural extension of his body.

The dragon didn't use magic. He *was* magic. It was a part of his DNA. She wanted to feel that confidently flowing power *everywhere*. If her magic belonged to him, then his belonged to her. It was only fair.

Trevelyan noticed the wispy precursors to his dragon-form floating around his body and swore softly, yanking his hand back. "Later." He let out a controlled rush of air. "Much later." He stepped back from her. It seemed to take all of his willpower to make it a foot away. "It would be... *better* to wait."

She had never seen Trevelyan so close to the edge before. His whole face was taut. Esmeralda's gaze slipped down to the front of his soft pants. He was so aroused, she had no idea how he was still standing upright. In response, her own desire cranked all the way up to a blazing inferno.

"Why do we have to wait?" She challenged. "Everyone's dead. I get my orgasms. A deal is a deal."

He rolled one shoulder, like he felt stretched in his own skin. "It's just not a wise idea for me to touch you, when I'm like this."

"If we postpone sex again, you'll just do something new to piss me off and I'll never get laid. Right now is *perfect*. I want you. You want me. What's the problem?"

"I *do* want you." He shook his head. "But the monster inside of me wants you, too. It wants *out*. It wants to hold you down and fuck you right here on the floor. *That's* the problem."

Oh.

CHAPTER SEVENTEEN

Pick your perfect nail polish from our unlimited selection!
Don't Look Back Blue: Wanna leave a trail of mangled bodies in your wake and still sleep like a baby at night? Well, this unforgettable navy cream has amnesia potion mixed right into the base. Put it on and you won't dwell on any of the horrible stuff you did, after you've had the fun of doing it. It will be wiped from your mind, as soon as you remove your manicure and you can begin your next reign of terror with a clear conscience.
(Also available in lipstick form, for those who want to kiss and not tell.)

Happily Ever Witch Cosmetics Website

The Club Castle

"Well, that's just silly." Maryanna, Queen of Clubs, shook her head. "Not even a dragon could defeat my army. We sent *legions* of knights. Didn't we send legions of knights, Hatty?" She looked over at her husband for confirmation.

The Mad Hatter nodded, no small feat, considering he was sitting upside down on his throne, with his legs pointed up in the air. He was twirling his pocket watch round and round his bare foot by its chain. The watch went arcing out like a yo-yo as far as it could in one direction. Then, he would flip his ankle and it would spin back the opposite way. Since that mechanism of cogs and gears sustained his literal heartbeat, she wished he'd be a tiny bit more careful with it.

"Reports were related to us as it happened, majesty. This is all slightly confusing, because we lost…. um… everyone. But, it seems that it wasn't actually Trevelyan who killed them all." The unfortunate playing card guard who'd been tasked with delivering the report swallowed. "It was the new Queen of Hearts."

"The witch?" The Queen of Clubs scoffed at that foolishness. "Impossible. Esmeralda is no queen. She's just a pawn in a game she barely understands. Good grief, she was sent to prison for scaring some teenagers, who were trying to eat her absurd gingerbread house."

The Mad Hatter squinted, as if he was imagining that architectural choice.

"Defeating my army would have taken a spell of incredible magnitude and Esmeralda doesn't have it." The Queen of Clubs continued. "She'd have to possess level five magic to pull it off."

At *least* level five magic.

The Queen of Clubs was a level five and she wasn't sure she could've vaporized thousands of men, all at once. No one could do that, except maybe that jackass from El Dorado and he was a level six.

Her breath caught. A level six. Was it possible...?

The Queen of Clubs glanced at her husband, again.

His swirling eyes met hers and she knew he was suddenly concerned. "Whose is fairest, Anna?" He asked, his gaze swirling round and round and round.

The Hatter might be mad, but their thoughts were often in clockwork synch. The Queen of Clubs wasn't sure what that said about her own sanity, but she knew it made them an unstoppable team.

Except the witch and the dragon had just beaten them.

Unable to help herself, the Queen of Clubs rose to her feet. She moved to the ornate golden mirror hanging beside her throne. It was shaped like a club and imbued with magic. Staring at her perfect, ageless reflection for a long moment, she rallied her courage. Her hair was black as ebony, flowing thick and long. Her skin was white as the snow that covered the icy Kingdom of Clubs. She was still beautiful, even after all these centuries. The spell she'd cast, so long ago, had been worth the price. To stay forever young, she'd needed to trade something of great value and so she'd given up her chance to have a child of her own. That had been hard. She was naturally giving and very maternal. But, she'd been smarter than the magic trying to constrain her. She'd found another way to become a mother. Now, she had her own dear family and she needed to ensure their future.

The Queen of Clubs took a deep breath. "Mirror, Mirror, on the wall... Whose magic is fairest of them all?"

Her magic was the fairest in Wonderland.

It *had* to be hers. It always was before, whenever she asked the question. According to the White Rabbit's Magic Matrix, the Queen of Clubs was fifty-five percent Bad. That was almost perfectly balanced with her Good. She was the epitome of fairness and order. No other queen could ever rule with more justice, or strength, or motherly goddamn devotion.

Wonderland would be hers, because she was destined to...

An image of that green-skinned witch appeared in the looking glass, obscuring the Queen of Clubs' reflection and cutting off her desperate thoughts.

The Mad Hatter stopped twirling his pocket watch and flipped himself around in his chair. "Oh bother."

The guard inched towards the door, sensing danger. "I'll just be going..."

The Queen of Clubs' beautiful face compressed in fury and she stabbed a finger in the playing card's direction. He was instantly blown off his feet in an unholy gale. His flat body tumbled out the closest window. A panicked scream echoed, as he plunged downward and was shredded by the landscaping of the formal garden far below.

Carnivorous rosebushes were always a bitch to fall into. Especially from five stories up.

"Why wasn't she stopped?!" She screamed at her husband, pacing around the throne room. "I hired that idiot Florian to ensure my army succeeded and instead *this* happens!"

"We shouldn't have let him leave, until after the battle." The Mad Hatter lamented. "We'll never get a refund on his consulting fee, now."

"Trevelyan must have done something to amplify the witch's magic. He's behind all of this, not *her*. I told you that bastard was clever." The Queen of Clubs didn't know all the details of what had occurred in the Heart Kingdom, but she knew the Green Dragon was directly responsible for ruining her plans. *Again*.

She'd nearly had the key to the damn spell years ago, but he'd escaped the Wicked, Ugly, and Bad prison before Snow White could get it from him. He'd used her poor stepdaughter and wrecked the Queen of Clubs' scheme, all in one night.

"We should just kill him, Anna." The Mad Hatter's head tilted this way and that, as his thoughts traveled along twisted, unnatural pathways. "The dragon's dangerous to have alive. And the witch is his True Love. When a villain finds his True Love, there's no telling what he'll do."

"Dragons don't care about True Loves. Everyone knows that. There must be more to his scheme."

The Mad Hatter didn't seem convinced. "Regardless, we control three of the kingdoms, already. Forget about Hearts, for now. Focus on clearing those bigoted, anti-magic humans out of Diamonds." He made a face. "I should have gotten rid of them, while I was there. I can't stand the Gyre."

"They're *humans*. Anyone can handle humans."

"And yet their numbers keep growing, in every known land."

She snorted in derision. "I'll stop them before they expand into more of Wonderland. For now, they're useful. The more magical people they execute on that beach, the less there are to challenge me."

"And when they come to execute *us?*"

"We'll kill them, of course." She scoffed dismissively. "The Gyre is still small here. Confined to the Diamond Kingdom. I have much bigger problems than those zealots. You've seen the calendar! Tove is coming up." That damn extra day wormed its way into weeks where it didn't belong, creating all kinds of chaos.

"The eighth square is on schedule..." The Mad Hatter's voice trailed off as a bread-and-butterfly buzzed past.

Slowly lifting his pocket watch, he pressed the stopper on top and froze the insect in midair. The bug hovered there, suspended in motionless flight. Giggling like it was the funniest thing he'd ever seen, the Hatter grabbed it between his thumb and forefinger, and popped it into his mouth.

"I've asked you not to eat those." The Queen of Clubs muttered distractedly. He used his amazing magic for the most ridiculous things sometimes.

She blamed his bloodline for his lack of couth. His great-grandfather had been a yeti. The Queen of Clubs preferred not to know how a hatter and a yeti mated. Yetis were big, grunting animals, so she doubted there had been much romance involved. They also fed on magic and the Mad Hatter had inherited that hunger. He needed to gorge himself on Goodness at regular intervals, to replenish his energy.

It was a small issue, though. There was always some innocent little maid he could suck dry. The death of a few anonymous girls was a small price to pay for his enormous powers. As a species, Hatters' magic was always linked to time and her husband's skill was particularly extraordinary.

Her eyes went to the window, admiring the Mad Hatter's greatest achievement. The Chessboard Tower was situated so it could be seen from the throne room. The Queen of Clubs loved the game. Her husband didn't even play chess --Again, his bloodline wasn't the most erudite-- but he'd put all his talents into building the tower to make her happy. He'd given it to her on the day she donned the Club Kingdom's tiara and become queen.

It loomed over the courtyard, its forbidding exterior tiled in a spiraling, black-and-white checkerboard pattern. Unlike an ordinary, round-faced clock, with numbers and hands, the Mad Hatter's tower had a gigantic chessboard at its top. It kept time with ever-shifting pieces. They moved back-and-forth in their proper patterns through mechanized magic.

Keeping track of each moment, until she was promoted to empress.

Only a few pieces remained in the countdown and they showed the white side was the clear frontrunner. There was no way the reds could win. It was preposterous.

So why did it seem like her time was running out?

The Queen of Clubs shook off the uneasy sensation. Her attention switched to the table in the corner. It was piled high with every color and brand of sealing wax ever invented. Made of every possible material and substance. From every known land and three unknown ones. Created from magic, bought at stores, melted, unmelted, stolen, given as goddamn unbirthday presents... And none of them worked in that impossible spell. *None* of them.

She'd done everything right. She was sure of it. The fault had to lie somewhere else. The Magic Matrix only put the Queen of Clubs at fifty-five percent Bad. *That* was the real issue. While it allowed her to be completely fair, she just wasn't dark enough. She was a *mother!* Loving and selfless to her core.

The ethereal white queen on any chessboard.

Clearly, only someone evil could cast the spell. A dark, super-powered villain, like Trevelyan, Last of the Green Dragons. He was a level five and he'd spent time studying the damn spell. Trevelyan knew how it worked. And his magic was pitch fucking black.

To ensure the glorious future of Wonderland, she needed that spell to work. She wasn't some power-hungry lunatic, only out for herself. This was for *everyone*.

Wonderland needed to change. Other kingdoms mocked its wackiness, polka dots, and revolving procession of beheaded queens. She was sick to death of ruling over one tiny corner of a laughingstock backwater. The whole kingdom had to be fixed. The whimsy ripped out by the roots. The anarchy tamed. The kaleidoscope of colors changed to elegant black and white.

As empress, the Queen of Clubs would create order from the chaos. She'd elevate Wonderland to its rightful spot on the international stage. Media. Celebrities. People who *mattered* would soon call it home.

Once she made Wonderland prosperous and popular, everyone would admit that she was incredible at her job. Hatty would be so proud. Her daughter would have a successful role model. She would finally be applauded and thanked for her many sacrifices. This plan was the only way to have it all.

And like any working mom, the Queen of Clubs deserved it *all*.
"No." Her blood-red lips pressed together. "Nothing is lost."
She refused to accept that. "The situation is just… evolving."
She would have to adjust and compensate for other people's stupidity. Her family was counting on her.

The door to the throne room opened and Snow White came wandering in. "Mommy?"

The Queen of Clubs' instantly focused on her precious stepdaughter. "Dearest, you should be resting." She hurried to her side, already fussing over her. "You need to look your best for our family dinner tonight."

Snow White's wide eyes blinked up at her, with no trace of intelligence or calculation. It was so sad. Once upon a time, her stepdaughter had been brilliant. A doctor! The Queen of Clubs had paid a fortune to put her through medical school. And now… She sighed. Now, Snow White was as helpless and blank as a doll.

Thanks to Scarlett Riding-Wolf pushing her into the Lake of Forgetting, the real Snow White had been erased. She'd been reduced to a shambles of the capable, confident, independent woman the Queen of Clubs raised. This girl couldn't come up with an original thought, if you held a vorpal blade to her heart. Could barely recall her old life, at all. Couldn't care less about restarting her career. She just sat around, waiting for her prince to come. The disappointment was never-ending.

But a mother loved her child, no matter what.

When the Queen of Clubs first came to Wonderland, she'd had no intention of staying in this wretched place. But then she'd met her True Love. That changed everything. At the time, the Mad Hatter had been married, with a baby daughter. She'd quickly slain his interloping wife, of course. What else could you do with a homewrecker? She'd intended to kill the infant daughter too, so she and her True Love could begin their happy marriage with a clean slate.

But when the Queen of Clubs had looked into the cradle and seen that tiny, innocent face, she'd stayed her hand. Instead of a rival for her new husband's attention, she'd seen the answer to all her prayers. Snow White gave her back the opportunity to be a parent. In return, the Queen of Clubs protected her, and guided her, and granted all of her wishes.

No matter how sickeningly bland.

"I couldn't wait, anymore." Snow White wore a pink ruffled dress and a ribbon in her dark hair. The former-her would have been appalled at the ludicrous fashion choices. "Is he here yet?" She asked eagerly, bouncing on her heels. "Is he? Is he?"

The Queen of Clubs closed her eyes briefly at the inane question. That bitch Scarlett Riding-Wolf would pay for what she'd done. And the cost would be any woman's most prized possession:

Her family.

The Mad Hatter sighed. As Snow White's father, he shared in this tragedy. He couldn't feel it as deeply as a *mother*, but he still mourned their lost daughter and did his best with the shell they had left. "For the eleventyth time: He's here. But he's still getting ready, Snow. Soon."

"Yay!" Snow White clapped her hands. She went skipping back out of the room, black ringlets bouncing. Only one topic in the world kept her attention for more than a nanosecond and he was presently chained in the dungeon, being fitted for a tuxedo.

The Mad Hatter glanced at the Queen of Clubs, again. "Remember, this is *your* project, Anna. I still say she can do better."

"And I know what my baby wants."

"Are you sure Bluebeard can even do this? The guy seems like a putz to me."

"He'd *better* do it, putz or not." Her brow furrowed, wondering if that imbecile with the turquoise facial hair really was up to the job. All her research indicated he was the very best with this sort of magic, but the Mad Hatter was right. The man was beneath them. "If Bluebeard can't do it, we'll kill him and start again." She decided with a firm nod. "There *has* to be a way to give Snow her happily ever after."

You didn't give up, even when the whole world conspired against you.

Not when your little girl was counting on you to make all her dreams come true.

CHAPTER EIGHTEEN

**Pick your perfect nail polish from our unlimited selection!
Slay and Run Sapphire: This reflective glitter polish will help the
modern evil-doer stay fashionable, as you dash through your busy
day of torturing minions, performing dark magic, and enslaving
hapless men.
(Legal Notice: We are not responsible for damages which result from
torturing minions, performing dark magic, or enslaving hapless men.)**

Happily Ever Witch Cosmetics Website

The Heart Castle

Esmeralda's heart pounded, as she stared up at Trevelyan.
"Your dragon wants me?"
"It always wants you. You're our mate. But seeing your magic..." He swallowed, stepping back farther, like there wasn't enough space between them on the balcony. "I am --*he* is-- too keyed up, right now. He just wants to claim you, over and over and *over*."
"That sounds great!"
He shook his head, scraping a hand through his long hair. "Sex would be... rough. Without finesse. He can't get out without magic, but he's in my head."
"The dragon is *you*, Trev. You're him. No matter which of you is at the helm, you're still in control." She didn't doubt that for a second. The man was the biggest control freak she'd ever met. "Just have fun with it."
"Fun?" He frowned, like that was crazy talk.
"Yeah. I just defeated an army. I'm in a cheerful mood. I want

my two orgasms. Let's go."

"Sex isn't about fun." He'd retreated all the way back to the balcony's railing, which showed how antsy he felt. Trevelyan never retreated from anything, certainly not from her. "I'm very serious about my proficiency."

"You don't take *anything* seriously. A fire-breathing monster just attacked and you were ready to make popcorn, by the end."

"But, I'm excellent at sex. It's my very best skill. I'm not going to be less than excellent with you, of all people."

"I don't care how 'excellent' you are. I care how much you want me."

Green eyes found hers, infinite, feral, very Bad desire glowing out of them. And all of that ominous longing was for her. "If you knew how much I wanted you, you'd run away." He said darkly.

Oooooh... *That* was more like it.

"Okay." Esmeralda grinned at him. Her magic had actually worked, her True Love was desperately in lust with her, and she was about to have out-of-control sex in her great big castle. The morning was looking bright.

"My God." He whispered, his gaze riveted on her smile. "I can't stop him, if you look at me like that. We like it when you're happy." The mix of pronouns was working for her. It was like something uncivilized and otherworldly had her in his/their sights.

"You can't stop *me*, at all." She backed towards the door. "But give me a thirty second head start."

"What?" Trevelyan's whole body jerked, finally processing what she planned to do. "No! Dragons are hunters. Whatever you do, *don't run*."

Esmeralda took off running.

"*Ez!*" It was literally a roar.

Laughing with wicked delight, she picked a direction and sprinted off in it. She quickly found herself in a spiraling hallway. The damn thing curved up onto the ceiling and then back down again, like a waterslide turned on its side. It was enchanted, though, like everything else in the Heart Palace. As long as you kept going, your feet stayed firmly planted on its surface. Esmeralda dashed forward, as fast as she could. Space was key to sustaining this game.

"*I warned you!*" Trevelyan didn't last thirty seconds. She knew he wouldn't. "Now, it's too late. I'm going to have you wherever I catch you, even if it's in the middle of the yard!"

"We can't even reach the yard, through the force field." Esmeralda shouted back. "We're going to have to play inside today."

There was a teeny, tiny door sitting right in the middle of her path. It wasn't attached to the wall. It was just a miniature door, kind of hanging out in space. No *way* could Trevelyan fit through it, so Esmeralda bent down to throw it open and crawled inside. Wherever it led, it gave her some added distance in the chase.

"Esmeralda!"

She ignored Trevelyan's shout and hauled herself into the new space. Turned out it was the room next to the royal suite, meaning she was basically back to where she started. Whatever.

The Cheshire Carpet's many smiling mouths smiled, like it had been expecting her. "Oh hello there, your majesty." Lips appeared and vanished on its pink-and-purple surface, moving at the relaxing speed of a lava lamp. "Did you stop the invasion?"

"Yep. The army is yellow-ish smog, now."

"Oh, that's nice. Did you know the Heart Kingdom's colors are pink-and-red?"

"It's certainly what I would have guessed." It was a bit unnerving to walk on something that was maybe, sort of alive, so Esmeralda carefully made her way around the fringe edges of the carpet.

"The Spade Kingdom's colors are black-and-red. The Diamond Kingdom's colors are red-and-white. And, of course, the Club Kingdom's colors are white-and-black."

"Super." Esmeralda headed for the normal-sized door. "Great to know." She poked her head out into the hallway, scanning for Trevelyan. He was nowhere in sight, but she could hear him shouting her name.

"I'm totally winning this game." She murmured to herself.

"A game?" The Cheshire Carpet repeated eagerly. "I adore games! Would you like to play chess? I especially adore chess!"

Again, it struck Esmeralda that the rug was probably lonely. She glanced back at it, momentarily distracted from tormenting the dragon. "How long have you been cooped up in this room, all alone?" She asked, before she could stop herself.

"Oh *ages*. Alice didn't much like me." Mouths appeared and vanished on its surface as it talked. And talked. "Neither did the queen before her. Or the queen before *her*. But I just know things will be different now that *you're* here. We'll be great friends!"

"Sure." Esmeralda had spent her whole childhood in an orphanage. She knew what it felt like to be unwanted. She was in a fabulous mood this morning, so she couldn't bring herself to hurt the rug's feelings. "Um... We'll play chess tomorrow." She promised.

"Really?" It cried excitedly. "Oh, I would enjoy that. Can I be the white side?"

"Absolutely. I'll see you, then." Esmeralda slipped out of the room, still on the lookout for Trevelyan. Everything seemed quiet, now. He wasn't calling her name anymore. Had he given up? She tiptoed to the corner and peeked around it.

Instantly, he appeared at the other end of the hallway. "*There* you are." He growled.

Esmeralda gave a laugh. She darted away, running to no place in particular. She could've come up with an actual plan to escape him, but she sucked at plans. Besides, escaping wasn't the point of the game. Getting caught was half the fun. The other half was driving your control-freak True Love past his limits.

Trevelyan went in a different direction, trying to cut her off. "You wanted 'kind.' I tried to give it to you. I told you to stop this, before you even started it. But you didn't listen!"

Esmeralda ducked into a random, hearted-all-to-hell bedroom. "I never said I wanted you to be kind! You *can't* be kind. I might as well ask you to be a Koala bear."

"You said your type was *kind* goddamn guitar players, with *kind* goddamn smiles." It was a furious accusation.

She rolled her eyes. "If you're going to try one of those qualities, go with the guitar playing. Not with kind. Why would you pick *kind?* Have you met me?"

He made an aggravated sound, right outside the room. "It doesn't matter. We're past all of it now, Mate. Now, you just get *me*." He rattled the knob, finding it locked. "Are you standing away from the door?" He asked in a quieter tone.

"Yeah. Why?"

It exploded. Trevelyan's powers were weakened, but his foot obliterated the wood just fine without them.

Esmeralda grinned. Forget guitar players. She loved dating a Bad guy. At least *this* Bad guy.

There was an elaborate armoire in the corner, wearing eyeglasses. Esmeralda yanked it open and climbed inside.

"You might have asked first!" It chided.

"Sorry." Esmeralda said, even though she wasn't. She crouched inside of the armoire, just as Trevelyan crossed the threshold of the bedroom.

She gave him a triumphant smirk. "Really? You thought it would be that easy?" She closed herself into the small space. One quick wave of her hand and, when she opened the door again, she was downstairs, in the pink-on-pink-on-pink ballroom.

"*Fuck!*"

Even from a floor away she heard his frustrated bellow. Esmeralda couldn't have been more pleased. Right now, she had magic and he didn't. That was keeping her in play. She raced into the foyer, trying to decide which way to go next. The basement levels were pretty maze-like. She could lose him down there. Perfect. There was a spring in her step, as she headed for the stairs. Evading the dragon wasn't so hard...

Something moved overhead.

Standing in the middle of the foyer, Esmeralda looked up at the open landing to the second floor. Trevelyan was already at the gilded railing, staring down at her.

"How'd you get there so fast?" She demanded.

"Dragon." He explained succinctly and vaulted right over the bannister.

"Holy *shit!*" Esmeralda took off running, back into the ballroom.

Trevelyan landed in an animalistic crouch, already on her heels. Beaming at him over her shoulder, she slammed the ballroom doors behind her. Then she sealed them with her powers, although that wouldn't hold him for long. She stood there for a beat, breathing hard.

He crashed right into the magically-enforced doors and instantly began looking for a way through. "Esmeralda." His voice was an evil croon. "You're just making this harder on yourself. Come out of there and give me what's mine."

She waved a hand, turning the back wall of the ballroom into a tunnel, lined with endless doors. Maybe that would slow him down. Once he got into the ballroom, he wouldn't know which door she went through.

Caught up in the chase, Esmeralda wasn't thinking before casting the spells. They just blasted out, one after another. She didn't even realize how much power she was using.

Trevelyan did.

He could feel it in the air, the same way she'd felt his, when he'd moved all the canons. "Oh yes..." His hungry groan reverberated across her nerve-endings. "I feel your energy like my own, Ez. I'm going to come deep inside of you, with all of that pretty, green magic wrapped tight around me."

"You'll have to catch me, in order to do that. And I'm winning this game, so far." She headed through one of the multitude of doors, into the atrium. Ducking through the giant talking flowers that grew there, she hoped that all the green growing things would hide her scent from the dragon.

And that the chattering plants didn't rat her out to him, if he came this way. They seemed to be pretty snobby.

"My how rude." One of the gigantic hydrangea bushes chided, as she pushed passed it.

"Shocking," agreed a borogrove blossom, with a sniff of superiority. "Alice was a much better queen. That darling girl was positively mimsy."

Esmeralda ignored their opinions. She didn't like being in the atrium. The humidity beaded on the glass walls and water was never her friend. Exiting the overly-warm space, she found herself in the kitchen.

Wonderful! She could use some breakfast.

Taking a moment, she grabbed up one of the wabeberry tarts she'd made the day before and peered through the hole she'd left in the dining room wall. No sign of Trevelyan. Ha! She'd known those hundreds of doorways would lose him for a while. Loud guitar music blasted through the castle, like a classic rock anthem played on full blast.

Esmeralda laughed in delight and then slapped a hand over her mouth to muffle the sound. Shoot! He'd just tricked her into giving away her position. Such a clever dragon. She hurried into the dining room and took a bite of the tart.

Electric, pulsing and played with perfect virtuosity, the magical guitar music was way better than any record store owner could've produced. Trevelyan's powers were bouncing back faster than she'd thought they would. That probably meant he was healing from his long sleep.

It also meant he was going to find her soon.

"Ez." He called from somewhere off to the left. She could sense him stalking through the rooms, searching for her.

"Come out, come out, wherever you are..."

She waved a hand and made her skin heart-patterned to blend in with the wallpaper. One thing Esmeralda always had total control over was her appearance. Blonde, brunette, bridge ogre... Glamours came easy to her.

"God, I *feel* your powers." His voice was a snarl of lust. "You're using so much of it, it's in the air. No one else's energy feels like yours, darling. That's why you smell as succulent as you do. You're just pure magic."

Esmeralda ate her tart and waited him out. Trevelyan went past the dining room, so he must not have spotted her.

Excellent. Another win for her team. Turning her skin back to green, she tried to decide on her next move.

The cabbage-y, corkscrew, sailboat-ish "rog" that she'd

accidently created in the basement went rolling past like tumbleweed. Lord knew why. Esmeralda ignored it.

Instead, she drew the outline of a heart-shaped door onto the wall with her fingertip. Adding a circle for the knob, she turned it and walked right through. She couldn't really predict where it would lead, but it didn't much matter. Her only objective was to play with Trevelyan.

It was probably why her magic was working so well, come to think of it. There was no pressure. No Good or Bad. No Cauldron Society. No rules or plans. Just having fun with her True Love.

She ended up in some kind of study. Esmeralda glanced around. She hadn't seen this room before. Not a huge shock, since the castle seemed to change on a whim. Wonderland's magic fed on illogical nonsense. She got the feeling the Heart Castle enjoyed having villains in residence, because she and Trevelyan contributed to the chaos that made everything thrive.

The study had a portrait of a red knight over the massive fireplace, and rugs made from the skins of a frumious bandersnatch on the floor. But there were no exits. Not even a window. She looked back at the heart-shaped door, but it had vanished, too.

When she turned towards the fireplace again, Trevelyan was standing there. He was just somehow *there*, right in front of her and gloriously naked.

"So, you *did* know I was in the dining room." She deduced.

His head tilted to one side, only focused on her. "Dragon." He reminded her. It wasn't so much a word as a growl.

Esmeralda took a step back from him, but he was already moving. Her nightgown was ripped off her body before she even hit the ground. Wow! Esmeralda's eyes went wide as she found herself pinned to the thick carpet. She had no idea how he'd done that, but it was awesome. Just to see what would happen, she tried to move...

He made a snarling sound at her halfhearted attempt to get free, his rock-hard-body holding her still. His fingers found the edge of her underwear without looking, shredding them. Now, she was naked and at the mercy of the Baddest man she'd ever met.

About time.

Her eyes fluttered shut in lust and she stopped struggling.

"You're never getting away from me and you know it." It was an evil purr, tempting and cruel. "Submit to the inevitable, my darling."

"I'm not submitting to anything." She panted. "I'm just... regrouping to..." She trailed off with a whimper, as a massive hand tangled in her hair.

"What I capture belongs to me." He murmured into her ear. Then, he licked it. "And I've got you, now. You're not going anywhere."

Yeah, the most monstrous part of him was at the reins, for sure. "My skin bruises easily, dragon." She warned breathlessly.

Glowing green eyes slashed over to meet hers.

She smiled at him.

He blinked. Nodded. No matter how wild he got, he was still careful with her. "Open your legs." His other palm was already between them, readying her for his possession. Long fingers pushed deep, wanting everything as fast as possible.

A cry of total, mindless desire escaped her, her thighs parting to accommodate his demands. This wasn't like he'd been in the interrogation room. He wasn't coaxing her. He was just *taking*. He groaned when he felt how wet she was for him. "See? You know you belong to just me." He relaxed the tiniest bit, feeling more confident in his claim. Big mistake. "You know that all this is mine. You're so ready for me, you're going to come on the first stroke."

Esmeralda finished regrouping.

She pushed him, using his distraction and overconfidence to her advantage. Magic gave her a boost of extra strength and she heaved him off of her and scrambled to her feet, just to see what would happen. Just because driving Trevelyan to the edge was fun and she liked...

She hit the rug, again.

Her freedom had lasted approximately half-a-second, and then Trevelyan had her. He cushioned her fall so nothing was bruised, but the dragon within him was seething at her defiance. "We'll do it the hard way." Trevelyan flipped her over. Now, she was on her stomach and he was behind her. On top of her.

Uh-oh.

Instinct had her squiggling forward, but he dragged her towards his body. One hand found the back of her neck, holding her in place like any predatory creature subduing its mate. Oh shit... She *seriously* liked that. She'd had no idea she'd like that. Who the hell could have guessed she'd like that?

Trevelyan, apparently.

"I told you not to run from me." His voice was so dark that it was causing spasms in her womb. "No matter how much magic you use, I will track you down. You will never be out of my sight for long."

Esmeralda stilled, swallowing hard, her forehead resting on the carpet.

"Mine." His free hand touched her body with authority, as if he had a right to every inch of it. In this position she had very little control and he knew it. He *wanted* it. This wasn't only about sex to him. This was conquest. "You're just mine, aren't you?" The whole chase had turned her on more than anything ever had. And, for some perverse reason, his dominance was now pushing her over the edge.

There was a rumble of dragon-y possession. His fingers were reverent as they brushed over the skin of her inner thigh. "Give me what I want and I'll give you what you want, Mate."

"What do you want?"

"Everything."

Esmeralda would explode if he didn't take her soon, but she certainly wasn't making it *that* easy for him. "I've never had sex in this position." And she'd seemingly been missing out, because she'd never been so aroused in her life. "Why don't we go upstairs and do this in a..."

Trevelyan cut her off. "You're going to have sex with me in every way possible and some I'm going to invent." His free hand lifted her body and adjusted it to his liking. Now, she was on her elbows and knees, totally open to him. "Be a Good girl and submit."

"Nope."

That earned her a dark chuckle. "I like this game."

God, so did she. Esmeralda gave a slight tug against his hold, to see how tight he was gripping her and she couldn't move, at all. Trevelyan was *not* letting her go. It reassured her. Made her feel wanted. Her hips rocked back, seeking more. "I really am going to come fast." She got out breathlessly.

"Not until you beg me to make you mine." He nudged against her swollen flesh and made her see stars. "And maybe call me 'sir' a few times. You started this, so you don't get to come until you show some repentance."

He thought she was going to resist that order, until he tortured her into a screaming frenzy and finally won her acquiescence. Trevelyan had no idea who he was dealing with. Only one of them was claiming victory and it sure wasn't the dragon. Esmeralda turned to look at him over her shoulder, her eyes filled with mischief and desire. "Please, sir." She whispered sweetly. "Make me yours."

That won the game.

Of course it did. The man was a deadly villain, but he was also putty in her perfectly manicured hands. Trevelyan's jaw sagged in shock, when he heard her playing-along. It was like he wasn't even sure how to process it. And, for just a flicker, she saw the dragon inside of him peering out of his eyes. Totally, *totally* enthralled with her.

Sucker.

Esmeralda's grin got bigger. She had the feeling some of her lamentable virtue shone out, because Trevelyan gave a choked sound of hypnotized wonder.

And Esmeralda vanished.

Well, not *really*. She didn't disappear entirely. She just shrank herself down to three inches high. Simple to do, when magic controlled your body. One second she was witch-sized and caught in Trevelyan's grasp. Then, she was tiny and he promptly lost his grip on her. Then, she was witch-sized again, rolling onto her back to laugh up at him. "Gotcha.

She was only a foot away from where she'd been before, so he was instantly on top of her. His eyes were more intent, now. "Got *you*." The man was clearly done playing.

So was she. Esmeralda parted her legs for him and he slammed forward, driven by animal instinct. Maybe it was the dragon taking her. Probably, it was both. They were the same monster, after all.

"*Trev!*" She screamed his name, as he surged inside of her. Sensations bombarded her. The True Love bond snapped fully into place, linking them forever-after. Trevelyan filled her as far as he could go, sinking in so deeply that it edged on delicious pain. And Esmeralda came harder than she ever had in her life. Just like he'd promised.

Her scream went higher and wordless, as the orgasm rushed over her.

"Fuck, fuck, *fuck.*" He buried his face in her hair. "*Do not move.*" He sounded guttural.

She had no idea who he was talking to: her, himself, or the dragon. If he meant her, too bad. There was no possible way she could stay still. Her hips were rolling, her body in meltdown.

"No! Don't…" Trevelyan groaned and then he was thrusting, like he couldn't stop himself. His hand planted on the ground beside her face, instinctively wanting to keep her right where she was. "The dragon likes you at our mercy. It likes the smell of you and how you play. God, darling… He just likes *you.*"

"I like the dragon." She got out.

An otherworldly snarl sounded next to her ear. "You don't understand. I'll…" He pulled her up into more of a sitting position. Big hands covered her breasts, feeling them move with his thrusts. "I have never needed… I won't last long either, if you…." He began speaking in some language she didn't know and sank into her at a new angle, sending off another round of aftershocks.

Esmeralda gave a sob of pleasure, helplessly arching in his grasp.

Trevelyan watched her, his eyes glowing. "Christ, you smell even more beautiful after you've come. I'll have to kill every dragon in the world to keep them away from you." It didn't sound like a complaint.

"You'll probably do that, anyway."

"Not the way I'd do it over you. I will slaughter anyone who tries to take you from me. It'll become a legend of blood and horror." He sounded sort of worried about it. "I would do anything to keep you, Ez. It's frightening how far I'd go."

Another orgasm was already starting to build, from his hands and from his words. But he was distracted and she was mostly Bad, so...

Esmeralda made another halfhearted bid for freedom. She managed to partially dislodge him, but he was too strong for her to get off his lap. Big arms held fast. He casually pinned her to the floor again, so she was stretched out before him like a pagan offering.

The quick loss of that round set her off giggling. "Yeah, you got me." She admitted.

His teeth gleamed and she realized Trevelyan was really having fun. She knew she could teach him! "Damn right I do." He sank into her as deep as he could go. "Run and I will catch you, witch. Every single time." He bent his head to suckle at her taut nipple.

"Oh, God... Just like that, Trev. *Yes*."

Now that he'd claimed everything he wanted, he was all Trevelyan again. "Yes, *what?*" He taunted meaningfully.

"I'm not calling you 'sir' again, you degenerate." She bit down on her lower lip, pleasure building and building. "Well, not unless you do something *really* inspiring."

"*You* inspire me, darling." He pushed heavily into her quivering core, making her see stars. "See the fireplace?"

Esmeralda tried to focus, but it was becoming impossible.

"Behind you, Ez. That's my perfect mate. Turn your head and aim your magic at it."

She managed to tilt her neck back to look at the huge fireplace on the wall.

"Light it." His voice was tight. "Use your powers and light it. I want to feel your magic all around me, while I'm inside you."

She was already shaking her head. "I can't keep that kind of spell controlled. I'll end up melting that picture over the mantel, instead."

"It's a picture of a knight. Who gives a shit?"

"But my magic will..."

"Do it. *Now*." The heel of his palm pressed down, rotating just the tiniest bit and Esmeralda would've happily set fire to the world for him.

She felt a rush of heat and flames behind her. She felt her magic overshoot the fireplace opening and engulf the whole wall. She felt more power slam out than she'd intended to use.

...And she felt Trevelyan come harder than he ever had in his life.

She grinned in delight, as his whole body jolted. He made a gasping sound, his hand clenching, trying to hold back. But it was too late. He was a goner. His release wasn't at all what he'd planned. She could tell, by the sudden shock on his face. She'd just made the dragon lose all control.

"Ez!" His head went back in a roar of possession, slamming into her with no thought except pleasure. Out of his mind for her. "*Fuck*."

His climax triggered her own. Esmeralda screamed, the fire she'd created becoming a whirlwind of flames.

Trevelyan made a helpless sound, watching half the room burn around them. He shuddered, still coming. "Just mine." It was a whisper of ownership and pride and utter amazement. "My God..." He finally slumped back, his breathing ragged. "You have so much magic." He let out a groan of renewed lust, as a part of the ceiling fell and crashed to the floor in a flaming heap.

Esmeralda swallowed, tearing her eyes away from his reverent expression to look at the instant remodeling she'd inadvertently done. She wasn't worried about burning to death. Her powers would never harm her or her True Love. Since Trevelyan didn't seem in a hurry to extinguish the blaze, she just let it rage.

"I couldn't control it." She whispered. "I can never control it." The game they'd played had been the best her magic had worked since... well... ever.

"Why would you want to control something so beautiful?"

She glanced up at him again.

He smiled, his eyes glowing hotter than the flames. "You're a force of nature, Esmeralda. I have *never* felt magic like that before. Your spells want death or freedom, like any other wild thing that won't be contained."

Esmeralda blinked, listening to the thick, hot admiration in his voice. She'd been afraid he'd be disappointed in her subpar magical skills. After all, she'd just set the house on fire, trying to light a couple of logs in a fireplace. Instead, he seemed rapturous over the flaming chaos. "Death or freedom?"

"Yes! *No one* has magic like yours. It's *everywhere*. Something so big can never be chained. You just have to let it go and believe."

"Since when do you believe in believing?"

"Since I met my mate." Trevelyan's hand slipped between her legs, feeling the combination of the slick juices. When his whole palm was saturated, he pressed it down right over her heart. "Mate." He repeated quietly, with a new and serious inflection in his tone.

Their combined scents coated her skin and she had the feeling it was some dragon-y ritual. It made her a little nervous, because Trevelyan was a wild creature, too. And she wasn't sure he could ever be tamed… but she also didn't tell him to stop.

He tilted his forehead down to rest against the handprint he'd left on her chest, as if he was savoring it. "You said you would only sleep with someone you liked." He reminded her after a long moment.

"Yep."

He was silent, like he wanted to say more, but he didn't know how.

Esmeralda was feeling generous with the big dummy. "I also said I liked *you*, dragon. …Most of the time. I guess this proves it."

Green eyes found hers, searching.

Esmeralda smiled at him again.

Trevelyan drew in a deep breath that expanded his chest and he slowly smiled back. "You *should* like me." He decided, sounding more like himself. "Our interests align. That's the basis for any great dynasty."

"Uh-huh." Esmeralda concentrated on the way he unconsciously stroked her skin and hair, like he just couldn't stop.

"Together, we have the strongest, darkest magic anywhere." He went on, oblivious to the gentle movement of his palms. "Our children can *rule* this world. Do you see that?"

"Sure... Unless you take it over yourself, first."

Trevelyan gave a chuckle. "My parents would have liked you, even though you don't want to join the Green Dragon line. They would have enjoyed your fathomless magic and your inner fire."

Her smile faded a bit at his words. "I never said I wouldn't join your line. You said I *couldn't*."

"No, I did *not* say that. Why would I say...?"

She cut him off. "You said I couldn't join your family, unless I helped you murder all mine." She arched a brow. "Right?"

He didn't respond, but she saw him suddenly thinking it over. He looked perturbed.

Content with that, for now, she cuddled closer to him.

Time passed. Trevelyan kept caressing her, but now he seemed more aware of it. He watched his hands smooth over her body and slowly exhaled. Touching her calmed him. "I'm usually very talented at sex." He eventually murmured.

"I noticed."

"No. I mean, I haven't had sex in a while. I wasn't prepared for what happened, between us. Chasing you is a fantasy for me and I..."

She cut him off. "It was perfect, Trev." Esmeralda would never forget it. After an eternity of being unwanted, *finally* she felt her life linking tight with someone else's. *Finally*, she belonged somewhere. *Finally*, she had her True Love in her arms. "I wouldn't change anything. It was just you and me having fun."

Trevelyan swallowed, as if he was trying to gather his thoughts. "I didn't... scare you?"

"No. You made me happy."

"No one feels happy around me."

"No one else is your mate." She kissed his jaw. "Do you believe me?"

"Yes." He whispered and, for a heartbeat of time, Esmeralda saw what it would be like to have this man belong completely to her. The wild, focused strength of his devotion. One elegant hand came up to cup her cheek, his thumb brushing her bottom lip. "My darling, you will *always* be happy around me." It was a vow. "I will kill anyone you point at with a frown. I give you my word."

Esmeralda grinned at that very Trevelyan-ish promise. "I believe you." She slid her fingers along the smooth, obsidian surface of his hair.

The dragon could learn everything she wanted him to. He just needed some time.

"Jesus." Trevelyan closed his eyes and buried his face against her shoulder. He stayed silent for a long moment, enjoying the feel of her hand gliding through the long, dark strands.

How many people had he ever allowed to touch him like this? She was betting exactly none. It wasn't easy to pet a dragon. They offered nothing but teeth and fire to anyone who got close. You had to be patient and persistent and preferably naked to break through.

Trevelyan let out a jagged breath. "This did not go how I imagined." He muttered.

"No?"

"No. As usual, you're confusing everything."

"I try."

CHAPTER NINETEEN

Pick your perfect nail polish from our unlimited selection! Power at Your Fingertips Glitter: In the mood to warp reality to your tyrannical will? Well, this crelly-based polish contains every color imaginable and two that *aren't* imaginable. ("Blinkle" and "Crimson-y Olive Sixish.") Because only *you* have the power to define your possibilities.

Happily Ever Witch Cosmetics Website

The Heart Castle

Not even Trevelyan could have sex all day, without a break for food.

He lounged against the kitchen counter, eating his dinner and thrilled with his life. He had everything a villain could possibly want: A willing, wicked mate, a kingdom to rule, scores of dead enemies, rapidly healing magical powers, and homemade wabeberry tarts for dessert.

He happily ate the sandwich that he'd put together, his eyes on Esmeralda's luscious body. It seemed logical that, after having sex, his interest in her would wane. That was what usually happened. The chase was always the most interesting part. But, apparently Esmeralda was different.

With her, the interesting part was *all* of it. The chasing part, sure. That had been world-altering. But catching her had been even more of a revelation. Hearing her laugh, and feeling her touch him, and being inside of her, and having her snuggle against him afterwards, like she trusted him to keep her safe... *All* of it. Now that he'd had sex with the witch, Trevelyan just wanted her more. She was addictive.

She was magical.

The whole experience *had* to be magic, really. She was doing something to enhance it. She *had* to be. Unconsciously elevating it all with her unique powers. However she created the sensations inside of him, it was the greatest spell he'd ever heard of. With Esmeralda, sex wasn't just physical. There was something else mixed in that he didn't fully understand. ...But, *oh* did he like it.

Hell, he even sort of, partially, maybe, slightly understood Marrok, now. The wolf had been... Well, not *right*. Trevelyan would never admit that son of a bitch was right about anything. But, he'd been *not wrong*, back in the WUB Club. Marrok decided to find his True Love, because he'd sensed she'd save him from his life. He'd been *not wrong* in his determination to have his one-and-only mate.

Now that Trevelyan had decided on his witch, no one else would ever do. All other women were superfluous, because he'd already claimed the very best one.

Thank God Trevelyan had insisted on that monogamy deal. He'd had so many flashes of brilliance over the years, but that one was his finest work. It had been difficult to convince her to give up guitar players, yet he'd persevered and won. (No one could negotiate like a dragon.) All other men would want what he had, but he'd already claimed his mate. It was done. Decided. Just him and the witch forever-after.

He was a goddamn genius.

"Only you can look smug while chewing." Esmeralda told him dryly.

"Eat your sandwich, darling. I slaved away making it for you." He took another bite of his own, watching her work. He'd rarely felt so relaxed.

Esmeralda checked on her latest nail polish project. It must've been the liquid gold one, because it looked shiny enough for even Kingpin Midas' tastes. "I'm not eating that sandwich, you monster."

"It's delicious."

"It's *ham*." She sent him a frown over her shoulder. "If I find out it used to be one of our hogs, I'm going to be pissed. I mean it."

"Even if it's just that horrible flying one, you dislike so much?" She looked outraged. "You better not have butchered the flying one!"

"You said he was bothering your favorite boots, so I got rid of him. You should be thrilled."

"Oh my God, tell me you're joking." She gasped. "I'm going to make that little guy a collar with a bow on it! I already have it designed."

He couldn't quite keep a straight face.

Esmeralda realized he was teasing her. She made an irritated sound, but her mouth was curved into a smile. "You are the worst person in the world."

"I try. And I promise you, none of our precious citizens were harmed in the making of dinner. Now eat. You need to keep your strength up. I've thought of at least a dozen more games I want to try." Since it had occurred to him that sex could be fun, he had all sorts of creative inspiration. "How do you feel about costumes, by the way?"

Esmeralda's hair color instantly switched to a platinum waterfall that fell to her waist. Instead of Trevelyan's half-buttoned shirt, she wore a sparkly prom dress. A black, pointy hat covered the diamond tiara. Witches always donned them for formal occasions.

"I'm *amazing* at costumes." She assured him smugly.

She was amazing at everything.

"Just don't ever change your skin." Trevelyan murmured. That petal-soft green flesh was staying put forever. He actually preferred the black curls too, but this blond look was also intriguing. "In my misspent youth, I once had some very scandalous impulses towards a random prom queen. I'm sure I mentioned that."

"It might have come up." She arched a brow. "How scandalous were these youthful impulses, exactly?"

"Oh, I was a precocious lad. They were absolutely *vile*."

She smiled, but somehow she looked troubled, as well.

Trevelyan's head tilted. "Tell me something true, Ez."

"I think you maybe started having sex too early." She blurted out.

He blinked. "What?"

"I think maybe you missed out on a lot of fun stuff along the way, because you were never really a kid. I think maybe you were always very... *you*." The word held a wealth of meaning. "And you like to think you're always in control of everything that happens, even when maybe..."

"I *am* always in control." He interrupted. "I'm a ninety-eight-percent-evil dragon. If I ever got out of control, I would do things beyond even my tolerance for Badness."

She nodded in agreement, but went on "I think-ing" and "maybe-ing" this strange conversation. "But, what if maybe your teacher was the one in control and she used it against you? I'm trying to imagine what *I* would have done, if my algebra teacher came on to me. It seems like that would be... *a lot* to process."

Trevelyan's first instinct was to dismiss that rush of words out of hand. "Dragons are very sexual beings." He argued without even stopping to consider it. "We mature quickly."

"I don't think you should have matured *that* quickly. I think maybe everyone --you included-- sometimes forgot you were a child. And I think your predatory teacher should be in jail. Or dead."

"She is dead. A house fell on her."

Esmeralda frowned. "She was a witch?"

"No, but that kills just about anybody." Trevelyan waved a hand. "Anyway, I didn't fight the idea of sleeping with her, so..."

She cut him off. "That has nothing to do with it. You were too young to consent. Just like *I* would have been, at thirteen."

He considered Esmeralda's words, picturing a much older man getting her alone, when she was a small girl. Fondling her delicate skin. Maybe forcing her to do things she didn't want to do. His mate feeling the shame and degradation he'd felt when Snow White had touched him in prison.

"Alright." Trevelyan allowed, with a slow nod. "I see your point."

Until that moment, he hadn't realized how closely he related

Mrs. Clyburn and Snow White in his mind. The resentment and the coercion underpinning the sex suddenly struck him as similar. That probably meant something, but he preferred not to examine what.

"I just wish I had found you sooner." Esmeralda met his eyes. "Like, in high school? I definitely would have kept you safe. …Even though we have separate lives and agreed *not* to keep each other safe. I would have made an exception."

His chest warmed in some weird way that he couldn't quite describe. It felt like a spark lighting in a very cold room. It made it easy to shove aside all the shit he didn't want to think about and focus on his beautiful mate. "Would you?"

"Yep. You probably took yourself too seriously, even back then. I could have shown you how to have way more fun. You needed that."

He needed *her*.

Trevelyan didn't like needing anyone, but there was no getting around the fact that Esmeralda was vital to him. It was astonishing how calm he felt in her presence. How *right* it all seemed. He was himself again, in a way he hadn't been since before the WUB Club.

The hungry, prowling dragon inside of him had never been so satiated. Restless anger that had been building for years was soothed by his mate. The dragon purred whenever she smiled. It wanted to rub up against her, basking in her scent.

"Of course, you were for *sure* the handsome, popular, cool guy in class." Esmeralda wrinkled her nose. "All the girls liked you, huh?"

He shrugged. No one ever liked him. He'd ruled his high school, but none of his terrified followers had *liked* Trevelyan. They'd just known better than to challenge him. If the witch had been there, she would have challenged him, though. And he would have been delighted by her fire.

"I wasn't very popular." She confided. "I was like those arty kids, who skip class, smoke hexed herbs, and do magical graffiti on walls. So, you would *not* have been thrilled to be seen with me."

It didn't matter which clique she belonged to, he would have joined it and seized control. Anyone who stood in his way would have fallen, screaming in agony and praying for death, until he held her in his clutches. Even as a boy, Trevelyan would have known his mate.

"And I'm *sure* you were a much better student than me." Esmeralda continued blithely. "You aced all the tests, am I right?"

"I was valedictorian."

She rolled her eyes. "Nerd."

"Some studious wizard-ling came within a few decimal points of me, so it was a close contest. ...Until he tragically disappeared." Esmeralda positively beamed at that sad news. "I got terrible grades, because I hated all the rules. I was kind of rebellious. I would have led you down the wrong academic path and wrecked your GPA."

The corner of his mouth curved at the idea of Esmeralda luring him into disrepute. "My darling, there has never been a time when *you'd* be the Bad influence in our relationship."

"Yeah, I would have been good for you, back then."

She was Good for him, now. Trevelyan had always scoffed at Goodness, until he'd been washed clean by Esmeralda's extraordinary magic. It was worrisome, how much he needed her. He'd never needed anything before, but now every single part of him needed his mate. He could *never* go back to not having her in his life

His contented thoughts grew darker.

"We would have flattened the school, flunked tons of subjects, and been expelled for making out in all the classrooms." She casually shrugged. "But it would've been a blast."

"You would have avoided me in high school." At least, she would have tried. "I'm not your type."

Esmeralda made a show of looking right, then left, then leaning closer to him. "Don't tell my True Love, because he's a little possessive," she stage-whispered, "but you're kinda *exactly* my type, dragon."

Her playful expression did crazy things to his heart. "You're kinda exactly my type, witch."

"I know." She grinned at him. "And I *totally* would have been voted prom queen, over that other girl. She would have tragically disappeared, right next to that wizard kid. You believe me?"

Trevelyan realized he had never in his whole life *liked* someone more than Esmeralda. Spending time with her was his favorite pastime. He couldn't stop his feelings for her. Couldn't deny them. Couldn't ignore them. They just *were* and nothing could change them. He needed the witch. It was simply a fact.

So what was he going to do about it?

The intensity of his emotions made him feel vulnerable. Why should he be the only one feeling vulnerable? Something would have to be done and only one something came to mind: Esmeralda needed to need him back.

"I believe you." He said quietly. "I quite honestly don't recall what that blonde even looked like. But I know no one could *ever* beat my mate."

"Damn straight." She watched him expectantly. "Your turn. Tell me something true, Trev."

He opened his mouth, but then that hideous blob of random parts she'd created the day before rolled past. It didn't seem to be sentient, but it lurched around like a drunken tumbleweed. It appeared to be a corkscrew, mixed with a sailboat, mixed with a cabbage.

"You never did explain to me exactly what that... *thing*... is."

She cringed a bit and it was adorable. "A rog." She muttered.

"A rog? What in the frozen-hells is a rog?"

"That is a rog." She waved a frustrated hand at it. "I have no idea why my magic created it. I have no idea why my magic does *anything*. You know that."

"Your magic is level six. Nothing it does happens by chance."

"Tell that to the rog."

Trevelyan stared at the glob of weirdness for a long minute and then his head tilted to one side. "Cabbage." He whispered. "Part of it is a cabbage."

"And part of it's a frigging sailboat."

"A ship." He slowly nodded and then pointed to his own chest. "And I'm a king, now." He looked at Esmeralda's boots. She was still wearing the damn things, even with her prom dress.

She loved them. "Shoes." He glanced over to the open window, where the hogs were playing outside on the lawn. "A pig with wings."

"What in the world are you talking about?"

"Your magic is tuning towards my magic." He should have realized it before. They were True Loves. Mates. "It's trying to help me."

"With a rog and my favorite boots?"

"With the spell." He met her eyes, feeling slightly dazed. "The spell the Queen of Clubs wants. The ingredients are almost all here. A ship, beloved shoes, three pig feathers, one large cabbage... If a king mixes them together in boiling salt water -- and adds the final, impossible piece-- the four tiaras of Wonderland will be united into one all-ruling crown."

"Do I even want to know what the impossible piece is?"

"Ceiling wax." He told her without hesitation. "It doesn't exist."

"Sealing wax exists. Old time-y people, like in Nottingham, seal envelopes with it. I'm sure we can find it in a craft store. Have you looked online?"

"No. *Ceiling* wax. With a C."

Esmeralda looked baffled.

"Lyon N. Unicorn misspelled the word. That's what I discovered, back in the WUB Club. It's why Snow White was after me." Trevelyan had died in some other timeline to keep that information secret, but relaying it all to Esmeralda felt natural. It felt right. "The wizard's typo is why no one can ever cast the spell. The final ingredient is always wrong, because no one is using *ceiling* wax."

"Oh." Her eyes traveled upward. "Who would want to wax a ceiling?"

"Nobody. Hence, the whole spell is impossible."

"Well, nothing's impossible in Wonderland, right?" She gave another shrug. "The magic around here likes things all topsy-turvy. Get a can of floor wax and turn it upside down. That's probably all it will take, in this dumb place."

Trevelyan's eyes widened at that blasé suggestion.

"Or *don't* do that, actually." Esmeralda continued. "I've got shit to do this week and I'd rather the world not end. My liquid gold nail polish isn't going to market itself... Crap." She sighed, because Trevelyan was already scrounging around in cabinets. He began tossing everything from under the sink, searching for a can of floor wax. There had to be one. Maybe there was a supply closet someplace?

"I don't even think you *should* cast the spell." Esmeralda complained. "Didn't you say it would end all of existence?"

"Only in the wrong hands..."

"Which yours almost certainly *are*."

"...And only potentially." He moved onto a different cabinet. "I think I can avoid existence ending."

"Still not filling me with confidence."

"This is going to work, Ez. I *believe* it."

He really did.

The next can Trevelyan grabbed was floor wax and he *knew* this was the answer. Casually using magic, he swept up the other ingredients.

Out on the lawn, the flying pig looked around in confusion as three of his feathers went soaring through the kitchen window without him attached. Esmeralda gasped like Trevelyan was a brute, even though the hog was perfectly fine. Trevelyan hadn't harmed the little guy.

"I'll make it up to him." Trevelyan promised. "Double apples for his breakfast." He dumped all the ingredients into one of the empty pots that Esmeralda used for mixing her nail polish.

"Do not mess up my best cauldron with that gunk..." She trailed off with a jolt as Trevelyan set it all on fire. "Poor rog." She *tsk*ed, as it was incinerated.

"I need your shoes next, darling.'

"Dream the hell on." She scoffed.

"We need them to take over Wonderland. Your shoes for an imperial crown. It's a fair trade."

"They're my favorite boots!"

"I'll get you a hundred more pair."

She pouted for a beat. "I want a record store."

"You're a queen, on her way to being an empress. What are you going to do with a record store?"

"I don't know. I just want one."

Well, whatever his mate wanted she should have. "Alright, then. I'll get you one of those, too."

"When?"

"Tomorrow?"

"You'll get me a record store *tomorrow?* You promise?"

"Yes, I promise." He'd figure out how to make that happen. How hard could it be?

Muttering curses in some witchy language he didn't speak, she reluctantly unzipped her boots. "Fine, but I hate you, right now." She threw them at his head, with a bit more force than necessary. "Why are we even doing this, when we don't have the other three tiaras, yet?"

"Because, I'm going to seal the spell inside of you." He tossed her boots into the caldron, ignoring her exaggerated wince. "Then, when the time comes, the tiaras will automatically unite on your head," he snapped his fingers, "and we win the game."

"I do like to win." Esmeralda admitted with grudging interest in the complicated magic swirling before her. "Do you have enough power to complete a spell this big, right now?"

"Not on my own, but your magic is supporting mine."

He wasn't sure how that was possible, but he felt it happening. The witch's strange, but familiar energy was helping him with this spell. It wanted him to succeed. And their powers were so close in color that they almost... That if he just focused, he could *almost*...

Esmeralda kept talking and his half-formed thoughts were lost. "Maybe we could do something safer. Like magic those brilligs of yours here to teleport us out."

"Even if I could get them here, which I can't, chances are they'd just get locked in, too. Then, they'd eat us."

"Eat us?" Her brow furrowed. "I saw some nature documentary about those weird things. Weird people keep them as weird pets. It didn't mention anything about them eating any owners."

"Well, it's not something the breeders advertise, but brilligs feed on rotting corpses. Sometimes they get hungry and *make* a rotting corpse for a snack." Trevelyan shook his head in exasperated affection. "Little scamps."

"Riiiight." Esmeralda drew out the word. "We'll just stick to *this* spell, then." She paused, watching him work. "You're *sure* it won't kill me and end all of existence?"

"I'm sure it won't kill you. I would never risk that."

She heard the evasion in his answer. "We *exist*, Trev. If you doom all of existence, it won't be great for me and you."

"Oh, I have enough power to shield us. It's only everyone else who will perish."

One blonde eyebrow arched at his flippant reply.

Trevelyan hesitated, trying to find the words to express his odd certainty. The only thing that came to mind was the truth. With Esmeralda, it always seemed easier to just tell the truth. It was very strange. "Ez, this spell... From the first moment I heard of it, I knew it was important. I knew I needed to solve the puzzle of it. I knew it was supposed to be," he lifted a shoulder, "mine."

Her expression changed, like she heard his sincerity.

"This spell was meant for me." Trevelyan had never been more sure of anything. "It will work, if I cast it. I promise you."

Esmeralda gazed up at him. "Okay." She said simply.

Trevelyan smiled. "That was shockingly easy. I think you're a little bit sweet on me, witch."

"Fuck yourself with a blender, Trev."

He chuckled and grimaced at the same time at that gruesome mental picture. "Ouch. Maybe you *are* the Bad influence in our relationship." Twisting his wrist, he inverted the floor wax. He already knew what would happen next.

He *believed* it.

The label on the can changed, the upside-down letters bobbing around and rearranging themselves. Now they were right-side up and read "Ceiling Wax."

Trevelyan smiled. "Fourth impossible thing." He told Esmeralda proudly and tossed the can of ceiling wax into the cauldron, as well.

Instantly, the flames changed color, burning white hot. The enchanted fire consumed everything in the pot, distilling it into pure magic.

Esmeralda lifted a hand to shield her eyes from the brightness of it. "Now what?"

"Now..." Trevelyan slowly closed his hand and the flames shrank down into a ball. "I'm going to put the spell right inside your Good little heart, where no one else will be able to access it."

"If it's going to hurt, I'd just as soon skip it."

Green eyes met hers. "I'll never hurt you." It was a promise to his mate and he meant it a thousand percent.

She nodded, trusting the greatest villain in the world. "Alright, then. Spell me."

Trevelyan felt a surge a pleasure at her faith in him. He waved a hand, manipulating the ball of magic and *poof*. It blinked away, sealed onto Esmeralda's beating heart.

Instantly, he felt relieved.

Taking over Wonderland was a worthy goal, but the spell was also an insurance policy. That was what he *really* cared about. The Queen of Clubs couldn't get the Heart tiara without beheading Esmeralda. That had been extremely concerning, because Trevelyan was an egomaniacal evildoer. He knew *exactly* what he would do in the Queen of Clubs' place. He'd send another army to decapitate the witch. For a villain, it just made sense.

But now the Queen of Clubs was checkmated. She couldn't get the spell if Esmeralda's heart stopped, so loping off her newly-blonde head was a lousy idea. The tiara was useless without the spell... and the spell was useless without the tiara. It was lose/lose for the Queen of Clubs. The predicament would, at the very least, stay that bitch's hand, if she came after Esmeralda, again.

Trevelyan loved plans that benefited him and fucked with his enemies.

Esmeralda looked down at her chest and then back up at him. "I don't feel any different. Are you positive it worked?"

"It worked. You don't feel it, because our magic blends together."

She nodded, like that was perfectly normal. It *wasn't* normal. He'd been serious the night before. It was impossible for high level powers to meld. Even the sparks of connection he felt with the witch's magic were rule-breaking.

Fortunately, Trevelyan loved breaking rules and Esmeralda hated following them. It was no wonder nothing had been normal since they'd met. He accepted their connected magic as par for the course. He couldn't explain it, but it didn't worry him. In fact, he quite liked it. It made him feel closer to his mate. No one else could ever touch him as deeply as she did and vice versa. They were made for each other.

"The Queen of Clubs will have felt that spell being cast." He theorized with cheerful unconcern. The woman held all the other tiaras. It was bound to reverberate through them. "It's going to enrage her." He smirked. "Such a pity."

"Well, maybe we've pissed off a villainous kidnapper, who wants us dead. But, you didn't end existence and it's not raining." Esmeralda winked at him. "So, things could be worse."

Trevelyan *so* enjoyed her Badness. He crossed to her. "Let's go have sex, again." He suggested, his mind going to other, funner matters. "We'll pretend we're in high school and I'm about to get you pregnant right before prom. Whichever one of us is leading the other astray, it will be incredibly scandalous."

"Okay." She agreed eagerly and then paused, like something had just occurred to her. Her forehead wrinkled in worry. "I'm having a really good time with you today."

"We've been having a very *Bad* time today, darling. Six very Bad times and counting."

"No, I mean, I haven't been thinking about Marrok enough." Trevelyan shuddered in disgust. "I should hope the hell you're *not* thinking of the wolf when we're in bed."

"But he's in trouble and I'm having fun with you." She seemed pensive, like she still wanted to help that mangy moron. "I wish I had better magic."

"There is no magic better than yours. Believe me. I would know."

No one else in the world could come *close* to Esmeralda's abilities. Once she learned to trust her powers, the woman would be unstoppable. Trevelyan was getting aroused just thinking about the chaos she'd create.

She didn't seem convinced.

"Marrok will be fine." Trevelyan persisted, wishing she'd just forget about that traitorous jackass. "The wolf is a survivor." Given his personality, he had to be or he would have been picked off long ago. Trevelyan had no doubt that he'd figure something out. "*I'm* the one in real danger, around here. If we don't get back into bed soon, I might die."

That dramatic lament earned him an exasperated snort. "I haven't even finished my sandwich."

Trevelyan quickly grabbed it with one hand and her with the other, eager to get moving. He pulled her into his arms, her back to his front and held up the sandwich. "Hurry." He prompted and pressed against her lovely ass so she could feel the direness of the situation. "My life depends on it."

"You're insatiable."

"You're irresistible."

"Crap. That line actually just worked on me. I'm embarrassed for both of us." She casually took a bite out of the sandwich, as he continued to hold it.

Oh, he *liked* that.

It was strange how much he liked it. Esmeralda might not "believe in him," but she trusted him to perform spells on her and ate the food he'd prepared. Trevelyan wouldn't have let an evil dragon perform mysterious spells on him or give him food. It was insane.

But he liked that Esmeralda let him do it, anyway.

He kissed the side of her blonde head, no longer in a rush to get upstairs. It was important that he feed her. Never in his life had he ever taken care of another person, but this was his mate. Trevelyan's free palm slid around her body to flatten against her heart. Right where he'd pressed his handprint after they'd had sex.

Just his.

She contentedly ate her sandwich from his hand, leaning against him like it was no big deal. "If you could perform *one* spell that you can't do now, what would it be?" She asked, as if she was still brooding about her magic.

"I can do every spell."

She flashed him a skeptical look.

"I can do all the ones *worth* doing." He allowed. "I can perform every type of wicked Badness there is."

"So, what *Good* magic would you do, if you suddenly could? Don't stop to think about the answer. Your first impulse is always right."

A love spell.

The thought flittered through his mind and he frowned. Love spells were Good, at least the harmless, protective kind that had popped into his head. He wanted his magic wrapped all around her, keeping her safe. That part was easy enough. But he also wanted her to feel happy and needed. He wanted to always be linked to her, so neither of them would ever be alone.

"I don't want to cast any Good spells." He muttered, instead of saying any of that.

Esmeralda took another bite of sandwich. "If I could only do one spell, I would blast through the force field around the castle." She decided with a thoughtful nod. She shot another doubtful glance his way. "Are you *sure* you can't do that, yet?"

He was sure he'd used all his magical reserves on far more important things. "I'm sure."

One eyebrow arched.

Trevelyan smiled blandly. "Can we have sex, now?"

"I have no idea why I like you so much."

Neither did he, but he figured it was only fair, considering how much he liked her. Really, the situation should be even *more* fair. Esmeralda should like him *best*. Best of everyone. He liked her best of everyone, after all.

Inside his mind, a new goal took shape. Or maybe it had been lurking there all along and now he was willing to examine it. She had to decide on him as her mate. That would be the *most* fair. It was the only way to ensure she needed him the way he needed her. He should have all of her. Every piece. Why should he have to settle for less than everything? He was a dragon! Trevelyan nuzzled the curve of her neck, breathing in her scent and silently plotting.

He had to convince Esmeralda to keep him.

CHAPTER TWENTY

Pick your perfect nail polish from our unlimited selection!
Ex Blood: It's like an Ox Blood burgundy shade, only siphoned from someone far more deserving of pain.
(Requires extra shipping time and the name of the former loved one you want drained.)

Happily Ever Witch Cosmetics Website

The Club Castle

It was an awkward date, by any measure. Things always got weird when a girl's parents came along.
The Mad Hatter was sitting at one end of a long table, in the Club Palace's onyx-black-and-icy-white dining room. He was drinking tea like it was hard liquor and putting globs of mustard on his jam sandwich.
"Jam yesterday and jam tomorrow, but *never* jam today." He announced to one and all, even though he was very obviously eating jam today.
Everyone else at the table was having Mock Turtle soup, as an appetizer. It grossed Bluebeard out, since his uncle had been a Mock Turtle. But Dijon mustard mixed with strawberry jam grossed him out even more, so he was swallowing the kind-of-cannibal-ish soup and keeping his complaints to himself.
Snow White was sitting next to her father. She was all decked out in a blue and yellow dress, her black hair curled into bouncy ringlets. Some might say the style was a little young for her, but Bluebeard was of the opinion that a woman could wear whatever she wanted to on a date. Her clothes were all gonna

come off anyway, so who gave a shit?

The Queen of Clubs sat at the other end of the table, angrily flipping through medical text books on witches. Because... sure. That made as much sense as anything else that had happened recently.

The Queen was in a rotten mood. Some sort of big spell had been cast earlier. Even Bluebeard had felt it. Whatever it was, it had *really* pissed her off. Since she had magical powers and a short temper, Bluebeard was doing his very best to stay inconspicuous. Let the wolf take all of bitch-mom's incoming fire. It was *his* fault they were in this mess, after all.

For her part, Snow White didn't notice the tension. She was too googly-eyed over Marrok Wolf to notice much of anything. The girl was totally enamored of his golden-boy, sports-star beauty. Her chin rested in her palm, her dreamy gaze fixed on the big, stupid dummy, like she believed he *wanted* to be at the table. Like maybe he'd *chosen* to wear that fussy tuxedo and top hat. Like he *hadn't* been abducted by her lunatic parents, and dumped in a dungeon, and then dragged to this dinner in magic-inhibiting shackles.

Like he didn't keep talking about his damn wife!

Bluebeard had met Marrok years before, when they'd both been in prison. Sooner or later, every villain worth his salt had washed up in the WUB Club. Bluebeard thought of his brief incarceration as a badge of honor, even though he'd only been in for a tax misunderstanding. Turned out, you could only jointly file with one wife at a time. But, anyway, the wolf had once been charming and clever. Now...? Not so much.

Marrok was arguing with Snow White, putting no effort at all into being a pleasant date. He wouldn't even shut up and focus on his soup, like Bluebeard was doing.

Granted, it was impossible for the wolf to pick up his spoon. There were chains cinched around Marrok's torso, tethering him to the chair and keeping his arms at his side. But he could still smile or something. It would seriously help the romance vibe. The fuckwit was going to get Bluebeard killed if he kept this up. Plus, he was ruining the first course.

"*Scarlett* is my True Love. There is nothing you can do to

change that." Marrok told Snow White, for the tenth time in as many minutes. "I am never going to be with you, because I'm married to *her*. Do you understand?"

Snow White nodded, without a drop of comprehension. "You have *such* pretty eyes." She told him sincerely.

Marrok closed said eyes in frustration. "You're an abusive maniac, who sexually harassed me when I was in prison." He reminded her through clenched teeth. "You did worse to other men. I don't care if you have your memory or not: *I don't like you*."

"We should go on a picnic tomorrow, out in the woods." She suggested guilelessly. "You would look so handsome in the snooooow..." She drew out the word in a baby-talk voice, her expression resembling an eleven year old girl who was looking at pictures of adorable kittens in bonnets.

Marrok's jaw ticked.

The Queen of Clubs sighed in impatience.

The Mad Hatter stood up, a mustard jar in one hand and a jelly pot in the other. "Move down!" He called, for no reason.

The Queen of Clubs and Snow White promptly got to their feet, grabbing their soup bowls. Bluebeard wasn't an idiot, so he did too. Everyone moved one seat clockwise and then sat down, again. Except Marrok, because he was chained in place and being a dick.

"I'm not going on a picnic with you." He told Snow White, who was now sitting to his right.

"It's so important that married people go on dates. It'll keep the romance alive between us."

"There is no romance between us and I'm not married to you. I'm married to Scarlett. My *wife*. You've met her. Red hair. Blue eyes. Pushed you into a lake."

"We should name our babies Marrok Jr." Snow White decided with a sudden gasp of inspiration. "All of them."

The wolf had had enough. He turned his head away from Snow White, pointedly ignoring her latest gibberish.

The Queen of Clubs' gaze cut over to Bluebeard. "This is the best you could do?" She challenged icily. "My beloved stepdaughter wants this man, so she'll have him, no matter

what it takes. Why is he not cooperating?"
Bluebeard slumped down in his chair. "I'm trying." He whined. "Wolves are crazy devoted to their True Loves and his connection to Scarlett goes even deeper than most."
"Try... harder..." Her words were spaced out like bullets.
A very young maid scampered into the room, doing her best to be unseen by her employers. It was hopeless.
The Mad Hatter's head whipped towards her, like he scented some new delicacy. Crap. He was going to suck the girl dry of Goodness and it was going to be gross. Bluebeard squeezed his eyes shut, not wanting to have his appetite ruined. The soup was terrible, but there was still hope that the entrée might be better. He couldn't risk his stomach heaving.
"What are you...? Holy *shit!*" Marrok exclaimed in horror.
There was a thump, as a body hit the floor.
Bluebeard opened one eye, checking to make sure the nasty part was over with. The maid was now a mummified corpse and the Mad Hatter was sucking on his fingers, satisfied with his snack. Considering where he was dining, Bluebeard was relieved it wasn't worse.
Marrok seemed jolted at the girl's death, his eyes staying on her body. Maybe he was finally realizing how seriously fucked-up this place was and he'd start behaving himself.
"Did you hear me?" Snow White asked Marrok in a louder tone, refusing to be ignored. She and her mother seemed unbothered by the murder. "I said we should name all our babies Marrok Jr."
The wolf didn't respond.
Snow White's lips formed into a pout.
"Move down!" The Mad Hatter called again.
Bluebeard sighed and trudged off to the next seat. Jesus, the meal was never going to end if they kept going round and round the damn table, every two minutes. Now, he was where Snow White had first sat, facing Marrok. The Mad Hatter was at the Queen of Clubs' original seat and the Queen was in the Hatter's old spot. It was just fucking strange.
"What's all this?" The Mad Hatter asked, spying the medical books piled around the Queen of Clubs' former chair.

"You know what it is." Her palpable frustration had found a new target. The Mad Hatter was stupid for drawing attention to himself. A smart man kept his mouth shut and his head down, when a woman was looking to blow her top. His many wives had taught Bluebeard that much. "I need to find a way to rip the heart out of that damn level six witch!"

Marrok's face snapped around, his gaze now on the Queen. The Queen of Clubs didn't notice. "Trevelyan put the spell on her *heart!*" She cried at the Mad Hatter. "I know he did. We all felt it. I have no idea how to get it off without another witch's help."

"Anna..."

She talked right over her husband, caught up in the melodrama of whatever-the-heck her problem was. "Dragons don't even care about their True Loves, but for some reason Trevelyan's thrown in with that little green bitch. He's protecting her!"

Marrok's jaw dropped.

"Esmeralda is nothing." The Mad Hatter soothed. Reasoning with her wouldn't make a bit of difference. Bluebeard could have told him as much. Once a woman got started, a wise man just nodded and apologized. "You said yourself she's just a pawn. I don't even play chess, but I know a queen can easily block a pawn."

She sniffed and didn't respond.

The Mad Hatter kept going, still vainly attempting to pacify her. "Esmeralda won't beat you, dragon or not. Even if her magic is fairest of them all --which it's surely, *surely* not-- she's too late! You've already claimed three of the tiaras."

"They're useless without the Heart Kingdom's." The Queen retorted. "I have to find a way to get the tiara *and* that damn spell. Only Trevelyan's rigged it, so I can't get one without destroying the other. He's helping her stay alive."

Bluebeard was following enough of the argument to know the frigging Green Dragon was somehow involved. Great. Trevelyan had a gift for making every situation worse. They'd done time together, too. Bluebeard had barely survived it.

"Trevelyan is too dangerous to keep alive. I told you that."

The Queen of Clubs drummed her fingernails on the tabletop,

disregarding her husband's I-told-yo-so-ing. "He's stymied me unless I find a way to rip out her heart, *while* keeping it beating, *and* beheading her at the same time!" She was fuming mad. The dragon did that to people. Their share circle therapy sessions had been the scariest time of Bluebeard's life. Maybe even beating this dinner party. "You know, you could be helping me, Hatty."

"I *am* helping you." He said around a mouthful of jam and mustard.

"How? You're supposed to be my king! We are a family of cooperation and fairness. The *white* side of the game!" She pointed towards the window. The huge checkerboard-ed Chess Tower was illuminated with spotlights, so everyone in the kingdom could read the time.

Not that Bluebeard had any clue how to read time on a chessboard.

The Mad Hatter's brow furrowed, as he studied the clock-that-wasn't-a-clock. "Huh." He said mildly. "I always thought we were the red pieces."

"Our daughter's name is Snow *White*." The Queen of Clubs reminded him with an impatient huff. "Like most of our kingdom is *white*. Like your hair is *white*."

"I'm not old." He interjected firmly, as if that was a vital fact to enter into the record. "It's the yeti genes that make my hair this color. The same with Snow's name. It's important to honor my yeti heritage."

The Mad Hatter was part yeti? Well, that explained the lack of table manners and the sucking people dry of magic.

"I hope the yetis don't attack our picnic." Snow White told Marrok. "Sometimes yetis attack people in the woods."

"That is a hurtful stereotype against my ancestors." The Mad Hatter objected. "And only sometimes true."

"I *said* 'sometimes,' Daddy! Marrok, tell him I said 'sometimes.'"

Marrok stayed quiet. He seemed to be thinking, which was probably Bad news.

The Queen of Clubs wasn't interested in justice for yetis. "Hatty, the Chess Tower only has white pieces left, except the red king and queen, and that horrible pawn." Her voice was strident. "You *made* the clock! How can you not know that?"

"I told you, I don't play chess." The Mad Hatter seemed to measure out the sixty-four squares of the chessboard with his hands. He moved his palms every-which-way and puzzled about something. "Strange that the other side is red. And Hearts' colors are pink and..."

The Queen of Clubs kept complaining, drowning him out. "You always do this. You always change the subject. Meanwhile, I've been doing research on witches' biology and it's very triggering to me. Do you have any idea how easily they can make reproductive choices? While I had to work *so hard* to become a mother..." She trailed off like it was all too much to talk about.

"The struggle just made you more determined to be the best mom in the world." The Mad Hatter assured her, his attention drawn by her unhappiness. He pulled his creepy eyes from the window and lost whatever train of thought he'd been trying to board. "And you *are* the best."

"You say that but no one appreciates me." She swept an all-encompassing palm around the table. "Not one of you understands all the work I do around here to keep this family happy."

Bluebeard did his best to look grateful for her sacrifices. He wasn't currently being blamed or beheaded, and he planned to keep it that way.

Marrok seemed riveted by the argument raging. His gaze went back and forth between his new in-laws, like he was memorizing details for their family Christmas letter.

Snow White didn't like the wolf's distraction. "How come you're not paying attention to me?" She whined. "You're my husband. You're supposed to be paying attention to me."

Marrok shot her an impatient look.

"Daddy!" Snow White wailed at the Mad Hatter. "Make him pay attention to me!"

"Talk to your mother." The Mad Hatter suggested.

"See?" The Queen of Clubs exclaimed triumphantly. "Everything *always* falls on a mother's shoulders."

The Mad Hatter rolled his spiraling eyes. "Because this boy is your project." He gestured towards Marrok. "I wanted her to marry William."

"William? The *lizard?* Are you out of your mind?"

"William's got style. This boy didn't even want to wear the top hat I found for him. I had to tape it onto his head." He pointed Marrok's way, aggrieved over the fashion slight. "I don't like him."

The Queen of Clubs didn't care. "Snow can do better than some social-climbing Tea-Partier. At least the wolf is famous. Having a famous son-in-law can only help our prestige as rulers of Wonderland. And he did break out of that prison, so he must have some hidden brains. And he's certainly handsome."

"*So* handsome." Snow White opined breathlessly.

"And Snow is very fond of him." The Queen of Clubs finished with a firm nod. "The wolf will do much better for her than *William*, for heaven's sake. Once he's leashed, everything will be fine."

Marrok joined the fray, his topaz eyes on Snow Witless' crown-wearing mama-bear. "Give it up. I'm not Prince Charming. She's not Cinderella." He jerked his reluctantly-top-hatted head towards Snow White. "And Bluebeard doesn't have Trevelyan's magic. I'm *never* going to think I'm in love with anyone, except my wife."

He had a point. Trevelyan was far more powerful than Bluebeard. The dragon had once enspelled Prince Charming to think he shared a True Love bond with the wrong girl. That was impressive. But, Bluebeard's magic was more hyper-specialized. Marriages were his forte and he could do exceptionally nuanced shit with them.

Bluebeard could convince Marrok that Snow White was his blushing bride. It would just take a little time. It would help if the wolf stopped fighting him.

And if Snow White wasn't such a frigging weirdo.

And if the Queen of Clubs wasn't making him so nervous with her cold stare and death threats.

And if the Mad Hatter stopped finger-painting with jam all over the tabletop. Damn it. If they had to switch seats again, Bluebeard was going to end up sitting there, sooner or later, and everything was going to be sticky.

The Queen of Clubs glowered at Marrok. "Do you have children?"

"Not yet."

"Then you can't possibly understand what it's like to be a parent. You can't understand the lengths we'll go to, to ensure our children are happy." Her ruby-red lips were flattened into a thin line of displeasure. "My daughter was *impaired*, because of you and your ugly stepsister of a wife."

Marrok's head tilted in a very dangerous way. "My wife is *not* ugly."

The Queen of Clubs ignored that opinion. "Snow White will always be like *this* now." She waved a hand at the girl's simpering smile. "Did you think you could just walk away after attacking my family? Altering our future, for your own selfish goals? Why should you get a happily ever after, when Snow White doesn't?"

"Because she's a desperate, delusional bitch, who no one sane will *ever* love." Marrok delivered that news with casual brutality. "…Just like her failure of a stepmom."

Bluebeard cringed a bit at the many layers of insult packed into so few words. His gaze slipped over to the undeniably *in*sane Mad Hatter, who was now adding mustard to his tea.

Deliberately offending Snow White's helicopter parents didn't seem like the best move, but then wolves were never known for making wise choices.

"Told ya I don't like him." The Mad Hatter chimed in smugly, stirring his Darjeeling and Dijon with his finger. "We should have gone with William."

A muscle jumped in the Queen of Clubs' cheek, her wrathful eyes on Marrok.

Marrok's answering smirk was all the arrogance in the world distilled into a facial gesture. Like the untouchable bully of your childhood, who'd just punched you while the teacher's back was turned, but somehow *you* were the one who got detention for disrupting class. It was a wonder he didn't get blasted to smithereens right then and there.

No way was Bluebeard going down with this sinking ship. "I can amp up the magic I'm hitting him with." He told the Queen of Clubs swiftly, wanting to avoid a bloodbath. "It might fry his brain, but I can convince him he's married to her. I swear."

She flashed him a dark look. "Do it, then."

Lupine gold eyes swung Bluebeard's way. "You're not strong enough to enspell me." Marrok sounded contemptuous of the very idea. "You're a third-rate nobody, from nowhere. You've never been on a date with a cognizant woman. You can't do *shit*."

Bluebeard stifled a wince, as the barbs hit home. All his life, showier villains had looked down on him for his fashion choices, and strange abilities, and hypnotized girlfriends. Anger took hold and he bounded to his feet. "You son of a bitch! At least I'm not tied to a fucking chair! Look at where you are, right now, wolf! You really think you're better than me?"

"I *am* better than you." Marrok leaned closer to him, his smile confident and cutting. Filled with all the arrogance of someone who'd been born beautiful and talented and special, it was downright taunting in its superiority. "Even *you* know it."

Bluebeard snapped. Digging deep, he called on every drop of magic he possessed. Every ounce of power. Every skill he'd ever developed. And then he slammed the full force of his energy into Marrok's mocking face.

The explosion of magic knocked the wolf backwards, his chair hitting the floor. Marrok let out a grunt of pain as he fell, unable to brace for impact with his arms tied. He landed on the ground. *Hard*. The taped-on top hat came loose and tumbled from his head, rolling along on its brim. The condescending bastard finally stopped talking.

Bluebeard stood there, breathing hard and impressed with himself.

The Queen of Clubs gave a satisfied sniff.

The Mad Hatter ate his teacup.

Snow White cried out in alarm and rushed to the wolf's side. Falling to her knees, she ran a hand over his golden hair. "My handsome husband!"

Marrok stared up at her in confusion. ...Then something began to happen to his features. Bluebeard's magic took hold and the wolf's expression softened. Tenderness replaced the anger and derision. He smiled at Snow White, like this was the someday when all his dreams came true. "My beautiful wife."

CHAPTER TWENTY-ONE

Pick your perfect nail polish from our unlimited selection!
Happy Ending Emerald: SOLD OUT!- Sorry. Looks like everybody got
a bottle of this one except you.

Happily Ever Witch Cosmetics Website

The Heart Castle

Esmeralda had always been a morning person.
She did her best thinking as a new day was born. It was when all her shiniest nail polishes got mixed and her greatest recipes got written. If inspiration was going to strike, it usually struck Esmeralda around six a.m.
The day before, the Queen of Clubs' army had attacked. That had interrupted Esmeralda's prime contemplation time. This morning was different, though. With Trevelyan sprawled out asleep in their bed and the rain falling outside the only sound for miles, Esmeralda had plenty of time to focus.
And all her focus was on the creepy, heart-shaped mirror. Trevelyan had moved it, because she didn't want it in the royal bedroom. Now she sat cross-legged on the floor of the hallway, staring into its silver depths. Her head tilted, watching her slightly-wrong reflection tilt its head, as well. There was a lag to the movement, like the looking glass took a moment to catch up. The heart-patterned wallpaper on the wall behind her wasn't exactly right, either. In the mirror, the tiny red hearts weren't just hearts. They were also spades and diamonds and clubs.
Esmeralda had known something was off about the damn thing, from the first time she'd seen it. Now she knew what it was.

Inspiration had struck her in the morning light, as it usually did when she was onto something *big*. The mirror wasn't just a mirror.

It was also a rabbit hole.

A portal, just like the vortex that had brought her to Wonderland. She recognized it, because she'd fallen through one, back in the Northlands. A girl always remembered her first inter-dimensional kidnapping. Someone had tamed this rabbit hole, harnessing it into a gilded frame and turning it into a looking glass. Its magic was controlled. If you went through it, you could direct where you came out. It was a gateway to other lands.

This was how she could get to Marrok. Every magical cell in her body told her so.

Her phone *bing*-ed with a text message. Esmeralda glanced down at it. She'd known Scarlett would call. Maybe her magic was getting stronger, because she'd been waiting.

Trystan Airbourne and Sir Galahad will be there in half an hour.
Esmeralda typed out a reply. *Good. I'm going for Marrok.*
No. The spell around the Heart Castle is too strong. I've got every magical Baddie in the Enchanted Forest looking into it and they all agree it won't work.
It WILL work.
Wonderland is still in lockdown. Galahad and Trystan think the confinement spell will affect them, too. So, the Club Kingdom is a COMPLETE no go.

Esmeralda made a face. Typical. Wonderland always had to be a pain in the ass. She glanced up at the ceiling. "Come on... I know you like chaos, but you're being unfair."

Galahad & Trystan CAN get inside the Heart Palace. Scarlett said in a new text bubble. *They won't be able to leave the grounds and get through that force field, but they can rescue YOU.*

Esmeralda glanced at the ceiling, again. "Better." She praised and then typed out a response to Letty. *I know a way out of this castle, but only using magic. Do they have any?*
No, they don't. And I don't want you using yours!!

That meant Trystan and Galahad wouldn't be able to come with her to the Club Kingdom as backup. Alright... Well, Esmeralda would just do it by herself. She was great at doing things by herself.

EZ!! You're not listening! You're going to end up dead. Come home. We'll figure out a new plan to get Marrok.
Snow White has him.

There was a long moment of silence from Scarlett's end, like she was trying to process that news. *I should have killed that bitch, when we had the chance.* She finally typed and there was palpable hatred in every word.

NOW is the chance. That psycho needs to die, for what she did to Trev. We can't leave Marrok with her, when I have a route to him.

Silence.

Scarlett was usually the one talking people into crazy schemes, but where her husband's safety was concerned, she was down for any idea that even had a chance of working. Esmeralda already knew it, because she'd feel the same way if Trevelyan was kidnapped by a madwoman.

Esmeralda's fingers flew over the keys, trying to tip the scales. *I can make it work, Letty. You KNOW I can.*

More silence.

Will the dragon go with you? Scarlett finally asked, deciding to trust her.

Esmeralda smiled at the sisterly show of faith. *No. I want Sir Galahad to bring Trev out of Wonderland.*

He'll leave you there?

Sure. Trev's not an idiot. The Queen of Clubs is still after him.

Even more silence.

Esmeralda kept going. *I'll get Marrok and then you can send Galahad back for me later.*

Your True Love is really letting you do this alone? ...Or are you just not telling Trevelyan your plan?

I've told that jackass what he needs to know. Don't worry. I'll call when I have your handsome husband.

Esmeralda shut off the phone, before Scarlett could respond with a long lecture.

"Your majesty!" Someone suddenly called. "Hello? Might I talk to you for a moment, before you go?"

It took Esmeralda a second to realize the voice belonged to the Cheshire Carpet. Frowning, she got to her feet and poked her head into the bedroom next to the royal suite. Sure enough the pink-and-purple rug was wide awake.

"Yeah?" She asked cautiously.

The Cheshire Carpet's multitude of mouths appeared and vanished, as it talked. "Are you ready to play chess, now? You did promise me a game today."

Crap. She *had* promised it. It had seemed lonely and she'd been in the middle of seducing Trevelyan. She'd forgotten all about it. "Um, to be honest, I don't really know how to play chess. So, I doubt I'd be much of an opponent for you."

"Oh, I don't know how to play either." It answered cheerily. "The rules are confusing, so I just make them up as I go."

That was how Esmeralda played most games, too. "I hate rules." She agreed.

"Shall we try a game, then?"

"I'm right in the middle of..."

"I'll be white." It interrupted. "White goes first." A chessboard appeared on a table that *also* appeared. "The goal is to move your pieces as quickly as you can."

Esmeralda debated the wisdom of pissing off a magic carpet. She wasn't clear what it could do, magically speaking, and she didn't need it causing her problems today. She was already dealing with enough trouble. And she *had* promised it.

"Can we do this later, maybe?" She tried.

"Pawns are useless." The rug said, by way of an answer. "I like moving my queen the best." The white queen slid across the board, with no one and nothing touching it. "You can win in eight moves, if you play your queen right. Won't take a moment."

Esmeralda reluctantly went into the room and moved the red queen. Eight turns shouldn't take long. She had no idea how to use the piece, so she just dropped it in the middle of the board. "This okay?"

"That's four spaces." The rug chided. "A queen only moves one at a time."

She was pretty sure that wasn't so. "You said we were making up our own rules." She argued.

"But we're not *savages*. Now I get to move my queen three more times to catch up."

Esmeralda rolled her eyes, as the white queen zigzagged around the board. For a creature with no hands or head, the Cheshire Carpet was agile. "What's the point of this?" She asked, as the rug cheated horribly.

"To win, of course. Or, contrariwise, to make others lose." The rug laughed. "If you get all the way across the board, you're *double* queen. And everything counts double-y double today, because it's Tove."

"Today's that weird extra day, added into the middle of the week?"

"Oh yes! It's always a merry time. Especially this year, with the empress being crowned."

Esmeralda remembered seeing a little crown drawn on Tove's calendar date, down in the lab. Shit. "The empress is supposed to be crowned on Tove? Great. That probably makes the Queen of Clubs even more dangerous than usual."

"I don't like the Queen of Clubs."

"Because she's a kidnapping murderer, trying to take over the kingdom?"

"Because she doesn't know how to play chess properly. She won't do for an empress, at all." The white queen hopped off the board and bounced in a semi-circle around the table top to reenter the game on the other side. "Checkmate!"

Esmeralda frowned down at the arrangement of pieces. Some of them were mismatched tokens from other board games and one was a salt shaker. She didn't see how any of them had boxed in her king, since she didn't have one. "This is checkmate?"

"No, I just like saying it."

"Right. Well, that was about seven moves, so now *I* get to catch up."

The two of them randomly jumped the pieces around, talking about nonsense and nail polish for a few minutes. The Cheshire Carpet didn't have hands, but it was sure a manicure would look just lovely on its fringed tassels. Esmeralda promised to work on a special formula. The Cheshire Carpet requested pink. Esmeralda was actually having a good time, but she needed to get on with her wolf rescue. "Double queen." She slammed the red queen down on the far side of the board, pleased with her victory.

"Doubly-double." The Cheshire Carpet reminded her with a happy sigh. "I just love Tove." The chessboard vanished again. "That was fun! We should play again, when you get back from the Club Kingdom. Next time, we'll use a properly colored board. Pink and red."

"Those are the Heart Kingdom's colors." Esmeralda recalled the rug telling her all about it.

"Exactly! I'll be the pink side and you can stay red. The Heart Queen should always be red. Coincidently, I far prefer pink. Or purple! What do you think of a pink-and-purple chess set?"

"We'll play whatever colors you'd like, when I get back." Esmeralda paused. "*If* I get back."

"Oh, you'll be back. I can tell you're ever-so-much harder to behead than the usual Heart Queens. I've been in this house since the Carpenter built it, you know. No one understands Wonderland better than me. I've seen many a wannabe empress, in my time. You're the only one who may have a chance at unifying the crown."

That was gratifying to hear. "Any tips on how?"

"Try to be less like you and more like Cinderella."

"Right." Esmeralda said again and headed for the door. Letty's depraved nutcase of a stepsister was *just* who she wanted to emulate. Cinderella had wanted to enslave the Westlands, for God's sake! And her manicure was always horrible. "I'll be going, now."

"Happy Tove!" The Cheshire Carpet called after her. "Remember the eighth square."

Esmeralda wasn't even going to bother asking about the eighth square. She'd just get a twenty minute gibberish lesson. She needed to get the hell out of the Heart Kingdom, before Sir Galahad showed up. She had a feeling Camelot's best knight ever was not going to like her taking off on her own. It went against his whole "hero" mandate.

But she wasn't leaving without one last look at Trevelyan. Taking a quick detour, she headed back into the royal suite and stared down at her True Love for a moment. Trevelyan was lying on his stomach, naked and relaxed and beautiful. Esmeralda let out a sigh, irresistibly drawn to the big idiot. The night before, he'd been playing with her still-blonde tresses, while they talked in bed. "I miss the black." He'd told her, curling one long strand around his thumb.

"I'm keeping this hair color, for now." Esmeralda liked to change her appearance often, so the platinum was working for her. Glamours were her favorite kind of magic, because she felt like she had total control over them. "I might go red next. Maybe blue."

"Green." He'd suggested with a persuasive nod.

That had amused her. "Green." She'd agreed. She'd been lying on his chest and she'd tilted her head to kiss one of the tattoos. Watching the inked flames move fascinated her. "You still owe me a turn, by the way. You never did tell me something true, Trev."

"Alright. Well, I think your magic is working without your knowledge."

"Yeah?"

"Yes, I think when we have sex your powers are," he'd made a vague gesture with his free hand, "somehow making it all *more*. It's incredible! I have no idea how you're accomplishing it, but don't ever stop."

Esmeralda had stacked her chin on her hands, so she could look into his face. "Interesting." She'd tried to keep her voice as neutral as possible. "You really think this is 'more' than usual sex?"

"Of course! I've had a lot of usual sex and this isn't anything like that. This is *much* more. This is..." Dark eyebrows had suddenly slammed together. "Wait, you don't think it's more than usual sex?"

She'd lifted a shoulder. "I mean, it's *fine*... I guess." She'd given his chest a consoling pat. "You're trying your best. That's all that really matters."

His head had tilted.

"Don't worry. I'll teach you." Esmeralda had tried very hard to keep a straight face when she offered that assurance, but he'd caught on to her teasing.

Trevelyan's chuckle had been dark and smoky. "We should practice more, then. See if I can't move things beyond 'fine.'" He'd leaned up, like he was instinctively going to kiss her and her heartbeat had accelerated. Then, he'd suddenly pulled back, recalling she'd told him not to. "Sorry. I..." He'd frowned and shook his head. "You believe me, though? About your magic making sex between us *more*."

"I can certainly see how you'd think that." She'd murmured, instead of answering directly. Because *of course* Trevelyan would look for magic in something that was far simpler. Still, no one could learn by somebody else just giving them all the homework solutions. They needed to solve the problems themselves.

...A hint now and then wouldn't hurt, though.

"Hey, why do you think the dragons are always so close to extinction?" She'd asked in a "gosh-I'm-just-musing-about-life" tone. "You're one of the most powerful species in the world."

"We're *the* most powerful." He'd corrected instantly.

"Okay. So, why do the super-powerful dragons keep getting enslaved by weaker groups?"

"We're outnumbered by our enemies. If the forces were equal, there would be no contest."

"Too bad there isn't a way to fix that. Like... for instance... if you guys sometimes helped other people, they might be willing to help you, too. With allies, you'd be even stronger."

He'd made a face, completely missing the point. "I'm not helping any other dragons and I know those assholes wouldn't help me. You recall Haigha trying to kill us, don't you?"

"Well, maybe some *different* allies would be less asshole-ish."

"Or maybe allies would all turn on me." Green eyes had narrowed in brooding thought. "Just like Marrok did."

"Trev..."

"I don't want to talk about him." He'd interrupted, as if suddenly guessing where this conversation was going. "The wolf is the whole reason we're here. You realize that? He put me in a mystical coma and *that* made it easy for the Queen of Clubs to kidnap me to Wonderland. It's all his fault."

"I'm pretty sure you were threatening Letty, when he put you in that coma."

Trevelyan had scoffed, like that was silly to even mention. "She was just a way to get to Marrok. If I'd wanted to *actually* hurt Scarlett, I would have actually hurt Scarlett. I didn't."

Esmeralda had met his gaze, because it was important that he hear this part. "I love Letty. She is my chosen sister."

"I didn't hurt her." He'd insisted.

"You *threatened* her. I can't have that. You wouldn't like it, if I threatened Maid Marion."

He'd opened his mouth. Then closed it again, like he was considering her words. "Alright." He'd conceded.

"You and Marrok have a history together. I get it." Esmeralda had stressed, in case he was working some angle she'd missed. "But Letty is not part of that mess. *Do not threaten her.* Not for any reason. Promise me. One of those thousand-percent dragon promises."

"I won't threaten her. I promise you a thousand percent. She is in no danger from me. I think I could like Scarlett, as a matter of fact. If you wish, I'll tell her so myself, at Marrok's funeral."

Esmeralda had scowled at him. "That's not funny."

Trevelyan's mouth had twitched. "It's a *little* funny."

"Someday, being so terrible is going to get you into trouble that you can't get out of on your own. Having allies would help you survive. That would be cool, right?" She'd tried one more time to get him to see reason. "If you don't like dragons or wolves, you can expand your horizons to some other species."

Like maybe a witch.

Trevelyan grunted, missing the subtext. "I don't like any other species, either."

Esmeralda had let it drop, at that point. Nothing she could've said would sway him and she didn't want to argue in circles. Sooner or later, he'd realize why their sex was "more" and why their magic linked up so perfectly. Until then, she'd have to do this on her own.

Gazing down at him in the early morning light, Esmeralda found herself smiling.

Wild things wanted death or freedom. That's what he said to her by the fireplace and it applied to them both. Finding your True Love was a confusing time in any girl's life. The bond was so all-encompassing and powerful you could get lost in it. You needed to makes sure you were still *you*, even when you were connected to him. You needed to make sure you were true to the very core of yourself.

And Esmeralda's core was her family. Every single exasperating one of them.

She kissed her thumb and then pressed it to Trevelyan's cheek. "Ez." He murmured, but didn't open his eyes. He always slept soundly when they were together. His magic sensed she was there and posed no danger to him. With her, the dragon was content and satiated.

She felt the same way around him. All her life, his voice had been in her head when she was scared, comforting her through her fear.

With me, you are always safe, my darling. I love you more than magic itself.

Some version of him had soothed her throughout the worst terrors of her childhood. She'd heard him in her head a hundred times. Esmeralda didn't know how that was possible, but it didn't matter. Her True Love's voice had reached her, when she'd needed him most.

"With me, you are *always* safe, my darling." She whispered. She wasn't giving him the rest of the words. Not unless he said them first. She wasn't a masochist. Of course, knowing Trevelyan he'd probably *never* say them, just to piss her off. Even Avenant was a more sensitive True Love than Trevelyan and her other honorary brother had spent *years* bitching about Belle, before he set his mind to winning her. The dragon was not going to profess undying love to her anytime soon. Jackass.

She reluctantly walked out of the room, leaving her big, stubborn, wild thing peacefully sleeping. Five minutes later, she'd written that idiot dragon a note, packed herself a lunch, and was back in front of the creepy mirror.

Alright, so she'd need magic to use an enchanted portal thingy. Sadly, Esmeralda's spells weren't the most reliable. She didn't relish the idea of ending up in the middle of the Lyonesse Desert, because she took a wrong turn in the reflection. How was she going to accomplish this?

Well, only one spell even kind of worked for her lately. Maybe she should do what Trevelyan suggested and go with it. She leaned close to the mirror and blew out a long breath against the glass.

Fog.

In the vapory mist clinging to the smooth surface, she drew a club with her index finger. Instantly, the looking glass began to move. It reminded her of someone throwing a pebble into a pond, causing ripples to radiate outward.

Well shit! The dragon had been right. She'd set her magic free and it had given her a pathway out of the Heart Palace. Too bad she couldn't tell him about it. Too bad she had to go alone. She glanced over her shoulder, towards the bedroom. Towards Trevelyan.

Then, she took a deep breath and walked through the mirror. The magic felt cold and heavy against her body, as she moved forward. She instinctively switched to warmer clothes, barely even thinking about the power it took to perform a spell inside another spell. Magic always came easiest to her when she didn't think about it.

Inside the mirror, passages spiraled in different directions, beckoning her to a thousand faraway lands. Only one misty tunnel mattered, at the moment. The path directly in front of her was illuminated with a subtle pulsing energy. Inside the twisting fog surrounding it, she could see tiny clubs floating like confetti in the gale.

Esmeralda headed straight for that tunnel.

Around her, everything was gray and shifting. It would be so easy to get stuck in a place like this. Without the tunnels, there would be no way to escape the infinite nothingness. She was grateful to leave the billowing vapor, even though she was headed someplace just as horrible. The pathway widened, daylight appearing at the end.

Esmeralda emerged from the mist and into a frozen field. One second she was inside the mirror, the next she was back in reality. Or as much "reality" as Wonderland ever achieved. She was standing alone in a clearing surrounded by periwinkle pine trees and steaming geysers.

Okay, so this wasn't the Club Castle.

Still, she'd clearly landed in the right kingdom. There were hundreds of club-shaped pinecones and snowdrifts on the ground. For her, that was pretty good aim. Except for the part where she'd landed in the frigging snow. Witches did not do well with water, even when it was in the form of ice crystals. Esmeralda quickly manifested herself a pair of boots, so none of the horrible stuff would touch her feet. This was Trevelyan's fault. He'd burned her lucky shoes in that dumb spell of his. Now she'd have to make do with her second-favorite pair. And if he thought she was going to just forget about him buying her that record store, he was sadly mistaken. He'd promised her one today, as a matter of fact, and she was holding him to it.

Why had she ever wanted to date a guy who ran one? Screw that idea. She'd just get her own. She was incredible at owning businesses! Happily Ever Witch Cosmetics almost turned a profit sometimes. It was time to expand. ...Just as soon as she killed the evil queen and saved her goofy brother.

In the distance, Esmeralda could see a frosty white castle. The thin turrets and jagged roofline were beautiful. And ominous. Perched on a cliff side, it watched over the land for infidels and intruders. Threatening. Impregnable. Treacherous. That *had* to be where she was headed. The palace looked like it was made from magic, and icicles, and the blood of enslaved children.

Wonderful.

Sighing in frustration, Esmeralda started for the fortress of chilly death. It could be worse, she supposed. It could be raining. Or snowing. That would be a real big problem for her. She could handle some evil spells, but not the damn weather...

Beneath her feet, the ground began to quake.

Esmeralda's eyes widened in horror. Oh God...
As she watched, the rocky geysers surrounding the clearing emitted thicker smoke and frosty bursts of deadly water. The force of the eruption vibrated the land itself. Loud and unstoppable. She took off running, even though it was already too late.

An explosion of water came straight at her and Esmeralda knew she was about to die. She'd melt into a puddle under the torrent. There was no chance to avoid the attack. No opportunity to brace herself, or run, or pray. She had exactly enough time for one word to filter through her head and then she was being doused with the deluge of acid-y liquid.

Trev.

Icy death splashed over her fragile skin. Burning her and...
Wait, why wasn't it burning her?
There was no burning, at all.

Esmeralda automatically glanced down trying to figure out why she wasn't dead. Or even wet. Nothing had happened. Her clothes were dry, her hair was dry, even her second-favorite boots were dry. Instead, there was a liquid pool all around her, in a perfect semicircle. Every single droplet had been stopped a foot from her body and fallen to the ground, like rain hitting against a window. Trying to make sense of it, Esmeralda scanned for some sort of explanation.

Two seconds into her examination, she sensed the spell.
The enchantment was like nothing she'd ever seen. Dazzling in its complexity and yet elegantly simple, it was applied with the precision of a surgeon. It enveloped every cell of her body like a watertight bubble. A flood could hit her and she'd stay dry.
Trevelyan.

Disregarding her orders and *way* overstepping boundaries, that tricky bastard had waterproofed her! No one else would have done it. No one else *could* have done it. This must have been why he'd been so low on power when the army arrived. This was the spell he'd exhausted himself on.

How had he even concocted such a specialized enchantment, given his weakened state? It probably drained everything he had. Plus, that son of a bitch had somehow cast it discreetly enough that she hadn't noticed it. Their magic was so similar that his powerful green energy had just blended in with her own.

Trevelyan hated not getting his own way. He'd wanted his powers sealed tight around her and so he'd made it happen. Because he *always* thought he knew best. Because he had freaked the hell out when that grog hit her in the library and he'd realized how vulnerable she truly was.

Because she was just *his* and he'd decided to keep her. Esmeralda's mouth curved. Now that she'd seen the enchantment, she could disable it if she wanted. Instead, she left the protective spell in place. Trevelyan had kept her safe. Even though it violated their "separate lives" agreement… Even though it must have depleted a huge amount of his recuperating energy… Even though he hid his underhanded efforts from her… He'd protected her.

He'd made sure his magic would catch Esmeralda, if she fell. Feeling lighter and happier than she had all day, she started across the snowy landscape towards the Castle of Clubs with new confidence. Maybe things were looking up. Maybe this whole rescue mission would be okay. Of course it would! She'd return to her True Love's side by tomorrow, ready to claim her happily ever after. Everything was going to be great!

And that's when the yetis grabbed her.

CHAPTER TWENTY-TWO

Pick your perfect nail polish from our unlimited selection!
Dying Alone Rose: Tragic romance got you down? Well, as you waste
away to nothing but a ball of pain and sad memories, at least your
manicure will match your despair. This wilted pink polish is the exact
shade of the floral arrangements from your cancelled wedding and
scented like never-ending tears.

Happily Ever Witch Cosmetics Website

The Heart Castle

Trev.
His eyes snapped open, all his nerves jangling. "Ez?"
His hand instinctively moved beside him to touch Esmeralda, but she wasn't in the bed. Anxiety swelled, an acidic rush of panic and mysterious emotions. She'd said his name. For one impossible second, there had been total unity with their powers. He'd heard her in his head, reaching for him. ...And something in her tone had sounded like goodbye.
Inside of him, the dragon went still.
"Ez!" Trevelyan bellowed, but there was no answer.
God*damn* it.
He was instantly on his feet, his heart pounding in his chest. "Esmeralda!" Naked and desperate to find her, he headed for the hallway.
He tried to tell himself that he was overreacting, just like he had that first morning in the castle. She'd probably gone to play with her liquid gold nail polish, again. She was an early riser. She was up to trouble before the sun even rose.

Except it was raining outside.

And he couldn't feel her perfect chaotic energy, anymore. His magic was strong enough now to sweep out. He sent it searching and it didn't touch with hers. The dragon roared so loud it nearly fractured his skull. Esmeralda was gone. He had no idea how or why, but she was *gone*.

Someone was sure as hell in the castle, though. Two men. He could sense them plain as day. Eyes narrowing, he headed straight for them. He planned to kill those motherfuckers, and every *other* motherfucker in the motherfucking world, until his mate was returned to him.

Trevelyan slammed into the kitchen. The door hit the wall with enough force to send a jagged crack up the pink plaster and across the pink ceiling. His furious gaze sighted on the strangers. "Where is my witch?" Four words that would doom the entire universe, if he didn't like the answer.

His soon-to-be initial victims glanced up from their coffee. The biggest of the men had wings and enough sense to be wary of an incensed dragon. His arm moved, like he wanted to reach for the weapon on his back.

The monster inside of Trevelyan snarled, eager for a battle. The winged-man didn't pull the double-bladed axe free, but Trevelyan could tell that he wanted to. He only hesitated for fear of the situation turning bloody.

Which it was absolutely about to.

The familiar-looking, human one wasn't bright enough to notice. "Woah! Pants would be nice." He held up a palm to block the bottom half of Trevelyan from his sight. "I thought gryphons didn't care much about modesty, but *wow*... I guess dragons are even more --um-- open."

Trevelyan frowned at that unexpectedly innocent remark. The winged-guy put a hand on the other man's arm, as if preparing to physically yank him out of danger. He thought Trevelyan was a threat. It was a wise guess.

The human smiled, continuing to avert his eyes. It almost seemed like he was deliberately ignoring the brewing violence. Either that or he was a dimwit. Trevelyan was betting on a dimwit. "Hi, I'm Galahad Airbourne. You must be Trevelyan."

Some of Trevelyan's aggression faded, because he recognized this puritanical man, now. He was indeed Sir Galahad of Camelot. There wasn't a sentient organism on the planet who couldn't identify the knight. He was famous for charity work, and his glistening handsomeness, and his TV shows. He'd also helped wipe out the entire gryphon race, if the rumors were true, and now Esmeralda said he was married to one.

Trevelyan's eyes flicked back to the winged-guy, who was silently watching him. A gryphon. These were the men Scarlett Riding-Wolf had hired to save Esmeralda from Wonderland. He relaxed slightly.

"Trystan Airbourne?" He surmised. "Midas sent you?"

The gryphon inclined his head, still waiting for a fight to break out.

As if Trevelyan didn't have bigger problems than some flying asshole and his celebrity husband. Gryphons were so hostile and paranoid.

Impatient now, Trevelyan waved a hand to create a pair of drawstring pants for himself. "Where is my witch?" He repeated in a marginally less dire tone. "Did she go back to the Enchanted Forest?" That made sense.

If Trevelyan wasn't a heartless monster, far beyond having his feelings hurt, his feelings would perhaps be *slightly* hurt that she didn't even nudge him awake to say goodbye, but... no. Obviously, he wasn't upset, at all.

Obviously.

Esmeralda wasn't in any trouble. That voice he thought he'd heard in his head was nothing. His mate had simply run off, fleeing his company and forsaking their True Love bond. Not a big deal. He was barely even bothered.

Obviously.

It would be a pain in the ass to go get Esmeralda again, but at least she was safe. And Trevelyan needed to level her ridiculous homeland into a hellscape of blackened rocks anyway, so a trip to the Four Kingdoms wasn't out of his way. He would simply retrieve his errant mate, kill her meddling family, and all would be well.

Raining or not, things could be worse.

"Esmeralda went to go find Marrok." Galahad told him, dropping his hand in relief now that Trevelyan was dressed. "She left you a letter, I think." He pointed over to an envelope on the counter.

Trevelyan's insides slid towards his knees.

Things were worse.

Esmeralda had gone to the Club Kingdom? She'd been *serious* about rescuing the wolf? No. That was impossible. The witch was too smart to do something so rash. How did she even get through the force field around the Heart Palace? She wouldn't go off into Wonderland alone. No. She knew the Queen of Clubs was plotting her death.

"No." He heard himself say out loud.

"Yes. She texted Scarlett about it. Said we're supposed to save you and then come back for her later." Galahad gave an earnest nod. "Scarlett was a little put out about the idea. I've been instructed to threaten you, about how she's not going to let you keep Esmeralda, if you can't be a more supportive True Love." He leaned closer to Trevelyan. "Letty's not your biggest fan. You're *really* going to have to work at being a great brother-in-law, if you want to gain her approval."

Trevelyan stared at him.

"Did I mention the letter?" Galahad prompted guilelessly.

Trevelyan went stalking over to grab it. Esmeralda had written his name on the front, in her large feminine script. He suddenly recalled telling her multiple times that he'd leave a note if he ever ran out on her. His teeth ground together so tightly it was a wonder they didn't shatter.

Galahad kept talking, without a care in the world. "Trys and I would like to help Esmeralda free the wolf, but we're trapped in the castle, too." He adopted a thoughtful look. "I guess it's because we weren't in Wonderland when the spell was cast, so it views us as interlopers. Hey!" He looked at the gryphon, bubbling with ideas. "When do you think you actually become a legit 'citizen' of somewhere, anyhow? Like does it take a certain amount of time? Or is it some events have to take place to emotionally link you to the spot? Or do you have to take some affirmative step to distance yourself from your former

home...?"
The gryphon cut off the merry avalanche of words. "Knight?"
"Yeah?"
"Stop."
"I'm not doing anything."
The gryphon slanted him a meaningful look.
Trevelyan ignored them both. He viciously ripped open the letter, shaking out the page so he could read it:

Trev,
Have gone to find Marrok, like we discussed. I went through that creepy mirror that you put in the hallway. Good call on it being enchanted BTW! You leave Wonderland with Trystan & Galahad, once they get here. I'll catch up with you later. Just try not to kill the knight.
Ez.
PS: If I die, you can have Happily Ever Witch Cosmetics. It's my baby, so don't screw it up. And remember to put a warning label on that nail polish that makes people invisible or you'll get sued. Trust me. It happens a lot.

Trevelyan read the ridiculous words twice, a muscle by his eye twitching.
Alright.
He slowly crumpled the paper in his hand, wadding it into a ball so tight his knuckles went white around it.
So apparently, she *had* been serious about saving Marrok. *Fine.* Trevelyan had told her the risks. If she decided to do it anyway, that was on her. Esmeralda was a level six witch. She'd be fine out there on her own, provided she actually used her fathomless magic for more than logs and hogs. Or perhaps she could turn herself into a dema*gogue.* That kind of rhymed with "frog." She could incite the Club Kingdom citizens to rebel against the current queen and join her, instead. Either way, she'd made her choice and that was... fine. Everything was fine. Obviously.
The paper in his grasp went up in flames.
He opened his fingers and let the smoldering ashes fall to the

floor, shifting his shoulder uncomfortably as the dragon stormed within him. He hadn't felt so close to the edge of mindless, blackout rage, since the night he escaped the WUB Club. "So, when do we leave?"

Trystan Airbourne watched him with unreadable brown eyes. "Now."

Right that second? "No." The word came out before Trevelyan could stop it. "We can't leave *now*."

"Why not?"

Trevelyan tried to think of one logical reason for his instant denial. "I need time to..." Fuck, what did he have to do? He had no idea. There was nothing left in the Heart Palace that he cared about. "Prepare." He muttered anyway. "Give me a moment to prepare."

Galahad nodded like that made perfect sense. Knights were dumb, so it was no surprise the he accepted the half-assed explanation. "Where would you like us to take you?" He asked in a friendly tone. "Where's your home?"

"I don't have one." Trevelyan stalked over to get coffee. It gave him something to do and it was hot. Was the palace colder than usual? It felt colder. Surely the witch's presence hadn't changed the temperature, though. The emptiness chilling the air was all in his imagination. He just needed to take control.

Or maybe he needed to burn down all of Wonderland.

That idea had real potential. It would certainly generate some heat. He looked out the window, into the rainy gardens. He'd ensured that she'd be safe from the weather, but there were so many other dangers. The realm suddenly seemed huge.

And deadly.

Goddamn it, he'd heard her voice in his head. She'd called his name. It had woken him up. It was *impossible*, but it had happened, right? Esmeralda said she'd been able to hear him, as a child. Maybe his powers had somehow manifested that idea into reality to warn him when she left the castle.

Esmeralda had been in the Heart Palace with *him*, since he'd met her. Now, she was off somewhere and Trevelyan was here alone. No part of him liked that situation.

At all.

He should start leveling the whole godforsaken place until the problem was remedied. That might drive home the point that the greatest villain in the world didn't appreciate it *when his mate went fucking missing.*

Trevelyan squeezed his eyes shut and saw flames. Bright and cleansing and wrathful. Losing control really would be… Bad. On some level, he knew that. He cleared his throat and opened his eyes, again. It didn't help. Everything was still on fire in his mind.

Trystan Airbourne watched him, like he could feel the dragon struggling to get out and destroy everything it saw.

"I didn't have a home until I found Trys." Galahad said, still having a normal conversation. "I live in Camelot, but *he* is home."

Gryphons were supposedly born without emotions, but Trystan Airbourne somehow smiled. His gaze stayed on Trevelyan, though. Awaiting an explosion.

Trevelyan hated them both. He sloshed coffee into the mug Esmeralda usually used. It had a Happily Ever Witch Cosmetics logo on it. Apparently, that made it his, now. As soon as his mate perished from her recklessness, he'd be a small business owner.

The edges of his vision clouded with ominous, scorching smoke. "Neverland." He muttered, because it was the first place he thought of through the thunderous frenzy consuming his mind. His room at his sister's beachside estate was where he stored his valuables. He slept there more than anyplace else. "I'll go to Neverland."

"Oh, great choice." Galahad nodded and headed over to refill his mug, as well. "I've gone pearl-surfing near the Mermaid Lagoon."

The knight had invented the damn sport. It had revolutionized Neverland Beach's tourist industry and made Maid Marion another fortune to add on top of her *other* fortunes. Galahad was allegedly one of the most creative, clever, charmed beings in the world. He must hide his talents well, because Trevelyan had rarely met anyone so sunnily, nauseatingly, idiotically positive.

(It never failed. Trevelyan was forever surrounded by morons. ...Except when he was with Esmeralda. She was the only one who never bored him or made him despair for the world's collective IQ. Everyone else was useless.)

Trevelyan drank his coffee without even tasting it. "How long ago did Ez leave?" He asked, although he wasn't sure why he bothered.

"Half an hour." Galahad leaned against the counter, casually at ease. "You know... I bet you could catch up with her, if you figured out a way through the magic mirror. Maybe if you reflected on it and..." He trailed off. "Reflect on the magic mirror! Hey, that's funny."

Using a pun just jumped Galahad straight to the top of Trevelyan's "needs to die" list. He restrained himself from slaughtering the knight, but only because homicide might spill his coffee.

His eyes stayed on the window, wishing he could see even a glimpse of the witch's dark hair in the distance. (Or whatever the hell color her hair was today.) He just wanted to *see* her.

"Of course I could figure out how to use the mirror." He muttered. "I'm a dragon. There's nothing I can't do."

"You can go after Esmeralda, then."

"Why would I want to? Esmeralda and I have agreed to live separate lives."

The gryphon scoffed at that news, moving to stand next to his husband. He was visibly worried about Galahad being so close to an unstable villain, his large body maneuvering so it was between the knight and Trevelyan.

Galahad rolled his eyes, but allowed Trystan to push him backward a few steps. "I have this handled." He complained.

His husband ignored him. "Separate lives will never work, dragon. Why would you let the witch suggest such a ludicrous thing?"

"It was *my* idea."

"That is even stupider. You've underestimated how much trouble a True Love can cause. Why would you wish to have less knowledge of what yours is plotting?" He flashed Galahad another look. "And they are *always* plotting."

Galahad shrugged, like he had no clue what Trystan was talking about.

"Separate lives is often a tempting thought." The gryphon muttered and then looked back at Trevelyan. "But the inevitable pandemonium that follows will just cause a man more headaches." He gestured around the empty castle. "Does this result seem wise?"

No. In retrospect separate lives was the worst idea he'd ever had. Trevelyan rubbed at his chest, trying to ease the ache that had started. God, she could be *anywhere.* With her powers, impossible things were simple. If she wanted to, Esmeralda could save Marrok and simply disappear. The note said she'd find Trevelyan, but what if she changed her mind?

Why would she *ever* come back to him, when she could be with her family?

"Is it cold in here?" He muttered. "It feels cold in here."

"The temperature is fine. You are just emotional. It's the nature of your species." Trystan Airbourne reached for a wabeberry tart from the tray on the counter.

Trevelyan's head whipped around. "Steal my tarts." He challenged ferociously. "I fucking *dare* you."

The gryphon arched a brow, but dropped his hand away from the desserts. Too bad. Trevelyan would have relished a fight. The dragon clawed to get out. Desperate to find their mate. Swirls of green smoke appeared above Trevelyan's skin, the precursor to transformation. His powers were healing.

He didn't care.

Trevelyan resisted the urge to pace, restless agitation driving him. "Esmeralda should have told me this was her plan." He informed the other men, needing to vent. Granted, the witch *had* told him her plan, but she should have been clearer about it. She'd tricked him by telling the truth. Why couldn't she lie like a normal person? "She left when my back was turned, because she knew I'd stop her."

"How could you have stopped her, when you were the one who suggested that she separate her life from yours?" The gryphon retorted, clearly still bitter over his failed plot to rob Trevelyan of his tarts.

Trevelyan didn't know how to answer that question, so his mind went back to savage destruction. That was understandable and familiar.

He could destroy the Four Kingdoms, if she didn't return. That would get her attention. Of course he planned to destroy it anyway. Esmeralda knew that. He could switch his plan and hold it hostage, perhaps? Say he *wouldn't* flatten the abysmal place, so long as she came back to him. That was a fair trade. He would spare the Enchanted Forest if it won him the bigger prize.

His eyes narrowed, thinking and fuming... and *not* hurt. "She didn't even ask me to help her in this suicidal lunacy, you know that? Ez just assumed I'd say no." Her lack of faith in him was galling. "I'm her True Love! She's supposed to rely on me. Confide in me. Need me! It goes to show her *complete* inability to trust."

"Did you offer your help?" Galahad inquired pleasantly.

"*I'm not helping her!*" Trevelyan roared back. "Why would I help? Why would I lift a finger? She went to save the man I intend to murder. She considers Marrok her brother. She gives all her loyalty to her beloved goddamn family."

Galahad tilted his head. "Seems like you're not showing much loyalty either, if you're trying to murder her brother."

Trevelyan shot him a killing glare. Literally. He was going to kill the man. He didn't care if it ruined his coffee and marooned him in Wonderland forever. It was worth it.

The gryphon stirred. "Knight?"

Galahad blinked over at him with wide purple-y blue eyes. "Yeah?"

"*Stop*. I see what you are plotting and it is a pointless idea." Galahad frowned. He abruptly looked shrewder than his grinning, blond exterior suggested. Maybe he wasn't so dimwitted, after all. "But he's going to regret this, Trys. You know he is. Look at him!" He gestured towards Trevelyan. "Without his True Love, he's going to implode."

"So? Let him ruin his life, if he chooses. The dragon would have undoubtedly done terrible things with his remaining years, anyway. He's a terrible person. He once stole the moon."

"We have to help him. Just a nudge in the right direction. He'll thank us later."

"You want to help *everyone*. It brings us nothing but trouble."

"It's the right thing to do. If the witch dies..."

"*She's not going to die!*" Trevelyan shouted, slamming his mug down.

Galahad and Trystan looked over at him.

Trevelyan put a hand over his eyes, trying to find some kind of control. He should feel vindication and righteous fury over her choice to assist Marrok. Instead, panic and desolation were eating at his insides. He could barely focus on what the other men were talking about.

Esmeralda had sounded scared when she'd called his name. But that was impossible. It was his unconscious mind playing tricks on him. You couldn't just call for someone in your head. Magic didn't work that way. She had *not* reached for him. Why the hell would anyone reach for him, if they were scared? He was a literal monster.

"All people die." The gryphon finally intoned. "A clan --a *family*-- works to keep *their* people alive as long as possible. Even the ones who are crazy and irritating. The witch is correct in her impulses and you are wrong in yours. It is very clear."

"*No,* I'm right about everything and she is wrong about even more." Trevelyan stabbed a finger off in the direction of the Kingdom of Clubs. "She left me here and ran off to save the man I *hate.*"

"He is her brother and he is in the custody of a magical madwoman."

"Who gives a shit? He betrayed me."

Galahad looked at his husband expectantly.

The gryphon sighed, as if he was giving in. "You will repay me for this later, knight."

Galahad beamed a smile very similar to the one Esmeralda wore when she'd just won an argument. "Thank you, Trys."

The gryphon grunted and refocused on Trevelyan. "I once stood at a similar crossroads, dragon. In a hotel room in St. Ives, I had a list of men to kill. It was my dream. But, my knight told me if I pursued my vengeance, he would forsake me and give his love to another."

"I never said that!" Galahad protested.

"We remember the event differently." One winged-shoulder lifted in a shrug. "But I had to choose: My past or my future. I could have my family or I could hunt my enemies. I could not walk both paths. I could not have both dreams. Neither can you, dragon. No one can."

Trevelyan saw his point and he didn't like it. "My family is gone."

"Your True Love lives. For now, at least. What greater family is there?"

That drew Trevelyan up short. He was still adjusting to the idea of a True Love, but he did know about mates. He'd watched his parents interacting for years. He vividly recalled their frequent screaming matches. They'd had some truly epic fights, filled with broken objects and vows of revenge. They'd both been powerful, arrogant, and prone to drama. Three houses had been incinerated. There'd been a graveyard full of possible romantic rivals out back. Holidays had sometimes become hostage situations.

But if something was *truly* important to his father, his mother would roll her eyes and acquiesce. And his father would do the same when his mother was the one being stubborn. When it really mattered, they'd always given in to make their relationship work.

Trevelyan's parents were the foundation of his self. He'd loved them. Modeled himself after their examples. And one of the most important things they'd taught him was that dragons never, ever compromised.

...Except with their mates

Because nothing was more important than your mate. Not pride or revenge or anger or hurt. *Nothing.*

Trystan Airbourne absently ran a hand over his husband's golden hair, waiting for Trevelyan to figure things out. Galahad sent the huge gryphon another shining smile. And there was a spark in his eye.

It caught Trevelyan's attention and gave him something to

focus on, aside from his runaway mate, the memories of his parents, and all the aggravating shit the gryphon was saying. He'd never seen those strange sparks appear in a man's eyes before. Probably because he hadn't looked for them. Women were always more interesting.

This would have been another clue, if he still gave a damn about his science experiment. Except, he didn't. The only eyes that interested him were crimson, and filled with wicked virtue, and headed for the Kingdom of Clubs.

Trystan Airbourne's head tilted, watching Trevelyan watch his husband. "Do not." It was a warning.

Oh for fuck's sake. "Relax. I prefer women."

"Many men swear they prefer chocolate. ...But they would happily try vanilla."

Galahad sighed, as if he was used to his husband starting random fights over him. He probably was. Like dragons, gryphons chose a mate without a lot of superfluous bullshit. And, like dragons, once they chose that mate, they were territorial lunatics.

Still, even knowing gryphons were unhinged, Trevelyan couldn't believe he was being accused of hitting on a knight. He *hated* knights! He'd sooner sleep with a bear trap. "I have a True Love. One I've promised to be monogamous to."

"A dragon's promises mean little. Especially, when the dragon is you."

Trevelyan's jaw ticked. "I keep the promises I make to my mate. A thousand percent."

"You have claimed the witch as a mate?" Trystan Airbourne's tone changed. Possibly the two species really were closer than gryphons and dragons liked to admit, because he understood the significance of that word. "If you have a mate, why do you look at mine?"

"I'm *not* looking at yours. I was looking at his eyes."

"Which are attached to him."

Trevelyan rubbed his forehead, not giving a damn about any of this. Why was he even speaking to these assholes? (Maybe because he needed someone to listen to him and convince him to do what he already knew he was going to do.) "Sometimes, mostly in Good women, I see a spark." He muttered. "It's rare and I don't understand why it's there, but Galahad has it. Life and purity and ideas. Some sort of strange, unguarded magic glowing."

"My knight is *always* guarded. By me." It was a statement of fact. "That is what warriors do. We guard our lights. Regardless of how annoying our True Loves are, with their persistent need to help evil-doers and idiots, we aid them in their pointless quests."

"I don't want to help her save Marrok!"

"And I do not want to be talking to you. Yet here we both stand."

"You can leave anytime you feel like it."

"As can you. Yet, neither of us is rushing for the exit and we both know why."

Trevelyan stayed quiet, his fist clenching and unclenching at his side.

Trystan Airborne didn't seem surprised. "There are some things you can't unknow. Once you've beheld them, there is no going back." Dark eyes x-rayed everything inside of Trevelyan, like he was seeing *all* of him, now. "Once you have found your mate, the world is different, yes? You can fight it, but the knowledge will not change. It changes *you*."

"Why should *I* be the one to change? Let *her* change."

"What would you change about your witch?" The words were calm and knowing. "What would make her more special to you?"

Nothing could make her more special.

Trevelyan adored everything about Esmeralda, from her virtuous smile, to her bitchy remarks, to her amazing green magic. He didn't want to change her. He just wanted... her. He *needed* her and she needed to need him back. Nothing else would do.

"Fuck."

Esmeralda was gone and he *had* to get her back. He'd never felt like this before. The dragon was going insane, insisting their mate was in danger and the goddamn palace was freezing. Without Esmeralda, nothing in the whole world felt warm.

Trystan Airbourne nodded sympathetically at the muttered curse. "I have been where you are." He repeated. "So, I know that you must either adapt to this new chaos, which is an essential part of your mate's maddening glow... Or you must return to the familiar darkness alone. Where you will never be challenged. Where you will be comfortable in your old ways." He paused with great meaning. "Where you will always be cold."

Trevelyan unconsciously shook his head.

No.

No to all of that. No to everything that didn't get him what he wanted. He was a dragon! He wasn't settling for half measures with his mate. He *didn't* want separate lives. He *didn't* want to panic when he opened his eyes, not knowing where she was. He *didn't* want any ambiguity as to their relationship.

Trevelyan wanted Esmeralda.

His brow furrowed. So what was he willing to compromise to get what he wanted?

Trystan Airbourne seemed to read the conflict on his face. "Galahad and I are leaving in five minutes." Big palms rested on the countertop, like the gryphon was no longer anticipating a battle. "Pick your own destination carefully, dragon. Your past or your future? Which looks to be the brighter path for you to travel, this morning?" He arched a brow. "Decide."

Chapter Twenty-Three

Pick your perfect nail polish from our unlimited selection!
Nude (But Not in a Fun Way): If dieting was a nail polish, this would
be the color. This conservative, neutral shade is perfect for boring
shit, like job interviews, court appearances, and lunch with your new
mother-in-law.

Happily Ever Witch Cosmetics Website

The Club Castle

"I'm going to put the witch's heart in an enspelled box." The Queen of Clubs decided with a firm nod, as she paced around in the morning chill. "Very classic and simple. I have a friend in the Spade Kingdom who can help me keep the heart beating, so I can still access the spell. Then, I'll be able to decapitate the witch and get the tiara. Trevelyan's magic probably didn't account for that." She looked over at Marrok. "Do you think his magic accounted for that?"

Marrok didn't respond verbally, but his lips curved like her question amused him.

The Queen of Clubs' own mouth thinned, resisting the urge to gut him right there on the veranda. For the moment, the house was quiet and she intended to keep it that way.

The Mad Hatter was in his workshop, fiddling with his pocket watch. The damn thing was mystically linked to his heartbeat, so he liked to keep it in proper working order. Hopefully, he didn't accidently kill himself by removing some vital cog or spring.

Snow White was at a session with her dwarf therapist, who was vainly trying to cure her memory loss. It wouldn't work. The

Queen of Clubs knew that. But, her optimistic mother's soul wouldn't let her give up on her poor, wounded child. She insisted that Snow White spend hours each day with the man, although they wasted most of that time on silly complaints Snow had dreamed up about her loving family.

Mothers *always* got blamed in therapy.

The Queen of Clubs had been forced to kill at least three of Snow White's former doctors, because they encouraged her daughter's ridiculous tendency to find fault with her supportive, stable, two-parent home. Those quacks were now fertilizing her rose garden. This dwarf psychiatrist would no doubt be joining them soon.

Everything else was going well. The Queen of Clubs' plan to become empress was working. Her carefully plotted plans *always* worked. Self-confidence, organization, and positivity were vital tools for any successful woman.

Her gaze flashed towards the Chess Tower in the courtyard. Most of the pieces were shifted towards the white side of the game. See? Perfect for this time of Tove. Right on schedule. Except, the red queen was standing alone, in the center of the board.

That was a bit odd. Nothing to worry about, of course. Just a small blip. The white pieces were all but guaranteed a win, regardless. Most importantly, the pesky red pawn was positioned at a2, far from promotion and safely under control.

The Queen of Clubs refocused on Marrok. He wasn't any worse for wear, after a night in the dungeon. She wasn't about to leave him alone with Snow White, so he'd slept down there. He *seemed* restrained, but best to be certain. Presently, he wore magic inhibiting chains tethering him to the patio table. Level five powers or not, the Queen of Clubs wasn't about to risk tangling with a wolf. They could transform into monsters. But really the shackles were just a precaution, given his enspelled state. It was safe to keep an eye on him by herself.

That wouldn't be a hardship.

Galling as it was, the Queen of Clubs half-understood Snow White's fascination with the wolf. He was truly, *truly* beautiful. And ever since Bluebeard had enspelled him, Marrok had been a perfect gentleman with her daughter, despite his bestial DNA. He could do the same with her. The wolf was the only one who could offer information on Trevelyan and the damn sealing wax spell. His cooperation was mandatory.

She arched a brow at him. "Trevelyan sealed the spell inside of that dreary little witch. It's obviously designed to keep me from killing her, the second we meet. Would he have anticipated me carving out her heart to beat his little trap?"

"It's impossible to fathom how much evil Trevelyan can anticipate." Marrok told her, with dark certainty. "I hate the man and even I'm consistently stunned by how horrible he is."

The two of them were alone on the wide porch, where the Queen of Clubs spent most of her mornings. It overlooked the frozen kingdom, providing stunning views of the courtyard and all the mountainous acreage she controlled. Snow-flurries fell softly, but the Queen of Clubs was never bothered by the cold. She was warmly dressed in an elegant white cape and had a comfortable spot in the sun.

She hadn't bothered to offer Marrok a coat. Let him freeze. Maybe it would motivate him to be a more pleasant captive. Her eyes stayed fixed on his perfect face. "Why did Trevelyan seal the spell inside of the witch and not himself? That would have been the smart move, if he was angling to stay alive. You were in prison with the man. You must have some theories as to what he's plotting."

"According to you, Esmeralda's his True Love."

"Yes, but dragons don't care about that."

"Says who?"

"Everyone! Every book. Every speciologist. *Everyone*."

Still... there weren't many dragons left in the world. How much did researchers really know about them? Dragons were untrustworthy and secretive. They might have lied about their feelings towards their True Loves, just to cause disruption. God knew, they lied about everything else.

Marrok arched a brow, reading her sudden doubt. "I know Trevelyan well enough to know that *nobody* really knows Trevelyan." He said, answering her earlier question. "Nobody can tell you exactly what he'll do, if you steal his True Love." He gave an exaggerated wince. "...But I can imagine some possibilities that aren't real pretty."

"That's ridiculous! How much thought would someone of Trevelyan's reputation really put into protecting a random, nobody witch?"

Esmeralda was *nothing*. Her magic wasn't the fairest in the land. It couldn't be! Maybe she was a level six talent, but who had even *heard* of the woman? She was barely even Bad, and a lackluster entrepreneur, and the Queen of Clubs was positive that she'd unnaturally augmented her skin tone. There was simply no way that someone so dead-average would be born with such an exceptional color.

"You have a True Love." Marrok raised one wide shoulder in a graceful shrug. "How much thought would you put into protecting the Mad Hatter?"

How dare he compare her eternal bond with her beloved husband to anything that overrated witch shared with the dragon! "It's not the same thing, at all!"

"No, it's not." The wolf agreed, a smirk curving his lovely mouth. "Because you might be a murderous psycho, trying to take over a kingdom and kill everybody... but Trevelyan is *worse*."

The Queen of Clubs' eyes narrowed, not bothering to take offense. Technically, the dragon *was* worse. Ninety-eight percent wicked. No one could match that level of Badness.

"Dragons don't care about True Loves." She insisted again, just as she'd insisted that the Mad Hatter was wrong when he'd said the same thing. "Most Bad folk will protect their True Loves. *Yes*. But the witch won't matter to him."

"Let's say you're right. Let's say dragons *don't* care about True Love." Marrok's head tilted, tawny hair glinting like gold in the sunlight. "But they sure as hell care about keeping what's theirs."

She frowned. Pathological greed *was* a defining characteristic of the species. It was hard for her to comprehend that level of self-centeredness. Being a mother, her natural instinct was to give.

"So, imagine you're Trevelyan." Marrok urged, his tone almost hypnotizing. "A merciless force of horror, whose blood runs rancid with evil spells. Imagine being handed a pretty little witch, who says she's your True Love. You've never had a person of your own before, but now this pretty little witch *belongs* to you. She's *yours.* Imagine the obsession that begins to brew in your violent and twisted brain."

The Queen of Clubs' scowl grew deeper. That was true, as well. Dragons were little more than animals. Even Florian, the scholarly one, had the cold eyes of a soulless beast. And just being around Haigha had made her skin crawl, because he'd been so base. If you threatened an animal's mate, they'd instinctively strike out. It was territorial behavior.

"Now, imagine," Marrok went on, "someone is threatening your pretty little witch. Trying to steal from *you.* Plotting to beat *you.* Challenging *you.* …How far would you go?"

The Queen of Clubs felt a chill that had nothing to do with the weather.

"I don't know *exactly* what Trevelyan will feel for a True Love." Marrok finished, topaz eyes gleaming. "But I guarantee he'll topple the goddamn world before he gives up what's his. And he'll laugh as it falls."

The Queen of Clubs closed her eyes in brief frustration. "You think he's laying a trap, *expecting* me to rip the witch's heart out and put it in a box."

"Where Trevelyan's concerned, I think it's impossible to be *too* paranoid. He's up to something. Don't kill him or Esmeralda until you know what tripwires he's set up. In fact, if you *really* want to win this, forget about murder. …You need to arrest him."

She outright scoffed at that advice.

"I'm serious." Marrok insisted earnestly. "I was Trevelyan's cellmate and I saw how those bars affected him. He was melting down, by that last day. Screaming and raving. He was *terrified.*"

That analysis matched what Snow White had once told her about the night of Trevelyan's escape. The man had been acting very out of character. "There was a fight between the two of you." She remembered.

"Prison was just too much for Trev. He cracked. It happens to some people, especially egomaniacs with control issues." Marrok didn't sound very sorry about Trevelyan's mental struggle. "I know that he'll do *anything* to stop himself from going back into a jail cell. Put him on trial and sentence him to life behind bars. He'll make a deal with you to avoid that."
"Why would I trust anything you have to say?"
"Because I hate Trevelyan, even more than I hate you. I think you're stronger than he is. You can win." Marrok's expression turned malevolent. "And I want him to lose."
Wolves were always simple in their thinking. "Your prison fight was so long ago. You're *still* holding a grudge?"
"Not for that. For what he did afterwards. I'm married to my precious Snow White, now. But I'll *never* forget what Trev did to what's-her-name, my first wife. He frightened her. Threatened her." There was genuine anger in Marrok's tone. "It was disrespectful to *me* and he needs to pay."
The Queen of Clubs' barely restrained herself from rolling her eyes.
"I want Trevelyan dead." Marrok assured her, his flawless jaw firm. His pensive expression was even more attractive than his taunting one. "I'll take a truth potion to prove that, if you want. I've never been more honest about anything."
"Oh, I believe you. *Everyone* wants the dragon dead." The Queen of Clubs shrugged. "You're trying to stop me from harming the witch, though. You and she are friends."
"I love Ez. She's family. Which is why I will do everything I can to get Trevelyan away from her." Marrok met her gaze and it was like being drawn into an exclusive club. Like they had some deeper connection that lesser people could never fathom. "You understand that, I think."
The wolf's charisma was simply off-the-charts. The Queen of Clubs was far too savvy to fall for a gorgeous man, with silken words and bedroom eyes, but she could appreciate how *other* women might.
"Why would I understand your feelings for that level six bitch?" She challenged.
"Trevelyan slept with Snow White. Does that make *you* feel all

warm and fuzzy inside?"

She shuddered with revulsion.

"*Exactly*." Marrok nodded in deep sympathy. "It's repulsive to even contemplate his hands on her. I can't stand the thought of him touching Ez and he deserves to die for defiling my cherished new bride, before I've even kissed her." Wolves were such possessive creatures. "So, you and I can work together. The enemy of my enemy is my slightly-less-hated enemy."

"What exactly are you suggesting?"

"If you agree to spare Esmeralda, I will help you bring down Trevelyan at a big showy trial. He'll be forced to make a deal. His tricks will all be nullified."

The Queen of Clubs considered that offer. "How can you be sure?"

"I *know* him. You said so yourself. And I know Trev's rigged it so only he can despell Ez. I promise you that heart-in-a-box idea won't work, until you deal with him. And he'll have an insurance policy, so you can't kill him outright. You see it, too, right?"

"I *was* thinking something similar." The Queen of Clubs reluctantly agreed.

"Of course you were! It's all so clear. The dragon will make it so his magic is the key to some vital lock, the sneaky bastard." Marrok sounded furious on her behalf. At least *someone* understood the pressure she was under. "He thinks we're both idiots. ...But that's how we'll break him."

She sniffed. "Trevelyan is overconfident."

"A classic narcissist." Marrok concurred. "He'll make sure he's the most important piece on the board. If he dies, he's probably set some trigger that will murder Ez, too. Then, you won't get the spell, at all."

That sounded *precisely* like something Trevelyan would plot. Selfish asshole.

"He'll never see this plan coming though." Marrok went on. "He has no idea I'm even involved. He'll be blindsided and off-balance. We can use that."

The Queen of Clubs pursed her lips, her eyes on Marrok. His dislike of the dragon was palpable. No one was a good enough actor to fake it and everybody who knew the two men was aware of their feud. Plus, Bluebeard's spell was making him loyal to Snow White. Surely that magic would carry over to her doting mother, even if the wolf was still somewhat annoyed over the chains and kidnapping.

Was there a downside to working with him? She couldn't think of any. Marrok was still safely controlled, in restraints and magic. It made a lot more sense to use him for her own ends. "Do you give me your word that you'll help me defeat Trevelyan?" Wolves were simple creatures, in so many ways. Even the Bad ones tended to honor deals.

"I swear to you on my beloved Snow White's life, I will help you *annihilate* that smug son of a bitch." Marrok pledged with predictable vehemence. "I want him reliving his worst nightmare, sobbing on the goddamn ground, and I will do my best to make that happen. Just promise me you won't harm Esmeralda."

"Very well." The Queen of Clubs waved a hand. "We'll arrest Trevelyan and threaten to sentence him to life in prison, unless he despells the witch. Once he does that, I'll execute him anyway and let Esmeralda go."

She had no intention of keeping her half of that bargain. The witch had to die. The Queen of Clubs wouldn't allow anyone else to challenge her. That green-skinned nobody would *not* have the fairest magic in the land.

Marrok was too caught up in his hatred of Trevelyan to realize that Esmeralda would never leave Wonderland alive. He sagged back in relief, smiling widely. "See, I knew this was the way to go with you."

He had a wonderful smile. So full of genuine gratitude. How pleasant to have someone grateful for all she'd done. Lord knew, her family rarely appreciated her. "I think we'll both get what we want, if we…"

"Majesty." William, the obnoxious lizard from the Tea-Partier set, came stumbling onto the veranda, interrupting her very productive meeting. His words were garbled by the bandage wrapped around his tongue. "Thank God!"

The Queen of Clubs looked William up and down in dismay.

Typically, he was well-dressed, which was why the Mad Hatter approved of him. Her husband was quite the fashion plate, with the perfect purple top hat for every occasion. At the moment, though, even Hatty would agree that William looked like he'd been mauled by coyote-shifters. Vicious teeth-marks covered his scaly skin. His natty suit had been shredded. He seemed to be missing some fingers.

Who in their right mind came before their *queen* in such sorry shape?

Her nose wrinkled in distaste. "What in the world…?"

"Gingerbread men attacked me. Only they weren't normal gingerbread men. They were more like monsters. *Mutants*." William half-crawled towards her. "I barely escaped with my life."

Marrok's eyebrows soared. "Ginger-mutants." He murmured to himself. "Huh. She finally got the spell to work."

The Queen of Clubs blinked. "Who did? The witch? *Esmeralda* did this?"

"Yes!" William answered around his sodden tongue bandage. Drool was pooling from his mouth, as he tried to talk. It was quite disgusting. "Her and the dragon. They attacked me unprovoked." He made it to the balcony railing, his mangled hand leaving bloody smears on the glossy stone. "You must stop them."

"I plan to." The Queen of Clubs edged back from the injured man and all his various fluids. She was wearing white, for God's sakes. "Why are you here, William?" Honestly, she thought she'd poisoned him along with the caterpillar and the March Hare, back in the Spade Kingdom. It was hard to keep track of all the various hangers-on.

"I need help!" He wailed.

"Well, I'm not a doctor or a…"

William rudely cut her off. "Then get me one! A reputable one, not some glorified village nursemaid. I've been hurt for days, but I can't get anyone worthy to show up and treat me. The whole kingdom is in chaos. People turned to hogs, and wars in rose gardens, and someone even said Sir Galahad was coming, all the way from Camelot!"

Marrok's head tilted.

"Sir Galahad?" The Queen of Clubs was actually interested in that rumor. Even though she'd locked down all access to Wonderland, she was hardly going to ban a superstar. Maybe the knight wanted to arrange a royal visit. It could become a media event. That would raise her international profile as a monarch, even more than having a wolfball player for a son-in-law. "Well, if *he* wants to come, we'll need to throw a grand ball."

"Majesty, please..."

She cut him off. "I only hope the wretched whimsy of this place doesn't embarrass me, in front of Sir Galahad." Sometimes she felt like Wonderland's chaotic magic actively plotted against her. "Once I'm empress, I'll be taming the rough edges of this land and making some big changes to..."

"I'm dying!" William shrieked, focused solely on himself. "You *have* to help me. I helped you plenty of times."

Of all the nerve! "I'm a queen! When did I ever need *your* help?"

"I got you the three brilligs!" The words were all slurred and wet. "You owe me a favor."

The Queen of Clubs' lips parted. The brilligs! Of *course.* She'd used them to get the wolf from the Enchanted Forest and it had worked perfectly. Why stop there?

She waved a hand at William, done with his selfish nonsense. Her magic blasted the nagging lizard right off the edge of the balcony. He went careening into the courtyard below, with a screech of terror and his reptilian eyes bugging out of his head. It was quite ghastly to watch. A Tea-Partier should have more dignity in death.

Marrok gave a slight wince at the echoing sound of William hitting the checkerboard cobblestones. He craned his neck to watch the carnivorous white roses grab hold of the lizard's body with their thorny branches. They dragged him into their flowerbed, starving for his nice, hot blood.

She furrowed her brow. Hmmm... Were lizards warm-blooded? Pat, the pigeon gardener, would be annoyed if William damaged the blooms with his unappetizing, reptile corpse. Pat was proud of the white roses. He only liked to give them high-quality victims. Good-looking, naked women were his particular preference. The Queen of Clubs didn't ask questions about where the girl's clothes went, before Pat tied them up for the feedings. Pat was an artist. No sense interfering with his methods.

Although, between the tedious innocents the Mad Hatter sucked dry of their Good magic and the roses' veracious appetite, it was a wonder the castle ever got cleaned. They went through six maids a week! No one in the Club Kingdom much cared where all the girls went, but still floors needed sweeping and beds had to be made. Why were mothers the only ones who understood what it took to run a household? Marrok grunted as the flowers devoured William. "…Or you could've just called a doctor for him." He remarked, like she'd asked for his opinion.

On the Chess Tower, the red queen shifted towards the white side of the board.

The Queen of Clubs didn't notice. "Oh, who cares about William?" She waved everything aside, because she'd just had a brilliant idea and she needed to share it. Having other people admire her brilliance was the best part of being so brilliant. "I know how we can arrest the dragon!"

CHAPTER TWENTY-FOUR

Pick your perfect nail polish from our unlimited selection!
Incognito Indigo: Want to walk away from your problems? Wishing that no one knew who you were? Well, this is the polish for you! Magically imbued with glamour-inducing pigments, this blurply shade will change your looks, so you can start all over again. Wear it and you'll instantly be transformed into a whole new person.
...On the outside, anyway.

Happily Ever Witch Cosmetics Website

Near the Club Castle

Yetis ate magic.
Esmeralda had known that zoological fact in the abstract, the same way she knew brilligs were excellent trackers and rocking-horseflies mated for life. It was one thing to hear dry information recited on some nature documentary. It was another to be living it in real time. A pack of enormous yetis had captured her and had carted her back to their cave for a feast.
And she was the feast.
The biggest of them was merrily making a fire to roast her on, while the others debated side dishes in their grunt-y language. All eight of them were covered in white fur and uncaring about Esmeralda's protests. The scent of her magic was all they kept rumbling about, as they eagerly awaited their dinner.
"Look, I'm telling you, the Queen of Clubs is *much* more delicious than me." Esmeralda argued for the hundredth time. "And I am totally willing to help you eat every last succulent piece of that bitch, if you just let me go."

Nothing.

The yetis acted like she wasn't talking, at all. She supposed she should be grateful that they were epicurean monsters and not just eating her raw. They flipped through a recipe book on barbequed magic, thrilled with their meal planning.

Esmeralda sighed in aggravation. So far, her mission to rescue Marrok was not going well. Not only was she trapped in a cave and about to be slow-cooked on a spit, but the yetis had broken her phone. That had hurt. For real. Finding another one in Wonderland was going to be a royal pain. Not to mention, she still had to hike to the Club Castle and fight a bunch of people. And she had to escape.

She needed to use a spell to get free of this mess. It seemed to be the only option. She could do that. It was just a matter of concentration and focus. She *focused* on the biggest yeti, who was still preparing to cook Esmeralda alive. She *concentrated* on getting her powers to cooperate, for once. Magic swelled within her...

And a television set fell from the sky.

It was one of the old-fashion console ones that weighed a ton. It crashed down on the yeti, the impact crushing the creature's head like a watermelon. Esmeralda squinted at the boxy, blood-covered TV and the twitching body beneath it.

Well... okay.

Maybe not the *best* spell, but at least it killed her abductor. She hadn't exactly been trying for death-by-television. Still, it had kinda worked. That's what mattered. How many more electronics could she conjure? At least seven, hopefully, because now the other yetis were real unhappy. They leapt to their feet, bellowing and furious.

"You started it!" Esmeralda shouted back at them. "You broke my phone!"

The yetis' cave was built into the side of a mountain and furnished in a neo-primitive style. The walls were hewn into solid stone. The sparse furnishings were made from animal skins and branches. The lighting was all torches and campfires. It was extremely atmospheric, if you were into dinosaurs and rocks. Esmeralda wasn't a huge fan of either.

Time to go.
The yetis had chained her to one of the gray walls by her wrists, but that didn't much matter. Her magic might be iffy when it came to most spells, but she was really good at changing her appearance. Her hand shrunk down, easily slipping out of the restraints.

Her eyes cut towards the entrance to the cave, which seemed a far way off. The yetis were charging at her, blocking her escape. Crap. There were a lot of them.

How had she accomplished that smog spell that disappeared all the knights? That seemed like a way better option than flinging more TVs. As usual, when she thought about her magic too hard, nothing happened. Esmeralda tried again, planning the spell out, but the yetis still wouldn't vaporize. Everything just got jammed inside of her and --*crap*-- they were getting super close, now.

Umm...

She weighed her options for half a second and then took off running. Since the path leading out of the cave was blocked by monsters, she went in the opposite direction, deeper into the maze of caverns. She had no idea where she was headed. Torches on the wall lit the way, as she followed the twisting stone passages farther underground.

Boom!

Splat!

A concussive explosion ricocheted off the stony surfaces of the cave's interior, followed almost instantly by a terrible wet *squish*. Esmeralda had no idea where the noise had come from, but it sounded disgusting. She spared a quick look over her shoulder. More yetis were following her, their yellow eyes slightly illuminated in the dim light. She was wandering deeper and deeper into their lair and now there were at least two dozen of them.

Crap.

Esmeralda turned a blind corner, already casting a glamour. Instantly, she'd transformed herself into a yeti. As disguises went it wasn't her favorite look, but it would do. She stood perfectly still trying to look like she belonged amid the hairy denizens of the cave. As soon as the yetis went past her, she'd casually walk the other way, right out of the cavern's entrance. Simple.

Except where were all the yetis?

Boom! Boom! Boom!

Splat! Splat! Splat!

The weird repetitive noise kept echoing. At least ten times in a row and getting closer. Panicked yeti yowls were now accompanying the *booms* and *splats*. It sounded like a war. Esmeralda's thick fuzzy eyebrows drew together and she stuck her head around the corner. What the hell was happening? Why hadn't the yetis already gone racing by her hiding spot, looking for her?

And why did she suddenly feel an ungodly amount of magic? She stepped out into the main corridor, her heart beginning to pound.

A yeti came tearing down the tunnel, making terrified *rawhhhhhs!* Four more of its kind followed close behind. They weren't searching for Esmeralda. They were fleeing for their fuzzy lives.

Boom!

Splat!

One of the creatures exploded.

Fileted yeti parts sprayed all over the walls and Esmeralda jolted in surprise. The yeti's huge body detonated, splattering blood and entrails everyplace. Okay. So that solved the mystery of the noise.

Other monsters roared out in horror, as they were coated in sticky red goo and matted bits of their buddy's fur. Then another yeti exploded. And another. And *another*.

They were being magically picked off with ruthless precision. They tried to evade the unseen force killing them, but it was impossible. No one could escape a spell that strong.

Esmeralda didn't even try. She didn't have to.

She stood in the middle of the carnage, clean and safe. None of the gore touched her. None of the yetis got close. None of the deadly magic even mussed her own thick fur. All the chaos washed around her, like water around a rock. There was really

only one way in the universe that could have happened.
Her attention stayed on the end of the corridor, not willing to believe it, until she saw him with her own two eyes. Then, Trevelyan walked into view, long coat swirling like a cape, and Esmeralda's breath caught.
He'd come after her! The man was literally killing mad, but she didn't care. He was *here*.
Trevelyan's focus instantly latched onto her face. Even though she was disguised as a yeti, he knew it was her. Dragons were scent-based. Still, a girl wanted to look her best, when her True Love showed up to save her from monsters. She transformed herself back into her actual body, only this time she turned her hair green, because he'd requested it and he deserved a reward.
Something sparked in Trevelyan's gaze.
Seeing she was all in one piece, his wrathful attention switched to the yetis who were still alive. Two of the shaggy white creatures took fearful steps back. Trevelyan rotated his wrist in a quick turn. The top half of their bodies went one way, the bottom half of their bodies went the other, like towels being wrung dry. Bones crunched. Yetis screamed. Trevelyan gave a particularly cruel smile and exploded them, too.
Esmeralda winced a bit.
Maybe she should have warned the yetis that her True Love was an evil dragon.
Another yeti dove for cover and was summarily folded in some complicated, origami-ish way that turned it inside out. How the hell did Trevelyan even know a spell like that? Wait, what was she thinking? Of *course* he knew a spell like that. The man's DNA was nothing but dark magic and unbelievable hotness.
The last yeti seemed to realize it was screwed. It lunged for Esmeralda, wanting to use her as a shield against the dragon's wrath. It made it exactly one step in her direction.
Trevelyan's gaze flicked towards it. His hand waved out in a swift downward motion.
And the yeti... unzipped. Its body split cleanly down the center, as Trevelyan's powers opened it up like a jacket. The two sections of muscle and fur peeled away from each other,

resembling something out of a horror movie. All of the yeti's insides splooshed out in the middle and the bisected halves fell sideways, hitting the ground in opposite directions.

Ick.

Trevelyan didn't seem to notice the carnage. His targets eviscerated, he focused his rage on Esmeralda. Green eyes pinned her, glowing with power so vast it seemed fathomless. "I told you before: Run and I will catch you, witch." The promise was sealed in blood and flames. "*Every. Single. Time.*"

Esmeralda ran for him.

Trevelyan caught her.

He hadn't been expecting that response to his dire threat. He barely had time to open his arms, before she was throwing herself into them. Her lips found his and she kissed him passionately.

There was half a second of stillness, as Trevelyan tried to process what the hell just happened, and then he was kissing her back. His mouth opened over hers, like he couldn't get enough. Like he'd been suffocating and she'd just offered him oxygen. Esmeralda wasn't sure if he'd lifted her or if she'd shimmied up his body, but somehow she was wrapped all around him. Trevelyan held her off the ground.

"You're kissing me." He got out, in case she hadn't noticed.

"I know." Esmeralda dragged his lips back to hers.

A desperate groan escaped him. His tongue was in her mouth, tasting and demanding. His hands memorized her body, crushing her against him. Dying for her. His grip was so tight that she might just be absorbed straight into his skin. One palm found the back of her neck, his fingers tangling in her hair. Her hands tugged at his jacket, wanting more.

Trevelyan drew back long enough to help her strip off his shirt. "You said you *wouldn't* kiss me." There was a dazed expression on his face. She'd apparently shocked him out of his anger, at least temporarily. It just went to prove how awesome she was at kissing. "Not until you believed in me."

"I believe in every single piece of you, Trev."

"You're smarter than that." His eyes drifted shut in pleasure, as she caressed his hair. Then, he seemed to rouse himself. "Are you alright?" He tried to take stock of her body, without putting her down. "Do you have a head injury?"

"No, I..." She gazed at him. "You came after me. I never expected that."

He looked annoyed by her surprise. "I'm your *mate*. Granted, for the first ten minutes I realized you were gone, my thoughts weren't pleasant. But there was no possible reality where I let you go off and die in the Club Kingdom."

"You *said* you were going to let me go off and die in the Club Kingdom, though."

"I lied! I'm ninety-eight percent Bad. I say all kinds of shit. Why would you pay any attention to it?" Trevelyan sounded frustrated. "Jesus, you must have seen that I'm violently obsessed with you. Nothing and no one could *ever* keep me away. I would drown Wonderland in blood and fire, until I had you back."

For a wicked witch, that was poetry. "You could sink the whole damn world and no one could stop you." She assured him. "It's *such* a turn on."

For an evil dragon, that was poetry. "Frozen-hells, I missed you, Ez." His mouth slanted over hers again, hungry and seeking more. Kissing seemed to be a new part of his violent obsession with her, because he didn't want to stop. Keeping their lips sealed together, he carried her towards the nearest wall. "I've been losing my mind without you."

Esmeralda toed off her not-favorite boots and wound her legs around his hips, needing to be even closer to him. "I was only gone a few hours. You couldn't have missed me *that* much."

"You shouldn't have been gone, *at all!* I'm fucking pissed at you. I mean it. I'm not..." He lost his train of thought, back to kissing her. He seemed to want to drink her in. His lips worshiped hers, his hand moving to her cheek. He held her face, like he'd die if she slipped away.

Esmeralda sure wasn't trying to escape. "I'm not getting naked in front of the dead guys." She somehow got out. "I'm a villain, but I'm not *that* Bad."

Trevelyan didn't even glance towards the yetis' remains. He just waved a negligent hand and every drop of blood vanished.

Esmeralda had no idea where the mangled body parts had gone. She didn't care. The casual use of dark, deadly power jacked her arousal up even higher.

She whimpered against his mouth. Not kissing him until now had been a huge mistake. The man was incredible at it. He was incredible at everything. His lips slipped down her throat and she did her best to unfasten his belt.

"We need to have a serious talk about your magic." He pulled back long enough to frown at her. "You are going to *have* to try Good spells. There's no reason a level six witch couldn't take out some yetis."

"I don't want to perform Good magic." She complained, even though she suspected he was right. "I was just going to walk right out, without a fight. It would have worked."

"Just kill your enemies and be done with it." He shook his head, like he was her disapproving homicide coach. "You're sure as hell willing to fight *me* and I'm eight-million times more dangerous than a pack of yetis."

She kissed his chin. "Not to me, you're not."

His forehead rested against hers. "No, my darling. Not to you." He agreed, breathing in her scent. "You're the only one I've ever wanted to be kind to."

"And you almost *are*, some of the time." She nodded encouragingly.

Trevelyan snorted. "Kindness doesn't come naturally to me." He allowed. "Killing things does, though. If you won't do Good magic, then you need to involve me in your plans, so I can *help* you. You see that, right?"

"I don't really do 'plans.' I'm just trying to save Marrok. And you said you didn't want to help me…"

He cut her off. "I will *always* help you, whether I want to or not. You should *know* that."

She rolled her eyes at his outraged tone. "How could I possibly know that?"

"How could you *not?*"

"Because you seemed pretty against the idea of coming to the Club Kingdom. In fact, you specifically told me…"

"I don't care what I told you, before! I'm telling you something *true*, right now."

She blinked, because neither of them screwed around with the Tell Me Something True Game. "You are?"

"*Yes*." His voice was certain. "I don't have much to offer you, but I am loyal. One thousand fucking percent." Green eyes burned into hers. "And all my loyalty is yours. Every bit of it. So, if you find that doing Good magic is too abhorrent for you... Fine." He still looked aggravated by her resistance, but he waved it aside. "You can stay right behind me and be safe, instead."

Esmeralda was mesmerized. "You want to keep me safe?"

"I *will* keep you safe." Trevelyan's hand cupped her face, again. "Your enemies will break against me, like waves hitting the shore. I will stand between you and them, and I will kill them all." He made it sound simple and certain. "But in order to do that, I need to be *with* you."

"If it makes you feel any better, you kept me safe with that waterproofing spell."

That didn't make him feel any better. It just upset him more. "You nearly got wet? How the fuck did *that* happen? You were gone a few hours and nearly died ten different ways."

"But I *didn't* die." She kissed him more gently than before. "Thanks to my True Love."

His sighed against her lips, like she was the one who cast the spell on him. "Protecting you is all that matters." He murmured.

"I appreciate you taking care of me. Really. But, you should not have cast something that big, before your powers healed. You could have seriously hurt yourself."

"And you could have melted." He wasn't the least bit repentant. "It seems like you almost *did*."

"The geysers didn't melt me and I even killed one of the yetis, as a matter of fact. It was a big one, too."

"The corpse in the other room was your doing?" He promptly answered his own question. "Obviously it was. No one else would murder a yeti with an old television set."

"The TV was an accident." Esmeralda didn't really want to discuss that part, so of course he wanted to discuss it. She resisted the urge to pout. Mostly. "Damn frog spell never works right."

Trevelyan paused thinking it over, but he still didn't get the connection. "Log, hog, grog, smog...?" He trailed off questioningly, his head canting to one side.

"Analog." She muttered. "The TV is ana*log*."

His slow grin was breathtaking. "You are *never* boring, Ez."

"I'm glad you're so entertained by my misfiring powers."

"I'm entertained by you, just being *you*. Do not *ever* leave me, again." Trevelyan refocused on getting her naked, lust hot in his eyes. "What the hell were you *thinking?*"

Esmeralda helped him strip off her pants. "Can we argue later? I want you inside me, now."

"I can multitask." He assured her, fully invested in both undressing her and ranting. "I am *really* goddamn irritated that I woke up and you were gone."

"I left a note."

"What the hell difference does that make?"

None, but Esmeralda felt the need to defend herself somehow. "I also discussed all the 'separate lives' rules with you. You said we didn't have to share everything..."

"The rules are changing." Trevelyan interrupted, angry and gorgeous.

"Why do you get to change the rules? I hate following *any* rules and I'm sick of you trying to switch things all around, just as I get a handle on how to bend them."

"Well, I'm sick of trailing you through the damn snow!"

"That's only happened once."

"And it's never happening again. The separate lives rule is *done*. All of it. How did you even talk me into that idea, in the first place?"

"You're the one who came up with it!"

Trevelyan kept talking. "*Done*." He repeated furiously. "Our lives are now so enmeshed, they're a Mobius strip." Her bra got tossed over his shoulder and he paused to lick the valley between her breasts. A sound of intense satisfaction left him, when she ran another hand through his hair.

"Trev..." Her body was on fire for him.

"If you leave me, I really will burn down the world." He whispered against her flesh. "I am not in control, when it comes to you. I never will be. And when I get out of control Bad things happen." His volume rose with each word. "Unless you really do want mindless wanton destruction across every known realm, *you'll stay fucking put.*"

"I missed you, too." She agreed breathlessly.

The admission calmed him. His thumb brushed tenderly over her lower lip. "...Did you?" The question was hesitant and surprisingly vulnerable.

"A lot." She swallowed. "Can I tell you something true?"

"Always, my darling."

"A thousand percent of my loyalty belongs to you, too. That is why I would never risk your safety for mine."

He made a face, like that concern was ludicrous. "I'm not at risk. I'm a dragon. Destroying people is one of my many gifts."

"And I'm a witch. Do you think our relationship is one way? That only you want to keep your True Love safe?"

His brows compressed. "...Yes?" It sounded like a guess.

"*No.*" Esmeralda corrected. "I will try Good magic. And I will include you in all my ideas. And I won't leave without telling you. But I will *not* stand behind you, while you risk your life. It's always the two of us, when the army shows up to attack." She wrinkled her nose. "And I feel like that's probably gonna happen to us *a lot*. When it does, we'll face things side-by-side. Deal?"

"Deal." Trevelyan's face was absolutely enthralled. "You and me, witch."

"You and me, dragon." She smiled, pleased with how quickly he'd learned. "I'm glad you're here, you know. Not just because you rescued me, but because I don't like being without you."

"Not even for a few hours?"

"Nope. I've gotten used to you, I think. A couple days ago, I was ready to beat you to death with a broomstick. But now..." She lifted her shoulder in a shrug. "I don't ever want us to be apart."

He gazed at her, his mouth curving at one corner. "Well, I guess you should decide to keep me then."

CHAPTER TWENTY-FIVE

Pick your perfect nail polish from our unlimited selection!
Fucking the Bad Guy Fuchsia: Deep down, you know you want to give it a try.

Happily Ever Witch Cosmetics Website

Near the Club Castle

Dragons could hold simultaneous, yet directly competing worldviews.
They were wholly self-centered, but their families meant everything to them. They were slow to trust, but suicidally loyal. Cruel, but playful. Isolated, but needy. Protective, but reluctant to show any care. They delighted in breaking rules, but they wanted absolute surety that their mates could never escape.
That last conundrum made wedding customs among the dragons' confusing for outsiders to understand. Dragons liked to be married. It was a territorial marking. An invisible sign that proclaimed, "This is *my* mate and not yours."
Possessiveness in dragons went even deeper than magic and marriage meant they didn't have to worry about rivals.
Well, dragons *always* worried about rivals, but marriage mitigated their concerns. It was an unmistakable boundary that only the very stupid tried to circumvent. Those dumb bastards were viciously and summarily slaughtered, as a warning to others. It was a wonderful system.
Dragons didn't care about some wizard or religious authority actually *declaring* them legally wed, though. Hell, no. What

gave some outsider the power to tell a dragon anything? *They* decided when they were married.

And Trevelyan decided he was married.

"You think I should keep you, huh?" Esmeralda grinned, oblivious to the fact she was now his wife.

"I think you might as well, since I'm not going to leave." He wound her shiny green hair around his finger. It looked almost as pretty as the black curls. "It'll save us both a lot of trouble."

"You like causing trouble."

"I like waking up with my True Love in the same kingdom. So, I think we're going to need to make a deal. I'm offering an even trade: You for Marrok."

She blinked.

"It's very fair." Trevelyan pressed, ready to sell the idea. "I help you save the wolf. I won't burn the Four Kingdoms to cinders. I'll give up my revenge... And in exchange you accept me as your mate."

"What are you talking about? I've never stopped you from calling me your mate."

"You need to decide I'm *your* mate." He stressed. Why should he be the only one married in their marriage?

Esmeralda frowned suspiciously, like she was looking for loopholes in the deal.

Trevelyan smiled, as if he had nothing to hide. Given the fact that she'd refuse to go along with his plan if he explained it, he saw no upside to explaining it. The only time she'd ever brought up marrying him, it had been to scoff at the very idea. It seemed far smarter to make the deal that secured him as her husband and then fill her in at some later date. Sometime far, far in the future.

He arched a brow. "Deal?"

Esmeralda stared at him. "Sort of a lopsided agreement, isn't it?"

He made a face. "Alright, you're clearly doing more. But, I detest your useless family. Also, it's cold here and I hate the cold. So, I am giving *something* up."

"No, I mean, I'm going to keep you either way." She leaned up to kiss him smartly. "I've been looking everywhere for you,

Trevelyan. For years and years. You *are* my family."

Something within him relaxed. "*Finally,* you realize that."

"I've realized it from the first moment we met. I told you right then: family sticks together." She pulled back to frown at him. "You wanted me to pick you or Marrok and that's not how this works. I'm sticking with every single one of you lunatics."

Trevelyan considered the arrangement. "But you like me best of everyone?"

Crimson eyes rolled. "Yes, Trev. I like you best."

Excellent. "I like you best, too. In fact, you can be Esmeralda of the Green Dragons, if you want." He offered that with studied nonchalance, even though his heart was pounding. "Being the last of my line gets tedious. You can join."

She happily nodded. "Okay. I've never been part of a line, before."

"Okay." He drew in a deep breath, relief and excitement filling him. He was winning. He knew he would. "So we have an agreement, then? You for Marrok?"

"Of course! It's win/win for me. But, you don't *have* to help Marrok. That's what I'm trying to tell you. "

His brow furrowed. It was unsafe for her to be so trusting. "No. You shouldn't make this deal without getting something in return."

"I *am* getting something, dummy. I'm getting you."

Trevelyan realized he didn't have a response to that. The woman was so sweet it left him defenseless, at times.

"You can come along with me to the Club Kingdom, if you want. But you don't *need* to." Esmeralda went on, ignoring his confusion. "And you don't need to get involved in the actual rescue process."

That idea was ridiculous. "I *am* the actual rescue process. It would be best if you went back to the Heart Kingdom and let me go after the wolf myself. I swear I won't kill him. Maim him...?" He seesawed his hand. "No promises. But not kill him."

"Nah." Esmeralda said easily.

He sighed at how difficult she was. "If you're going to be picky, I won't even maim him. Alright? Not permanently, anyway. I would just prefer it if you were safe, while I went and saved that worthless..."

"Nah."

Trevelyan rubbed his forehead. The woman complicated everything.

"We'll both go. Side-by-side." She offered instead. "Just like we agreed."

Did he have a choice?

Esmeralda was determined to rescue her moronic brother and Trevelyan was determined to seal their mating bond. Helping her was the best option. Besides, the quicker the wolf was safe, the quicker Trevelyan could get his witch away from the Club Kingdom. She was more important than Marrok. More important than anything.

His mate was all that mattered.

He *never* wanted to go through another morning like this one. Once he'd figured out how to walk through the magic mirror in the Heart Castle, it had been simple enough to follow her path. Simple to track her across a field of frozen geysers. Simple to know that she'd been snatched by yetis. Simple to imagine all the gruesome things they could be doing to her. By the time he'd arrived at the cave, he'd been ready to kill everything he saw. Even more so than usual.

That rage and terror had faded, once the witch was back in his arms. Now, he had to make sure she stayed there.

"Deal." He promised. "You decide to keep me and I'll make sure Marrok stays alive." There were plenty of other assholes he could murder, after all. Trevelyan was fortunate, in that regard. The world was full of people he hated.

"You sure?" Esmeralda asked, like she still couldn't believe his offer.

"I'm sure." Marrok would be pissed off if Trevelyan was the one to ride to his rescue, which would be almost as satisfying as slaughtering him. The man would absolutely despise that he owed Trevelyan his life. The thought was bolstering. "I have to go to the Club Kingdom, anyway. The Queen has your other three tiaras. I'll just kill her, instead of Marrok. Compromise is part of any successful relationship."

"I thought dragons never, ever compromised."

"We do with our mates," his mouth nipped at her ear, "Mate." Dragons were amazing husbands. (They were the first to say so.) And Trevelyan's father had often boasted that the Green Dragon line produced the very best husbands of all. His mother hadn't always agreed, granted, but they would both be pleased to see how easily Trevelyan was adjusting to the role.

Esmeralda was understandably impressed with his negotiating skills. "Well, I'd be keeping you either way... But lending a hand on my rescue mission gets you the bonus of making me very happy."

"How very happy?"

"*Really* very happy." Her smile was all wicked virtue.

"I want you to decide on me right now, Ez." Inside of him, the dragon was closer to the surface than it had been since he'd woken up from the sleeping spell. His powers had recovered enough that he could transform, but he wasn't about to do that. Green smoke rose from his skin and he ignored it.

Esmeralda didn't. "Does your dragon wish I was a dragon, too?"

"No. He wants you, just as you are. And that isn't going to happen, because in that form I would crush you. But you need to have sex with this version of me *right now*."

"I mean... sure." She shrugged, ready to go along with the plan. "But, I could *look* like a dragon, if it would make you really very happy. The same way I looked like a yeti. Or I could just be me, only really big. The same way I got really tiny and escaped you the first time we had sex. I'm amazing at glamours. I can look like anything."

Trevelyan stared at her. So did his dragon.

"It'll be fun." Esmeralda blinked up at him. "Big or dragon?" She prompted.

"Big." His voice was darker than usual. Even he heard it. The dragon was taking control and Trevelyan wasn't stopping it, now. He'd never been with anyone, as a dragon. It had never even occurred to him that it was possible. The idea was intoxicating. Having a level six witch for a mate was a never-ending adventure.

Esmeralda casually glanced upward, gauging the height of the ceiling. "That cave with the cooking fire is probably our best place to do this. Otherwise I'm not sure we're going to fit." Trevelyan was already hustling her back towards the larger cavern, moving her along in front of him. "Take your underwear off." He attacked the fabric, not waiting for her to comply.

"You're sure there's no one but us around here, right?"

"If anyone was stupid enough to survive, I'll kill them even harder this time." That was a heartfelt promise. He used magic and brute force to finish undressing her. "Fuck yes." He had her naked by the time they reached the massive chamber, his hands caressing her glorious skin.

"You shred two-thirds of my wardrobe." Esmeralda complained good-naturedly.

"It should be more. Covering your body is a crime against nature." His hands had claws, now. He gently grazed them over her skin, watching her nipples peak. "You have the most beautiful breasts I've ever seen."

Esmeralda's head fell back against his shoulder. Sighing in pleasure, as his inhuman hands caressed her delicate flesh.

"You say that to all your mates, I'll bet."

"I only have one mate."

"And it had better stay that way."

"It will." She didn't fully understand how seriously dragons took mating and there was no benefit in explaining it to her. Not when he was about to get everything he wanted. His teeth grazed the skin of her throat, marking her. He'd never fully understood why men did that to their mates, but now it all made perfect sense.

She didn't object to the feel of his teeth against her neck. Instead, she angled her head to give him better access. Like she wanted to be claimed. He could smell her growing arousal. Trevelyan took great pride in his villainous reputation, but he loved that she trusted him. That she was so sure she was safe in his arms.

"How much does your dragon want me?" She asked, excited for the game.

"Enough to cause a cave-in, chasing you down. Don't run from him."

She nodded, her pulse pounding.

He kissed it, enjoying the small sound she made in response.

"I'm very serious, Ez. This will be so much easier for you, if you just submit. In that form, I'll be less civilized and he's enormous. You understand?"

"Yes."

"You *promise* you understand?"

"Yes, I fully and completely understand, you control freak. Stop nagging."

Trevelyan stepped back from her, far from appeased. "Your forty-nine percent Goodness is always looking for an outlet. This is the moment. Be a Good girl, for once. Stay still and let the nice dragon fuck you."

She flicked him off, but her eyes were dancing with amusement.

Trevelyan grinned. Then, green smoke swirled and he was a dragon.

After the long confinement, the monster gloried in its freedom. His mind remained his own, but it was interlaced with something more primal. Something closer to the wild that beat at the very heart of him. All Trevelyan's senses were sharper. Everything looked brighter and sounded richer. ...And the poisoned-candy-smell of his mate was like a drug. It clouded his brain in want and possession. Need for her pumped through his blood.

Holy *God*. How had he lived even a day without her?

Esmeralda stared up at him, tiny and vulnerable and not the least bit afraid. "Oh wow."

In his dragon-form, he was towering. A beast of legend, somewhere between a serpent and a panther and a man, partially obscured by the green mist. His eyes stayed the same, though. Glowing. Fixed on her. Waiting.

Trevelyan's head canted to one side.

Esmeralda grinned... and took off running.

He'd expected nothing less.

The dragon snatched her up, shaking the cavern in his haste to

grab her. The mini-earthquake delighted her. Evil-doers loved natural disasters, especially when they caused them.
She tried to squiggle free of his hold, laughing.
Trevelyan's claws sealed around her, not letting her escape. Every dragon wanted to capture himself a damsel and now he'd done it. He lifted his prize right off the ground, which was simple to do when he was fifteen feet tall. Her soft little body felt glorious beneath his fingers. She tried to pry his thumb loose from around her waist, but he wasn't budging.
"Mine." His voice was dark and filled with smoke.
Esmeralda responded by making herself *sixteen* feet tall.
Trevelyan's exhilaration redlined. For the first time, his dragon had someone to play with and she wasn't going anywhere. The witch might be a foot taller now, but he was twice as strong. Sweeping her up in his arms was simple. He caught hold of her wrists and pinned her down. The green mist of his dragon-form coated her exquisite skin, mesmerizing him.
Esmeralda smiled, enjoying this tremendously. "I don't think it's my magic making sex between us more." She got out, her eyes bright. "I think it's just us."
Christ, he thought so, too.
"Your skin is green, like mine." She whispered. "I see it beneath the mist."
In this form, his body shimmered with iridescent scales in every possible shade of green, from grass to forest to sea. But the color still wasn't anywhere close to the magic of hers.
Trevelyan's mouth moved down her curves. No one else in the world had skin like his mate. It looked perfect. Felt perfect. Smelled perfect. It *was* perfect. He wanted to lick every inch of it, so that's what he did. In his dragon-form, his tongue was longer. Forked.
When it slid between her legs, Esmeralda made a sound of absolute rapture. "Please."
Oh, dragons loved it when their captives begged.
She arched, her pretty black fingernails sliding through his hair. The touch was like a balm, soothing and warm. His palms lifted her hips, angling her for his mouth. She tasted just as sweet as he knew she would.

"*Trev*." She breathed in awe. Her whole body trembled as he feasted. "Oh my God... Oh my *God*. Ohmygod!" The orgasm rushed over her less than a second later.

Esmeralda shrieked with surprise and ecstasy. One of her larger-than-normal hands slammed into the wall, cracking the foundation of the mountain above them. She didn't seem to even notice the colossal use of magic, her eyes closed in bliss.

Trevelyan had always been an arrogant bastard. (Although, was it *really* arrogance, if you were legitimately great at everything?) Still, at that moment, he'd never felt more smugly pleased with himself.

"You didn't even make it to the first stroke, that time." He moved back up her body, like the predator he was. "Are you *sure* you don't want to just submit, darling?"

Esmeralda responded by vanishing right out of his arms.

The dragon snarled in lust. Trevelyan totally agreed. Bedding his mate was always a challenge. He loved that too, even as it frustrated the hell out of him.

Esmeralda reappeared just out of reach. "How come I never get to chase you?" She asked breathlessly.

"We can play that game later." He glided after her, his eyes hot.

She probably would have responded with some wiseass remark, but she got distracted by the sight of his erection. He had no idea how she'd missed it before. Aroused dragons weren't small. Apparently, she'd been preoccupied with the swirling green smoke around his inhuman form and the sinister cast of his elongated features.

She blinked. "Um... I can make myself bigger if..."

The dragon was already on her. It took him less than a second to have her back on the ground. "Oh, I'll make it fit." He promised her, careful not to harm her extraordinary skin.

Esmeralda gave a gasp of surprise, like she hadn't expected him to move so fast. She was even more shocked when he flipped her over onto her stomach and pressed against her.

One of Trevelyan's hands lifted her into position, while the other tangled in her thick green curls, keeping her in place. "You wanted me to take you like this, back in front of the

fireplace. I could tell. Why did you stop me?"
"I don't know. I guess..." She swallowed and he realized she was suddenly anxious. "I told you, I've never had sex this way, right?"
Tenderness struck from out of nowhere. He had truly never been with anyone so innocent. "Well, this is your first time, then." He teased, just to distract her from her nerves.
"Excellent! Dragons love defiling virgins."
Esmeralda flashed him a glare over her shoulder, forgetting her nerves. "Oh, shut up, Trev."
He chuckled. Sex with her really was fun. His hand glided up the interior of her leg. "If it helps you get through this ordeal, just remind yourself that your evil mate is making you do all these Bad things. He's mostly an animal and he wants to claim you like one."
Her breathing changed, getting choppier, as his fingers eased inside her wet core. She made a small sound that had him growling with pleasure.
"That's right." Trevelyan's mouth found the edge of her ear, even as his fingers slid in and out of her. "See, you can be a Good girl. Just submit, darling. Give me what's mine."
"Shit." Her body grew even hotter, aroused by his words and his touch. "Your dominance kink is extremely twisted and wrong."
"Yes, I like it, too."
"A Good girl would *not* submit to a dragon. Just so you know." She undulated against him, like she just couldn't help herself and met his eyes over her shoulder. "Luckily for you, I'm fifty-one percent wicked and you kind of inspire me." Her grin was filled with playful Badness. "Sir."
His brain short-circuited. The woman was going to be the death of him. It was inevitable. "I need you, now." His voice was completely inhuman, the most bestial part of him seizing control. "Open your legs wider. There we are." He removed his hand and positioned himself behind her, his claws still clutching her hair. "Ready?"
"Yes, I... *Holy shit!*"
Her consent ended in a cry, as Trevelyan drove into her. He

sure wasn't giving her time to change her mind.

As he pushed forward, his head went back in ecstasy. All his senses were blazing. The feel of Esmeralda around him. Her taste on his tongue, and her glorious scent enveloping him, and the sounds she made, and the way she looked stretched out beneath him... This really was like the first time he'd ever been with a woman. With Esmeralda everything felt *more*.

"Holy shit..." Esmeralda got out again. "I love this." Her weight dropped forward onto her elbows, her hips instinctively rising to take even more of him. "Oh, I really love this. You should have told me how fun this was."

"*Christ.*" Smoke escaped his lips, as he gritted out the words. "Do not even *try* running, until I'm finished with you."

She liked that warning. He could tell by the way she instantly tried to move away. Because he knew she'd enjoy it (and because he just wanted to) he let go of her hair and grasped the back of her neck. Holding her down.

"*Trev!*" She was already close to another orgasm. She loved to be caught and he loved to chase. It was a perfect match. "You're so big and so *deep*."

The dragon relished his possession. Trevelyan had never been so enmeshed with the beast. So totally one. Their thoughts and feelings were exactly the same. ...And they were all Esmeralda.

He dipped his head and licked his tongue across the pulse in her neck, tasting where he'd marked her and every single part of him growled with satisfaction. "Just... *ours*."

Esmeralda's whole body shuddered with pleasure, like she knew Trevelyan wasn't alone in claiming her. Or maybe this was the most fully himself he'd ever been. Either way, she wanted to be taken by a monster. She pressed closer to him, eagerly accepting his heavy thrusts.

The dragon was on fire for her.

"I can feel how very, *very* Good you are, when I'm inside of you." Trevelyan got out, his tone ravenous. "Your Goodness is all over me."

"I can't help that. I've tried to get rid of it..."

He cut her off. "Do not change *anything*." It was a command.

"You... You want the Good?"

"I want every single piece of you, Ez. I *need* you. I want you to need me back." He moved his head to meet her eyes.

"Promise to keep me." Esmeralda was trapped beneath him, at his mercy, but it seemed pretty clear which of them had really submitted. "Please, my darling." He was prepared to cheat, beg, and die to have her as his mate.

He didn't have to, though.

Esmeralda gave him what he needed. "I'm keeping you. You know I am." Her body trembled as he hit a spot she really liked. "*Oh.*"

"Right there?"

"*Yes.*" It was a sob. "Please let me come."

He moved his hand to the front of her, clawed fingers carefully finding the tight knot of her desire. Scratching it lightly.

"*Trev!*" Her exquisite body clamped around him and sent him over the edge.

Ecstasy washed over him, blocking out everything but his mate. Fire and smoke spiraled towards the ceiling, as his roar of completion shook the cave.

Nothing else even came close to the feelings Esmeralda created in him. Whenever he was with her, it was like he'd discovered something bigger than magic. She was completely right. It was no spell making sex between them more. It was "more" because he was crazy in love with the woman.

Emphasis on the "crazy" part.

The emotion had been coming on for a while, but now it was all-consuming. Trevelyan wasn't known for his moderate approach to life. His love for her could mean a cataclysm for the rest of existence, because nothing else meant a damn thing to him. He could feel whatever common sense he'd once had drowning in the tide of his obsession. Lines and limits were washed away. Trevelyan's world reoriented itself, so one small witch sat at the center of all creation. He'd do anything for her. Literally anything.

And for a dragon "anything" was a hell of a lot.

Esmeralda shrank down to her normal size and her hair went back to black, like she was too replete to keep up the glamours.

But she didn't move away from him. Instead, she snuggled against his side, unconcerned with the difference in their sizes or the green smoke that coated his monstrous form.

The dragon purred, wrapping himself around her. No creature alive could have gotten her away from him. In that moment, she was the safest woman in the universe.

Her lips curved in sleepy contentment, as if she knew it. "Have I decided on keeping you enough, yet?" She asked drowsily.

Trevelyan's claws smoothed through her ebony curls. "Almost." He transformed himself back into his normal form, because that was how the ritual was traditionally done and he wanted every possible i dotted and t crossed. He was leaving her no escape route.

"Your eyes look different." She whispered, her gaze on his face.

"Changing back sometimes takes a moment." Although his eyes should have remained the same, in both forms.

"No, that isn't it." She yawned, not really focused. "What are you doing, now?"

Trevelyan took hold of her wrist and guided it between her legs. Esmeralda watched, not protesting, while he made sure their combined scents saturated her palm. Then, Trevelyan directed her hand back up again, flattening it against his chest. His fingers slid between hers, holding her hand over the elaborate tattoos of suffering knights and lovely flames.

He watched her expectantly. "Mate."

"Mate." She repeated, giving him what he wanted.

Finally.

Trevelyan drew in a deep breath, as the mating sealed. There were no wedding vows in a dragon ceremony, but the magic was just as strong. Ancient enchantments snapped into place. Spells so engrained in dragons that Trevelyan didn't even know how they were created. They just existed in his blood and bone, left there by his devious ancestors. For a thousand generations, dragons had used them to ensure their mates never got away. It was inspiring to come from a line of such feral madmen.

Satisfaction filled Trevelyan, as he felt all the invisible ties between him and the witch knot tight.

Esmeralda felt it, too. Her dreamy expression evaporated and she was wide awake. Those too-clever crimson eyes sharpened, searching his face. She didn't know exactly what had happened, but she knew it had been massive.
"What did you just do?" She demanded.
"Nothing."
"Troll shit."
"No, it's true. *You* did this. You decided on me, just like we agreed."
"Uh-huh." She wasn't buying it. "And what does that mean exactly?"
"You really should have asked that *before* you agreed to the deal." He chided. "Why would you trust an evil dragon to lead you through some mysterious ceremony, without questioning him a bit? If I wasn't playing nice with you, I could have just cast all manner of diabolical…"
She interrupted his helpful lecture. "What does 'deciding' mean in dragon-ese?"
"That I'm yours, of course. And you're mine. We belong to each other, forever-after."
Esmeralda seemed to like that idea. He could see it in her face.
"Yeah?"
"Is there even a doubt?"
"No." She admitted, but she still wasn't completely mollified. "And that's *all* it means?"
"Essentially."
"But not *entirely*, right? Because some kind of magic was just triggered between us. Something huge."
"Yes, I noticed it, too."
Her gaze narrowed, as if his very innocent tone had all her suspicions blazing. "How permanent is this very huge spell?"
"Oh, you're stuck with me for quite a while, I'm afraid."
"You can't undo it?"
"Nope." And he'd never felt more pleased about a limitation on his magic. The mating bond was specifically designed to be eternal. The dragons of old hadn't been idiots. They'd made sure their mates were tightly secured in their grasps.
Wheels turned in Esmeralda's head. "Did you just marry us? In

a goddamn *cave?*"

She didn't sound happy. Shit. He didn't like making the witch unhappy. Telling her the unvarnished truth would no doubt make her even *more* unhappy, so Trevelyan instinctively hedged. "Dragons are only married when we decide to be married. Everyone knows that."

"So, *that's* what the 'deciding' thing means?"

Dammit. He should have phrased that differently. Trevelyan was quiet, weighing how much trouble he was in.

She didn't appreciate his hesitation. (He was clearly in *a lot* of trouble.) "Answer me!"

"When a dragon formally accepts his mate and she decides to accept him in return, magic seals the bond." He said very carefully. "They belong to each other, after that."

"How is that different than being married?"

It wasn't.

"Um..." Trevelyan hunted for hairs to split. "Well, we don't need rings..."

Esmeralda sat up, anger on her face. "So you decided to do this dragon-y mating ritual and now we're magically bonded forever. Am I getting that right?"

"Essentially."

"Son of a bitch." Esmeralda got to her feet, glamouring new clothes for herself. The green jumpsuit covered too much of her skin, but at least the color was right and it looked warm. "No way am I going along with this. *I* didn't decide to get married and witches are only married when we *decide*. Just like dragons. I just decided that."

He shook his head. "You can't decide that."

"Why not? Seems like *you* can decide all sorts of shit."

"Because this is the way dragons have *always* done things. You can't just arbitrarily change the rules."

"I hate rules! Besides, you change rules, all the time. Look at the separate lives thing. I was following *those* rules and you undid the whole idea, right as I was getting the hang of..."

He cut her off, sitting up and scowling. "No! That was *you* finding loopholes to exploit." It still infuriated Trevelyan to recall how she'd vanished on him. The panic and the desolation had been worse than losing his magic. "So now I'm doing the same thing: liberally interpreting our agreement."

"I didn't exploit any loopholes! We were playing every dragon and witch for themselves."

Trevelyan's own temper sparked. "Not anymore we're not! I opened my eyes and you were *gone*. That changes the whole game." He pointed to his temple. "I heard you in my fucking head, calling my name, and I had *no idea* how to get to you."

"You said it was impossible to hear each other like that. That magic didn't work that way."

"Except, *I heard you in my head*." He repeated emphatically. "So, I'm thinking what's *really* impossible is predicting how level six magic works. I think you were afraid and you reached for me, just like you said happened when you were in that orphanage."

Crimson eyes met his and held. ...And he knew he was right. To every other being in the world, Trevelyan was a creature of darkness. But his mate instinctively turned to him for safety. His chest tightened with emotion and his voice softened. "I can't promise that nothing will ever frighten you, again. But I promise you, one thousand percent, I will kill anything that does." It was a vow. "Do you believe me?"

She gave a jerky nod.

"You belong to me." He knew she liked hearing that. Liked the reassurance of their bond. So did he. "There will be moments when you wish you didn't. But, nothing will ever change it. You can't get rid of me. I need you." The words were bare. "I don't like needing anyone, but I need *you*, Esmeralda. You're my family."

"I wasn't trying to get rid of you." She shook her head, her anger lessening. "I would never do that. I need you back."

Happiness flooded him. "Yeah?"

"Yes! You belong to me, just as much as I belong to you. And you know I'll kill anything that frightens you, too. I wiped out a couple thousand knights, because you asked."

He smiled at that treasured memory.

"I was coming back to you, Trevelyan. There is nowhere else I would rather be. I explained it all in the note."

His momentary relief evaporated. "Fuck the note! You *left* me. You ran off while I was asleep, because you knew I would try to stop you. I needed the mating ritual to ensure that it didn't happen again.

"I *asked* you how our separate lives deal worked and then I did exactly what you wanted." Esmeralda gave a lofty sniff. "The rules didn't say I had to wake you up, every time I leave the house. And anyway, that's all behind us."

"It's not behind *me*. I'm still furious about it. I plan to be for quite some time."

She kept talking. "*If* we get married, it will be because I say 'yes.' That's what we're focused on, now."

"We already negotiated that!" He sat on the floor, watching her pace. "We had a deal that you would decide on me, if I helped your dumbass brother. Well, you decided. You can't back out of it, now."

"You didn't explain the fine print of that deal."

"The rules didn't say I *had* to explain it." He taunted, tossing her words back at her.

They glared at each other for a long moment.

"Okay, time out." She abruptly made a T-shape with her hands. "As I've been saying all along, rules are not our friends. Villains shouldn't try to follow them. We suck at it."

He grunted, because that was true.

"From now on, let's just tell each other everything. It'll be so much easier."

He considered that proposal. "*Everything* we tell each other is true? Like the game never stops?"

"Yes. There needs to be honesty between us, all the time. Otherwise, we'll keep finding ways to bend the rules and this crap will keep happening."

Trevelyan nodded. "Deal."

"Deal." She pushed back a handful of dark curls and returned to arguing. "But, we're still not married. You tricked me into it."

Trevelyan promptly resumed the fight, too. "Because you would have refused, if I hadn't. This way I get what I want." He looped one arm around his knee, exasperated at how complicated she was making this. "It's too late. The spell is set, just like we signed a marriage scroll. Nothing can change it." Esmeralda's eyes narrowed, as if that was a dare.

Fuck.

He did *not* want to dare a level six witch to change something he didn't want changed. Trevelyan had faith in the craftiness of his ancestors, but he had *more* faith in Esmeralda's fathomless magic. Who the hell knew what she was capable of, if she got mad enough? He didn't need her brainstorming ways to get rid of him.

Trevelyan quickly backtracked. "It's still a fair deal. I'll save Marrok and be a good mate to you." He made a face, because they'd just agreed to be honest. "Well, I mean, not *Good* good, but I'm loyal and I proved to you I could enspell guitars. Surely you can work with that."

"I'm not married to you, unless I say yes." She reiterated stubbornly.

This was insane! The woman was already his. There was simply no denying it. Except she was denying it. How could he stop her from denying it?

Trevelyan thought for a beat. Witches' mating customs were different than dragons'. If he didn't give her the opportunity to choose him openly, she wasn't going to accept their bond. Esmeralda was too much like him, in too many ways. Death or freedom. Even if it beyond-a-shadow-of-a-doubt *existed*, she'd continue to view their marriage as illegitimate, if she felt trapped. That wouldn't do, at all. Everyone needed to know Esmeralda was his, especially Esmeralda.

"Alright." Trevelyan switched to a different tactic. Dragons kept trying strategies until one worked. It was how they racked up so many victories. "What will make you marry me?"

She blinked at him, like she hadn't expected that question. Trevelyan raised his eyebrows at her obvious surprise. "A mating ceremony in your culture is a wedding. We can have one of those."

Women liked weddings. At least his sister did. Marion planned another elaborate marriage ceremony to Nicholas ever year or so, dragging her poor True Love through a new mess of seating arrangements, cake tastings, and the occasional barbarian invasion.

Esmeralda looked wary, but at least she was listening.

"I told you, I can compromise with my mate. ...Even when she doesn't want to admit that she's my mate." Trevelyan persisted. "I want to get married, in a witches' ceremony. So we can *both* feel like we decided."

Her lips parted. He must be on the right track.

"Let's make another deal. What can I do to get a 'yes' from you?"

"I don't know." She finally murmured. She seemed calmer. He was winning. He could tell. "I guess you could try *asking* me to marry you."

Simple enough. "Will you marry me, Ez?"

"Nope."

Trevelyan tipped his head back and groaned. "Oh for God's sake..."

"I'm mad at you, because you're an idiot. I need time to calm down." She headed for the cave entrance, black curls bouncing. "Ask again later."

Shit.

Compromising was going to take some getting used to.

CHAPTER TWENTY-SIX

Pick your perfect nail polish from our unlimited selection!
Phony Magic Silver: This oil slick polychrome polish reflects every perfect shade you *wish* was there, but really isn't. Like sleight-of-hand, it's all an illusion dependent on a desperate desire to believe.

Happily Ever Witch Cosmetics Website

The Club Castle

Something wasn't quite right.
Bluebeard tried convincing himself that the vague sense of unease was just his imagination. That the situation was all going great. That the spell convincing Marrok he was married to Snow White was permanent. That Bluebeard had done his job. That the Queen of Clubs would soon let him go on his merry way. That this happy family meal wouldn't end in a bloodbath.
The only problem was: he didn't quite believe any of it.
"I think we should honeymoon in the Fae Islands." Snow White told Marrok, hanging onto his arm like parasitic moss. "They're supposed to be just mimsy! I've always wanted to see them."
"And I've always wanted to see you in a bathing suit." Marrok drawled and playfully poked her up-turned nose with his index finger.
Snow White giggled like that was just the height of wit.
Bluebeard tried not to retch in his mustard-flavored oatmeal.
The Mad Hatter had fixed a "surprise brunch" for the whole family and it was *definitely* a surprise. There were worms in the coffee and extra, extra, *extra* sugar in the butter. But no matter how repulsive the food, it was still more appetizing than

listening to Snow White and Marrok cooing at each other. God, something just wasn't quite right here.

"Gyre soldiers are in the Fae Islands." The Mad Hatter's huge purple top hat had been switched for a huge purple chef's hat. "*Lots* of them. And they're a much more organized group of warriors than those rejects in the Diamond Kingdom. Stay away from humans, Snow. Too many crazies."

Aside from calling-other-kettles-black, the Hatter was fully focused on his gourmet cooking. He even occasionally whistled while he worked. An off-key version of *Twinkle, Twinkle Little Bat* accompanied the rhythmic *slams* of a cleaver as he chopped up a live mouse. A make-your-own-omelet station was being arranged on the ebony wood buffet, against the wall. Bluebeard would be skipping the minced rodent, when he created his perfect egg dish.

He also didn't argue with the man's take on those magic-hating humans. Although, to Bluebeard's mind, the Gyre's murderous bigotry and the Mad Hatter's murderous lunacy were exactly the same. Get too close and you ended up like a mouse in an omelet: Sliced to pieces and wondering how the fuck you got there.

"Hatty, don't start complaining about the Gyre." The Queen of Clubs instructed. "I don't want any politics discussed today. I'm having a guest over later and I want everything civilized and polite. Grimhilde the Wicked Witch. You remember her?"

"Nope."

"Of course you do! She has a place in the Spade Kingdom. She's held in *very* high regard, for her seminal thesis on magical uses for still-beating hearts." The Queen of Clubs seemed pleased to know such an illustrious person. "Grimhilde has the exact expertise I need. With the witch's heart taken care of, we can decapitate that green bitch and get my tiara. Witches' biology can be so complicated, so an expert is really…"

"You said you were going to spare Ez." Marrok interrupted. "We had a deal."

The Queen of Clubs frowned impatiently. "We still do. I'm sure Grimhilde will be able to find some way to rip out your friend's still-beating heart without killing her. It *will* still be beating, after all."

"What about the decapitating part?"

"Oh, that's hardly ever fatal for witches." The Queen of Clubs assured him airily.

Marrok seemed to accept that explanation.

The spell must be messing with his mind, because anyone sober could tell she was lying. At least she wasn't focused on Bluebeard or on the undercurrent of not-quite-rightness filling the dining room, though. That was the important thing. Bluebeard's eyes stayed on Marrok, who went back to attentively listening to Snow White jabber about how pretty his tawny hair looked. The wolf couldn't have seemed more enthralled with every word the weirdo spoke. Except his left hand was on the table, shackles on his wrist and his fingers restlessly drumming.

And his wedding band was still visible.

A wheeze escaped Bluebeard, as he finally realized what was wrong. His spell should have erased the ring, as Scarlett vanished from Marrok's mind. His spell *would* have erased it, if it had actually worked. Nothing could remove the ring totally, of course, but it should have become invisible. Nobody else would understand that detail, because they didn't understand Bluebeard's specialized magic. *He* knew it, though.

Just like he suddenly knew that Marrok was faking.

The wolf wasn't under a spell, at all! He was pretending and plotting and... *holy fuck.* This was terrible. This was so, *so* terrible. Whatever Marrok was up to, it was a disaster for Bluebeard. Brunch was for sure going to end in a bloodbath. He could tell.

Bluebeard must have made some sound or the smell of his increasing fear must have hit the wolf's senses. Marrok's topaz gaze swung his way, like a hunter spotting game in the woods. Bluebeard glowered at him. Hating the man for not being enspelled, like he was supposed to be. For screwing up everything, with his stubborn, unbreakable, animalistic loyalty to his damn True Love. For beating Bluebeard's wonderful magic.

Marrok's head tilted to one side and there was something

predatory in the movement. Beneath the campus-hero good looks and affable charm, the Big Bad Wolf was a villain. He couldn't presently transform into his lupine self, but he could still sniff out the perfect weak spot.

Marrok slowly smiled.

And Bluebeard knew he was in a race for his life.

His frantic gaze cut over to the Queen of Clubs. Shit! What could he say that wouldn't get her enraged at him? He couldn't admit that the spell hadn't worked, because then she wouldn't need Bluebeard anymore. He'd have demon-mom trying to kill him, too. No, he needed someone else to blame.

Scarlett.

He'd blame Marrok's True Love! He'd convince the Queen to turn her wrath on that ugly stepsister. He'd say that as long as Scarlett was alive, the magic wouldn't hold, because wolves were too primitive. Bluebeard would insist that getting rid of Scarlett would solve the problem. Hell, that might do the trick for real. You never knew, right? Might as well give it a go.

"Majesty, we need to talk about…"

"Who wants strawberry jam in their mice and eggs?" The Mad Hatter asked, talking right over him.

Marrok leaned closer to Snow White, whispering in her ear.

"Don't we have apples?" The Queen of Clubs complained to her husband. "Hatty, you know I like apples in my omelets."

Bluebeard spoke louder, desperate now. "Majesty! I'm sensing that Scarlett Riding-Wolf is doing something to disrupt…"

Snow White let out a bloodcurdling scream of rage.

Everyone turned to look at her, except Marrok. The wolf leaned back in his chair, his smug gaze on Bluebeard. His expression was the same victorious taunting smirk that had pissed off everyone who'd ever crossed the man… Right before Marrok really fucked up their day.

Bluebeard felt himself pale.

"You're trying to ruin my happy marriage!" Snow White shrieked at Bluebeard. Her face was a thunderous mask of fury, her black curls bouncing as she leapt to her feet. "Marrok says you're trying to drive us apart!"

Marrok nodded, like it was nothing less than the truth. "Don't let him get away with it, honey."

"Snow," The Queen of Clubs began, flashing a suspicious look Marrok's way, "let's take a moment and calm down."

"Nothing will get in the way of our love!" Snow White stomped her foot, her face flushed with the force of her passion. "Nothing! Nothing! *Nothing!*"

"Snow!" The Queen of Clubs said again, more sternly now. "You're becoming overwrought. The wolf isn't going anyplace. Calm down."

"You've never liked Marrok, either!" Snow White screamed at her. "You were against my marriage from the start, Mommy! My husband told me so!"

The Queen of Clubs' mouth thinned, her deadly gaze zeroing in on the wolf. "What are you doing? We had a deal."

"We still do." Marrok drawled, throwing her own words back at her. "I'm just making sure we all know that I hold some cards in this game." He lounged there, casualness personified. "Snow'll take my side, if you and I have a falling out. The little woman's *crazy* about her new hubby."

Snow White's big, damp eyes swung towards her father.

"Daddy!" She wailed at an octave that had the crystal chandelier ringing. "Bluebeard's trying to ruin my marriage and Mother isn't stopping him!" She broke down in hysterical sobs, her arms flailing. "*Why is this happening to me!?*"

The Mad Hatter fished the oversized pocket watch out of his "Kiss the Cook" apron, fully occupied with his mustard omelet. "Fine, Snow. I'll help you kill the man. Just stop crying."

"You always give into her tantrums." The Queen of Clubs turned her ire towards her husband, throwing up her hands in frustration. "*That* is why she's like this!"

"Wait, who are we killing?" Bluebeard demanded, his eyes cutting around the room.

"Do *you* want to listen to her caterwauling all day, Anna?" The Mad Hatter clicked the plunger on the top of his watch. "No, this is simpler."

Bluebeard froze. Literally *froze.*

He tried to move, but it was impossible. That pocket watch trapped him in time, somehow. It was the same magic the Mad

Hatter had used by the Pool of Tears, when he stopped the Queen of Diamonds and chopped her head off. Only now *Bluebeard* was the one stuck in some fixed moment and awaiting death. Everyone else in the room was still moving and talking, but he was suspended like a living statue. Imprisoned in his immobile body.

Marrok's eyebrows shot up, like he hadn't been expecting that outcome.

The Queen of Clubs barely even noticed Bluebeard's plight. "Raising a child isn't *supposed* to be simple." She told the Mad Hatter angrily. "You want every day to be an unbirthday. That is not how we should co-parent. I'm always stuck with being the mean one, because *you* don't enforce boundaries with her."

"Bringing the wolf here was *your* idea." The Mad Hatter reminded her. "I thought Snow could do better. ...But, I guess William won't be marrying her, now." He shot the Queen of Clubs a pointed look. "Since that pigeon gardener of yours fed his body to the roses."

"Is *that* what your mood is about? Me killing some stupid tea party lizard?"

"I'm not in a mood. But, you would be pissed too, if I murdered any of your friends. In fact, you *have* been. Remember that ugly duchess?"

"Don't you *dare* compare the situations! Just because you don't like spices, you bludgeoned a noblewoman to death with crockery."

"She was getting pepper in my jam!"

Snow White selected a knife from the table, turning it over in her hand. Frowning, she shook her head and set it back down again. "Too small." She picked up another, examining the blade and finding it lacking, as well. "Too big."

"Is Bluebeard really worth ruining brunch?" The Mad Hatter asked the Queen of Clubs, like he was trying to defuse the whole situation. "Let's just give Snow her way."

"Well, I'm not dealing with the mess." Turning on her high heel, the Queen of Clubs went stomping towards the door.

"Not again."

"Anna..."

"No!" She turned back to him. "The eighth square will happen *today* and the empress will be crowned." She sounded frustrated to the point of tears. "I need that spell to claim my rightful position as empress! Only I've gotten new reports from the Heart Kingdom. Trevelyan and the witch aren't there, anymore. The palace is *empty*."

The Mad Hatter's brows went low over his spirally eyes. "How did they get out of the castle?"

Marrok's mouth curved. "Level six witch, that's how."

The Mad Hatter and the Queen of Clubs sent him identical glowers, then went back to scowling at each other.

"Even if Esmeralda found them a path somehow, Trevelyan is still the one to worry about." The Mad Hatter insisted. "He's a merciless villain and he'll shield his True Love. It's biology. I *told* you he was too dangerous to keep alive."

"I can't kill him, until I arrest him."

Marrok nodded, like that was a very wise decision... which probably meant it was total bullshit.

"*Arrest* him?" The Hatter scoffed.

"Yes! The brilligs are tracking Trevelyan, now. Once they bring him here, we'll put him on trial. We'll force him to undo any traps he's laid. Then, we can finally get the spell off the witch's heart and the tiara off her head."

Snow White selected another knife and turned it this way and that. "Just right." She decided. Looking calmer, she strolled towards Bluebeard with a spring in her step.

"Hang on... Now the damn *brilligs* are involved?" The Mad Hatter had clearly missed some planning sessions.

"I can control them." The Queen of Clubs sniffed. "You're being ridiculously quarrelsome."

"No, 'ridiculous' is you blocking all the Bad magic in the castle!"

"Are we back to that, now?" She demanded. "You should be glad that I blocked Bad energy. It will be easier for you to sniff out Goodness to eat."

"I know you're not going to pretend you did it as a favor to *me*."

Bluebeard began to seriously panic. No one was stopping Snow White. No one was even paying attention to her, like they already knew what was about to happen.

The Queen of Clubs tried a different tactic with her husband. "You always do this. You put everything you're annoyed about into one pot, so all the small arguments become one *big* argument. We can never discuss one thing at a time."

Snow White stopped to admire the eviscerated mice on the buffet, a dreamy look on her angelic face. She daintily popped a still-wriggling mouse tail into her mouth, sucking it down like a strand of spaghetti.

"You're blocking Bad magic." The Mad Hatter repeated slowly, like maybe the Queen of Clubs didn't understand his point. "We didn't 'discuss' that, at all. You just did it *your* way."

"Because all the ways belong to me! The queen is the only piece on the board who matters."

The Mad Hatter crossed his arms over his chest. "Really?" He deadpanned.

The Queen of Clubs blew out a breath, as if realizing she'd gone too far. "You know I didn't mean that the way it sounded. I'm just under a lot of stress."

He grunted, more exasperated than offended.

Bluebeard continued to struggle, trying to get free of the Mad Hatter's spell. No matter what he did, he couldn't move. Not even an inch.

"Bad magic will be back this afternoon." The Queen of Clubs promised. "I timed it to the eighth square. Everything is right on schedule."

Marrok frowned, clearly trying to understand what the eighth square meant.

The Queen of Clubs didn't bother to explain it. "Think of this like a big chess game, Hatty."

"I don't know how to play chess."

"What difference does *that* make? Until the eighth square, we're both Good enough to cast spells without Bad magic. Your pocket watch works without it. Bluebeard's spell on the wolf will stay in place without it. ...But without Bad magic, Trevelyan is screwed. All he *is* is Bad. He won't be able to strike at us."

"The witch has more Good magic than either of us, though."

"You think I'm afraid of her? Esmeralda's not a queen. She's a pawn and I can keep a pawn controlled. I have magic sensors on every gate and all the doorknob sentries alerted, just in case she tries to come here. Not that she *will*. She knows she's overmatched."

Marrok glanced towards the window, like he already expected to see the witch down there, headed their way.

"I researched Esmeralda's so-called 'fairest magic in the land.'" The Queen of Club continued scathingly. "Even the other witches know she's useless! The Cauldron Society barely even acknowledges her as a member."

"Who the hell is the Cauldron Society?"

"The international federation of accredited witches. Grimhilde is their president. They're very elite!"

The Mad Hatter groaned like that answer was the stupidest thing he'd ever heard.

The Queen of Clubs stomped a foot. "Why do you never support me?"

He pinched the bridge of his nose, trying to calm down. "I'm supporting you. When have I not supported you? I'm even making breakfast. But I'm not going to tell you an idea is smart when it's crazy." He pointed to his temple. "And when *I* say an idea is crazy, it's *really fucking crazy!*"

Snow White stopped directly in front of Bluebeard. Her grin was nothing but emptiness and horror. "I don't like you, anymore." She told him sweetly.

Oh Jesus...

"I'm not *just* a wife and mother, Hatty. I also have a career." The Queen of Clubs proclaimed. "I will be empress of Wonderland by tonight. To do that, Trevelyan needs to be captured and this is the best way to accomplish it fast. Do you not understand the kind of pressure I'm under?"

"Which is why it's better to let Snow do as she wants." The Mad Hatter circled back to his original objection, triumph in his tone. The Queen of Clubs had a point. He *did* bundle arguments together into one big pot. "None of us will have a moment's peace until she's killed him, so let her kill him. What's the big deal?"

Marrok's eyes were on Snow White, who'd hefted the knife. "Holy shit." He whispered. "She's really going to kill him."

Bluebeard screamed in his mind, even as the rest of him was still.

Terrible impulses had lurked in Snow White's head, back when she'd had all her memories. She'd been able to gloss them over with civilized manners, so only her patients ever glimpsed the real her. Now, all her depravity was unmasked, revealing the depths of her power-hungry, sadism for everyone to see.

"No one's ever, ever, *ever* taking Marrok from me!" Snow White plunged the knife into Bluebeard's chest with a gleeful laugh. "He's mine, mine, *mine!*" Each word was punctuated by another vicious stab.

Bluebeard couldn't escape the blade. Couldn't make a sound of protest or try to fend off her attack. He could only sit there as Snow White murdered him and the smell of omelets filled the air. It dragged on and on and *on*. Frozen in place, he couldn't even die. He just lingered in a timeless space, filled with pain and terror.

"Well, I hope you're happy, now." The Queen of Clubs swept from the room, with a parting glare in her husband's direction. "Since you're such an expert on parenting, *you* can clean up the body this time."

"I'll feed it to your carnivorous roses, like *you* did to poor William." The Mad Hatter called after her. "Pat the gardener will be thrilled and God knows we have to keep the overpaid pigeon happy."

"I can*not* talk to you when you're in a mood like this." She swept out through the doorway, high heels tapping on the tile floor.

The Mad Hatter glowered after her, his face both irritated and regretful.

Satisfied with her work, Snow White stepped back from Bluebeard, breathing hard. "Daddy?" She said sweetly. "I'm done now."

The Mad Hatter sighed and clicked the pocket watch, again. Bluebeard fell from his chair, freed from the immobilization spell. Landing on the floor, he felt the life seeping from his body. Saw the blood pooling around him. Knew he was going to die. It was almost a relief.

"This is the last time, Snow." The Mad Hatter scolded. "I mean it. I won't have your poor mother upset."

"Sorry, Daddy." She didn't look sorry. She looked thrilled, in an unwholesome, vaguely sexual way, as Bluebeard perished at her feet. Lifting a hand to her mouth, she daintily sucked the blood from her fingers.

Even the wolf seemed uneasy about what he'd unleashed. The last thing Bluebeard saw was Marrok's frown. Maybe golden boy was pondering how many wolf-killing spells the dragon had memorized over the years. Or maybe he was contemplating how quick his in-laws would finish him off, once they realized he wasn't really enthralled. Either way, it didn't seem like Marrok's future was much brighter than Bluebeard's. Every psychopath in Wonderland hated his guts.

Well, except for his "wife" and she was the scariest of them all. Hopefully, the wolf was terrified and miserable and stuck in his new marriage for a very long time. He deserved it. It was all his fault that... Marrok had ruined... If only...

The world went dark and Bluebeard went still, again. This time forever. He'd known brunch would be a bloodbath.

CHAPTER TWENTY-SEVEN

Pick your perfect nail polish from our unlimited selection!
Violent-ish Violet-ish: Falling for some handsome villain who's about to wreck your life, empty your bank accounts, and leave you a sobbing mess on the floor? Wanna smash something? Preferably him? Well, this vampy metallic shade of black-and-blue will magically strengthen your fists into weapons of stylish destruction! (Requires indemnity wavier to purchase.)

Happily Ever Witch Cosmetics Website

Near the Club Castle

"The Queen of Clubs is definitely doing something to block my magic." Trevelyan complained. "I'm getting real damn sick of only having partial powers."

The two of them were trekking through the frozen woods. Everywhere they looked was another picturesque scene of mountains and fragrant pine trees. Pristine and mysterious, with a magic all its own, the Club Kingdom had welcomed them into its timeless forest. Being inside of it made a person feel small and joined to some greater, eternal whole. Clean air filled their lungs and the breathtaking perfection of nature surrounded Trevelyan and Esmeralda, as they walked.

It annoyed the crap out of them both.

Villains didn't hike.

Luckily, they were getting closer to the Club Palace, so they could kill people soon. That would be a welcomed relief from all the icky, unspoiled beauty.

From this distance, Esmeralda could already see a tall, black-and-white clock tower looming. For some reason, she sort of liked the strange structure. It seemed like there was a chessboard on top of it, rather than a numbered dial. Frigging bizarre, sure. But, it made her think of the Cheshire Carpet and *that* reminded her of the Heart Castle and, weirdly, *that* association wasn't so terrible, at all. Thinking about the Heart Castle was actually soothing.

Homey.

God Knew, nothing else in the kingdom was calming. Certainly not the weather. A lifetime of dreading water meant Esmeralda had automatically recoiled, when snow began falling. But Trevelyan's waterproofing spell kept her warm and dry.

As her instincts gradually caught up with her mind and body, her confidence grew and a smug sort of happiness took its place. Despite the unappealing wholesomeness of their pine-scented surrounds, things could be a lot worse. She was walking in the snow with her True Love! It was like a frigging Christmas song. Without giving herself time to think about it, she reached out to take hold of Trevelyan's palm.

He glanced down in surprise and didn't pull away. Instead, his fingers slid between hers, linking them together. His lips curled up at the corners.

Esmeralda bit back a smile. She might be pissed at the man. -- He still wasn't tamed and never really would be... He was always setting stuff on fire... He was *completely* trying to trick her into marriage.-- But no one could deny that he belonged to her. A thousand percent.

A girl could do worse for a mate.

"I still think the Queen of Clubs is only blocking the Bad magic." She told him casually, because they'd been talking about this for a while. His incredible powers were one of his favorite topics, ranking just after sex and his assortment of hated enemies. "Some of my energy is still okay."

Not that her Good half would do her much --ya know-- *good*. She could feel it within her, but she didn't exactly know what to do with it.

"I'm not sure how this new spell of hers even works. Especially, at a distance." He sounded distinctly pouty. "There shouldn't be any spells that I can't dissect."

"I told you the magic here is --like-- it's own thing. It's going to amp up every spell to make shit even crazier." Esmeralda gestured to the winter Wonderland they were walking through. Every not-so-unique snowflake was shaped like a tiny club. "This whole kingdom thrives on chaos."

"I thrive on chaos too, but not when it's working against me. And it seems like it's *always* working against me, in this misbegotten land."

She considered that. "Maybe that's a feature, not a bug."

"Oh God... Are there bugs here?" He looked around in distaste. "They're probably ridiculous and chattering, like every other creature in Wonderland."

"No, I mean maybe the magic here is targeting you and me, because we're the ones trying to rule this place. It wants to make sure we're up for the job, so it's throwing weird-ass tests our way." She arched a brow. "Have I mentioned I suck at tests?"

"Don't worry. I'm a dragon. I excel at everything."

She rolled her eyes. "I'm just saying, maybe Wonderland wants to see you excel *without* using your powers as a cheat-code. Maybe prove that you can make some allies."

...Which meant for her, it was probably the opposite. Esmeralda typically got through her life with minor spell-casting. Wonderland probably wanted to see her rely on her magic, for a change. God, that was a stupid plan, even for this stupid place. Her Bad powers were disastrous enough. Just using Good spells, they were outright doomed.

"But, magic is what *makes* dragons excel." He grumbled. "Without it, no one can be a true villain."

Esmeralda glanced his way, surprised by that crack in his supreme confidence. "You can. Magic is *not* what makes you the best at being Bad, Trev. I told you before. You're just as big a deranged maniac without it."

"You think?"

"I *know*. You've barely had any powers since I've met you and you've been absolutely awful the whole time."

"Sweet of you to say so." He gave her fingers a squeeze. "Horrific villainy *is* an innate talent of mine, I suppose."

Esmeralda snorted at his boastful tone, but she was pleased to see his normal arrogance return.

"Still, if my powers weren't being blocked, I could transport us right into the Club Castle and the Queen would already be dead." He went on. "I hate waiting for my enemies to suffer."

"She'll be horribly murdered soon." Esmeralda consoled, nodding to the ominous, white palace in the distance. "And you got us this close to the castle."

Trevelyan grunted, not fully appeased.

There was a huge tree toppled directly across their path, with weird icicle ivy growing all over it. He let go of her hand to climb up on top of it. The delicate frozen leaves crunched under his feet. Trevelyan didn't care about exotic vegetation, because Trevelyan didn't care about much. Mostly, just about him and her. That was kind of enough.

"Here, my darling." He put a palm down to assist her over the log.

She could have climbed up there on her own, even in her not-favorite boots. Still, it was cute of him to offer her help, so she let him grasp her hand. He was learning, for sure.

Trevelyan pulled her up, onto the top of the fallen tree. He helped her balance on it, five-feet above the ground. "So, do I get half of your nail polish company, now?" He asked from out of nowhere. "Because I have ideas for a dragon-green polish that will revolutionize fashion."

"I'm not giving you half of my company. Why should I give you half of my company?"

"Married people share assets." He lectured, as if he'd somehow become an expert on matrimony. "What's yours is mine." He hopped down to the ground on the other side of the log.

"We're not married! And even if we were married, what's mine is still *mine*." Villains weren't naturals at sharing. "You already owe me a record store."

"I promised to get you one today and I will."

"Well, I'm not giving you half of that, either. What are you giving *me* as a shared asset? Do you even own anything?"

"I own a lot of gold. Does that count?" He couldn't sound more

blasé. "I'm the second wealthiest person on Neverland Beach."
Esmeralda looked down at him in shock.

"My sister's knowledge of future inventions made me rich." Trevelyan explained, seeing her surprise. "Well, stealing made me rich. Investing my ill-gotten gains with a time-traveler made me *enormously* rich. It's a lovely system, where I get to cheat twice."

She blinked.

He arched a brow. "I have magic powers and no conscience. Did you think I was poor?"

"No I just..." Neverland Beach was full of disgustingly well-off people. Like private-yachts-for-their-race-horses levels of well-off. It was their diamond-encrusted native habitat. It had never occurred to her that Trevelyan had that much money. "You're really the second richest person on rich-person island?"

Trevelyan frowned, as if mentally tallying up his bank accounts. "Possibly, I'm only the *third* richest citizen in Neverland, now. It depends on how much Clorinda's made, while I was in my coma. Marion is number one, of course. My sister breathes and money rains down. But she's inexplicably fond of Clorinda, so that horrible woman's investment portfolio always over-performs."

Esmeralda sat on the edge of the huge log and pondered his words for a beat. "I figured if I ever dated a rich guy, he'd be more into boring suits and business meetings, and less into wholesale slaughter."

"You'd be surprised at how well wholesale slaughter pays." He held up his hands to help her down. "And we're not 'dating.'"

"No?"

"No. We've moved on to the next stage of our relationship." He gripped her waist to lift her to the ground. "The True Love bond is confusing you, for the moment. Once you begin to..."

Esmeralda cut him off. "How is the True Love bond confusing me?"

"It's still primary to you." He carefully set her on her feet, steadying her on the snow. "It's always been secondary to me."

Her brows compressed. "Secondary?"

"If another woman was my True Love, I would leave her. It's

not even a question." Trevelyan dismissed the most important bond in a person's life like it was a lousy blind date. "Dragons value their mates above all and *you* are my mate. I knew it the morning after we met, in the kitchen. You made pancakes, and threatened to fuck a guitar player, and I chose you over all other women. I *decided*. After that," he shrugged, "True Love or not, you belonged to me. No one else would ever do."

She blinked.

"Now *you*," Trevelyan continued, "value True Love over all else. The True Love bond is primary to you, so you follow it. But you didn't *choose* me. So, when I say I'm your mate, it doesn't resonate with you, as it does with me."

"I did choose you."

"You'd pick a different mate, if you could." He started to walk, again. "Someone smiley and kindhearted. Except you *can't*. The True Love bond wins out over all other considerations, for you." He didn't sound particularly sorry that she was stuck with him. "It's a cultural issue. We have both bonds, but we're prioritizing them differently. ."

She caught hold of his arm. "I chose you, Trevelyan." She repeated.

He stopped and frowned, like he didn't believe her.

"They're the same bond. Not two." She held up two fingers. "*One*." She crossed them to show the interconnection. "Your mate *is* your True Love."

He looked a little confused by that idea. "No."

"*Yes*. You *always* have to decide. You *always* have to choose to fight for it or fight against it. And we're both fighting for it. Nothing can stop people like us. Not when we know what we want. We don't quit."

His head tilted. "Death or freedom." He quoted.

"Death or freedom." She agreed. "I have fought *for* my happily ever after. That is my freedom. I need my True Love to make that happen. And the dragon I'm mated to…?" She arched a brow. "He's the one."

Trevelyan stared at her, listening intently. "And if he *wasn't* the one?"

"He's ninety-eight percent Bad. If *wasn't* my True Love, that evil bastard would just figure out a way to create a True Love bond between us. Because he would never, *ever* risk sharing me with anyone else."

Green eyes gleamed, tension easing from his shoulders.

"Dragons don't share." She gave him an arched smile.

"Marriages, True Loves, mates... That's the most complex magic in any land." Trevelyan reminded her piously. "Very advanced. Messing with that is taboo."

She leaned closer to him. "I've seen you do it, though. In the Four Kingdoms, with Cinderella and Prince Charming. I've seen you cross every line that got in your way."

His mouth curved.

"Would you cross lines to have me, Trev?"

"My darling, there *are* no lines, where you're concerned."

That made her laugh. Yeah... the man would never be tamed. Wildness and rebellion were a part of him. She wouldn't have it any other way.

His hand reached out to toy with her hair. "I don't have to use a spell. Everything between us is real. But, we both know I would drain every drop of dark magic in the world, if that's what it took to steal you away from someone else."

She wrinkled her nose in delight. "You see why I chose you? You're a fucking lunatic for me! A witch needs that in her life. *You* are my happily ever after." Her hand cupped his cheek. "All the bonds between us --True Love and mating and marriage-- They're just different names for what we both already know: It's you and me, dragon. Forever."

He dropped his forehead to hers, breathing deep. "If they're all the same, why is there an issue? Marry me, witch."

"Nope. Still pissed. Ask again later."

His smile was a thing of beauty. "You'd better eventually say yes. ...I *really* want my half of that nail polish company."

Esmeralda grinned back at him. "You're not coming near Happily Ever Witch Cosmetics. You'll hunt down the first person who leaves us a bad review online."

"So?"

"So, we can't kill our customers. Dead people don't make for repeat business."

He frowned at that logic, searching for a loophole. Dragons were not a natural fit for customer service. "Oh." Learning he couldn't just pick-off any troublesome clientele had him rapidly losing interest in the cosmetics industry.

Esmeralda decided to throw him a bone. "I can do dragon-green polish for you, though." She caught hold of his hand again. "Maybe it'll be my new bestseller."

Trevelyan watched with interest, as she brought his fingers to her lips and blew across his nails, painting them with her powers.

If Wonderland wanted to see her excel at magic, she might as well start with her biggest talents. Every bit of Esmeralda's energy went into giving Trevelyan the very best manicure she could. Amazingly, using her Good powers wasn't hard. Once she tried, it came naturally. It made her think maybe she used them all the time in her transmogrifying, and she just didn't notice. That's why it was the one type of spell that worked.

Trevelyan looked slightly awed, as his nails became lacquered in iridescent green. The shade was an exact match for the scales of his dragon, shimmering with a million subtle colors that didn't exactly exist, and the sparkle of unadulterated magic, and a whole lot of feelings she couldn't quite hide. It was the best work she'd ever done.

Trevelyan clearly thought so, too. "Oh, we're never selling this color." He decided, moving his hand to watch it shift in the light.

"No?"

His eyes lifted to hers. "No," he leaned in to kiss her softly, "this one is just mine."

She smiled against his lips. "You think everything's just yours."

"I may be greedy…"

"You are."

"…But, *I'm* not the one refusing to share assets with my True Love, am I?"

Esmeralda made a face, because he had a point.

Dark eyebrows rose in dragon-y smugness.

"Oh, alright, *fine*. You're the rich one, so we might as well split it all." Esmeralda wasn't against the idea of spending his money. There was a ton of pretty stuff she could buy. "We'll be one of those annoying, share-y couples, who are always..." Her agreement was cut short when Trevelyan's head suddenly snapped up.

His body stilled, even as she felt the dragon within him restlessly stir. Green eyes flashed to the left and he inhaled some invisible scent. "Fuck."

Before Esmeralda even processed what was happening, he'd swept her right off the ground and literally *threw* her back over the massive log. Esmeralda gave a yelp of astonishment, as she landed ass-first in the snow. If her skin was unbruised, it would be a miracle. "What the hell, Trev?"

"Stay down! Something is... *Shit!*"

His shout had her scrambling to her feet and peering over the top of the fallen tree in concern. "Shit!" She agreed.

A huge mushroom creature had grabbed Trevelyan. It was three times Trevelyan's size, so there was simply no evading it. It came whiffling from the woods; an unstoppable force. The monster's weird fingers jutted off in extra directions, with too-many knuckles and a coating of fuzzy mold. All of them dug into Trevelyan's arm.

Half a second later, the creature and Trevelyan were both gone. Just *gone*. Vanished in a puff of polka-dot smoke.

Esmeralda's lips parted in shock, finally catching up with what was going on.

Brilligs. Three of them. The biggest one had just kidnapped Trevelyan. Now, the littler ones were charging at the log, trying to get her. Unless she figured out a way to stop them, she'd be teleported, too.

Her mind raced, desperately trying to recall any useful details from the nature documentary she'd seen on them. Brilligs were somewhere between animals and plants. Walking fungus, with the IQs of gerbils and an appetite for rotting meat. Their muscular flesh was patterned like poisoned toadstools, while their oversized jaws were filled with yellowed rows of razor-sharp teeth.

Oh, and magic.

Brilligs had inexplicable magic, which wasn't Good or Bad. Their uniqueness was why powerful people kept them as pets. It didn't take a genius to figure out these particular brilligs belonged to the Queen of Clubs.

How was Esmeralda going to kill these things? The damn nature documentary hadn't mentioned that part. And she really, really needed to figure it out. The brilligs began clawing at the log, desperate to reach her. Chunks of bark went flying, as their massive fists beat at the wood blocking their path. Esmeralda took a stumbling step backwards. Trevelyan had bought her time. He'd protected Esmeralda by putting her behind the fallen tree --even though they'd agreed to stand *beside* each other during a fight, dammit-- and that gave her an extra moment to plan. She generally sucked at planning, but she wasn't about to let him down. She needed to do this.

Yes... She could do this.

Crap... She couldn't do this.

Brilligs were way, *way* bigger than giving Trevelyan a stunning manicure. Good magic was a mystery to her. Nothing she tried would work! She knew that without even trying. Nothing *ever* worked right, for her.

The log splintered into twigs and the brilligs surged forward. In her panic, the damn ginger-mutant spell was the only thing that popped to mind. Cookies were food. Mushrooms were food. That was common ground, right? Trevelyan had said the ginger-mutants didn't obey her, because she'd used too much Bad magic. Maybe unadulterated Good magic would make the spell work better.

It wasn't like she had another option.

Esmeralda lifted her hand and let loose with every bit of her power. Good energy slammed out. Green and glowing, it glittered like springtime burning through frost. The spell arched forward, in a joyful fireworks display of wholesome command and unstoppable sparkles.

The force of the magic hit the brilligs full-blast, knocking both of them off their feet. The mushroom monsters toppled to the snowy ground and broke into a million pieces. It was like shoving over a gumball machine and watching the candy explode everyplace.

Were they dead?

Breathing hard, Esmeralda edged closer to the fallen creatures, wondering what the hell she'd just done. She craned her neck forward to peer down at the remains and then squeaked in alarm when something moved.

Then *more* things moved.

What had once been two huge brilligs was now a thousand *tiny* brilligs. The size of actual mushrooms, the itty-bitty beings were alive and well. And apparently a lot happier.

Her eyebrows soared, stunned that her magic had kind of worked.

Some of the little brilligs pranced around, holding hands in cheery circles. Some sang in high-pitched unison, like something out of a cartoon. Some of them scampered off into the forest to explore. Within seconds, the others followed that group, eager to play with their friends. Her Good energy had turned them into joyful, childlike, mini-monsters.

"Hang on!" She called after them, coming out of her shock. "I'm not just letting you leave without telling me where Trevelyan is!"

The brilligs giggled madly and dashed away, vanishing into the woods. They had no intention of obeying her. Esmeralda might be a villain, but she couldn't very well stomp on frolicking babies. Also, they were too fast for her to catch. Sweet and defiant little jerks.

She ran a hand through her hair, breathing hard. Good magic was clearly a pain in the ass. How was she supposed to find her True Love, now? The first brillig must have taken him to the Club Castle. Right? That made sense.

What if it hadn't, though?

What if Trevelyan was hurt? What if the Queen of Clubs was already torturing him? Damn it, she needed to make sure he was okay! Esmeralda blew out an aggravated sigh, trying to think. If only she could talk to him somehow. Get reassurance. She hadn't been this scared since she was a kid, huddled in the orphanage, hiding from the rain and reaching for her True Love. Esmeralda's eyes widened in sudden inspiration. ...And she wondered just how strong her Good magic could get.

CHAPTER TWENTY-EIGHT

Pick your perfect nail polish from our unlimited selection!
Accidental Turquoise: Whoops!

Happily Ever Witch Cosmetics Website

The Club Castle

The gigantic brillig transported him straight into a dungeon and then quickly teleported out again. Maybe it sensed its life was in mortal peril if it stayed. Trevelyan didn't have time to react, before it was gone.

It must have been following the Queen of Clubs orders, because it *had* to belong to her. None of his other enemies were organized enough to enlist a brillig to fetch him. They were exceptionally rare and expensive to keep. Not to mention, they tended to eat their owners. Flying pigs were much better pets, really.

As pissed as he was, Trevelyan was not disappointed to see the brillig go. Fighting it without powers would have been a real bitch. It was the largest one he'd ever seen, with teeth like a shark and empty black eyes like --well-- *also* like a shark.

Fuck.

The damn brillig had tossed him into a wall, so he wasn't at his most articulate. It was an evil monster and, as much as Trevelyan generally approved of evil monsters, he hoped that particular one died. A lot. When he got free, he fully planned to help that happen. That was the bottom line.

In the meantime, at least he'd finally made it to the Club Palace. Because this was definitely the Club Palace.

He held a palm to his forehead, checking for blood, as his eyes took in his surroundings. Given his personality, Trevelyan spent a lot of time in lockup. He'd seen enough cells to tell the worst from the *really* worst. This particular one was mid-range horrible. It got some credit for having no visible rats, but it lost points for being freezing cold.

He was alone. No other prisoners were trapped in the dungeon and no other brilligs were arriving with Esmeralda. Had she escaped? Had they captured her and taken her someplace else? Was she hurt? Scared? Looking for him?

Instinctively, he headed for the barred window, sitting high on the wall. Hoisting himself up, he peered out of the small opening and saw a slim view of the aggressively checkerboarded courtyard. As he watched, the Chess Tower shifted, for no reason at all. Trevelyan frowned as the red queen edged towards d1. He had no idea why there was a huge chess game looming over the landscape.

Or, more importantly, why it was making such a pointless move. The queen was all by herself, heading forward with no apparent strategy. Pawns could get promoted, if they reached the opposing side of the board. They could become a queen. That was a rule. No other piece gained anything by moving there, though. So where was that queen going? Who was controlling it? Why was everything in Wonderland so dumb?

And where in the frozen-hells was his mate?

He squeezed his eyes shut in frustration. ...And he suddenly smelled the wolf.

Trevelyan's eyes popped open again. Marrok's scent was all over this dungeon. He'd been locked down here, very recently. Trevelyan dropped back down to the floor and headed over to the corner of the space, where a dirty mattress was pushed up against the wall. Marrok's scent was strongest there, so he must have slept on the makeshift bed the night before. Chances were the wolf was still alive.

Trevelyan wasn't sure why, but he was inexplicably relieved by that fact. *He* didn't care if Marrok was murdered. Obviously. In fact, he was all for it. But, he knew Esmeralda would mope all afternoon about her brother's grisly demise. She favored that idiot and Trevelyan didn't want Marrok's death ruining her day. Perfectly understandable.

(And even if he *was* personally a little glad that Marrok survived, it was just a temporary pause in his hatred of the man. Trevelyan might have a concussion, after all. Some mental confusion was expected.)

He crouched down to examine the hideous checks plastered all over the walls. Maybe the decorating was part of the torture. Why else would someone choose such an eye-spinning pattern? All the paint was in pristine condition, except for a small patch by the mattress. Some lovesick bastard had carved the name "Letty" into the stone, marring the black-and-white color scheme with his heartfelt pining.

Trevelyan rolled his eyes.

The wolf had been pathetically far gone over his True Love, before he'd even met the girl. Now that he had Scarlett, he was clearly even more insane. Trevelyan was so much stronger than that jackass, thank God.

Trev?

His heart stopped. "Ez!" He jumped to his feet, his gaze cutting around, desperate to see her. "Where are you? Are you alright?"

Nothing.

What the hell…? He was still alone in the dungeon. He didn't see or smell his mate. She wasn't there.

Trev, are you there?

It was a whisper in his mind. Esmeralda's voice. He stilled, wondering if he'd fractured his skull and he was hallucinating.

Can you hear me? I feel like you can hear me.

The breath shuttered out of him. It was real. She was talking to him in his head, just like he'd heard her that morning.

Trevelyan knew magic from every land imaginable and he'd never heard of two people being able to mentally communicate over large distances.

But there was only one level six witch.

Furrowing his brow in concentration, he focused inward. He had no idea how to answer her, because the spells to do that hadn't even been invented. He'd figure this out, though. He was a dragon! To reach his mate, there was nothing he couldn't do.

Closing his eyes, he searched for a connection. With all dark energy blocked, ninety-eight percent of his powers were stifled. Useless. That made it easier to find what little magic he still had control over. He dove into himself, down, down, down, to the bottom. To the very deepest part.

And he found that last two percent.

No wonder he'd never felt it before. The thin, golden strand barely even existed, but it was there. Not just some blip in the margin of error. No, it glowed strong and bright in the pitch black. The very best part of him.

And it stretched straight to his True Love.

Ez?

Who else? You okay?

Relief. The emotion came from both of them, vibrating all along the connection.

I'm fine, my darling. Are you alright?

I'm great. ...Except we agreed to stand beside *each other during a fight and instead I wound up behind a huge log, while you faced a brillig alone!*

It was instinct.

Troll shit.

It's true. I'm a selfish being. Faced with the prospect of losing the one person I can't lose, my inherent self-interest kicked in and I protected you.

That's the excuse you're going with? For real?

I can't fight my nature.

Well, you'd better learn how, real damn fast. I am not going to let you die over your stupid control issues. I need you, too, dipshit.

Warmth spread in his chest. *Do you?*

Yes! Lucky for you, we're both alive, and my ginger-mutant spell kind of works on brilligs, or I'd be really *pissed.*

You killed them?

Not exactly. I used the ginger-mutant spell to shrink them down to action-figure size.

His mouth curved, pride filling him. His mate. Just his.

They're now a super-cute invasive species that ran off into the woods. It's probably going to screw-up the whole Club Kingdom ecosystem. Using Good magic has still got some kinks that I need to work out.

Work them out back in the Heart Palace. I will handle things here.

It's like we have the same conversation, but you never actually hear it. We go together. *It's part of that True-Love-sharing thing you're so fond of.*

We're sharing bank accounts, not death sentences. I know I agreed to this idea of facing things side-by-side, but it's proving very hard on me. I want to renegotiate, so you're never put at risk.

Can't hear you. La-la-la-la!

Stop singing over me!

You're lucky it's not a Pecos Bill song. I know all of them.

He looked up at the ceiling, frustrated and a little frightened.

Esmeralda, I promise you a thousand percent, I will find Marrok. (Just as soon as he escaped the dungeon.) *You'll be detected if you enter the Club Castle. I'm sure the Queen has traps set.*

Don't worry so much. I'm gonna come to the palace and save the day. It'll be fun! I'm amazing at sneaking into places. I've never once paid for a movie ticket, concert admission, or amusement park ride.

To get the sealing wax spell, the Queen of Clubs will rip right through you.

Hanging up, now. ...Oh wait! I need to gloat first. I told *you I used to hear you at the orphanage, didn't I? You talked in my head, night after night. This proves it!*

What did I say to you, back then? You avoided telling me that part, so I imagine it was interesting.

Don't change the subject. When I find you, you can apologize for ever doubting me.

I never doubted that you sensed me. I simply failed to understand exactly how impossible your magic can get. And you're *the one changing the subject. DO NOT COME HERE. By the way, I've decided to say 'yes' the next time you ask me to marry you, so try not to do anything stupid. I'm already marrying a bossy control freak. I'd just as soon not marry a dead one.*

There was the sensation of her kissing his cheek and then she was gone.

Ez? Ez!

Nothing.

Trevelyan didn't have enough magic to keep the connection going on his own. He could still feel it, but it was silent. Shit! He banged a fist against the iron bars of the cell. The woman would drive him insane one of these days and it wasn't like he'd been so incredibly stable *before* she'd arrived.

He'd been wrong earlier. Marrok's desperate need for Scarlett was fully rational. In fact, it was calm and fucking sensible, compared to Trevelyan's violent obsession with Esmeralda. Having their mate soothed the dragon and enabled Trevelyan to function at an even keel. ...But losing her would detonate him like a bomb and wipe out the goddamn galaxy.

Did she not understand that? Why did she insist on risking herself? He *said* he'd save the wolf. Did she not trust Trevelyan to keep his word?

The dragon stirred at his core. Suppressed, but awake. Trevelyan and the dragon were the same. That two percent of Goodness threaded through them both. The dragon wasn't brooding about their mate's stubbornness, though. It was annoyed at Trevelyan. "Do you not trust *Esmeralda?*" it seemed to ask. She said she could get into the Club Castle undetected. Did he believe she could do that?

Was he willing to risk his life --his *mate's* life-- on blind faith? Trevelyan drew in a deep breath. Yes. Because, his faith *wasn't* blind.

No one had magic like Esmeralda. It was a simple fact. The witch had just casually spoken to him in his mind, because it didn't even occur to her that it was impossible. Because, she'd apparently been connecting with him all of her life. Because, no one ever told her she couldn't or, if they *had* told her, she wasn't paying any attention. If anything, she consistently underestimated her abilities.

If she said she could get into the Club Palace undetected, then she could get into the Club Palace undetected. Trevelyan trusted that. He trusted her. As her loving husband, it was his job to support her villainy. To help her believe in her own power.

Keeping her safe was vital, but he needed to balance that with ensuring that she was happy and fulfilled. The slow evolution of his priorities solidified in its new and permanent orientation. So only one truth remained:

Esmeralda was all that mattered.

He slowly exhaled, feeling calmer.

A movement outside the cage drew his attention. A cadre of nervous looking playing card guards stood there. Rather than a show of intimidation, the large force seemed to be for their own protection. They were terrified of him, which was gratifying, but also annoying.

Not even Trevelyan could escape two-dozen armed men, with no magic. If they'd been a bit braver, and come in as a group of six or eight, he could've easily slain them all and escaped. It wasn't fair to give them any actual credit for thwarting his plans, of course. No. They'd stumbled across the tactic by complete accident. The playing cards had lucked into survival through their own cowardice and ineptitude.

(Sadly, sometimes stupidity paid off. Trevelyan knew that better than most. No matter where he went, it was the same: Gaggles of morons surrounded him.)

Trevelyan flashed the guards an irritated look. "If you're here to execute me, I should warn you, my mate wants me alive. ...And I make sure my mate gets what she wants."

"We're not here to execute you." The leader of the men swallowed audibly, his unpleasant face scrunched up in distaste and fear. "You're just ordered to come with us."

Everyone in the Club Kingdom seemed particularly unlikable. Trevelyan had only met a few of its denizens, so far, but he'd killed or was planning to kill one hundred percent of them. It was a grim statistic, even for a dragon.

"Where exactly are you taking me, if not to the gallows?" He asked.

The guard edged closer to the cell door, poised to flee at the

first sudden movement. "We're escorting you to the trial."
Trevelyan stared at him blankly. "The what?"

***

Glamours didn't set off magic sensors. At least, not when Esmeralda used them.

So long as she didn't go too big with her spells, her powers got disguised right along with her outward appearance. She was pretty sure that it didn't work that way for all witches, but transmogrifying came naturally to her. She barely even had to think about using her Good energy to make it happen. A little dash of magic and poof!

Esmeralda strolled through the gates of the Club Castle and the magic sensors never flickered. She was just another hardworking playing card guard.

Getting used to her new very, very thin form was the most challenging part of the mission. It felt like a stiff breeze would blow her away. Playing card guards had short limbs, so she had to swing her whole body on the diagonal to walk. It was completely ineffective. No wonder it was so easy to beat these dopes.

A few other guards walked past her and saluted. Esmeralda nodded in reply. She'd made herself a nine. That seemed like a high enough rank that no one would question her movements, but not so exalted that she'd get recognize as an imposter. It was all working great!

Nobody looked twice, as she walked right into the palace courtyard. Now, she just needed a way to get inside the castle and find Trevelyan.

Unfortunately, there were talking doorknobs on all the doors and they seemed to be some kind of security system. Being as inconspicuous as possible, Esmeralda watched people come and go through them. Each time someone approached, the doorknob would ask them some nonsensical riddle.

"What is down and up, whenever it goes sideways?"
"Why is a river fish like a teaspoon full of tennis shoes?"
"How can you be in two places at once at three in the

afternoon?"

Everyone had to solve a riddle properly, before the doorknobs would let them pass. And "properly" seemed to mean saying the very first thing that popped into your head, no matter how stupid.

Esmeralda was tempted to try and brazen through. How wrong could her responses really be? No one else's answers made any sense and they seemed to work fine.

Question: What is a loaf divided by a knife? Answer: Red. Seriously, *what the hell* did that even mean? Nothing! It was pure gibberish. Esmeralda was pretty sure she could bullshit her way through some word-salad riddle. If no answer was right, then no answer was wrong.

But what if there was more than just whimsical inanity happening here? What if the craziness was actually a code? Everything in Wonderland was stupid, but it wasn't always *purposelessly* stupid. If she approached a door and gave the wrong ridiculous answer, the knob might alert the Queen of Clubs. That could be disastrous for Marrok and Trevelyan. She needed to find another way into the palace.

Muttering curses in the forgotten language of witches, Esmeralda moved around the perimeter of the castle, looking for an unguarded entrance. The whole place was locked up tight. At least on the ground floor.

Her eyes went up to a balcony, jutting out from a higher level. Hmm...

Even if she'd had a broomstick handy, which she didn't, flying would for sure draw attention. That was out. But, maybe she could get up there a more surreptitious way. Esmeralda wasn't about to risk any powerful spells, out in the open. Nothing that even *hinted* at frogs. Some smaller magic might do the trick, though. She could create a ladder, like when she manifested herself a hairbrush at bedtime. Simple. Harmless. Low key. Anyone could do that.

Concentrating, she focused all her energy on creating a nice, safe ladder.

What she got was a three-story, loop-the-loop circus slide. Esmeralda blew out an aggravated breath. Fucking Good magic. It seemed to douse all of her spells in acid-tripping happiness.

At the top of the adorable slide there was a gigantic clown face with a glowing red nose. If anyone was dumb enough to ride it, they would travel through the clown's gaping mouth, as they rode down his twisty tongue. Esmeralda wasn't dumb enough to ride it. Not only couldn't she climb up the smooth, shiny surface of the clown's tongue, but she also wasn't thrilled with the idea of crawling passed his giant glittery teeth. They chomped up and down amid calliope music and mechanized laughter.

The damn thing was already attracting attention.

"What in the world is *that?*" A dwarf in a doctor's coat asked from behind her. He'd stopped walking to frown up at the multicolored spectacle that Esmeralda had inadvertently created.

"How dare you question our brilliant Queen of Clubs!" Esmeralda snapped back, counting on her playing card guard disguise to brazen through. "If she wants a carnival slide for her balcony, we build her a carnival slide. They're all the rage in elite decorating."

The dwarf stroked his long beard. "Is it for Snow White's wedding to the wolf?" He asked, almost to himself. "Does she want a clown-themed reception? Has she slipped that far into madness?"

Esmeralda gaped at him, forgetting to stay in character. "Snow White isn't marrying Marrok!" She yelped. Scarlett would flip out, when she heard that idea.

"Snow White thinks she's *already* married to him. She just wants a new wedding, because she can't remember the one that never happened." That demented explanation was delivered in a bored tone. "As her therapist, it makes my job easier to just go along with the delusion." He gave a dismissive shrug, clearly indifferent about keeping patient-doctor confidentiality.

"As her therapist, you should stop her from holding the fake-groom captive."

"Marrok Wolf played for the Southlands' Wolfball team." The

dwarf informed her loftily. "I voted for the *Eastlands.* That bastard cost me a fortune, over the years. Screw him." He went stomping off, muttering to himself about sports gambling and the grim subconscious meaning of red clown noses.

Jesus… Esmeralda liked being a bitch, as much as the next Baddie. But the citizens of the Club Kingdom just plain sucked. Shaking her head, she distanced herself from the clown slide and followed the cobblestones around the courtyard. It felt like she was going in circles, because the path was laid out like a spiraling chessboard. The design had probably been super expensive to have installed and the effect wasn't worth the money. It created an optical illusion that made you feel like you were falling, even with your feet firmly planted on the ground. Not to mention, it all mixed in with the Chess Tower, which was *also* covered in checks. And the icy white castle. And the big black fence. And the white snow. And the ominous black gallows, in the square. …The black-and-white color scheme of the Club Kingdom was crazy monotonous.

Aside from the rainbow slide, the only splashes of color were the red chess pieces on the tower and some red roses in the garden. Wait. Esmeralda skidded to a halt.

Red clown noses.

What is a loaf divided by a knife? Red.

The Cheshire Carpet said the Queen of Hearts should always play red.

In the WUB Club, the most dangerous inmates, like Trevelyan, Marrok, and Esmeralda, had the red designation.

And now there were a few red roses, in the otherwise starkly white landscape.

Yeah… Wonderland was for sure using codes.

Esmeralda changed directions and headed towards the garden. The closer she got, the more her mind struggled to process what she was seeing. Had someone *painted* the roses? What kind of dumbass painted roses red?

And that's when she realized it wasn't red paint, after all. The roses' petals were smeared with blood.

Esmeralda's eyes widened in shock. Tangled in the thorn-covered bushes were bodies. She recognized William the lizard and several half-skeletonized women in handcuffs. The plants seemed to be drinking from them, weaving vines around them like cocoons.

She was standing there, gaping down at the ghastly sight, when a door swung open beside the flowerbed. It was small and built right into the castle wall. It must have been a servants' entrance, because it wasn't decorative or spade-shaped. In fact, it vanished completely when it was closed.

And it didn't have a doorknob.

The man who came out of the service door seemed to be the gardener. He was a completely ordinary-looking, overall-wearing, anthropomorphized pigeon. Nothing at all noteworthy about him.

Except for the body he was dragging.

"Your dirty blood best not hurt my babies." He told the corpse in a grouchy voice. "They only like mimsy young girls. Keeps their pedals pure white."

Esmeralda's stomach lurched. The dead man was Bluebeard and he'd been stabbed. A lot.

The gardener stopped by the carnivorous roses, chatting to them and careful to stay out of range of their grasping thorns. "Here we are, my babies. Old Pat's got ya more junk food. I'm not taking off his clothes, like I do with the females, though. No fun in it, for me."

Using a shovel, he levered Bluebeard's corpse into the flowerbed. Instantly, hungry vines cinched around it, dragging the dead man deeper into the bushes.

Pat the gardener barely noticed. Leaning against the closed door, he dug into his pocket for a cigarette. He continued to talk to the plants, as if this was a day-to-day routine. "Next time Snow White slaughters someone, I hope that fruitcake does it *down* stairs. Hauling corpses is hell on my back."

Clearly, disposing of murder victims was no big deal to him, aside from his sciatica. Excellent. The fact that he was even more of an asshole than the rest of the Club Kingdom made this *so* much easier for Esmeralda.

The Cheshire Carpet had suggested that she be less like herself and more like Cinderella. Suddenly that advice seemed pretty sound. Esmeralda dropped her playing card disguise and glamoured herself to look exactly like Scarlett's evil stepsister. Only her version of Cinderella was naked. Really, really naked. Cindy had always been blonde and innocent-looking, which was sure to catch the pigeon's beady eyes. Also, she had great breasts for a lunatic. What better victim could a psychotic murderer ask for?

"Whoops!" Esmeralda hurried towards the pigeon, a "me-oh-my!" look on her face. "I was in such a hurry this morning, I forgot to get dressed. Can you imagine?"

Pat's expression became one of lustful stupefaction. The cigarette tumbled from his beak unnoticed. He must've used all his brainpower gossiping with the flowers, because he seemed incapable of communication with another person. Or possibly he just wasn't used to nude princesses approaching him. Whatever the reason behind it, he didn't call for help. Didn't order her away. Didn't even nod. He just stood there and gaped at Cinderella's naked form. Esmeralda walked right up to him and he didn't do a damn thing to stop her.

Villainy was almost too simple sometimes.

Esmeralda halted two inches from his feathered-chest and smiled her sweetest smile. "Can you open that door for me?" She asked, gesturing to the one he'd come out of. "I'm all alone and very vulnerable."

The gardener's eyes turned crafty. He wordlessly passed a wing over some invisible panel and the door reappeared. She could see him mentally sizing her up for plant food. There was no telling how many other girls had disappeared into his garden, after falling into his sleazy grasp.

Even Cindy could aim higher than this prick.

"You know, Bluebeard was an evil little shit." Esmeralda held the edge of the door with her foot, so it couldn't close again. "But he deserved a better funeral than that."

And then she shoved the scumbag pigeon right into the roses. She caught him so totally off-guard, that she barely had to push, at all. Pat's muffled squawk was quickly drowned out by all the leaves sealing themselves around his feathered skull. The bushes swallowed him up, the same way they'd swallowed up

William and Bluebeard and all the other countless bodies. The killer gardener was compost and now Esmeralda had a way into the Club Palace.

Admiring the verdant crime scene, Esmeralda felt pretty proud of herself.

Sometimes a plan came together perfectly, even when you didn't exactly have one. She glamoured her newest body a leather mini-dress and fishnet stockings. For once, Cinderella looked presentable and not like a cupcake with too-much frosting. The depraved nutcase should thank her for the fashion upgrade.

"Checkmate to my friend the Cheshire Carpet." She said out loud.

See? She'd told Trevelyan it was great to have allies.

CHAPTER TWENTY-NINE

Pick your perfect nail polish from our unlimited selection!
Gray Area Gray: On Sale! Better make up your mind about this
enigmatic shade fast, because you won't get another chance.

Happily Ever Witch Cosmetics Website

The Club Castle

It was weird they weren't killing him.
Trevelyan had expected the Queen of Clubs to murder him (or at least try) as soon as she got him into the Club Palace. Instead, he'd been tossed into the dungeon and now he was being dragged into some kind of insane courtroom.
Just from William the snobby lizard's descriptions, he identified the Mad Hatter sitting on a raised dais. The gigantic top hat was distinctive. The man's fingers were drumming on the arm of his throne, like he was unhappy with this whole situation.
"How long is this trial going to take, Anna?" He complained. Beside him, a regally beautiful woman lounged in her own golden chair, looking smug and in control. Three interlocking tiaras rested on her head. Spades and diamonds on the sides. Clubs in the middle.
The Queen of Clubs. Obviously.
"Oh, it shouldn't take long." She crooned as Trevelyan came forward. "We already know the sentence, after all. We just need the verdict." She cast a meaningful look towards a group of playing-card guards, who were seated in rows of six on the right hand side of the room. They must've been the jurors, because they all obediently nodded at her pointed words.

Trevelyan's eyes flicked to the figure sitting in a smaller throne off to the side. Snow White. Her scent was just as rank as he remembered. Rotting syrup and deceit. He'd always thought the dragon would fly into a blackout rage, if he ever saw her again. They'd both hated the woman, for so long. They *still* hated her, but it wasn't white-hot and mindless anymore. Esmeralda anchored them, now. Trevelyan was in control of himself and his emotions.

It was freeing.

Snow White seemed oblivious to his chilling stare. One finger twirled in her ebony curls, all her attention focused on a fashion magazine about bridal gowns. Her current clothing was covered in childish ruffles and dried blood, so whatever she was shopping for was sure to be an improvement.

Beside her, chained to a gaudy wooden chair, was Marrok. Trevelyan instinctively frowned at him.

The wolf stared back with watchful topaz eyes.

A side door opened and a stately woman, with gray hair and the smell of magic swept in. The pointy hat she wore was the preferred formal-wear of witches everywhere. She wasn't *Trevelyan's* witch, though, so she didn't matter.

"Why is there a clown slide in the courtyard?" She asked no one in particular. "It's playing calliope music and ruining the aesthetic of the castle."

"Calliope music?" The Mad Hatter echoed in confusion.

The Queen of Clubs faltered for half a second. "I'm sure it's just as small mishap by the grounds-keeping crew." She clearly didn't want to lose face and admit that she had no idea what the woman was talking about. ...Even though it was obvious she had no idea what the woman was talking about.

(Neither did Trevelyan, but he was willing to bet his mate was behind it. Maybe "clown slide" rhymed with "frog" in that witchy language she liked to use to swear at him.)

"I'm glad you accepted my invitation, Grimhilde." The Queen of Clubs went on. "Hatty, you remember Grimhilde, President of the Cauldron Society, don't you?"

"Nope."

She pretended not to hear his bored reply, her welcoming smile aimed at her guest. "I have to rip the heart out of a witch later and I'll need your vast, murderous experience."

Trevelyan's eyes narrowed.

"Which witch?" Grimhilde demanded imperiously. "Nobody important, I trust."

"No, no. Just Esmeralda."

"Never heard of her." Grimhilde sat down, with a studied sweep of her ornate black robes. "Is there anything noteworthy about this girl?"

"She's got a high percentage of Good." The Mad Hatter chimed in, something ravenous flashing in his horrible eyes. "I'm looking forward to sucking it out of her, before she dies."

Inside Trevelyan, the dragon snarled.

"Esmeralda's nothing." The Queen of Clubs assured Grimhilde, continuing to disregard her husband. "Certainly, no one you'd be interested in saving. I just need her heart in a box."

Grimhilde's green skin was clearly pampered, but the color was a pale imitation of Esmeralda's luminous shade. "To do that, you'll have to reinstate Bad magic around here, Maryanna. I can't very well work with Good."

"Don't worry. The spell blocking Bad powers only lasts until the eighth square."

"It's an effective enchantment." Grimhilde said grudgingly. "For a non-witch."

"Well, my magic *is* fairest of them all."

"Is it?" Grimhilde didn't seem convinced. "In any case, it shouldn't take long to rip out this Esmeralda's heart, once I have my full powers. Whoever the girl is, I'm sure she's no match for me."

Trevelyan mentally added Grimhilde to his endless list of enemies. He supposed she'd already been on it, really. The Cauldron Society had been mean to his mate. They all had to die. It was simple cause and effect. Really, it was convenient that so many people he hated were gathered in one place. It would cut down on his travel time.

"According to Rule Forty-Two of the Uniform Code of Wonderland, I hereby call this trial to order." A Knave of Clubs called out, reading from a long scroll held up in front of him.

"The People of the Kingdom of Clubs vs. Trevelyan, Last of the Green Dragons."

"That's not my name."

The interruption threw the Knave of Clubs off-script. He blinked at Trevelyan. "Not your name?" He repeated blankly.

"No. Dragons' full names change throughout their lives, as their familial circumstances evolve. I *was* 'Trevelyan, Last of the Green Dragons.' Now, I am 'Trevelyan of the Green Dragons, Mate of Esmeralda.'"

Marrok was listening with unnerving focus, like he was trying to gauge the honesty of that claim.

Trevelyan kept going. "She is 'Esmeralda of the Green Dragons, Mate of Trevelyan.' When we have children, their names will be added. 'Trevelyan of the Green Dragons, Mate of Esmeralda, and Father of So-And-So.' They will be 'So-And-So of the Green Dragons, Child of Trevelyan and Esmeralda.' Until they find a mate themselves, at which time...'"

The Queen of Clubs cut him off. "Is all this necessary?"

"Only if you'd like to avoid looking like an idiot." Trevelyan lifted a bored shoulder. "Which, granted, doesn't seem to be a particular concern of yours."

Her lips pinched in displeasure.

"Rule Forty-two says that every insult to her majesty adds another year to the dragon's life sentence." The Knave instructed. "Jury, you can begin tabulating them now, if you'd like."

The jury opened their club-patterned notebooks and obediently tabulated.

"*This* is the mighty Trevelyan?" Grimhilde eyed him up and down. "How curiouser. Given his vile reputation, I expected him to be far more special."

Trevelyan didn't bother to look her way. "Who are you?"

Dragons excelled at insulting people, even when they weren't trying. With a modicum of effort, though, they could cause decades worth of psychological trauma with a few cutting words. Just the tone of Trevelyan's voice had Grimhilde flinching.

It was so gratifying to have talents.

"I'm the wickedest wicked witch in the world, boy." She proclaimed, her voice an over-compensating mix of defensive and superior. "The very best at being Bad."

He outright laughed at that claim. It wasn't a pleasant sound. "The dragon once stole the moon." The Mad Hatter was happy to inform her. He might just dislike the older woman even more than Trevelyan. "Ninety-eighth percentile of evil."

Trevelyan appreciated it when other people bragged about him. It saved him the trouble of doing it himself.

"He's clearly just a pretty face who got lucky with some spells." Grimhilde decided dismissively. "Evildoers today are all just social media stars and fly-by-night hoodlums. No innate depravity. None of them can inspire the *true* terror of my generation." She preened a bit. "I once removed a witch's hands so she was unable to cast spells, just for the fun of watching her scream. ...And she was my favorite granny."

"Oh, that *is* inspiring." Trevelyan drawled and not even the Wonderlandians were dumb enough to believe his smile.

The jury cringed in perfect unison, slinking deeper into their seats.

The Mad Hatter and the Queen of Clubs exchanged a sideways look.

Grimhilde gave a supercilious sniff. "No respect from villains today." She grumbled and went back to snubbing him.

Trevelyan didn't care. He had far more important issues to deal with, before he got around to slaughtering her. Like, for instance, figuring out what was *really* happening here. The Queen of Clubs should have killed him as soon as she had the chance. The spell was in Esmeralda's heart, so she didn't need Trevelyan, now. It was outright stupid to keep him alive and nothing the Queen of Clubs had done up until this point had been stupid.

Why put Trevelyan on trial? Who had convinced her that this was a bright idea?

His gaze fell on Marrok, again.

Marrok arched a brow.

Trevelyan's head canted to one side.

Oh.

From out of nowhere, he recalled why he'd befriended the wolf in prison: The two of them were apex predators. While they might not have always liked each other, Trevelyan and Marrok saw the wisdom of cooperating. Things had gone to hell the night of Trevelyan's escape, but the logic of their initial arrangement held. Why waste energy fighting each other? Mutually assured destruction helped no one but their opponents.

The enemy of your enemy is your slightly-less-hated enemy. Marrok was disappointingly moral at his core, however the man's deviousness was never in dispute. He always had an angle. Right now, there was no plotting, seething, promise of revenge in those lupine eyes. No call to resume their personal war. Instead, Trevelyan just saw a question.

"Your sister's been looking for you, wolf." He called testing the waters.

One tawny brow arched ever-so-slightly. Recognizing that calling Esmeralda Marrok's sister was Trevelyan acknowledging their family bond. Dragons didn't fuck around when it came to families. "Is Ez okay? Have you hurt her?"

"She's my mate." Trevelyan answered simply.

Marrok settled back in his chair. He understood what the word "mate" meant to dragons. He knew it was a no-bullshit answer to his silent question. An acceptance of the offer. "Alright." He said mildly. "For now."

"For now." Trevelyan agreed.

That fast, they had a deal.

Marrok's mouth tilted at the corner.

Trevelyan's eyes gleamed.

In unison, their attention swung towards their prey.

Oh, this was going to be fun.

"So, what's he being charged with?" Marrok asked lazily. "Because I have some *great* suggestions."

The Queen of Clubs waved a dismissive hand. "We'll figure that out later. Knave? Call the first witness."

"First witness!" The Knave of Clubs shouted towards the door.

"I don't leave witnesses." Trevelyan assured them all.

"That's a fair point." Marrok nodded. "I once watched him kill a guy, who saw him kill another guy, who'd seen him kill *another* guy. I was lucky he didn't kill me for seeing it."

"I tried." Trevelyan reminded him.

The Mad Hatter began counting off the various bodies and degrees of separation in that story on his fingers.

"I want a new wedding." Snow White announced to the world. "I don't even remember my first one. My therapist says I'm right to think that's unfair. He says I have to trust my feelings."

"Damn dwarf." The Mad Hatter grumbled. "He still owes me twenty gold pieces from the last Wolf Ball Championship."

"There must be silence in the court!" The Knave shouted. "Rule Forty-two says that every outburst will add *another* year to the dragon's life sentence. Jury, write that down."

The jury dutifully marked their notebooks.

"Where's my lawyer?" Trevelyan wanted to know.

"I *am* your lawyer." The Knave retorted.

"Well, who is the prosecution then?"

"I'm that, too."

"Are you the judge, as well?"

"No. Their majestic majesties are the judges."

"They already think I'm guilty."

The Knave shrugged. "Because you are."

Marrok nodded like that made sound judicial sense.

The Mad Hatter rolled his swirling eyes. "Since I'm finding him guilty anyway, can I just go? I'm missing tea."

"Don't be silly, Hatty. We haven't heard all the evidence, yet." The Queen of Clubs was relishing this. "We have to learn *why* he's guilty."

Grimhilde cackled, enjoying Trevelyan's hopeless legal position. Clearly, she was a cruel and malicious person. Too bad that Trevelyan planned to kill her. Under other circumstances, he and Grimhilde might have gotten along famously.

"First witness!" A Three of Clubs came marching into the room carrying a hunk of wood on a velvet pillow.

Trevelyan blinked as the familiar looking log was paraded past him and carefully set on the witness stand.

Marrok squinted in confusion. "What the fuck is that?"

"Obscenity!" The Knave shouted. "Under Rule Forty-Two,

that's another mandatory year added to the dragon's life sentence."

The jury wrote that down.

"Thanks a lot." Trevelyan told Marrok.

Marrok made a face. "You're getting life anyway."

The Queen of Clubs made a sound of smug amusement. "Swear in Queen Alice." She told the Knave. "We're ready to begin questioning."

The Mad Hatter frowned at the log. "Didn't Alice used to be blonde?"

"I don't even remember what my first wedding dress looked like." Snow White pouted. "Marrok, sweetie, what did my wedding dress look like?"

"It was hideous." He told her sadly.

Trevelyan glanced between them, wondering what *this* was about, now. Whatever it was, Marrok was using it to feed the madness. If Esmeralda was right (and she usually was) Wonderland thrived on chaos and it was testing Trevelyan. Anything that added to the escalating disorder could only help him win.

Snow White's eyes went wide. "My wedding dress was hideous?"

"I *dreamed* of you wearing a beautiful gown, my precious pearl." Marrok lamented. He might not know the nuts-and-bolts of Wonderland's thirst for anarchy, but it didn't matter. Mayhem came naturally to him. "You wanted it, too. You would have looked like an angel of sunlight, and cartoon fawns, and those adorable parasols in sugary drinks. ...But *your mother* insisted you wear the ugliest gown in the kingdom."

"What?" The Queen of Clubs' head snapped around, only half-hearing that lie over the Knave's questioning. "What about me?"

The Knave just talked louder. "Isn't it true Alice --if that *is* your real name-- that Trevelyan transformed you into a log, thereby seizing control of the Heart Kingdom and directly threatening the rule of her imperial greatness, the Queen of Clubs!?"

The jury looked at the log.

The log sat there.

"She doesn't even deny it." The Mad Hatter complained with a *tsk*.

The Knave tapped his forehead knowingly. "A clear sign of guilt."

"She has the right to remain silent." Trevelyan argued.

"Under Rule Forty-Two, you do *not* have the right to remain silent." The Knave told the jury.

The jury wrote that down.

"What are you telling my daughter, wolf?" The Queen of Clubs glared at Marrok, her attention on whatever he was up to. "If you think I'm going to let you…"

Marrok cut her off. "Oh no, don't turn this around on me. *I'm* not the one who made poor Snow White wear an ugly wedding gown."

"I didn't make her wear an ugly wedding gown! Are you insane?"

"Under Rule Forty-Two, you *do* have a right to plead insanity." The Knave told the jury.

Grimhilde's spiteful smile slowly faded into befuddlement. Her head whipped back and forth, as she tried to follow the tornado of arguments.

Marrok watched the Queen of Clubs with gleaming menace. "You know… The wedding is sorta foggy in my mind, too. If she didn't have an ugly dress, then let's get the photos out. We'll look at them together."

The Queen of Clubs' eyes glinted like the magic mirror that hung on the wall, next to the throne. Cold and flat. "I'm not getting any photos out." She snarled.

"Why not?" Marrok challenged. "Why can't Snow White see the pictures of our wedding?"

"Yes, why can't I see the pictures, Mommy?"

The Queen of Clubs paled, like she was trying to see her way out of a trap. A lot of people looked that way around Marrok.

"I call the Mad Hatter to the stand." Trevelyan interjected.

The Knave glowered at him. "We're not done questioning Queen Alice."

"She's clearly a hostile witness and the Mad Hatter has vital information about my innocence."

"You're guilty." The Mad Hatter shot back. "How can I have information on your innocence?"

"That's *exactly* what you'll be explaining to the jury." Trevelyan countered. "Under Rule Forty-Two, the judge must testify if he's wearing a top hat." He had no idea what Rule Forty-Two said, but this was Wonderland, so no one else did either.

"You can't fight that kind of legal precedent." The Knave allowed and looked over at the jury. "The Mad Hatter is called to the stand."

The Mad Hatter trudged over to the witness box. He shoved the log aside, so it crashed to the floor, and sat down. "Fucking waste of my time."

"Obscenity." Marrok gleefully chimed in.

The jury wrote that down.

"Ladies and gentlemen of the jury." The Knave put his hands behind his back, walking back and forth in front of them. "Before you sits an innocent man. Falsely targeted by this unhinged lunatic, who is…."

"Objection!" Trevelyan pounded a hand on the table in front of him. "'Unhinged lunatic' is prejudicial. I demand you apologize to his Highness, the Mad Hatter."

The Mad Hatter's crazy, swirly eyes fixed on the Knave. "Did you just call me an unhinged lunatic?"

Trevelyan nodded. "Under oath, no less."

Grimhilde looked dizzy.

"I want to see my wedding photos." Snow White shrieked at the Queen of Clubs. "Why can't I see them?"

"Well, because… they're… not here, Snow."

"Your mother got rid of them." Marrok surmised. "All our treasured memories. *Gone*."

Snow White let out a wail of horror and fury.

"You son of a *bitch*." The Queen of Clubs got to her feet, stabbing a finger at Marrok. "You're not under a spell, at all! I will turn you into a throw-rug for this!"

"What spell?" Marrok taunted. "Explain what you mean, *Mom*."

The Knave's panicked expression stayed on the Mad Hatter. "Sire, I didn't call *you* an unhinged lunatic. I called *Trevelyan* an unhinged lunatic."

Trevelyan shook his head. "You can't change your testimony, after you've already given it. The jury's written it down."

"I'm not testifying! I'm the attorney."

"And *he's* the judge." Trevelyan gestured towards the Mad Hatter. "Smart lawyers don't insult the judge. I find you guilty. Jury?" He looked their way.

They all looked at the Mad Hatter for a ruling.

"Guilty." The Mad Hatter intoned. He stood up, pulling out a katana. "The sentence is off with his head."

Trevelyan had a feeling that was *always* the sentence.

The Knave backed up a step.

"Mommy, what spell?" Snow White repeated, stomping a foot. "How can you be so mean to Marrok? Why did you destroy my wedding pictures?"

"Snow, not *now*." The Queen of Clubs snapped. "Mother is talking."

Marrok kept his attention on Snow White. "She wants to keep you a child forever. *That's* what this is about."

"My daughter is not listening to you, wolf. None of this will work. You're going back to the dungeon!"

Marrok ignored the Queen, his eyes on Snow White. "We need to get our own place, honey."

Snow White brightened. "Like an apartment for just the two of us?"

"Exactly! Living with the in-laws never works."

The Queen of Clubs gave a harsh laugh. "Oh, you're not going *anywhere*."

"You can't keep us here!" Snow White screeched back.

"I'm your mother and you'll do as I say!"

Marrok's gaze never wavered from Snow White. "We can't lead our own life, with her meddling. You see that, right? Untie me and let's get out of here. She'll respect you more, if you stand up to her."

Snow White rushed over to start unfastening his chains.

"What are you doing?" The Queen of Clubs quickly moved to intercept her. "Snow, I swear if you don't stop that immediately, I will…"

Her dire threat was cut off by the Knave of Clubs' terrified howl. "Stop!"

The Mad Hatter didn't stop. He advanced, an oversized pocket watch in one hand and a sword in the other.

Trevelyan's eyes fixed on the watch. William the lizard said it was synched to the Mad Hatter's heartbeat and could control time. Trevelyan only had access to two percent of his powers. Not enough to do anything useful or Bad.

But, exactly enough to piggyback off one of Esmeralda's not-quite wicked spells.

In his whole life, Trevelyan had never believed in anything he couldn't see, hear, touch, scent, or taste for himself. It was his bedrock principle. ...But he believed in Esmeralda. He believed his True Love was a part of him. He believed that her incredible powers could somehow meld into his own, even though every rule of magic said otherwise. He *believed* it, a thousand percent.

Fifth impossible thing.

Trevelyan's fingernails were painted in the enchanted color that Esmeralda had made for him. Her magic was literally *on* him. The microscopic amounts of Good energy he possessed reached for it. Instantly, Esmeralda's powers surged beneath his command, flowing like his own. Enough to help him and give his almost-margin-of-error-Goodness the boost it needed.

His gaze flicked to the Alice-log, which was also seeped in Esmeralda's beautiful, green magic. Filled with the one spell she cast, again and again. Calling to him, with all its poetic possibilities.

Log, hog, grog, smog... *Cog.*

Pocket watches were made of gears and springs and cogs. It's how they kept time. If some deranged maniac just happened to vaporize all those cogs, who knew what might happen to the watch?

Trevelyan was just the deranged maniac to find out.

Esmeralda's words came back to him. Her sweet little pep talk, as they faced down an army with limited magic and no clue how it would all turn out: *You're the best at being Bad. That's got nothing to do with your powers. You're just a horrible*

fucking person, through and through.
The Mad Hatter's swirling eyes cut in Trevelyan's direction, somehow sensing his own sudden peril.

"You threatened my mate, right in front of me." Trevelyan's smirk held all the darkness in his soul. "That might just make you the stupidest man alive. ...But you won't be for long."

The Mad Hatter's mouth opened to scream, but it was too late. Trevelyan ruthlessly exploded all the cogs in the pocket watch. Bad magic or no Bad magic, there was nothing he couldn't destroy. It was a gift. Springs loudly *spronged,* from within the mechanism. The case bulged and cracked open. Bits of glass and metal rained down, scattering across the black-and-white floor.

The Mad Hatter let out a cry of shock, clutching at his chest. His fingers dug into his purple shirtfront, as his heart slowed and his magic ebbed. His body hit the ground, writhing in pain, his lips already turning blue.

Trevelyan blew across his nails, satisfied with the man's suffering.

"Hatty!" The Queen of Clubs screeched.

Even Snow White was distracted by her father's distress. "Mommy, what's wrong with him?"

Forgetting about Marrok, they both raced to the Mad Hatter's side.

"Grimhilde, help me!" The Queen of Clubs cried. "You have to keep his heart beating!"

"How can I, without Bad magic?" Grimhilde demanded, even as she rushed forward. "I'm a wicked witch!"

"You wrote a whole thesis on using mystical spells on hearts!" The Queen of Clubs shrieked. "Do something!"

As everyone else aided the Mad Hatter, Trevelyan headed for Marrok. God only knew why, but he couldn't leave the wolf behind. His powers weren't strong enough to break through the enspelled chains, but he was *physically* strong enough to help Marrok break the damn chair. Wonderland wanted to see him succeed without magic? Fine. He'd create havoc with his bare hands.

Trevelyan slammed his weight down on the back of the chair to hold it in place. At the same time, the wolf wrenched up on the armrest, using all of his strength. Wood splintered and the chains slipped free.

"Go!" Marrok roared.

Trevelyan was already moving. The two of them bolted from the room, before anyone could try and stop them.

And so seven years after they were cellmates in prison, Trevelyan and Marrok finally escaped together.

CHAPTER THIRTY

Pick your perfect nail polish from our unlimited selection!
Simple Revenge Taupe: ATTENTION: THIS PRODUCT HAS BEEN
CANCELLED. We know that everybody's been looking forward to
seeing this uncomplicated shade of justified vengeance, but the
formulation is impossible. Not even magic can keep the pigments
from getting all muddy and the color from becoming something
wholly unintended.
We're sorry for the inconvenience.

Happily Ever Witch Cosmetics Website

The Club Castle

The second Trevelyan managed to get the damn chains off Marrok, the ungrateful bastard punched him.

"What the *fuck*?" Trevelyan roared, grabbing his very-close-to-broken nose. "Are you out of your mind?"

The two of them had ducked into some overly-decorated room, with black walls and solid white furniture. Maybe it was a formal parlor for royal guests. It seemed as good a place as any to get their bearings. Esmeralda would be there soon. He needed to quickly devise a plan to steal her crowns.

"You're lucky I don't gut you right here." Marrok snarled at him, with no consideration for Trevelyan's schedule. "When we get out of this place, I still might."

"Try it. I've been fantasizing about ways to skin you since the WUB Club, so I have a head start on planning."

"You're still pissed at me over the jailbreak? Well, I'm even more pissed at *you*."

"For what?" Trevelyan demanded incredulously. *He* was the injured party here. Literally.

"You threatened my True Love!"

"Oh, for God's sake... I wasn't going to hurt Scarlett." Trevelyan swiped a hand under his nose. Blood dripped from his fingers onto the ivory, club-shaped rug. "I was just trying to annoy you."

"It worked." Marrok said darkly.

"You can't *possibly* think I'd actually harm your mate."

"Can't I?"

"No." Trevelyan was a little insulted the wolf had bought into his theatrics so wholeheartedly. He also didn't have time to fight about this nonsense. "I was perhaps a bit dramatic, but...."

"You were out of control!"

"I'm never out of control! I didn't even use magic on her. Or you."

"But you turned *yourself* into a dragon!"

"And I didn't put a claw on her! Snow White..." He tried to find the words to explain something he'd rather not discuss. "Well, you've slept with people you didn't choose." Wolfball players were always sexually exploited. It was an open, dirty secret. "You understand that it's not... enjoyable."

Marrok's head tilted.

"Do you *really* think I would have done something like that to a woman?" Trevelyan asked again. "I didn't have my mate then, but I have a sister."

"Troll shit. You don't have a sister..."

"Marion." Trevelyan interrupted. "I claim her as my sister, just as you claim Esmeralda."

Marrok paused his ranting, his eyes searching Trevelyan's face. Trevelyan met his gaze. He was speaking the truth and the wolf knew it.

"You talked about Maid Marion a lot in jail." Marrok allowed.

"It's how I knew to invest money with her. Now, I'm making like eighteen percent a year. It's also why I've been questioned by bank regulators, at least four times. She's fiendishly, ruthlessly, possibly *criminally* ingenious, when it comes to making villains rich. Every Good folk in the world hates her."

Trevelyan nodded. "My sister."

"Huh." Marrok mused, like he was suddenly seeing the resemblance.

"If you believe nothing else, believe I'd never risk my relationship with Marion. And she would *not* have forgiven me if I harmed an innocent girl. Most other crimes, I think. But not that." He shook his head. "I went too far with frightening Scarlett." He didn't like admitting that, but they were in a hurry and it was true. "I spent two years in a coma for it and that's fair. But it never would have gone as far as you think."

"As far as you *threatened* it would go, you mean."

"Why am I blamed for every single thing I say?"

Marrok made a scoffing, snarling sort of noise at that defense. Trevelyan kept going. "I'm a Bad person! Even I can't keep track of the thousands of threats I make, but I don't carry them all out! You no doubt know every crime I've ever committed. Were any of them for assaulting some unwilling girl?"

"No."

"No." Trevelyan agreed, disgruntled that this was an issue. "I know what it feels like, so I would *never* sink so low. And I certainly wouldn't have hurt your True Love. Not even I'm that big a bastard."

Tension eased from Marrok's shoulders.

"I was quite impressed with Scarlett, as a matter of fact." Trevelyan went on. "She can do *far* better than you, if you want my opinion. You're being completely unreasonable."

"To get at me... you scared Letty." Marrok slowly reiterated, like Trevelyan still wasn't understanding something.

"But you're the one who..."

Marrok cut him off. "*You scared my mate.*" He stressed each word for emphasis. "How angry would you be if somebody scared Ez?"

Trevelyan's righteous indignation hit a wall.

Marrok arched a meaningful brow.

"Alright." Trevelyan said after a long moment. "I see your point. We've both crossed some lines in our friendship."

"I didn't cross any lines." Marrok insisted. "I did nothing to ruin our friendship. That was all *you*. My mate is half your size and has no magic. She is *Good*. You terrified her! Reverse the goddamn situations and tell me again how I'm overreacting."

Shit.

Trevelyan closed his eyes. He remembered how furious he'd been when he'd learned that the Walrus had dragged Esmeralda into that interrogation room. The panic he'd felt when Haigha had sighted on her as a prize. His violent wrath at the yetis who'd trapped her in that cave.

No one would ever touch his mate and live. Not for long, anyway.

"I screwed up." Denial was a losing position, so Trevelyan abandoned it. "But now I have Esmeralda and I am a kinder person. Scarlett is giving me another chance."

Marrok suddenly looked worried. "No. *No*. Letty's *not* going to give you..."

"She's at least considering it." Trevelyan interrupted. "She told Ez that I should help you and so here I am helping you." He spread his arms. "I've been sent in to hero this situation, dickhead. You're welcome."

Marrok pinched the bridge of his nose and sighed, like his wife's Goodness was a never-ending struggle. "Scarlett and Ez *really* believe we can work together and not kill each other?"

"Our True Loves think we're better people than we really are."

Marrok grunted. "Speak for yourself. *My* True Love is going to be blown away by my non-violence. I'm even impressing myself. The fact that I'm not ripping your throat out shows how goddamn magnanimous I am. ...And proves that I'm a *way* better friend than you are."

"I'm a fantastic friend!"

"In my place, you'd be setting me on fire and you know it." Trevelyan made an aggravated sound, because he couldn't argue otherwise. "My God, you're always so stubborn. I've apologized for scaring your mate and *still* you can't..."

"You didn't apologize for anything!"

"I'll apologize to *her*. And you haven't apologized to me, either!"

"What do *I* have to be sorry for? *Not* blowing up the WUB

Club?"

"I would have died, if I stayed there." Trevelyan pointed off towards the Four Kingdoms, even though he wasn't certain which direction it was in. "That was supposed to be my last day alive. Marion knew the future and she told me that I *had* to get out. You refused to help. What kind of friend is *that?*"

"You were supposed to die? For real?"

"*Yes.*"

"Well, you didn't tell me that!" Marrok snapped. "If I'd known it was literal life-and-death, I would've helped you with an escape plan. I thought you were just bored and homesick. I still wouldn't have rigged a bomb to wipe out a hundred people, but I'm sure we could've come up with something to save you."

"I did come up with something. I slept with Snow White. And I was *never* the same. I've always been Bad, but I was worse after that. The dragon raged for five goddamn years and --yes!-- I got out of control. At least partially. And I *hate* being out of control."

The wolf frowned.

Trevelyan ran a hand over his face. He knew Esmeralda had been right when she said he'd had sex too early. Mrs. Clyburn had been a predatory bitch. It seemed obvious, now.

Trevelyan had spent years afterwards inoculating himself with more and more meaningless bed partners. That just made things worse.

But, he'd never *felt* out of control. Not until Snow White. That had been the moment that changed him. When he'd decided to survive, yes... but the means of his survival hadn't *really* been his decision. After that, all the little shit that he'd been previously ignoring, coalesced into something huge. His resentment of Snow White and Mrs. Clyburn had mixed together in his head and crashed down on him. Trevelyan had wondered if he'd ever get back up. He almost hadn't. He'd done things that even he knew were wrong.

"It wasn't until I found Ez that I felt like me, again." He said aloud. Trying to work it all out, so they'd both understand. "The dragon finally settled and my mind cleared. And I was fully in control, again."

The wolf was listening.

Trevelyan sighed. "God, Marrok. I did *not* want to sleep with Snow White."

"I know." Marrok's tone changed, becoming less cold. "I shouldn't have said what I said about that, back in the Westlands. When I implied you must have wanted her back. I know you didn't."

Trevelyan shrugged, staring at the wall and hating this whole conversation.

Marrok wasn't done. "But, we have our mates, now. Whatever we did to get them is worth it. We endured it all and *won*, because we found them."

Trevelyan was quiet for a moment. "When I scared Scarlett, I wasn't thinking beyond my fury at you. I have very few friends and I was... upset with you for not helping me."

"You need to not be such an asshole. Then maybe you'd have more friends."

"Possibly." He returned his eyes to the wolf. "I'm sorry."

Marrok crossed his arms over his chest and thought for a beat. "How much did it just hurt you to say that?"

"A fucking lot."

"Good."

Trevelyan expelled an irritated breath, because he might as well say it all. "I understand what you meant in that jail cell. All those times you said your True Love would save you, I thought you were being ridiculous. But I get it, now."

"I know you do. You wouldn't have come for me or be saying any of this, if you didn't love Ez."

"She wants you alive. Lord knows why. She'll be here soon to save you. I told her to stay away, but I'm sure she'll ignore me. And she'll be able to feel my magic, even with the block on Bad energy." That golden strand still connected them. It always would. "We need to wait here, until she shows up."

"Trev, she'll come for *you*." Marrok corrected. "For both of us. But mostly for you."

"You have no idea how desperate she's been to find you."

"And I've been desperate to find her. But *you* are her True Love. Nothing will stop her from reaching you. Esmeralda will rain down nail polish and gingerbread mutants on anyone who keeps you from her. Trust me. She's a villain. Just like us."

"She's better than us."

"She is." Marrok agreed. "But that just makes her stronger."

"She has the greatest magic I've ever seen." Trevelyan said with genuine pride. "No one anywhere can match it. Not even me. What she can do is *impossible* and yet she does it without even seeing how special it is."

"Doesn't surprise me." Marrok flopped down on one of the pristine white sofas, getting comfortable while they waited for Esmeralda. "When the Tuesday share circle escaped the WUB Club, I was the muscle, Scarlett had the plan, Benji and Avenant got us across the Lake of Forgetting... But Ez's glamours made all of it possible. Even with those magic detectors everywhere, she could find ways around the rules."

Trevelyan smirked. "She hates rules."

"If you don't take care of her, I'll kill you." It wasn't a threat. It was a flat warning. "If you have a sister, than you know that I will."

Trevelyan nodded, because he did know.

Marrok grunted. "This was a good talk. Very healthy. Much better than you ever did in group therapy. Are we calling a truce here?"

"Fine." Trevelyan had bigger enemies than the wolf, after all. "Tuesday share circle sticks together, yes?"

Marrok's mouth curved a bit at the family motto. "Yes. You weren't actually *in* our Tuesday share circle, though."

"I was in *a* Tuesday share circle. That counts. It was very bonding. ...Except when I killed Bluebeard, during that one session." He made a face. "Although somehow he's seems to have survived it."

"Bluebeard you just beat half to death. It was *Gold*beard we killed."

"You're kidding."

"Nope. *I* killed Bluebeard, a couple hours ago. Well, Snow White did, technically. Goldbeard is the guy we buried in the garbage dumpster and then let The Count of What's-His-Face take the blame for it."

Trevelyan blinked in genuine confusion. "Who the hell was *Goldbeard?*"

Marrok lifted a baffled shoulder. "I thought *you* knew that."

"I never heard of him."

"Well, why did we hate him, then?"

"I thought *you* knew that."

"I have no clue! I was just following you."

They looked at each other.

"Huh." Marrok finally said. "Well, he was probably a jerk."

"So was Bluebeard." Trevelyan dismissed the mix-up, because what did it really matter? "They're both dead. We're not. Let's keep it that way."

"Agreed."

A commotion sounded from outside the room. "Where the hell is my dragon?"

Trevelyan's head snapped around. That wasn't Esmeralda's voice, but she was the person using it. The poisoned-candy scent was unmistakable. His mate was here! She'd found him. And for some damn reason she sounded like Cinderella.

CHAPTER THIRTY-ONE

Pick your perfect nail polish from our unlimited selection!
Ass-Kicking Aubergine: Ideal for storming castles and flattening enemies, this luscious gel polish has a super glossy finish that holds up in any combat situation. Plus, its slithy mix of blackened-violet and actual venom will look spectacular when you're finally decked out in the enormous diamond tiara* that you so richly deserve.
*Enormous diamond tiara stolen separately.

Happily Ever Witch Cosmetics Website

The Club Palace

"Is that Cinderella?" Marrok jumped to his feet. "What is *she* doing here? I thought we locked up that depraved nutcase." Trevelyan was already at the door. He wrenched it open, stepped into the hall, and was nearly flattened by a stampede of playing cards. The guards were fleeing from a very pissed off witch.
Esmeralda stalked after them, dressed in Cinderella's body and fishnet stockings. Her disguise was off-putting, of course. (Marrok was right, for once. Cinderella was indeed a depraved nutcase.) But Esmeralda was *Esmeralda*, no matter the glamour. Seeing his beautiful mate had his mood soaring. Esmeralda was safe and whole and out for blood.
"One of you is going to tell me where Trevelyan is or I will *make* you tell me."
She was asking about him? Not the wolf? Trevelyan leaned against the doorframe, intense satisfaction filling him. She *did* like him best. His mate needed him, just as he needed her.

This was excellent news. It was only a matter of time before she loved him. After all, he was a dragon! Who wouldn't love a dragon?

Esmeralda was so caught up in her search that she didn't notice she'd found him. "I know you've got him someplace close-by. Stop!" A manicured palm waved out... and the escaping guards became a cheery hurricane of magazine pages. Glossy pictures of toys. Photos of brightly wrapped packages. Images of smiling women in pretty dresses. A confetti of colorful advertisements rained down, like a tickertape parade. Trevelyan's eyebrows soared.

"What the hell is this, now?" Esmeralda grabbed one of the bits of paper and squinted at it. "Cata*logue*." She finally muttered in disgust, tossing it away, again. "That damn frog spell still won't work. Good energy just makes *happy* rhymes."

Love spread through Trevelyan's chest. Hotter than fire and more real than magic. "You need to use *all* your powers to have balance." He told her. "Good and Bad together."

Esmeralda's fake-face snapped around, wrong-colored eyes widening. "Trev!" She ran for him, believing that he'd catch her.

And he always, *always* would.

Esmeralda jumped up and Trevelyan's arms wrapped securely around her, holding her close. "I've been waiting for you, my darling." Kissing her blonde temple, he carried her into the formal parlor, before someone else came along and saw them. "I got here as quick as I could. Have you ever tried climbing a mountain in heels?" She pulled back to look him over, her legs looped around his hips. "Are you okay? Are you hurt? I've been so worried!"

"Hey, Ez." Marrok said dryly, heading over to them.

"Hey, Marrok." She shot him a quick, beaming smile and then turned back to Trevelyan. "Did someone hit you?" She ran a hand over his face, like she half-suspected he was hiding some grievous wound from her. "Why is your nose bleeding?"

"Marrok did that." He might have an uneasy truce going with the wolf, but Trevelyan wasn't about to miss an opportunity to score points. "After I rescued him from certain death, he punched me. But, I forgive him, because he's your brother." He endeavored to look noble. "I'd suffer through anything to please my future bride."

Esmeralda stared at him, like he really was her happily ever after.

"Asshole." Marrok flipped Trevelyan off, without any heat.

Trevelyan ignored him. "Why do you look like Cinderella?" He asked Esmeralda.

"Oh!" She instantly dropped the glamour, so she was herself again. Much better. "Right. Sorry. I had to get naked to kill a gardener and I used her body to do it."

"*Naked?*"

"Relax. The gardener didn't touch me."

"But he saw you!"

"He saw *Cindy*." She rolled her eyes. "I just needed a distraction."

Trevelyan was far from appeased. Even if it wasn't his mate's *real* body, dragons didn't share. "You're sure this gardener is dead?" If he wasn't, he soon would be.

"Yep. I pushed him into some carnivorous roses. It was a terrible way to go. You'd be thrilled."

He was glad the man had suffered. Still... "You pushed him with your *hands?*" He shook his head, because that news was even more upsetting than her nakedness. "No, darling. We need to work on ways for you to kill people at a distance. I don't like that you got that close to him."

Esmeralda hopped down out of his arms, disgruntled now. "Pushing him worked just fine. Stop nitpicking my villainy."

"I'm not nitpicking. I'd just rather you not get beheaded. Our honeymoon will be a lot more fun for me, if all your body parts are attached."

Marrok gave a bark of laughter. ...Which he quickly tried to turn into a cough, when Esmeralda scowled at him.

"I can always tell Letty that you died during the rescue." She warned, jabbing a finger in the wolf's direction. "I'm already pissed that you hit my True Love."

Marrok held up his hands in mock surrender, fighting a grin. Clearly, he was thrilled to have Esmeralda back, which made

Trevelyan soften towards the man. Slightly. "You've met Trev, right? You know he deserved a bloody nose and a lot more."
"I don't care! He's still my True Love, so I'm on his side."
Trevelyan preened at the show of solidarity. Esmeralda had given him her loyalty. She looked for him *first*. Stood by him *first*. It was exactly what he wanted to hear. What *any* dragon wanted to hear. Except she still hadn't told him she loved him. What was the hold up? Loyalty was vital, but so was love. It turned out, he needed both.
"You shut up, too." Esmeralda ordered, even though he'd been too busy puzzling over his unsettled emotions to say anything.
Marrok moved to wrap an arm around Esmeralda's shoulders, giving his sister a hug. "I missed you, Ez." He kissed the top of her head. "I think you did a great job of getting in here to rescue us, even if the dragon doesn't appreciate it."
Esmeralda leaned into his side, looking sulky. "Thank you."
Trevelyan pushed aside the restlessness that still lurked at his core. "Why are you listening to this meddling liar? Marrok's a verbal arsonist. He sets shit on fire, just by smiling and fucking with people. He literally went to jail for it."
"Only twice." Marrok moved to sit on the arm of a club-patterned, club-shaped club chair. "And who are you to talk? You're an *actual* arsonist."
"You're that, too!"
Marrok hesitated, as if recalling his fifty-count rap sheet. "Okay. Yeah. *That*."
Trevelyan focused on Esmeralda again, because he always focused on Esmeralda. "Darling, I completely support your villainy. I just want you to be safe about it. I worry about you, like you worry about me. It's what mates *do*."
She made a slight face, but couldn't dispute his words.
Trevelyan raised his eyebrows in innocent inquiry and pushed his luck. They were fighting magical enemies and taking over a kingdom, but a man had priorities. "Speaking of mates, are you ready to accept my proposal, yet? You agreed to agree the next time I asked."
She continued to pout. "Whatever."
"Is that a yes?"

"It's an 'I'll marry you, if I don't kill you first.'"
"Which is a yes?"
"Yes." She muttered, still annoyed at him.
A win was a win! She hadn't admitted that she loved him, but this was still a huge step forward. Trevelyan gave her a smacking kiss, not concerned over her grouchy acquiescence.
"This moment is *just* how I imagined it." He teased.
She gave a snort of reluctant amusement, her lips curving. Trevelyan's heart swelled. He loved making her smile.
Marrok groaned, his too-handsome face falling into his palms.
"Custom dictates that *you* pay for the wedding." Trevelyan told him smugly. "The bride's family always foots the bill. My sister is very clear on that rule."
"Let's discuss vendors later." Esmeralda urged. "I want to get out of here sometime today."
"Oh, we can't leave." Trevelyan protested. "The Queen of Clubs timed her spell to the eight square. It must be a ceremony, of some kind. She thinks she can use it to keep her position secure and then she'll be safe." His eyes narrowed in thought. "Instead, we'll kill her and everyone else standing in our way."
"God... how many times have I heard you say that?" Marrok lamented.
"Well, it's always a reasonable plan."
Marrok was less enthusiastic. "This is *not* the right time for an attack."
"I swear, if you start lecturing me about the supposed 'immorality' of slaughtering a bunch of people," Trevelyan added quotation marks around the word, "I'll leave you here to..."
Marrok cut him off. "It's not morals, dick face. It's *logic*. The Mad Hatter is dying, because of you. You murdered the Queen of Clubs' True Love! She's going to be out for your blood."
Esmeralda's lips parted. "You murdered the Mad Hatter?"
"Murdered?" Trevelyan seesawed a palm, unconvinced about the charge. "When you kill someone in a courtroom, it counts as a legal maneuver. My lawyer will probably agree."
"You have a lawyer?" Esmeralda sounded skeptical.

"I *did*. He might be dead, now." Such a tragedy for the legal community. "The point is, the Queen of Clubs is distracted with her husband's dwindling heartbeat, so this is a golden opportunity to get your crowns. Attack when your enemy is weakest."

"You murdered her True Love." Marrok stressed. "The woman isn't weak. She's never been more dangerous. And with Bad magic blocked, you and I have barely any powers to fight her."

"Bad magic will come back at the eighth square. You said so yourself."

"We don't even know what that *means*."

"Chess." The answer flashed into Trevelyan's mind, as he recalled the huge tower in the courtyard. "Somehow it's related to chess. There are sixty-four squares on a chessboard. Eight in either direction."

Esmeralda and Marrok stared at him.

"What? I like chess. It's a game of strategy and control."

"The Cheshire Carpet made me play chess this morning." Esmeralda said, looking suddenly thoughtful. "It was going on about double queens and inventing rules. I think it was trying to tell me something important."

"You're befriending our rug?"

"Who the hell cares about chess and rugs?" Marrok retorted. "What does that have to do with anything?"

"I'm not sure, yet." Esmeralda shook her head. "Half of everything in Wonderland is nonsense. ...But the other half *isn't*. It speaks in codes, if you listen."

"If *you* listen." Trevelyan corrected. Wonderland's cheerful anarchy seemed particularly tuned to the witch. It liked her wicked virtue and impossible magic. "It wants you to be empress." It was the only explanation for all the oddness that came their way.

Marrok grunted. "Well, I'd like to tell Scarlett I'm alive, before I die. The Queen of Clubs was talking about Sir Galahad earlier. Saying he was coming to Wonderland. I know my wife is responsible for that, because she's working with Midas."

"Letty sent Galahad to retrieve us." Esmeralda told him. "She's been frantic to get you home."

"So, let's go home! You have no idea the shit I've been through, just today. I had to fake being under a love spell, and listen to Snow White talk about the pekapoo she wants us to adopt, and pretend to make a deal with the Queen of Clubs, so she didn't murder *this* bastard on sight." He pointed at Trevelyan. "And that last part took some fast talking. Have you ever tried to brainstorm convincing reasons *not* to kill Trevelyan? There aren't very many!"

Trevelyan casually flipped him off.

Esmeralda frowned. "What's a pekapoo?"

"A cross between a pekinese and a poodle. Does it seem like a *wolf* would do well with a cross between a pekinese and a poodle?" Marrok didn't wait for an answer. "Snow White is dangerous and insane. This whole fucking place is! I have watched them murder two people, during family meals. One was some perfectly innocent maid." He shook his head. "We should come back *later*, when we have the element of surprise, bigger numbers, and a lot more magic."

"No one here has more magic than Ez." Trevelyan didn't want to retreat. As usual, he wanted to play offense. "She's got *far* more Goodness than the Queen of Clubs has. She can beat her."

He believed it.

Esmeralda didn't seem so sure.

"What about Grimhilde, the fancy-ass witch." Marrok crossed his arms over his chest. "That woman knows how to rip out hearts or some shit. I don't like the idea of Ez facing her…"

Esmeralda cut him off. "Grimhilde is here?" Her voice rose in alarm. "She hates me, when she bothers to remember who I am! She's kicked me out of the Cauldron Society a dozen times, for misfiring spells."

Trevelyan lifted a shoulder, because he didn't see an issue. "So, we'll kill her, too." (It was just *always* a reasonable plan. How did everyone not see it?) "You are half Good. She isn't. You're a level six witch. She isn't. You are my mate. She isn't. You will *win*."

"Against Grimhilde *and* the Queen of Clubs?!"

"Against anyone."

Esmeralda still looked doubtful. "Maybe I can send them out for an exhausting *jog*, but otherwise…"

He cut her off. "Your powers fight you, because they're confined and separated. Let them go --Good and Bad-- and *believe* that they will know what to do."

Esmeralda studied is face for a beat. "Death or freedom." She whispered.

He nodded. "Wild things need freedom. They have to *decide*. Your magic will do what you want, but you can't force it. It's too big to ever plan for or control. Just trust it. *Believe*."

"But, I only have Good magic, right now. My spells are all… cute." Her tone was an embarrassed lament.

"Cute?" His brow furrowed.

"Yes! It's *horrible*. How can I achieve any genuine evil with nothing but frigging candy-coated joy blasting out everyplace? A wicked witch needs…"

Her protest was cut short by a rush of power. The brillig burst into the room, knocking the door right off its hinges. Esmeralda went flying backwards, as it barreled past her. One huge hand seized Trevelyan, the other Marrok, and then all three of them were *gone*.

The brillig transported the men right out of the palace.

A fraction of a second later, Trevelyan landed face down in the sand. What in the frozen-hells…?

He lifted his head, taking stock. The brillig, Trevelyan and Marrok were now on the edge of a huge lake. Inflatable beach balls and lounge chairs dotted the shore. A cadre of human dipshits stood nearby, gaping at the intrusion with typical human intelligence. Magical creatures were strapped to posts around them, apparently suffering some form of public execution.

The Diamond Kingdom.

It had to be, given the summertime heat, the murderous humans, and the incessant harlequin patterns on everything. Off in the distance, a giant sandcastle rose out of the desert, diamond-shaped windows glinting in the sun. God, that was actually worse than the Heart Castle. And the chafing here would be the stuff of nightmares.

Not that it mattered. He wasn't staying long. Now that Trevelyan was out of the Club Kingdom, his Bad magic was back. Even more than he'd had in the cave. For the first time since he'd woken up from the coma, he had *all* of his power. It filled him with a rush of dark fury and unfathomable energy. *Finally.*

Above him, the brillig roared. Marrok must have gotten his magic back, too. He started transforming into a wolf, but the brillig was too big to stop. It threw Marrok backwards, crashing him through a red-and-white beach umbrella. Mist covered Marrok's wolf, his body growing and his strength increasing, but it wouldn't be enough to stop an enraged brillig. Thundering forward, the creature prepared to crush him with its giant feet.

Trevelyan slammed magic into the brillig's back, deliberately drawing its attention away from Marrok. It would have been gratifying to witness his brother-in-law getting stomped like a grape, but he rose above the inclination.

(Truly, Trevelyan was a *wonderful* friend. How dare the wolf even question it! Look at how he was selflessly saving that moron's life.)

The brillig was knocked sideways by the bolt of Trevelyan's power. It wasn't a lot, because he had to cast the spell while sprawled in the sand. But, it was enough to draw the creature's wrath and singe off one fungus-y ear.

Apparently, no one else had ever scored a hit against it. The brillig screamed out in surprised anger. Changing direction, it charged for Trevelyan. It was huge, incensed, and intent on killing.

...But it was no match for a dragon.

Trevelyan was transforming before he even finished standing up. Green smoke swirled all around him, as he released his own beast. The dragon roared its satisfaction. It had been too long since it was free to hunt enemies. The brillig had taken the dragon from its mate, so the brillig would die. Obviously.

The Queen of Clubs' pet monster slowed its attack, like it was reconsidering its headlong charge, now that Trevelyan was fifteen-feet tall.

Too late, asshole.

Dragon fire burned out, so hot it turned the sand to glass. Liberally applied flames were always so useful in battle. The brillig broiled alive, right where he stood, the smell of roasted mushrooms filling the air.

"Shit!" Marrok covered his head with his arms to avoid getting flambéd.

It was the shortest fight ever recorded against a brillig. Trevelyan expected no less, considering he was the best at being Bad. Wonderland had shown him that he could be a deranged maniac, even without using dark spells. That was encouraging to know. With his powers, though, his manic derangement was a force of fucking nature. That was even better.

"Stop the magical infidels!" Not content with their general stupidity, the humans sunk into the annals of the historically idiotic. Drawing swords and guns and any other weapon they could find, they charged at Trevelyan. "Strike down the dragon!"

At least eighty humans headed his way, across the beach. Trevelyan smirked. He'd been planning to kill the Gyre, anyway. His very magical True Love wasn't safe with them milling around Wonderland, executing magical beings. He might as well wipe them out of existence, right here and now. It wouldn't take long. Some might call that overconfidence. He just saw it as fact.

"Who the hell are *these* guys, now?" Marrok leapt to his feet. "Goddamn it, everyplace you go is filled with people who hate you, Trev. Think about why that keeps happening." He didn't bother to wait for a response. He just began fighting the soldiers, stopping the first wave from reaching Trevelyan. When an army attacked, Marrok stood beside him. Both Trevelyan and the dragon were pleasantly surprised by the show of loyalty. Esmeralda had been right. Having allies was a welcome change.

In this case, though, it was also wholly unnecessary for Marrok to wade into the fray. There was a reason dragons were so often enslaved as super-weapons. Because, nothing could stand against them for long. Maybe stronger, smarter, better organized members of the Gyre had managed to takeover other places, but it would take a million men like this pathetic group to conquer Wonderland.

This kingdom belonged to the Green Dragons.

The power he unleashed was like the creation of a universe. Or the destruction of one. Multi-forked lightening split the sky, edged in glowing-green and hotter than hell itself. One thought from Trevelyan had the deadly bolts arcing downward and striking his foes. Sparks flew a hundred feet in the air, as they found their targets.

Even the humans were bright enough to know how Bad it was about to get. A few of them screamed and tried to retreat, but the bolts of energy tracked them. Like hungry snakes, the lightening slithered after its prey. Tracing them. Jumping from man-to-man. Striking, again and again. Incinerating the soldiers to ash, one-by-one. Nobody escaped his wrath.

Trevelyan had forgotten how marvelous it felt to destroy foes with his full powers! Even without his magic, he still always won. (Dragon.) But *with* his magic, there was nothing alive, dead, or necromanced that stood a chance against him.

The Gyre didn't like magic? He would give them a reason why. Even Marrok looked shocked by the devastation. He stopped fighting, just watching the carnage. In less than a minute, Trevelyan had slaughtered every human in the Diamond Kingdom. It was like a buzzsaw of fire and death cut through them. When it was over, blacked piles of ash were all that remained of Trevelyan's many enemies. Exactly the way it *should* be.

This time the dragon's roar was one of triumph.

Marrok slowly made his way over to him, back to his too-handsome self and looking thoughtful. "I think maybe you were telling the truth before." He scanned the smoldering battlefield. "I think you could have killed me and Letty, back in the Northlands, if you wanted."

Trevelyan transformed into his usual form, as well.

"Obviously." He agreed, out of breath from the exertion.

"So, why didn't you?"

"When it all comes down to the wire…? I never want you quite as dead as I *think* I do." Trevelyan was already focusing on the only thing that mattered: Esmeralda. He'd been away from her for about three minutes and that was *way* too long. "I have to get back to Ez."

"How?" Marrok shook the sand from his hair. "Bad magic is still blocked in the Club Kingdom."

"I'm going to connect to my half-Good mate."

Marrok's brows slammed down, following his thought process. "*You* can't use Esmeralda's powers. No one can meld magic like that. Not even True Loves."

"Ez and I can. Our magic is the same." Esmeralda had never cast a transporting spell, though. At least not that he knew of. He couldn't piggyback off of her work, like he had with the log/cog trick. "I just need to access her energy and use it to power one of my own spells. Once I figure that part out, I can get back to her."

"It's literally impossible."

"I know. But I believe it, anyway."

CHAPTER THIRTY-TWO

Pick your perfect nail polish from our unlimited selection! That Sophisticated Mauve Shade All the Other Girls Wear: Trends are for the anxious. Sure, you can buy this boringly popular color, but do you even like it? We recommend skipping the headache of trying to be who you're not. Instead, choose a unique nail polish, perfectly suited to your own exceptional taste.

Happily Ever Witch Cosmetics Website

The Club Castle

"Look at what that demented dragon did!" The Queen of Clubs shrieked, as Esmeralda was hustled into the throne room. Two seconds after the brillig disappeared with Trevelyan and Marrok, a dozen playing card guards had burst in and arrested Esmeralda. She hadn't bothered to resist. Esmeralda probably could have paper-shredded them all and climbed out the window, but fuck it.

Her True Love had been kidnapped by a brillig. Again! Esmeralda was sure Trevelyan and Marrok were safe. Between the two of them, they were damn near indestructible. That didn't mean she was any less pissed about it, though.

There came a time when a witch needed to stand her ground and fight.

Especially, when she was suddenly almost understanding the Cheshire Carpet's earlier words. Wonderland really did like secret codes. The rug said everything counted doubly-double on Tove. Doubly-double was four. Four tiaras made up the Wonderland crown. Therefore, Esmeralda needed to be doubly-double queen in order to claim the throne. Right? Right.

...Only she had no idea what that actually meant.

Esmeralda stepped away from the playing card guards, her gaze cutting around the throne room. The space was setup like a courtroom, so she imagined this was where Trevelyan had maybe killed The Mad Hatter. Which would make sense, since a man with a purple top hat was sprawled on the checker-board floor. His hair reminded her of a yeti.

The Queen of Clubs and Grimhilde from the Cauldron Society were kneeling beside him, doing their damnedest to keep his heart beating. Meanwhile, Snow White was searching around the perimeter of the room, calling for Marrok to stop playing hide-and-seek with her.

As much as she hated all four of them, Esmeralda hated Snow White the most. That psycho had forced Trevelyan into sex and she deserved to die for it. Granted, *all* these rotten people deserved to die, but Snow White's death was an absolute necessity.

"The dragon exploded Hatty's pocket watch." The Queen of Clubs continued, her beautiful face pulled taut with panic. "I can't fix it without *all* of my magic and Bad magic is blocked until the eighth square."

"Well, whose fault is that?" Esmeralda retorted, planting a hand on her hip.

"Yours! All of this is because of *you* and you're going to fix it! Then, I am going to kill you, become empress, and force Wonderland under control. With *me* in charge, none of this madness will ever happen again."

"Wonderland needs madness." Esmeralda said honestly. "It can't survive, if you take that away." Anyone could see that the kingdom thrived on breaking the rules. ...Just like her.

The Queen of Clubs didn't want to hear that truth.

"Wonderland will do what it's told and so will you! Save my True Love. *Now*."

"I recognize this witch." Grimhilde spared Esmeralda a quick, repressive frown. Her pointy hat and refined bearing made her the very picture of a successful, modern evildoer. "Didn't we expel you from the Cauldron Society?"

"Several times."

"You're the one who lied about being a level six on the official application." Grimhilde recalled with a disapproving *tsk*. "As if we wouldn't see through *that* foolishness. You couldn't even hex yourself a proper familiar. The society-approved cobra turned into some wretchedly huggable hedgehog."

The hedgehog's name was Milo and he granted good fortune to whoever petted him. He now lived in the Enchanted Forest, with Scarlett's grandmother. She rented him out for extra cuddles whenever some villain needed luck on a crime-spree. He was the most popular resident in town.

Esmeralda didn't bother to tell Grimhilde any of that. The Cauldron Society didn't matter to her, one little bit. Her attention stayed on the Queen of Clubs. "I'm not saving your True Love. Not when you tried to kill mine."

Esmeralda planned to return that favor by killing Snow White. That loony bitch was presently looking for Marrok under the edge of a club-shape mirror. It didn't seem to be a converted rabbit hole, like the looking glass in the Heart Palace. This was just a typical magic mirror. So, there was no way Marrok could possibly be hiding inside or behind it. That didn't stop Snow White from checking for him though.

Fucking stalker.

It bugged the crap out of Esmeralda that the woman was still walking around free. She wanted Snow White dead. The only question was: what spells could she possibly use to make that happen? It wasn't like she had a lot to choose from. The ginger-mutant enchantment wasn't going to work, because none of these people counted as food, and the damn frog spell was always a failure.

Believe.

The word seemed to whisper in her head. Trevelyan wanted her to trust her magic. To just let it free. That had worked to get her out of the Heart Palace, but her Good magic was in charge now and it seemed to be over-compensating, after years of getting shoved down. Every spell she cast was turning out cheery, twinkling, and disgustingly cute.

How could she inflict damage with cuteness?
Believe.
Her eyes narrowed, shoving aside her doubts. By being a wicked witch. That's how.

Of *course*, she could use Goodness in a villainous way. She'd defeated the brilligs, and gotten into the Club castle, and taken out those playing card guards with Good magic. She'd killed like ten people today! She didn't need Bad magic to be Bad. She was Esmeralda of the Green Dragons.

Wickedness was a goddamn part of her.

"You have no idea what's even happening here, you stupid little pawn!" The Queen of Clubs ranted, in full drama-mode. "The game is over and you've *lost*." She gestured towards the window and the Chess Tower beyond. "The white queen has won!"

Esmeralda frowned at the giant board, trying to make sense of it. She didn't know the rules of chess, but she felt like Wonderland didn't either. It would never choose an empress on the outcome of such a regimented game. That wasn't what it was testing today.

"I am going to rip out your heart and claim my spell." The Queen of Clubs continued venomously. "But first I need your repulsive magic to keep my husband alive until the eighth square."

Pawn… Game… White Queen… Eighth Square… Thoughts whirled in Esmeralda's head, fitting together into a pattern. Suddenly, the Cheshire Carpet's nonsensical words made a lot more sense.

You can win in eight moves, if you play your queen right.
If you get all the way across the board, you're double queen.
The Heart Queen should always be red.

Trevelyan said there were sixty-four spaces on the board, eight in either direction. That eighth square was where a new queen was crowned, if you could reach your opponent's side. And this was Tove, the extra day randomly squeezed into a week. The special date when an empress was crowned.

Wonderland wanted one of the queens to reach the eighth square on the chessboard… on Tove, the eight square added to a seven day calendar... and be doubly-double crowned empress of all four lands.

It was obvious to anyone ignoring the rules. Anyone who really listened to the silly clues. Maybe Wonderland was looking for an empress who accepted its nonsense and played along. Maybe that was the *real* game.

"Marrok?" Snow White searched for him beneath a table, her forehead creased in agitation. "Where are you? You're not supposed to leave. Mommy said I could keep you forever and brush your pretty hair!"

Grimhilde shot her a sideways look, disapproving and vaguely alarmed by the other woman's instability. "Is she *always* like this?"

"Do you have something to say about my little girl?" The Queen of Clubs demanded, flashing her a warning glare.

"*I* have some stuff to say about that psycho." Esmeralda volunteered in a not particularly helpful voice.

The Queen of Clubs attention snapped back to her. "I'm about to retain my crown and you're about to become an empty husk. What could you possibly have to say, that I'd want to hear?" She paused meaningfully. "Well, besides 'goodbye'?"

Outside, the red pawn exploded on the chessboard. The Queen of Clubs laughed, the sound slightly crazed. She must have used a surge of her own Good magic to destroy it, but Esmeralda wasn't sure why she bothered. The empress contest could only be settled by the queens. Anyone who understood Wonderland could see that.

"Anna?" The Mad Hatter drew his wife's attention. His chest barely moved, as he struggled to breathe. "You must take out her queen."

The Queen of Clubs still didn't get what was happening. Wonderland wasn't really her home. She just wanted to own it. To change it into something controlled and homogenous. But Wonderland wasn't like other places. It had a magic all its own. A sense of self that it would exert over any would-be rulers, if they threatened to erase its weirdness. Nothing could ever tame Wonderland. Not without a fight. Wild things fought for freedom.

"It will be the eight square any moment." The Queen of Clubs soothed the Mad Hatter, her eyes damp with emotion. "Once I'm empress, everything will be fine. Until then, the witch's magic will sustain you." She jabbed an oh-so-tastefully manicured finger at Esmeralda. "She's fifty percent Good."

"Forty-nine." Esmeralda corrected, amazingly calm. "And you know, I'm still not convinced you can quantify magic, with levels and percents. I think maybe it's bigger than all that bullshit."

No one else agreed.

Grimhilde sniffed with haughty distain. "What would you know about magic? Your powers are abysmal." She looked over at the Mad Hatter. "I doubt they'll be very appetizing."

"It doesn't matter what she tastes like!" The Queen of Clubs shouted. "Hatty," she lifted his head, trying to get him to focus, "you need to eat her magic. *Now*. It will keep you alive!"

His creepy, spiraling gaze opened just enough to fix on Esmeralda. For one horrible second, she sensed his attempt to suck the Goodness from her. It felt like he was ripping at her bones, trying to break through to the very marrow of her being. But he wasn't strong enough to hurt her.

None of them were. She *believed* it.

Her magic roared to the surface. For the first time in her life, she knew just what to do with her over-abundance of Good energy. She didn't know all the steps to get there, but she knew the result she wanted and she believed that her powers could achieve it. The rest would come naturally.

Esmeralda yanked back from the Mad Hatter's magical grasp and looked at the Queen. "You don't understand Wonderland, at all."

Unadulterated Good energy flowed through her, bright as a summer day. She threw a hand out, towards the Chess Tower, and shoved with all her might. Magic poured free, like gossamer morning dew and the happy darting of hummingbirds in a meadow. It was the purest, Goodest, most powerful spell she'd ever cast.

And it hit the chessboard like a wrecking ball.

The meticulous game was destroyed. All the carefully planned moves ruined. The remaining pieces toppled over in a hopeless jumble. ...Except one.

The red queen stood tall, as it slid forward into the eight square.

Outside, the Chess Tower started *bong-bong-bonging.* Unlike a clock striking, the chime was spaced all wonky and it wasn't counting down the time. It was signaling something much bigger.

One...

"Impossible!" The Queen of Clubs shrieked. "You can't win!" Her eyes went to her husband, like he might be able to do something. "Only a pawn can be promoted to a queen. No other piece gets rewarded for reaching the eight square. Only the pawn! A queen cannot become a *double* queen! And certainly not *doubly*-double."

The *bongs* kept slowly chiming. Two...

The Mad Hatter blinked. "I thought *all* the pieces who got to 'kings row' got crowned."

"That's checkers!"

"Well, you should have explained the rules better, before I built the damn tower." He sounded defensive, even through his pain. "I told you a hundred times, *I don't play chess!*"

Three...

Power surged. Not exactly Esmeralda's, but still hers. Green and strong and shared between True Loves. "Ez!" Trevelyan appeared in the throne room, slightly frantic, as he scanned for her.

"Hi, Trev." Esmeralda wasn't at all surprised to see him, even though his arrival was magically impossible. She could feel her own powers connecting with his, melding as if they were one. Grimhilde began to look worried. Anyone with a brain would be worried to see Trevelyan standing against them.

Four...

"You're cheating!" The Queen of Clubs jumped to her feet. "You're both cheating! This is against the rules!"

"She hates rules." Trevelyan headed over to position himself beside her, right where he belonged. There was sand on his clothes and he smelled like smoke, but the man had never looked better.

Esmeralda took hold of his hand, so they stood shoulder-to-shoulder.

"This isn't really my fight." Grimhilde told Esmeralda, edging towards the door. She knew her side wasn't winning. "I'll just leave you to your work, dear."

"Shut up, before I melt you." Esmeralda spared her a quick look. "I have a feeling Good magic can produce a real pretty waterfall, right on your fucking head."

Five...

"We're *witches!*" Grimhilde protested. "We have a bond of sisterhood and..."

Esmeralda waved a hand and sealed the woman's mouth shut with the stickiest, most indestructible, goddamn adorable-est taffy ever created by light magic. The President of the Cauldron Society clutched her jaw, desperately trying to pry it open.

Trevelyan's lips curved, watching her struggle. "Now, who's the best at being Bad?"

Six...

"Your magic is not the fairest! *Mine* is!" The Queen of Clubs launched an attack of her own.

The Good energy she unleashed was a textbook example of expert spellcraft. Once, Esmeralda would have been intimidated by the perfection of it. The Queen of Clubs knew exactly what she was doing and she had a lot of Good energy. Every molecule of her spell was planned. It should have struck her opponents like a rainbow missile, blowing them into glittering pieces.

Unfortunately for the Queen of Clubs, her opponents were protected by soap bubbles.

Esmeralda's powers manifested the translucent orbs with barely a thought. They whooshed around her and Trevelyan, a tornado of protective ferocity and shimmery magic. They deflected the Queen of Clubs attack without a single one popping. Playfully bobbing through the air, unstoppably strong and filled with iridescent layers of power.

Trevelyan watched them float past with a reverent expression. "Beautiful." He was a control-freak of the highest order, but he wasn't rushing to take charge. He believed she could win. He wanted her to believe it, too. The man really had learned to be a wonderful True Love.

Seven...

The Queen of Clubs screamed in fury.

The Mad Hatter coughed, back to arguing with his wife. "I told you, Anna. That damn tower was a pointless idea. Chess is a stupid way to keep time."

"It's supposed to be counting down to *my* coronation as empress. Not *hers*. I'm not going to let that little nobody take everything away from me! There's still more I can do! I *know* it." The Queen of Clubs grasped at her scalp, as if she wanted to forcibly hold onto the three tiaras sitting there.

Her fingers closed on nothing. The fortune in gemstones was no longer on her head.

Eight.

"My God." Trevelyan whispered, his attention on Esmeralda's hair.

Esmeralda reached up and felt the crown sitting there. All four tiaras interlocked. The spell that Trevelyan had sealed into her heart burned brightly, forever welding the magic to her body.

Badness rushed back into all of them, as the Chess Tower finally stopped *bonging*.

It was over. Wonderland had chosen a new empress. Someone who listened to its talking carpets, and created chaos with her weird magic, and appreciated the untamed.

Esmeralda was home.

She smirked at the Queen of Clubs and said *just* what the bitch had wanted her to. "Goodbye."

"No..." The Queen of Clubs breathed.

"Oh bother." The Mad Hatter's head slumped in defeat.

Grimhilde drew back a palm, ready to fire off a deadly spell. Not ready to give up without a fight. Wanting to strike down Esmeralda, now that her own magic was restored.

Except Trevelyan's powers had returned, too. His eyes slashed over to Grimhilde and the woman's hands disappeared.

Literally, they were *gone*. No blood. No scar. Her arms just ended at the wrist.

"I *loved* that story about your granny." Trevelyan taunted. "It really did inspire me."

Esmeralda had no idea what Grimhilde's grandma had to do with anything, but she had to admit Trevelyan's trick was effective. It was hard for a witch to cast anything without her hands and Grimhilde was too panicked to try. She cried out in shock, but her jaw was still glued shut. The sound came out as a painful, warbling, wheeze.

"I can be a monstrous villain even without my magic." Trevelyan assured Esmeralda, casually watching his newest victim suffer. "But using evil spells is just *so* much fun."

"Good magic has its moments, too." Esmeralda flashed him a grin and let her full powers explode out.

This time she didn't question or hesitate. Planning wasn't her style. It never would be. She let instinct guide her, instead. Good and Bad magic were woven together, like they were always meant to. The detonation of them looked like a graceful dance of swirling electricity, and soaring broomsticks, and dragon fire. The colossal torrent of energy engulfed the Club Kingdom, igniting the world in a cleansing green glow.

And as the spell cleared, she saw frogs.

The Queen of Clubs, and the Mad Hatter, and Grimhilde, and all the other unpleasant residents of the Club Kingdom had been transformed into harmless frogs. They hopped around, making *ribbiting* sounds, and it was the most beautiful sight Esmeralda had ever seen.

"You did it!" Trevelyan beamed in shared triumph and hugged her close. "I *knew* you could."

Esmeralda leaned against him, relieved and proud of herself. For the first time in her life, the magic had flowed like a natural extension of her body and mind. It had all felt... right. "When I mixed the Good and Bad together, the spell just seemed to work."

"Because *you* are Good and Bad together, my darling. The perfect balance of both." Trevelyan pressed a kiss to her temple. "And you look incredible in that crown."

"How incredible?" She tilted her head back to give him an arch look. "On a scale of one to shiny?"

"*Very* shiny." He brushed her lips with his own, visibly relishing the fact he could kiss her whenever he liked. "I can't wait to see you wearing it and nothing else."

Esmeralda smiled against his mouth. Forget the frogs. Trevelyan was the most beautiful sight she'd ever seen, now and forever.

"Give me back Marrok, *right now!*" Snow White suddenly screamed, ruining the moment. "I know you're the one who stole him from me, Trevelyan."

Trevelyan flinched at the shrill voice saying his name.

Esmeralda turned to glare at the other woman. She hadn't even noticed that Snow White wasn't frogified. It seemed like the Good and Bad powers had transformed everyone in the Club Kingdom *except* Snow White. Of course they had. Esmeralda wasn't the type of villain who needed to slaughter all her enemies. Transforming them into fly-eating, pond-dwellers would do just fine.

Unless they'd hurt her True Love.

"Are you about to freak out?" Esmeralda asked, concerned for Trevelyan.

"No. I might have, before I found you. I would have done something crazy." He squeezed her hand. "You told me not to break you, when we met, but *I* was the one broken. From her and Mrs. Clyburn, and all the shit in my past. You made me sort it all out. You put me back together."

"*You* put you back together." Esmeralda was proud of him. It showed real growth that he wasn't incinerating someone.

"I want Marrok!" Snow White stalked towards Trevelyan, fury twisting her expression. "Now, now, *now!*"

"I don't think she even remembers what she did to me." Trevelyan's whole body felt rigid, as he surveyed his abusive doctor. "Killing her for it would be... wrong, perhaps? I'm not sure. I'm only two percent Good, so kindness is always a challenge."

"Don't worry." Esmeralda patted his arm. "I know how to handle this."

"Do not get close to her." Even his tone was tense. "She's more dangerous than she looks."

"So am I."

"Give me my husband!" Snow White screamed. "If you don't give him back, I'll hurt you, dragon. I'll make you sorry. I'll…" Esmeralda lifted a hand and suddenly Snow White was inside of the club-shaped magic mirror. Imprisoned by the glass, she stood on the other side, flattened and helpless.

Trevelyan's brows soared.

"See?" Esmeralda smirked. "Handled… from a distance."

Snow White's astonished, empty eyes flew around the interior of the looking glass. "How did you do that? You're not allowed to do that!" Her palms came up to rest against the inside of the mirror, searching for a way to free herself.

Trevelyan made an impressed face. Probably, because Esmeralda had just invented the enchantment imprisoning Snow White. Magic was so much easier when she let loose and didn't worry about the rules. "What spell did you use, darling?"

"Whichever one rhymes with 'Don't fuck with the Green Dragons.'"

He gave a rumbling sound of pleasure. "I so enjoy your poetry."

"Let me go!" Snow White's volume was muffled, as she beat against the ornate looking glass. "I'll get you for this! I'll tell my mother!"

Esmeralda stepped closer to the mirror, her eyes locked on the woman. "With or without your memory, you're just a really lousy person." She flicked a fingernail against the glass. "Be glad Trev and I are so damn kindhearted… or I'd make this hurt a whole lot more."

The mirror fractured. One crack snapped into another, until it looked like splintering ice covered the entire surface. A heartbeat passed, as it all stayed frozen. Then, the mirror shattered into an avalanche of jagged shards. Snow White was reflected in all of them, screaming while the glass fell into nothing. As the pieces hit the floor, she vanished from them. Winked out of existence.

Gone.

Trevelyan stared at the destruction for a long moment. "Magic mirrors are expensive." He said at last. "We could have killed her in a far more economical way."

"This way was worth the cost."

"It *was* a lovely funeral." A moment ticked by and he swallowed hard. "Thank you, Ez."

"Snow White shouldn't have touched my mate." She walked over to him and stepped into his arms. They wrapped tightly around her. "Thanks for de-handing Grimhilde."

"She should have welcomed my wife into her silly club." He arched a brow. "Hey, do you think one of these toads is jumping around with no paws?"

"*Frogs*. And no. The spell is about continuation of energy, not an actual one-on-one transference." Although, two of the creatures seemed particularly keen on bouncing along together. The Mad Hatter and Queen of Clubs had been True Loves. Maybe those frogs were, too.

Or maybe they were just frogs.

Trevelyan made a face, scanning around the room. "These reptiles aren't nearly as adorable as the hogs."

"They're amphibians, not reptiles."

"Whatever they are, they'd look better with feathers."

"*No wings*. I mean it. They'll fly around and get slime in my hair." She shook one of the wart-y creatures off her boot, careful not to smoosh it. "Is Marrok okay? You didn't feed him to the brillig or anything, did you?"

"Of course not. We're getting along famously."

She looked around. "So, where is he?"

"I left him somewhere or other." The words were breezy with unconcern.

Esmeralda frowned. "We can't just abandon Marrok in some random place."

"It's not a random place. He's by a lake. I'm sure he'll be along soon. He's very self-sufficient." Trevelyan deftly switched topics. "You know, we'll need to rehome these frogs to a swamp. I'm not about to make pets out of these flightless bastards."

"We can take them to a *bog*. Don't worry. I accidently created one, back in the Heart Castle."

His mouth curved. "Is *that* why the bathroom is full of mosquitoes and crocodiles?"

"At least the tile isn't pink anymore."

He laughed in delight.

Esmeralda found herself grinning, as well. Standing in the kingdom they'd won, safe in her dragon's arms, she was finally right where she belonged. "Oh, shut up, Trev."

CHAPTER THIRTY-THREE

Pick your perfect nail polish from our unlimited selection!
Better-than-Before Berry: This glitter bomb makes everything in your
life sparklier than it used to be. Every time you look at it, you feel
stronger and safer and more loved. Trust us. You *need* it.

Happily Ever Witch Cosmetics Website

The Spade Castle

"Are you *sure* we can't do this later?" Esmeralda asked in a long-suffering tone. "I'm exhausted from wrangling frogs, I have to find a phone to call Scarlett, and we need to figure out where my brother is."

Night was falling, casting all of Wonderland in a purple haze. Relocating the frogs had taken more time than expected. The amphibians wouldn't have survived the cold weather overnight, especially since they seemed to love playing on the clown slide, out on the Club Palace balcony. Rounding them up had been the first priority. Now they were all safely living in the Heart Palace's bog and Wonderland's new royal couple could focus on more important things.

Trevelyan wanted to start off on the right nefarious foot, rounding up possible dissenters and renaming public buildings after himself, but his mate wasn't allowing it. She was very insistent that they not piss off Wonderland's remaining citizens, right from the beginning of her reign. She really was adorably Good, sometimes.

"I thought Marrok would be back by now." Esmeralda went on, with a suspicious glance in Trevelyan's direction. "You said you left him by a lake, safe and sound, right?"

"Yes. It's very scenic. There's a beach and everything."

She stared at him.

His smile was all truth and innocence.

Crimson eyes narrowed.

"The lake was in the Diamond Kingdom." He admitted casually. "Did I mention that part?"

"No, you did *not* mention that part. Marrok can't teleport. How is he supposed to get out of the frigging Diamond Kingdom?"

"Why would he want to leave? There's a beach! Everyone likes the beach. Marrok's happy as an oyster, I'm sure."

Having saved the wolf from Snow White's clutches, defeated his numerous enemies, and united the Wonderland crowns, Trevelyan was in a jubilant mood. But, he had one more vital task to check off his to-do list. Marrok would have to wait.

Esmeralda kept complaining about her beloved brother being stranded in the Diamond Kingdom, as if it was their most pressing concern. "I swear, if Marrok dies of thirst, crawling through a desert..."

"I'm telling you, he's *thriving*. All he has to do is hike over some sand dunes." Trevelyan waved the matter aside. "But, I'll go and look for him, if you're worried. God knows the man *is* helpless, these days. I just need you to see this, first."

"You'll find Marrok, if I humor you and admire whatever it is you want to show me? That's the deal?"

"Yes. I promise."

"Fine." Esmeralda agreed and refocused on the huge building in front of them. "What am I looking at?"

"A record store." Trevelyan announced with real pride. "I promised to get you one today and here it is! I'm the best husband in the world." (Green Dragons always were. It was simply undeniable.)

The record store idea had occurred to him, while he walked around the empty Club Castle and wondered what they were going to do with the place. The former queen had had abysmal taste and no way in the frozen-hells was Trevelyan living in such a cold climate. That thought had led inexorably to the realization that he and Esmeralda now owned four palaces. They might as well put them to some use.

He wasn't sure what to do with the Diamonds' sandcastle or the Clubs' ice palace, but the Spade Kingdom showed real promise. He'd only been there five minutes and he already saw the possibilities.

Esmeralda didn't.

"It doesn't *look* like a record store. It looks like a cottage-y castle, with a leaky thatched roof. Trust me, I know all about leaking roofs."

"It's nothing some magic can't fix."

She made a skeptical sound. "That's what every contractor says." She glanced around the deserted landscape. Each direction featured postcard perfect views of colorful trees and sweeping mountain scenery. "So, is everyone in this kingdom hiding from us or have you already killed them all?"

"Hiding. They've no doubt heard about my little showdown in the Diamond Kingdom, by now. And they surely know that you turned all the citizens of the Heart Kingdom into hogs and the Club Kingdom into frogs." Trevelyan lifted a shoulder. "As the last kingdom standing, it may take some time for the Spade citizens to recover from their survivors' guilt."

"I'm sure you'll work hard to win their hearts and minds."

"I'm the fairest emperor in the land."

"And if any of our subjects disagree, you can always banish them to your stolen moon."

He splayed a hand over his heart, in mock affront. "I'm not going to steal the moon, again. That was just a phase."

"Are you making puns, now? I feel like that was a pun."

"Don't be ridiculous. Puns are punishable by death. That's a day-one royal decree."

"You really are the worst person ever, Trev."

"I try." He slung an arm around her shoulders, using his free hand to gesture towards the Spade Palace. "Focus on our newest business opportunity. Picture how amazing your record store will look, housed in this place."

Esmeralda's eyes traced over the stone façade. "You want to remodel a hundred-room castle into a music shop?"

"Why not? It's not like we're going to *live* here. The lawn will be forever in need of raking." He cast a disparaging look towards the autumnal trees and the ever-falling leaves. "We'd need a whole team of gardeners."

"No gardeners." Esmeralda gave an elaborate shudder.

Trevelyan didn't argue. "On the plus side, I think the overly-colorful environment will encourage wealthy visitors to spend their afternoons browsing in our quaint record store."

"You would slaughter any tourists, just on principle."

"With excellent reason. Everyone is a moron, except you and me. Never more so than when they're on vacation."

"That should be the motto on our 'Welcome to Wonderland' sign."

"I hate people, but I love their money. Which is why this plan is so perfect. It keeps all the interlopers in the Diamond Kingdom. It provides the citizens here jobs to keep them busy. And it gives us all their lovely gold."

"Because the second-richest-man-in-Neverland needs more gold."

"No one becomes the second-richest *anything* without needing more gold, darling."

Esmeralda's forehead creased as she considered the scale of the remodeling project. "How do you intend to accomplish this grand commercial transformation?"

"Oh, I don't. I intend for *you* to do it."

She glanced his way.

He arched a brow. "But, you can use my powers to help with the project, if you like. It's going to take quite a big spell to fill a space that large with enough records. You might have to magically invent some new musical style, just so you can sell recordings at a ridiculous markup."

"You're the guitar player in the family. That'll be your job."

That made him laugh.

Esmeralda grinned back at him, leaning into his side. Two seconds later, he felt her magic swell. His own powers moved to support it, providing energy and guidance when she hesitated over some part of the spell. But she didn't need much help. Her confidence grew, as she reshaped the castle to her liking.

It felt so strange to have his magic engaged in Goodness. Nothing about Esmeralda's remodeling was evil. It hurt nobody. It was just beautiful and creative and he *liked* it. He'd never ever tell anyone else that, of course. Trevelyan had a reprehensible reputation to protect. But he enjoyed the light, joyful play of energy against his own. And he really liked the delicious hint of darkness around the edges.

He kissed the side of Esmeralda's head, basking in her wicked virtue.

"What do you think?" She asked, after a long moment.

Trevelyan dragged his attention off of his mate and took in the changes to the castle. Before, it had resembled an oversized chalet, with a steeply-pitched roof and half-timber walls. Nauseatingly charming. Completely unsuitable for any professional villain.

Now, the formerly pleasant exterior was far more... witchy. Multicolored cobwebs, bat-shaped windows, and an ominous bell tower dominated the exterior. Along with a huge neon sign that read, "Green Dragon Records." The glowing tubes curved into the shape of a mighty dragon, its jaw opening and closing with the blinking of bright green lights.

Trevelyan's mouth curved. "I approve of the teeth."

"I got the idea from the clown slide." Esmeralda surveyed her work in obvious satisfaction. "Let's just hope your nefarious infamy doesn't scare off all the customers." She headed for the palace, wanting to get a closer look at her efforts.

"It's your name up in lights, too." He called after her. "And you're far more likely to terrify people than me, now. Under our hopefully despotic rule, I'm just the lowly emperor. It's my empress who wears the crown."

Esmeralda gestured to the glitzy, interlocked tiaras on her head. "Four of them." She could remove the unified crown at will, now that it was hers. But now that it was hers, she didn't seem to be in a hurry to take it off.

"Four *so far*." Trevelyan stipulated. "There might be more lands in need of our leadership."

"Don't even think about it, you deranged maniac." She sent

him a saucy look over her shoulder and Trevelyan's heart stopped.

Her eyes had a spark.

Not just *a* spark. The brightest spark he'd ever seen. Life and purity and ideas, beamed out at him. *For* him. No spark had ever been intended for him, before. His magic had been able to see it in others, but he'd always known it was meant for someone else. Esmeralda's special shine was directed solely at Trevelyan.

It was his.

Just his.

And then Trevelyan suddenly understood what he'd been seeing in the other people with that glow. Understood why their mates were so passionately protective of them. Understood why he'd never been able to tempt the women away for meaningless sex to assuage his curiosity. Understood what that spark meant to anyone lucky enough to receive it.

It was love.

He was seeing the person's unguarded, absolute love for their mate. The life they shared, and the purity of their bond, and their ideas about their future. He'd been peering straight into their souls and he'd seen nothing but True Love shining back. And he'd had no fucking clue what it was.

How could he? Before Esmeralda came into his life, the very concept of love was foreign to him. How in the hell was Trevelyan supposed to know what it looked like, until his Good little Bad witch was there to teach him?

Trevelyan let out a shaky breath.

Esmeralda loved him. The evilest evil-doer in the land had just claimed the biggest prize of all. He'd known he'd come out on top! Was there even a doubt? No one could stop him. His treasure was held safe in his claws and he'd never let her go. Esmeralda didn't *want* to go. She'd chosen him. She'd decided. She loved him. He believed it.

That was the sixth impossible thing he believed and it was *everything*.

"You okay?' Esmeralda asked, seeing his stupefaction.

"How mad would you be if I seduced a girl with a spark?" He

whispered. "Just one. Only one."

Her eyebrows slammed down. "You would rue the fucking day. ...But not as much as that glittery bitch would."

He nearly purred at the witchy threat in her voice. "What if I told you, she had the most beautiful crimson eyes I've ever encountered and the spark makes them positively glow?"

"I don't give a shit if she's covered in chocolate sprinkles and orgasms, you're not going to *touch* her." Esmeralda marched back towards him. "I have never been so serious about..." She stopped short, abruptly processing his description. Big crimson eyes blinked. "Wait." She pointed a black fingernail at her chest. "Me?"

Trevelyan gave her a slow smile. "You."

"You never told me you saw a spark before." She shook her head. "You would've said something."

"It wasn't there before. I don't think you loved me, yet. Or perhaps you were too guarded to let it show."

Esmeralda stared for a beat. "That's what you've been searching for? Love?"

He nodded, his gaze intent. "And now I've found it in you." His words were certain, but his heart was pounding.

"Oh." She glanced away and thought about that. "Alright. Cool. Well, I'll be touring my new record store." She started for the castle.

Trevelyan shook his head. "Oh no." He glided in front of her, cutting off her retreat. "You have something to tell me, first."

She gave her hair an agitated toss. "Why should I tell you anything? You know it all already, right?"

"I want to hear it." His voice was fierce. "I *need* to hear it. It's mine."

"Fuck that. It's *mine*."

"You gave it to me." He gestured to her eyes. "I already see it!"

"If you already see it, then what's the issue if I don't say anything?"

"I need you to say the words."

"I'm not going to just..."

"Say you love me." He interrupted quietly and it was close to begging. "Tell me something true, Ez."

She gazed up at him, breathing too fast.

"Please?"

She closed her eyes and when she opened them again, the spark was bright enough to light up Trevelyan's whole world. "I love you, Trev. You believe me?"

"Yes!" He lifted her right off the ground, squeezing her too tight. He knew that, but he couldn't seem to loosen his hold. "*Finally!* Fucking hell, it took you long enough." He gave her a smacking kiss. "Now you've done it, though. It's you and me, forever after. You'll have to kill me, if you ever want me gone."

"You have the weirdest ideas about romance." She complained, but she was laughing as she said it. "You're lucky you fell for the Empress of Wonderland. Any normal girl would be getting a restraining order against your abnormal ass."

"I can be normal, if you want." He nipped at her jaw, with a playful growl. "I mastered kindness, didn't I? I'm a dragon. I can do anything. I even won myself a witch."

Her arms twined around his neck. "Can your very normal superpowers get us home, then? I'm worried that I'll end up marooning us on another planet, if I try. And I'd really like to be somewhere private, when I rip your pants off."

She hadn't even finished talking before Trevelyan was transporting them to the royal bedroom of the Heart Castle. He didn't consider the destination first. He just instinctively reached for it, when she said "home."

Interesting.

Esmeralda didn't seem worried about a dragon carrying her off to parts unknown. She also didn't seem surprised by their location, so she must've had the Heart Kingdom in mind, as well. "Your magic is so beautiful."

"It's exactly like yours." He assured her, although he appreciated that she trusted his powers. "I can feel your magic and it's strong. You can rely on it. It's capable of much more than you think." With time, she would believe that as deeply as he did.

Esmeralda dropped onto the bed, waving a quick hand. The clothing vanished off both of them, in a swirl of green sparkles. "How's that?"

"You're naked, so it's better."

That made her laugh. Reaching up, she dragged him down to join her on the bed.

Trevelyan didn't resist one little bit.

Esmeralda ran her fingers along his back, as he covered her body with his own. "Are we actually gonna have sex in a bed?" She feigned surprise. "This is a first for us."

He slid forward and her legs parted to make space for him. "Told you I could be normal."

Still, that didn't mean they couldn't *also* have fun.

Trevelyan's lips found hers, even as his magic licked up the inside of her thigh. His tongue couldn't be in two places at once, but he could make it *feel* like it was.

"Oh my *God*..." She breathed. "I didn't know you could do that." Her feet slipped around the back of his legs, clinging to him. "You should have told me, because you would've been doing it for days."

"Dragons can do anything we want. I believe I *did* tell you that." His powers found a spot she really, really liked. "And what I want most is you." Trevelyan smoothed a palm over her hair. "I love you, Esmeralda."

She gazed up at him, enraptured.

"Obsessively. Passionately. *Viciously*." He went on. "It's terrifying how much I love you."

"I don't terrify easy." Her hips arched upward, seeking more. "Love me all you want. I can take it." Her incredible skin glowed with happiness and magic. "After all, you're part owner of a record store, and you let me paint your nails, and I like your smile. You're perfect for me!"

"I *am* perfect for you." Trevelyan positioned his erection at her weeping entrance. "I'm even tragically normal." He pressed into her tight channel, while his powers did very Bad things to every part of her they could reach. "See?"

Her nails dug into his hips, dragging him even closer. "Don't ever stop being *exactly* this normal."

He dipped his head to nuzzle her magnificent breasts. "You are the freedom I fought for my whole life."

This time was different, between them. They both felt it. There was magic and teasing, but it was also... gentler. Somehow that made the experience even more intense.

He made a contented sound against her nipple. "How many times a day is it 'normal' for you to tell me you love me?"

"I don't know." Her eyes were glazed with desire. "Once?"

He scoffed at that completely unreasonable estimate. "I'm thinking twice an hour. I'm a dragon! We need constant attention or we set shit on fire."

Esmeralda's hands glided through his hair. "Sounds like the perfect kind of normal for a wicked witch." She drew him down to suck on his lower lip. "I love you so much."

Trevelyan forgot what they were even talking about. It was impossible to concentrate on anything except her. He thrust deep, and her ankles came up to lock around his waist, and he felt every single part of them connect.

Esmeralda's palm cupped the side of his face. "I see sparks in your eyes, too." She whispered.

"Obviously." He breathed, basking in her scent. "It's impossible to hide my feelings for you. They burn through every single part of me."

She smiled at him and he was lost.

He'd had sex countless times. (And he'd fucked even more.) With Esmeralda, it was beyond that, though. He was making love to her. *With* her. In the past, he would have scoffed at the softer verbage. Would have insisted that there was no real difference, except for a polite sheen on the words. But he would have been dead wrong.

Esmeralda undulated against him, her mouth parted in passion. As they moved together, her crimson gazed stayed locked onto his and he'd never felt so close to anyone. It wasn't just the physical act that was better than ever before. It was the emotion and the sense of belonging he had with Esmeralda. With her, he gave everything and she gave him back even more. When she came, it triggered his own release. Esmeralda arched upward with a blissful cry, holding him tight. That was all it took. Trevelyan shouted her name, as he spent himself deep inside of her. Perfect. All of it was perfect, because he was with his witch.

He collapsed forward, totally replete. Because he wasn't ready to let her go, he rolled onto his side, taking Esmeralda with him. She wound up sprawled across his chest. Neither of them seemed to mind.

It took Trevelyan awhile to catch his breath. "I *knew* doing this with a sparkly-eyed girl would be extraordinary. I'm always right."

"And so modest." She laid a palm over his heart. "Mate."

"Mate." He put his hand over hers, so their fingers slid together.

The intimacy of the moment struck him. Esmeralda was the only person he'd ever been truly intimate with and he found he liked it. Craved it. His blood began to heat again, stimulated by her and their connection. They really were True Loves. He finally realized what that meant. His love for her was the deepest, purest, truest part of him.

She snuggled closer, not missing his renewed arousal. "We can't go another round, right now. We can lay here for ten minutes and then we have to go rescue Marrok."

"*Again?*" He groaned. "Rescuing your brother is becoming our fulltime job."

"We haven't even finished rescuing him from the first time, yet. You left him stranded someplace."

"We'll go looking for him in an hour." He offered, always willing to compromise with his mate.

"Twenty minutes. And I'm telling him it's all your fault, when he's pissed at us."

"I can live with that."

Outside, it started raining.

Trevelyan frowned towards the window. He really did need to create a spell to control the weather. Even with her body magically waterproofed, Esmeralda was bound to be uneasy around storms. Nothing should ever make his mate feel uneasy.

"It's okay." She said, like she read his thoughts. "I'm not worried about rain, anymore." She pressed a kiss to one of his tattoos. "I feel safe with you here."

He closed his eyes against her hair, his arms cradling her against him. "With me, you are *always* safe, my darling. I love you more than magic itself."

She jerked back, an amazed expression on her face. "That is exactly what you used to say in my head! At the orphanage. I heard you, again and again, my whole life."

"You knew I loved you, from the beginning?" He gave a snort. "Well, that explains a lot. Like why you were never afraid of me."

"I didn't know you loved me then, because you didn't. But I thought you could be taught." She wrinkled her nose in an adorable way. "Which you were."

"Well, for a girl who paid no attention in school, you're wonderful at giving lessons."

Esmeralda snickered at that remark. "Besides, how could I ever be scared of someone who comforted me a thousand times growing up? Whenever I was frightened, I'd instinctively reach for you," she stroked his hair, "and you reached back."

He leaned into her touch, considering her words. "Our magic can meld. If you were ever in distress and some part of me felt it..."

"You'd reach for me." She finished firmly. "Which is exactly what you did. You wanted to help me."

Trevelyan tried to make her understand. "My magic is part of my DNA. It's keyed to my survival and my life is entirely tied to yours." He met her eyes. "I'm not sure the world would survive, if I ever lost you. I know for certain I wouldn't. It's possible my magic preemptively connected with you, knowing all that was inevitable. Knowing I'd fuck it up when we finally met. Wanting to prevent that from happening, by getting you used to me."

"Or maybe you just wanted to help me. Because you're sort of kindhearted, under the evilness."

"Sort of?" He repeated in mock annoyance. "I'm *exceptionally* kindhearted."

"We promised to be truthful with each other, remember?"

"I'm exceptionally kindhearted... with you." He stipulated. "I'm ninety-eight percent Bad. You're the only person *in* my heart."

Esmeralda smiled, her eyes sparking. "Well, that's Good

enough for me." She kissed him.

Trevelyan sighed reverently, his mouth opening over hers. Each time their lips met, it was new and special, but this kiss was the best one yet. It was soft and sweet and full of love.

Just like his witch.

EPILOGUE

Pick your perfect nail polish from our unlimited selection!
True Love's Rainbow: Exactly what you didn't expect and guaranteed
to be the color you've always dreamed of, this polish is our best
seller. Shipping on this one is unpredictable. It might take a while to
arrive. But we promise it is *so* worth the wait.

Happily Ever Witch Cosmetics Website

Two Weeks Later
The Heart Castle

The Heart Kingdom had grown on Trevelyan.
The plaid and polka-dot landscape no longer bugged the hell out of him. The endless heart-patterned rooms of the castle no longer gave him a headache. He played daily games of chess with the Cheshire Carpet, who now lived downstairs to fully participate in castle life and sported pink manicured tassels courtesy of Esmeralda. He tolerated the giant flowers in the conservatory endlessly gossiping about his sex life. (They were jealous.). He'd even repaired the killer robots in the library, just to have the fun of destroying them again.
This was Trevelyan's home.
It helped, of course, that he and Esmeralda had flattened, scorched, and transmogrified so much of the interior. The devastation fit their villainous aesthetic perfectly. The two of them ruled all of Wonderland, but they'd made the Heart Palace their very own evil lair. It seemed pleased to have them, adding new rooms just as fast as the old ones got burnt.
Trevelyan crouched on the balcony of the royal bedchamber and fixed a dragon-green bowtie around the flying pig's neck. Esmeralda had made it for the little guy and he looked quite dapper. Their pet was scheduled to be the ring bearer at their wedding that afternoon, so he needed to be presentable.

"Trev?" Esmeralda came bursting into the room. "Hide me."
"What?" He stood up, confused as to what was happening.
"Your sister wants me to wear *white* and Scarlett is agreeing with her." Esmeralda hurried to duck behind the edge of the fireplace. "Wicked witches do not wear white!"
"Alright. Calm down." Trevelyan held up his palms, prepared to smooth over the dispute. Dragons were natural mediators. "I'll talk to Marion. I can reason with her." He headed for the door, throwing it open. "Ez is not wearing motherfucking white!" He bellowed down the hall.
"Oh, now you're a goddamn fashion expert?" Marion shouted back. "The man who never takes off his trench coat, even in summer?"
"I don't like being cold. Is that such a crime?"
"No, but every *other* thing you do is a crime. Does your bride know you're a wanted fugitive in nineteen kingdoms? That's going to narrow the honeymoon options."
Trevelyan rose above that provocation. Reuniting with Marion was a blessing, regardless of her attitude. When she'd come stalking into the Heart Palace and laid eyes on him for the first time since his coma, her heartfelt greeting had been: "What the fuck is wrong with you?"
Marion had been born into the aristocracy. Her accent and features bespoke the highest breeding. The rest of her would always be a felon.
Trevelyan had started for her, happiness filling him.
"Do you have any idea how hard it was to find your worthless ass?" Marion had continued angrily. "I have been searching every known land! You couldn't maybe put a magical tracker on yourself? Is that so hard to do, Mr. Level Five Powers? Then, I'd be able to…"
The rest of her lecture had been cut short by Trevelyan hugging her.
He had never hugged Marion before. At least not that he could remember. The novelty of it had knocked her off-track. Instead of ranting at him, she'd frozen for a beat. Then, her arms had slipped around his waist and she'd held him tight. He'd heard her sniff into his chest, like she was suddenly holding back

tears.

"Shit, Trev. *Now* look what you did."

Trevelyan had smiled into her dark hair. "I love you, too." He'd told her in the dialect of Green Dragons. As far as he knew, the two of them were the only ones who spoke it. "In every single timeline there is, you are my sister. My family."

Marion had broken down sobbing. "You're my family, too. And I'd thought I'd lost you!" She'd given his shoulder an irritated whack. "I thought you were gone for good, this time."

"You should know better. I'm too evil to die, for long. I always find my way back."

"Yeah, well, one of these days, your evil luck is going to run out. Then what?"

"Then, you'll have to save me, Marion dear. Why else do I keep you around?"

"I keep *you* around, because I'm a glutton for punishment."

"And because a dragon livens up any home." He'd craned his neck, so he could look at her face. "Speaking of which, you haven't gone into my room, have you?"

"Of course I did. But, I didn't touch your precious brilligs, if that's what you're worried about. Except to throw them fresh rotting meat to eat. They've taken over the whole space."

"We'll just leave it to them, then. Keeping brilligs happy is always a wise idea. And I'm going to need to expand my room, anyway, so my mate and I can have a vacation place. Anything lavish will do."

Marion had glanced up at him, brown eyes wet with tears and amusement. "I'll build you a guest cottage. ...And we're putting a tracker on you. Deal with it."

Trevelyan figured he could deal with it.

After that, he and Marion slipped back into their usual routine of screaming at each other. Both of them were content with that arrangement. But that didn't mean she got to bully Esmeralda into a white gown.

"I've planned eight weddings." Marion reminded him. "How many have you planned, dickhead?"

"Every one of your weddings has ended in disaster. Nicholas is out of his obsessed mind for continuing to show up at them.

One day, he'll be saying 'I do' dead."

"Most of those disasters were *your* fault! The scorpions..."

"Those were *not* my fault! You always blame me for the scorpions."

"You wrapped them up in a box and handed them to my husband!"

"You have no sense of humor. That's *your* issue, not mine."

Marion was getting exasperated. "Forget it! Esmeralda has enough problems with you for a groom. I won't add to them. If she won't do white, how about blush?"

"What the hell color is that?"

"*Pink*, you oblivious moron."

"No! Find something green."

"I want to wear red." Esmeralda complained. "I've decided it's my signature shade, as empress."

He sighed and relented, because he really was the soul of compromise in his marriage. "Find something *red*." He told his sister.

Marion made an aggravated sound. "I liked you better in the coma, Trev."

"You're supposed to be Best Man. Figure this out!" He slammed the door shut and glanced back at Esmeralda. "Okay, I reasoned with her." He said calmly.

"You know, for two people who aren't genetically related, you and Marion are very much alike." Esmeralda pointed out, like she was trying not to laugh.

"Don't be ridiculous. She's violent, unreasonable, and always thinks she's right." He crossed over to kiss his mate's forehead. "...But, I'm taller."

Esmeralda gave up and laughed. Trevelyan felt like he'd won a prize, the same way he always did when he made her smile. He had cast every protective, loving spell he could think of on her, using her Good magic to power them. Esmeralda thought it was vastly amusing to watch him muddle through such light enchantments, but he didn't mind her teasing. Trevelyan wanted her safe and happy and connected to him. If he could get away with it, he'd have his arms wrapped around her twenty-four hours a day.

"If we get through this ceremony without bodies on the floor, it will be a miracle." She told him, still chuckling. "You know that, right?"

Trevelyan shrugged. A wedding with all their assorted friends and relations was bound to be a little unruly. It was only to be expected. "As long as it's just the wolf who's slain, I'll be fine with a little bloodshed."

Esmeralda made a face. "You said you'd get along with Marrok."

"I said I'd *try*." And he was. Sort of.

Since Trevelyan heroically rescued the wolf from Snow White, plucked him from the sands of the Diamond Kingdom, and reunited him with his True Love, Marrok was forced to be less hostile towards him. He seemed to grudgingly accept that he was stuck with Trevelyan, so he was trying to make the best of it.

Marrok still watched him with wary eyes, waiting for some nefarious plot to spring, though. The blatant mistrust inspired Trevelyan to be... friendly. *Sickeningly* friendly. The more nauseatingly, over-the-top friendly he was the more suspicious Marrok became. It had gotten to the point where the wolf sniffed his food at dinner, like he was convinced Trevelyan might secretly poison him. Trevelyan had responded to his paranoia with a pleasant smile and an offer of seconds.

Marrok now ate nothing but prepackaged Gala-chips, whenever Trevelyan was around.

Who would have guessed friendship could be so much fun?

Meanwhile, Trevelyan *was* making actual inroads with his new sister-in-law. Scarlett had cornered him the morning after she'd been reunited with her husband. Arms crossed over her chest, blue eyes watchful, she'd stood directly in front of him. Waiting.

The two of them had been alone in the kitchen, which had somehow made the whole conversation easier. Trevelyan liked the kitchen. It was the room he felt most comfortable, because it was the room he most associated with Esmeralda. She spent a lot of time there, baking minions and making nail polish. It was where he'd realized she was his mate. The room gave him support and he'd needed it.

He'd dug deep for a way to apologize to Scarlett and wound up going for something totally out of character: Telling the unvarnished truth. "You should never have been brought into my feud with Marrok. I targeted you, because I knew you were what he valued most. I knew he could never live without you."

One red brow had arched, still waiting.

Trevelyan had cleared his throat. "Having my own True Love makes me see how very screwed up my plan was. Because I could not live without Ez. Having her makes everything I did seem very, very… wrong."

Scarlett had kept waiting.

"It *was* wrong." Trevelyan had told her simply. "I'm sorry."

He'd meant it, too. And not just because Scarlett was Esmeralda's chosen sister, but because Scarlett was clever. Aside from him, she was the only one who'd ever come up with a plan to escape the WUB Club. Trevelyan admired cleverness. He was fairly sure he would like Scarlett and there were very few people Trevelyan liked.

Her lips had pursed. "You're sorry, huh?"

"Yes."

"*How* sorry?"

"Give me a chance to make it up to you and I will."

Blue eyes had narrowed in thought. "Well… you did save my husband and sister."

"Is that enough to earn me some goodwill, maybe?"

"No."

He hadn't thought so. "Would it help at all if I let you hit me a few times? Because I'd be okay with that."

"Hitting you wouldn't be very satisfying, if you're 'okay' with it. It defeats the whole point."

"Perhaps you could sneak up on me and attack me when I'm least suspecting it. Catch me off guard."

She'd snorted. "Ez would be upset if I bludgeoned you in your sleep."

"Would she?" He'd seesawed his hand. "It would depend on the day."

Scarlett hadn't cracked a smile. She'd had him over a barrel and she was going to demand everything she could get. Gaining her forgiveness would cost him a fortune.

It was worth it.

"What would you like?" He'd asked surrendering to the inevitable.

Scarlett had been waiting for that question. "The Enchanted Forest has to expand. We have a lot of Baddies in need of homes and we're running out of space. We need someplace where they're treated equally, and welcomed, and have a real chance at having successful lives." She'd pointedly looked out the window at the pastel landscape. "I'm thinking Wonderland will do nicely."

He hadn't been thrilled with that idea. Paying her heaps of gold would have been far preferable. "You seriously want me to open the boarders and let miscellaneous villains take up residence?"

"Yep."

"Can't I just buy you some other kingdom instead?"

"Nope."

Trevelyan had searched for another way out. "Did you talk to Ez about this plan? She's technically the empress. She may not like the idea."

"Oh, she said she's fine with it, because half your citizens are hogs and frogs, so you need a new tax base. But she insisted that you were co-ruler and you'd have to agree. I told her I was *sure* I could persuade you. I'm pretty talented at convincing people to do stuff they'd rather not do." Scarlett had paused. "Particularly, when they owe me."

The battle had clearly been lost. Still, dragons liked to make deals, so Trevelyan had at least tried for better terms. "Alright. We'll take *some* of them. They can live in the Diamond Kingdom. But, only if you forgive me."

"*Try* to forgive you."

Trevelyan had decided to take what he could get. "Try to forgive me." He'd nodded. "And if you work towards seeing what a wonderful brother-in-law I can be. Because I can be a *wonderful* brother-in-law. Loyal, charming, great at moving furniture... Ask anyone."

"Isn't Nicholas Greystone your brother-in-law? And didn't he punch you in the face, earlier?"

"Everything Nicholas says about me is a lie." Trevelyan had assured her, without missing a beat. Setting the gargoyle's clothes on fire had been a harmless prank, but Nicholas took everything so personally. "He's always been the black sheep of the family."

"He's a sheriff."

"I know. It's very sad." Trevelyan had kept talking. "The point is, you have to give me another chance. For real. And in exchange I will allow your precious Baddies into Wonderland. That's a fair trade."

Tension eased from Scarlett's shoulders. It wasn't just his acquiescence that made her start forgiving him. It was the fact that Trevelyan *wanted* her forgiveness. They both knew he disliked the idea of any other villains around. He was only doing this so she'd stop hating him.

"Deal?" He'd extended his palm.

"Deal." She'd shaken his hand.

Trevelyan had smiled, pleased with how well that had gone. It inspired him to begin renegotiating. "Wonderland is not going to become some criminal haven, where Bad folk do whatever they want, though. Everybody you send here has to follow my laws. Perhaps you could prescreen the applicants to weed out the troublemakers."

"They're villains. They're *all* troublemakers." Scarlett hadn't been eager to help with his immigration concerns. "Keeping your new citizens in line is *your* problem, not mine." She'd headed for the door with a spring in her step. "Just don't turn them all into pigs."

"Hogs." Trevelyan had called after her. "And that part wasn't promised in our deal."

Scarlett had made a "humph" sound and kept walking. "I'll negotiate it into the next one, then."

Trevelyan still felt smug, whenever he thought of that exchange. In time, he was sure he could win the woman over. She already hated him way less than most people he met. That was a great start.

Besides, he could put his new citizens to work rounding up customers for Esmeralda's record shop. The tourists might need some *encouragement* to spend. Bad folk were excellent at parting people from their gold.

In the meantime, Trevelyan had a wedding to get through.

"I'm going to wear a black pointy hat to get married." Esmeralda announced, back to her fashion choices. "It's very appropriate for a formal occasion. And I'm going to add a sparkly red veil, just because I want to. Let's see which one of our families complaints about it first. I'm thinking Avenant will have something to say. He usually does, the snob." She made a face. "You can slay *him*, by the way. I won't mind."

Trevelyan wasn't falling for that trick. Murdering any of her honorary-siblings would get him kicked out of bed for weeks. Marrok and Avenant's unkillable status didn't thrill him, but he'd endure it.

Why couldn't all her brothers be like Benji the bridge ogre? The large, blue fur-ball was contributing lovely flower arrangements and had thanked Trevelyan for "bringing Esmeralda back to us." Presently, Benji was the most likable relative on either branch of their family tree and he was a *fucking bridge ogre*.

The wedding party was in truly dire straits.

"If you want to be sure everyone survives the day, we could just forget this extraneous ceremony." Trevelyan cajoled his bride. "I've explained that dragons simply declare themselves mates and that's the end of it. So, you're *already* my wife. What do you say we just lock the door and begin our wedding night?"

"For the last time, *no*. Your name will be next to mine on an official marriage scroll, so you can never, ever escape."

He scoffed at the ridiculous idea. "I'm not going to escape."

"You're sure not. Because you will be married to me *forever*." She smirked. "Also, I have enough magic to track your ass down, no matter how far you flee." She gave him a quick kiss. "Now, I'm going to go do my nails, before your sister realizes you saw me on our wedding day and we have to do this all over again tomorrow."

Trevelyan made an irritated noise. "Remind me again why I'm agreeing to this craziness?"

"It must be your two percent Goodness at work." Her crimson gaze glowed up at him, filled with life, and purity and ideas. Filled with love.

Trevelyan pressed his lips to her temple. "All of me belongs to you, my darling." He closed his eyes breathing in his mate's perfect fragrance. ...And that's when he noticed something new.

The scent of another dragon.

Trevelyan's eyes snapped open again, his mind racing. Inside of him, his own dragon went still. "Esmeralda?"

"Hmmm?"

"Do you remember when we were playing that high school thing? And I may have mentioned that it was my intention to knock-up the prom queen? And you may have agreed with the idea?"

"Uh-huh." She cuddled closer to him, happy to be held in his unyielding arms.

"How seriously would your powers have taken that game?"

He felt his words register with her. A jolt of surprise when through Esmeralda's body, as her energy scanned and sensed what he had. "Oh shit." She pulled back, looking shocked. "How the hell did *that* happen?"

The question made him laugh. "I could describe the exact sequence of events, if you'd like. We were in the bedroom with the missing ceiling. I was naked and tied to the..."

"No! I mean that *shouldn't* happen. Not without me *letting* it happen." She shook her head. "A witch's magic regulates birth control automatically."

"Your magic likes me, Mate." He pressed his lips against hers in quick celebration. "It lets me do all kinds of impossible things."

Wide eyes met his, sparking and a little scared. "I think I might really be pregnant." She breathed in astonishment.

"Oh, I *know* you really are." Trevelyan realized he was grinning like an idiot.

Esmeralda's eyebrows drew together, as she considered the situation.

He waited for her to catch up, loving the new scent mixing with hers. It was so subtle that he'd barely noticed it, at first. But now that he'd caught hold of it, it would stay with him forever. A mix of Trevelyan's confidence, and the witch's sweetness, and a dash of something totally unique. He smiled, holding Esmeralda close.

His mate and his child.

"Just mine." The vow didn't come from Trevelyan or the dragon. It came from both of them together. From all of him. Every single piece.

Esmeralda still seemed overwhelmed. "I never seriously thought about becoming a mother. I guess because I didn't have one. What if I suck at the job?"

"You'll be wonderful at it." He promised. Inside of him, the dragon was purring with contentment. "No one is more loyal or loving or a stronger fighter." He rubbed his chin against her hair, fully prepared to level the universe for his new family. "I love you so much it's slightly psychotic."

Esmeralda gave a jerky nod. "I know. I feel the same way about you." She leaned into his hold, trusting him. "It's taking me a second here. But I think... I'm okay with being pregnant. Do you think you're okay with it?"

"I *know* I'm okay with it." Trevelyan had never been so pleased with himself. He'd already accomplished so much, but this was truly his best work. He'd somehow convinced the witch to create life with him. It was impressive, even by his own high standards of excellence.

Esmeralda met his eyes. "Do you feel its magic, though?" She whispered.

"Yes."

The small potential being inside of her was at least a level five. Obviously! Look at its parents. The magic in dragons' DNA developed quickly. It was the foundation of their biology. Already, Trevelyan could feel all the energy it was emitting and it wasn't even an actual baby, yet. It would only grow more...

"Oh, frozen-hells." He muttered, suddenly processing what she meant. "The child will be Good!"

Esmeralda looked grave. "Trev, it's *really* Good. Like ninety-eight percent Good. Like maybe nobody else in the world is as Good as this baby will be."

The two of them were quiet for a beat, staring down at her stomach.

"Well, it's still colossally super-powered." Trevelyan finally decided with a sanguine lift of his shoulder. "That's all any father can ask for, I suppose."

"At least a level five." Esmeralda agreed with a hint of pride. "Are there any other Good dragons?"

"Not that I'm aware of." He smirked. "Ours will be the first, my darling."

"Everything we do is amazing. Have you noticed that?"

"Exceptional people do exceptional things." His mother had often told him that and it was true. "We'll just have to lead our exceptionally Good child down the wrong path."

She chewed her lower lip. "You really think we can teach someone ninety-eight percent Good to be a genuine evildoer?"

"Of course!" Trevelyan fully believed in their child's horrific potential. "Look how much you've taught me about being a True Love." He kissed her again, because he never got tired of it.

That seemed to reassure her. "Goodness can be destructive, too. The more Good spells I cast, the more I see all the vile possibilities."

"Some of the worst people I've ever met were born Good." Trevelyan concurred. "Take Marion."

Esmeralda nodded with growing excitement. "Besides, Good or Bad, the baby is *ours*. It will be a natural at causing pandemonium."

"Exactly! Scandalous villainy is in its genes. It will just need some guidance. We can do that."

"Side-by-side we can do *anything*, Trev. I believe it."

"So do I. A thousand percent."

She looked at him, love sparking in her eyes. "This will be fun!"

"The chaos will be *extraordinary*." Trevelyan couldn't wait to see it. "The world might not survive, but at least it won't be boring." His hand found the curve of his mate's stomach and he sighed with immense satisfaction. "Now, there are *three* Green Dragons."

Author's Note

This book took a very long time for me to write.
A very, very long time.
To be fair, writing always takes longer than I think it will. My characters are often an unruly bunch and I tend to follow their leads. Also, I am fussing with every word on every page right up until my sister makes me stop. I would never publish something half-assed, just for the sake of publishing it. I try to make my books the best they can be, before I release them. Ideally, this is no more than a few extra months of struggle, because I am writing several different books at the same time. When I get stuck, I switch to another book until I figure out the issue on the first one.
In the case of *Happily Ever Witch*, though, it took years to get it right.
Esmeralda was not happy with ANY of the heroes I tried with her. Nothing I did clicked. None of the ideas panned out. Sensing my struggle, readers wrote in to recommend partners I might tempt her with. I thank all of you. I truly read and thought about each and every suggestion. The ideas were good! It should have been so simple to just choose one and get Ez on board. For example, Galahad was a popular pick for a hero. Seems like that would work in an "opposites attract" kinda way, right? Then, I got a few people saying maybe I should pair Ez with a female love interest, which was a good idea, too. And a lot of readers said maybe a Mad Hatter character should be her True Love, which made total sense in an Alice in Wonderland themed book.
But none of it quite worked.
Sometimes I have to write down parts of my stories to "screen test" the pieces. The process of typing words on a computer screen helps me see if the images in my mind will translate to the page. A few times, I got to a point where I would stick Ez

with a hero for a couple chapters and see if they could whip anything up together. This is how I stumbled across the characters of Midas and Trystan, who appear in *The Kingpin of Camelot*. Versions of them were first in rejected concepts for *Happily Ever Witch*, as I discuss in the Author's Note of that book.

If you are interested in reading the longest of Esmeralda's screen tests, I will include a link to it in the Star Turtle Publishing newsletter. Contact us at starturtlepublishing@gmail.com if you would like to join. Those of you who have followed the progress of *Happily Ever Witch* might be interested in seeing the sausage get made and track how the book changed.

Mostly, the alternate four-ish chapters stand as proof that I *was* working on this book the entire time. It just wasn't gelling. I tried *lots* of versions, with lots of heroes, and lots of plots. I would write the first chapter or two and then have nothing else to say. I have no idea what happens next in any of them. And then there was Trevelyan…

Right after *Wicked Ugly Bad* was published, I started getting letters asking when his book was coming out. I had never even *considered* giving him a book, when I was writing *Wicked Ugly Bad,* so the torrent of messages caught me by surprise.

I recall turning to my sister Liz and saying, "What am I missing here? Trevelyan can't have a book. He's *literally* the villain."

"You gave Kingu a book." She pointed out. She likes to bring this up, because she was initially opposed to the idea of *Treasure of the Fire Kingdom* and remains low-key annoyed that I was right about Kingu all along.

"Kingu deserved a book." I told her righteously. "Kingu never did anything evil."

Liz is a practical soul and she loves our readers. *Loves* them. I am not exaggerating about that. In her eyes, you are always right, while I am an introverted screw-up who can't even work Facebook. So at that point, she became Trevelyan's biggest booster. "Jesus, Trev doesn't do anything *that* irredeemable. When someone takes the time to write you about a character, you should listen."

She had a point. If people like a character, why shouldn't I give them a book? I want to make our readers happy, if I possibly can. And maybe they're spotting something I didn't.

Honestly, I still remained unconvinced that Trevelyan could pull it off. But, I told Liz I'd think about it and I did. Time past and the idea mulled around in my head... More and more people kept writing about Trevelyan... Maybe he *was* redeemable... And Ez needed a hero... Finally, I thought what the hell? I'll give him a screen test. What can it hurt?

And within five pages, that damn dragon completely won me over.

More importantly, he won *Esmeralda* over. For the first time, she was dealing with another character like they were her equal. Ez is a woman who likes extremes. Any middling, kinda Good/kinda Bad guy bores her. For better or worse, few men I've ever written are more extreme then Trevelyan. Once I realized she *liked* Trevelyan's ninety-eight percent Badness, it was like the heavens opened up with possibilities. The two of them never ran out of things to say, which made my job so much easier.

I began to conceptualize this True Love match as an arranged marriage. From Trevelyan and Esmeralda's point of view, they were suddenly tied to someone who was supposed to be their enemy. Someone they didn't trust and hadn't chosen. But they're now linked in this intimate way, and maybe they sort of like each other, and they aren't sure what they're going to do about it. The twisting loyalties and reluctant bond that develops are the fun of the story.

The first time I screen-tested Trevelyan as the hero of *Happily Ever Witch*, I knew it was going to work. Literally, I was awake all night dealing with them. (It was the initial draft of their confrontation in the lab, where he debones the executioner.) There were still problems I had to iron out. Like the actual plot of the story, for instance. That took a while. But after such a looooong time it was a massive relief to know that *finally* I had a hero that Ez loved.

That snarky, arrogant, damaged dragon saved my ass. Every scene with Esmeralda, I could feel Trevelyan wanting her. I could feel his determination. And I think that's what the book is about. It's about fighting for all the impossible things you believe in, because a stubborn, crazy-ass part of you just won't compromise on your happily ever after.

Before I finished this book, I added Trevelyan to *Seducing the Sheriff of Nottingham*, the fifth book in this series. That is where he interacts with Maid Marion and her gargoyle husband, Nicholas. I started this book first and then stopped after 40,000 words, so I could go back and set up additional plot stuff for it in *Seducing the Sheriff of Nottingham*. I was actually writing portions of the two books simultaneously, in order to keep things straight. The prologue of *Happily Ever Witch* and the epilogue of *Seducing the Sheriff of Nottingham* were written back-to-back over a two day period.

Going back ten years also allowed me to figure out how Trevelyan's mind really worked, behind the innuendoes and death threats. Seeing him through Maid Marion's eyes was a big help, because she was so casually bitchy with him and he was just delighted by it. It became clear that Marion's second big priority in *Seducing the Sheriff of Nottingham*, after saving Nicholas, was saving Trevelyan. That surprised me. And I was even more surprised at how quickly Trevelyan got attached to Marion. I anticipated them being more reluctant allies in prison, but then it turned out they ate lunch together every day. So, I just let them do their thing and they decided to become family.

Side note: I actually think Trevelyan likes Nicholas. He can't admit it, of course, but he also doesn't do anything to break them up. ...Which he would a thousand percent do, if he didn't secretly approve of his brother-in-law.

Anyway, with Trev pushing so hard to be the hero of this story, everything with *Happily Ever Witch* was finally right for me. FINALLY. So, I take back every rotten thing I ever said about the guy's hopeless villainy in *Wicked Ugly Bad*. In the end, Trevelyan got his second chance and he made the most of it. The dragon turned it all around and that's kinda the point for everyone, right? To live and learn and do better. He's now an actual hero, in my eyes.

(He would no doubt agree.)

If you've read any of my Kinda Fairytale series, you've possibly noticed that they are not faithful adaptations of the traditional stories. *Wicked Ugly Bad* is basically *Cinderella* and *Little Red Riding Hood* in a blender. *Beast in Shining Armor* is *Beauty and the Beast* meets the Greek Minotaur legend. I like mixing up the tales, tossing in some modern ideas, and creating something new.

That said, I always try to keep the key "stuff" of the story intact. I feel certain details and plot points make each particular fairytale different and special. If you're writing a Robin Hood story, you need to add arrows and Sherwood Forest. Omitting them would be altering the very fabric of the fable. I work hard to ensure that all the big pieces are there, even as I dismantle and reassemble everything around them.

There is A LOT of "stuff" in *Alice in Wonderland*. Especially, since half of the "stuff" we think of as *Alice in Wonderland* really comes from *Through the Looking Glass*. They are two books, packed full of amazing ideas. For example, *Through the Looking Glass* was published with a chess problem in the front. Readers could solve it by moving the pieces in ways that matched the actions of the anthropomorphized chess pieces in the book. But those moves *also* conformed to the rules of chess. The problem ends with Alice (a white pawn) on the other side of the board, eight squares from her starting point. I mean, how frigging cool is that?! I turned that general concept into the Chess Tower in the Club Kingdom, even though I play zero chess and have no clue how the pieces could possibly work as a clock. ...Or maybe *because* of that. The kind-of-confusing, kind-of-intriguing weirdness of it fits Wonderland perfectly.

On the other end of the inspiration spectrum, I actually got the idea for Lyon N. Unicorn's typo-riddled spell from the Disney cartoon version of *Alice in Wonderland*. As a kid, I had no clue what "sealing wax" was. When that Walrus and the Carpenter part came on, I assumed they were singing about waxing a ceiling. That is still where my mind first goes when I hear the words together.

I knew that including characters like the White Rabbit, the

Walrus and the Mad Hatter was necessary, from the very first draft of this book. The Walrus and the White Rabbit were actually introduced in *The Kingpin of Camelot*, in preparation for showing up here. But, I also felt I should toss in smaller *Alice in Wonderland* "stuff," like the 4,207 king's men. (I made them queen's men.) I started this project with a list of over fifty assorted *Alice in Wonderland* lines, references, and themes I could play with, because Lewis Carroll provided me with hundreds of pages worth of awesome "stuff" to crib from. I thank him for his boundless imagination.

I added most of that list to *Happily Ever Witch* in one way or another. But I did save a few ideas from *Alice in Wonderland* to possibly use in future Kinda Fairytale books. For instance, the caucus race with a dodo bird. Not sure what that will be exactly, but doesn't it put images in your mind?

I used the same process for the Snow White references. To me, the poison apples, the stepmother, the glass coffin, etc... helped to add some extra elements to *Happily Ever Witch*. This series always works best for me when pieces from different fairytales are all mixed together. Since Dr. White was an enemy of both Marrok and Trevelyan (and everyone else who's ever been in the WUB Club), the Snow White tale seemed like a natural match. Also, the magic mirror idea bridged both stories. They just fit together.

I didn't use the Huntsman yet, though. I feel like I already had plenty of characters and a future book might need something hunted. I don't like adding "stuff" just for the sake of adding it. I want it to enhance the overall story. ...Unless it's some random "Jabberwocky" word. Then, I tossed it in here regardless, because they're just *so* mimsy.

In any case, if you haven't read *Alice in Wonderland* and *Through the Looking Glass*, I urge you to spent a few hours and delve into these wonderful tales. They're free on the internet and fairly quick reads. Trust me, you won't be sorry. There's a reason that Alice's golden afternoon has lived on for a hundred and fifty years.

On a personal note, all the central characters in *Happily Ever Witch* are Bad. Maybe the fact that *everyone* was a villain allowed the cutaway scenes of the Club Kingdom to really stand out for me. The hostage situation/meet-the-family gatherings unexpectedly became my favorite parts of this book. I could have happily written Marrok, Bluebeard, the Mad Hatter, Snow White, and the Queen of Clubs annoying each other for endless chapters. I especially liked the "dinner date." It's not often that I reread my own work and laugh, but Bluebeard's whining, self-pitying observations about the jam getting everything sticky cracked me up.

Marrok, meanwhile, took a more proactive role in his kidnapping than I ever imagined. The climax of the book, where Trevelyan gets put on trial like Alice in *Alice in Wonderland*, was all the wolf's idea. I had no idea that was going to happen until it was already happening. When I conceptualized Snow White holding him hostage, I pictured Marrok more "waiting to get rescued" and less "maniacally scheming." I was kidding myself. *Wicked Ugly Bad* is the bestselling book I've ever written. At least part of its success is owed to Marrok's ability to be the sweetest guy on the planet, when he wants to be. ...And when he *doesn't* want to be, all sorts of Badness results. Few characters in the series enjoy causing trouble as much as Marrok. He uses exactly the wrong words at exactly the right time. Watching him manipulate things in the Club Kingdom's villainous soap opera reminded me of why he's always been one of my favorites to write.

Wrapping up this very long Author's Note, I would like to take a moment to talk about the glories of a stunning manicure. Reading any of my books, you'll usually see some kind of nail polish reference in there. This isn't so much *intentional* as it is a reflection of my own passion for varnish. I have hundreds and hundreds (okay thousands) of bottles. My favorites come from independent manufacturers.

There are so many talented nail polish makers, who do amazing work that's uniquely their own. Esmeralda's company pays homage to the small businesses who sell those fantastic concoctions of sparkles and shine. Be assured that when you buy my books, you are feeding my addiction to their whimsical new shades and also helping other entrepreneurs succeed.

Presently, I'm wearing Glam Polish's "She Preferred Imaginary Heroes to Real Ones," which is a shimmery red with scattered holo glitter. Super pretty. ...But you know it was the name that sold me.

If you want to discuss *Happily Ever Witch*, nail polish, Green Dragons, or anything you're curiouser and curiouser about you can contact me at **starturtlepublishing@gmail.com**_ The same email address can be used to sign up for our mailing list for news about our upcoming books. We also have a Facebook page, which we update fairly regularly, and a new and improved website at www.starturtlepublishing.com. I hope to see you there!

Also by Cassandra Gannon

The Elemental Phases Series
Warrior from the Shadowland
Guardian of the Earth House
Exile in the Water Kingdom
Treasure of the Fire Kingdom
Queen of the Magnetland
Magic of the Wood House

A Kinda Fairytale Series
Wicked Ugly Bad
Beast in Shining Armor
The Kingpin of Camelot
Best Knight Ever
Seducing the Sheriff of Nottingham
Happily Ever Witch

Other Books
Love in the Time of Zombies
Not Another Vampire Book
Vampire Charming
Cowboy from the Future
Once Upon a Caveman
Ghost Walk

Frightful Loves Series
Love vs. The Ooze Monster by Cassandra Gannon
Love vs. The Beast by Elizabeth Gannon

Sexual Tyrannosaurus Anthology
Lust and Fury by Elizabeth Gannon
Taming the Tyrant Lizard by Cassandra Gannon

If you enjoy Cassandra's books, you may also enjoy books by her sister, Elizabeth Gannon.

The Consortium of Chaos series
Yesterday's Heroes
The Son of Sun and Sand
The Guy Your Friends Warned You About
Electrical Hazard
The Only Fish in the Sea
Not Currently Evil

The Mad Scientist's Guide to Dating
Broke and Famous
Formerly the Next Big Thing

Other books
The Snow Queen
Travels with a Fairytale Monster
Everyone Hates Fairytale Pirates
Captive of a Fairytale Barbarian

Printed in Great Britain
by Amazon